JAMES OSWALD

WHAT WILL BURN

WILDFIRE

First published in 2021 by
WILDFIRE
an imprint of HEADLINE PUBLISHING GROUP

1

Cataloguing in Publication Data is available from the British Library

Hardback ISBN 978 1 4722 7614 8
Trade Paperback ISBN 978 1 4722 7615 5

Typeset in Aldine 401BT by Avon DataSet Ltd,
Arden Court, Alcester, Warwickshire

Printed and bound in Great Britain by Clays Ltd, Elcograf S.p.A.

HEADLINE PUBLISHING GROUP
An Hachette UK Company
Carmelite House
50 Victoria Embankment
London EC4Y 0DZ

www.headline.co.uk
www.hachette.co.uk

WHAT
WILL
BURN

By James Oswald

Inspector McLean
Natural Causes
The Book of Souls
The Hangman's Song
Dead Men's Bones
Prayer for the Dead
The Damage Done
Written in Bones
The Gathering Dark
Cold as the Grave
Bury Them Deep
What Will Burn

Constance Fairchild
No Time to Cry
Nothing to Hide

For all the witches

1

She always knew she would die like this.

They come in the night, crashing through the under-growth and pushing through the trees. They don't use the path that meanders up the slope from the road; that would be too easy. Neither do they come in one band, but surround her cottage as if she might slip away round the back while they hammer on her door at the front. She could no more slip away than stand, but that makes no difference to them. A mob knows no reason, and this is most surely a mob.

She glances towards the unlit fire, the cat lying hopefully in front of it. 'You should go. While you can. Find a safe home.'

It looks at her with wary eyes, ears cocked at the sound coming closer, ever closer. That stare is knowing, calculating. A moment's hesitation, and then it rises, stretches, nods its head once, and disappears. She is relieved. Her time may have come, but the cat still has many lives to live.

The sound of breaking glass comes a few minutes later. Stupid, really. The door wasn't locked. Someone curses loudly as they climb in through the back window, and she catches a whiff of blood on the breeze before it is overwhelmed by the stench of men. Where before they were loud coming through the trees, now they are silent. Not stealthy, but not speaking either. She doesn't know how many of them there are, although it feels like a multitude. Fit, strong, young. Angry. They swarm into her small room like cockroaches, start smashing things before they've even realised she is there waiting for them. Perhaps they thought she'd be in her bed.

She doesn't resist when they grab her; that would only encourage them. And besides, she is old and weak. Utterly at the mercy they so obviously lack. Her passivity only angers them more. She thought she was prepared, but nothing really prepares you for this. She hasn't many of her own teeth left now, but they knock them out anyway. Arthritis has swollen her knuckles, and the pain when they break her fingers makes her scream. With the sound, their bloodlust grows, their animal instincts taking over. Except that no animal would do what they are doing. Not to one of their own. She folds in under their savage fury.

'Don't kill her, boys. We need her still breathing.'

There's a familiar edge to that voice, but she's not sure whether she recognises it or simply the obedience it demands. She can taste blood in her mouth, feel the broken bones in her hands, her legs, the slide of fractured ribs that threaten with every breath to puncture a lung. It's nearly over now, but there is one last thing to do before the end.

'With my dying breath I curse thee.'

The words come out as a mixture of whisper and bloody gurgle. She had meant to look up at her killers, but she is too old, too weak, too broken. A rough hand grabs her hair, pulls her head back in a yanking motion that sends a bolt of pain down her spine.

'You say something, old crone?'

He is very young, the one who holds her. Not much more than a boy. Shaven head, tank top straining to contain his gym-and-steroid muscles. There's scarcely a spark of anything in his eyes, certainly not intelligence.

'With my dying breath.' She gasps in a lungful of pain. 'I curse thee.'

'Aye, well yer right about one thing.'

The hand releases its grip on her hair, throwing her back as it does so. To some unspoken order, the men step away. Something wet splashes her arm, and for a moment she thinks they're pissing on her. Then it hits her face, soaks into her clothes. Fumes reach the bloody broken mess of her nose, and she realises it is something far worse than piss.

She barely has the strength left to lift her head. Petrol stings her eyes as she blinks to see the blurred figure standing in front of her. The leader. He has something in his hands, although she can't see what it is. No need to see; she knows well enough.

'With my dying breath . . .' As she wheezes out the words, something flares in the man's hand. She traces its passage as he flicks it towards her, a tiny flame on the end of a matchstick, tumbling over and over in impossibly slow motion.

She always knew she would die like this.

After all, she's done it many times before.

2

The stench hit her long before she reached the crime scene. At first it was a lingering unpleasant scent on the air, but as she climbed the steep path from the woods, so it developed into something worse. Burned carpets, chemical reek and the unmistakable aroma of overdone barbecue. And underneath it all, a fug of decay that didn't sit with the bustle and activity around her. Detective Constable Janie Harrison had attended enough fires in her short career as a police officer to know the usual unpleasant smells, and this place had them all. The fact that she was even here at all meant at least one person had died, but the question she found herself asking was when, rather than who and how. She should really have been with a detective sergeant of course, but that wasn't going to happen any time soon. Never enough detectives, always too much to do.

'Is it far?'

The words were out before she could stop herself, and it left her with a feeling of having said 'Are we nearly there yet?' A false memory from a hundred or more dull car trips to the seaside or some boring ancient battlefield. Some kids might have reacted to that upbringing by taking to a sedentary life, and Janie had almost been one of them.

'Not much further, no.' The forensic technician who had met

her at the roadside wasn't one she'd met before. Or at least not one Janie could easily recognise from all that was visible of her face. Her overalls, hood tied tight, left little to go by. Harrison wore similar, although as yet she'd not pulled up the hood. The day was too warm for that, the air in the trees humid with the threat of yet more rain. Summer had been long and hot, but it was gone now, autumn making up for lost time.

The buzz of forest insects gave way to a hubbub of noise as they left the trees and entered a clearing straight out of a children's fairy tale. It was hard to believe the city was only a few miles away, although if she concentrated, Janie thought she could hear the dull roar of the bypass. Her attention was dragged away from idle musings by the cottage that stood a dozen or so metres away.

Quite what such a building was doing up here in the hills she had no idea. Perhaps it had been a gamekeeper's lodge or something, which would mean there was a huge mansion nearby, a great estate that would have built a tiny house out of well-cut stone and slate. She wasn't sure of the area, so it might well have been that the mansion house had long since gone, only this more humble dwelling left. Fire had taken hold at some point, then apparently given up, leaving far more of the building intact than she'd been expecting, or indeed than the heavy smell suggested. Janie followed a marked path up to a point where a small section of wall had collapsed outwards, splitting the roof open to reveal a burned mess inside.

'Reckon it's more or less safe as long as you keep to the middle.' The forensic technician who had shown her this far seemed reluctant to go any further. Janie could sympathise; fires were never pleasant, especially when people were involved.

She picked her way along the route marked, careful not to turn her ankle on fallen rubble from the wall collapse. A couple of white-suited figures crouched beside the remains of an old stuffed armchair, not much left of it but springs and scorched wooden frame. At the same time as she noticed the battered case beside them, the older of the two turned. He frowned, looked past her as if expecting to see someone else, then returned his gaze to her and smiled in recognition.

'Detective Constable Harrison. This is a pleasant surprise.'

'Doctor Cadwallader.' Janie nodded as the other figure turned. 'Doctor Sharp.'

'I take it you're alone?' Cadwallader asked.

'Aye. We're a bit short-staffed at the moment, what with Gru . . . DS Laird retired and, well.' She shrugged. The pathologist knew as well as any what the situation was.

'Still not sorted?' He gave her a sympathetic smile and a shrug. 'Well, you'd better have a look at our poor victim here before we move her, then.'

It was only as he said the words that Janie realised the blackened mess lying at the feet of the pathologist and his assistant was not, in fact, the remains of a burned feather bolster cushion. Intellectually, she had known it wasn't, but still the shock was visceral as her eyes took in more and more details. She swallowed down the bile that tried to rise up and choke her, took a shallow breath, and stepped closer.

'Female, old. I'd say in her seventies at least. We'll know more once I've had a chance to examine her back at the mortuary. From the way she's burned . . .' Cadwallader leaned in close to the grisly corpse. '. . . And the smell. I'd say she's been dead at least a week.'

A week? Janie gulped again. She was no rookie, knew she could do this without being sick, but that didn't make it much easier. She looked up from the body, around what little remained of the room. It was almost impossible to get a sense of the place, the person who lived here, anything really. 'An accident?'

Cadwallader stood up slowly, knees popping as he straightened. Beside him, his assistant tidied away the few instruments he had used in his examination before standing up herself in a much more fluid and graceful motion.

'I'll know for sure once we've done the post-mortem. We'll get a better idea of when she died too. This is a remote spot, and the fact that she's been here so long unnoticed would suggest she was a loner, wouldn't you say? Poor dear likely fell asleep in her chair and then something shorted out. Wiring in these old places is never the best, is it?'

Janie risked a glance down at the remains of the dead woman again, found she was able to detach herself from the horror of it and focus on what few details she could see among the rubble. The body lay on the floor, and she expected when forensics were done they'd show that the woman had been lying there before the fire started. Hopefully they could tell her where and how it happened, too. It felt off, though. There was something about this scene, this cottage and its setting that made her want to call DCI McLean. It was his kind of case, of that she was sure. If only he was available.

'Can you let me know when you're doing the PM, Doctor Cadwallader?' she asked as the three of them retreated from the building.

'It'll probably be a few days, unless you want me to prioritise it. Could maybe get her seen tomorrow if you think it's necessary.'

Janie wanted to say yes, but she was only a detective constable. This wasn't her call.

'No, get to her as soon as you have a space, but unless we turn up something suspicious here I don't think a few days' delay is going to make a difference.'

'You're probably right. She's waited a week already, after all. I'll email you the results as soon as I have them.' Cadwallader paused a moment as if considering something before adding: 'On one condition.'

'Yes?'

'Call me Angus. "Doctor Cadwallader" is such a mouthful.'

Janie wasn't sure whether to recoil or laugh, so she said nothing, and after a moment the pathologist gave her a little nod and headed off along the path, his faithful assistant Doctor Sharp trotting along behind him.

'According to the records I can track down, the cottage is part of the Bairnfather Estate. Council says it's occupied by a Cecily Slater. Born fifth July 1931. No one else at the address, so I guess it was just her there on her own.'

Back at the station, DC Harrison sat on an uncomfortable office chair in the CID room, trying not to feel dwarfed by the imposing bulk of DC Lofty Blane. It wasn't his fault that he was six foot eight to her five foot six and a bit, but she still couldn't get used to someone being quite so large. He made up for it by being a genius forensic accountant, and something of a wizard with computers, even if his hands splayed wider than the keyboard and his fingers sometimes hit four keys at a time.

'Do we know anything else about her? Next of kin? GP?'

'Give me a moment, Janie. We're not exactly overstaffed here.'

'Sorry, Lofty. It's been a bad day.' Janie glanced up at the clock over the door, disappointed to see that it was barely noon yet. A long afternoon lay ahead of her before shift end, and she had a horrible feeling she wouldn't be going home then either. 'How did we even find out about this? The pathologist reckons she'd been dead a week and nobody noticed.'

'Local farmer delivering her groceries, apparently. Talk about being cut off, eh? There's an old track goes right up to the cottage, but the bridge collapsed a few months back and everything has to come in by tractor.'

Janie made a mental note to add interviewing the farmer to the list of actions already piling up. 'Guess we'd better speak to him. And find out who else has been there recently.'

'Who's SIO on this then?' Blane asked as he laboriously tapped at the keyboard.

'We don't even know if it's suspicious yet, Lofty. Nothing at the scene to suggest it wasn't just a horrible accident. Let's see what the post-mortem brings up, aye?'

'You know when that'll be? Don't want to waste too much time on this if it's no' suspicious. I've enough work for two as it is.'

'Doctor Cadwallader said he'd let me know, but it might be a few days. Just need to make sure we've all the background on the poor old dear before then. I'll take what we've got to DI Ritchie soon as she gets back in from wherever she is right now. She can decide whether to make our lives more difficult than they already are.'

'You reckon we'll get any more officers soon?' Blane asked. It was a question that bounced around the echoing walls of the near empty CID room most days. The team hadn't exactly been large to start with, but they'd lost two detectives since the summer. One retired, one . . . well, who knew? Maybe they'd all be reassigned to other teams within the Specialist Crime Division. Still nominally based in the city but tasked wherever there was an investigation needing their skills. Or maybe there would be yet another reorganisation and something entirely new would rise from the ashes.

'Kirsty's asked. Many times. Doesn't help that they're still arguing over who's going to be the new station chief here. Nobody wants to make any staffing decisions until the top spot's filled.'

'Well maybe I have some good news for you then.' Blane clicked once more, sending whatever he'd been doing to the printer. He pushed back his chair, swivelled it around to face her. 'Word is the new boss starts next week. Apparently she's coming up from England. The Met, no less.'

'She?'

'That's what Jay says.' Blane nodded towards DC Stringer's desk, empty since he was on late shift and wouldn't be in until it got dark. 'He's been known to get it wrong from time to time, mind you.'

'Not on something like that.' Janie followed Blane to the printer, busily churning out twice as many pages as they'd asked it for. 'Wonder what persuaded her to come north.'

'Probably hit the glass ceiling down there. Reckoned she'd have more chance of promotion if she moved. Either that or she really likes haggis and whisky.'

'You're such a cynic, Lofty.' Janie grabbed the first few sheets from the printer and started flicking through them. Not much detail at all. Cecily Slater, so much a recluse that nobody noticed when her house caught on fire. Too old and frail to save herself from burning to death. What a horrible way to go.

'What's the plan of action?' Blane asked.

'Write it all up and pass it on. We're only lowly constables, after all.'

3

It was only a slap, for fuck's sake. You couldn't even see the bruise once she'd stuck some make-up on. What's all the fuss about?

Gary sits at the table in the stuffy meeting room and manages, for once, to keep his mouth shut. His suit smells of mothballs and doesn't fit properly. He's not worn it since . . . Christ, it would have been Bazza's wedding. That was some party, right enough. He frowns as he remembers that was where he first met Bella, too. Shame Bazza's marriage didn't last more than a couple of years. Trish walked out on him, right enough. Dozy bitch.

'. . . could be looking at a custodial sentence, Mr Tomlinson.'

Something in the lawyer's words cuts through his meandering thoughts. Annoying, expensive wee shite that he is, the man's supposed to know what he's doing, but that doesn't sound right.

'You what?'

'I said that you could be looking at a custodial sentence, Mr Tomlinson. Jail time, in other words. According to Miss MacDonald, her injuries were quite severe.'

It takes Gary a while to work out who the lawyer's talking about. Miss MacDonald. Makes her sound like a school teacher and not the useless junkie waster she is. MacDonald's her mam's name, not her da's. But then they never married either, did they?

Far as he knows nobody's ever called her anything except Bella.

'Barely touched her. She's putting it on just to make me look bad.'

The lawyer says nothing for a moment, and Gary reckons the slick fuck's trying not to sneer. This whole thing's getting out of hand, making him angry. He shoves his hands into his lap, fists clenched, right leg jiggling up and down as he tries to keep a lid on it. He needs to get out of this room with its shiny wooden table and metal frame chairs, its weird modern art on the walls and that smell of desperation and fear.

'Mr Tomlinson. Gary.' The lawyer's trying to put on a reasonable voice now, but it makes him sound like the wee kids in the school playground he and Bazza and Big Tam used to pick on for their lunch money. Gary tenses, lifts his chin so he can stare at the man down his nose.

'I barely touched her.'

'So you have said, and I'm sure it's true. However.' The lawyer flips open the thin folder he has with him, picks through some of the pages until he finds what he's looking for. 'Miss MacDonald was seen by her GP a few hours after the alleged assault. She referred her to the hospital for X-rays, which showed fractures to the jaw and skull consistent with repeated punching.'

'I slapped her once. An' only 'cause the stupid bitch wouldn't shut up when I asked her to.' Gary's fists are on the tabletop before he realises what he's doing. The lawyer lets out a small yelp of surprise, rocks back in his seat even though he's well out of reach.

'Please, Mr Tomlinson. I'm on your side here. Just laying out the case that's been presented to us.' He has his papers in his hands, held close to his chest like a shield. It's pathetic.

'There's no fucking case. Just her lies, aye?'

'Well, see . . . It's not quite as clear-cut as that, I'm afraid. Miss MacDonald could very well press charges, and in the current political climate a guilty verdict might see you in jail. You might be lucky, get a sympathetic jury, but cases like these they tend to believe the . . . ah . . . victim.'

For a moment Gary wants to flip the table, maybe give the lawyer a good kicking, then storm out of the building. All this talk of fractures and victims and fucking jail. It's doing his nut in. He gave her a slap, that was all. She'd been moaning at him that much she deserved it, right enough. And all he wanted her to do was go and quiet the wain down. Poor wee thing needed changing maybe, or a feed. What fucking use was a mother if she couldn't feed and change her own wain?

'What can I do then?' he asks once the urge to break things has lessened. The lawyer's face brightens a little at this, the tension sagging out of his shoulders as he manages a weak smile.

'Well, as it happens, I've had some communication with Miss MacDonald's solicitor, and she is prepared to not pursue charges.'

'Not . . . ? What does that mean?' Gary's leg stops its incessant jiggling and he leans forward, arms on the table, paying attention.

'It means you'd walk away with nothing but a caution. No trial, no jail time. You'd keep your job.'

'Aye, there has to be a catch, right? She's wanting somethin'.'

The lawyer puts down his papers again, looks Gary straight in the eye. 'Indeed she is, Mr Tomlinson. You and Miss MacDonald are not married, but you have a daughter?'

'Aye, Wee Mary. She's named after my nan, see?'

Something like a grimace passes over the lawyer's face. It puts Gary back on edge.

'Well, as I say, Miss MacDonald is prepared to let the assault go, but only if you agree to cut all ties with her and the child.'

Gary's leg's started tapping again, his hands balled into fists. 'You . . . She wants what?'

'Think about it, Mr Tomlinson.' The lawyer's got his wheedling school kid voice on again. 'If you're found guilty of assault you will go to jail. It's very likely the court will deny you visiting rights even after your sentence is served.'

'But . . . She cannae do that. Mary's my wain too. I've rights, ken? And that bitch is no' fit to be a mother either.'

'I'm truly sorry, Mr Tomlinson. But in these cases the overwhelming majority of times custody is given to the mother. If it went to court you would almost certainly lose, and we would be right back here where we are now. I know it seems very unfair, but believe me when I say you can save yourself a great deal of heartache, pain and money if you take Miss MacDonald up on her offer.'

'But my wain. My Wee Mary.' He's helpless, he knows. Like the lawyer says, the bitch has got him over a barrel. Courts'll believe her any day, and if the stuff he and Bazza got up to when they were still lads gets out . . . Gary feels the wetness in the corners of his eyes and that brings on the anger even more. 'She cannae do this to me,' he says, but now that snivelling tone is in his own voice and he knows that the bitch can. She has done. Shafted him good and proper.

He sniffs, runs the back of his hand across his nose and then sniffs again. This is not over yet. Not even close.

'Where do I sign, then?'

4

Janie Harrison had never been all that fond of the city mortuary, and especially not first thing in the morning. There was no real reason why she had to attend this examination either, except that in the days since the old lady's burned remains had been found, she'd grown increasingly uncomfortable with the idea of it being no more than an undiscovered accident. So when the pathologist's email had appeared, informing her that Cecily Slater would be the morning's first examination, she had replied letting him know she'd be there.

Angus Cadwallader himself greeted Janie at the door. 'Come through, my dear. We're all ready to go.'

He led her down the squeaky clean corridor and into the examination theatre, where the body had been laid out on the central table and covered with a white sheet. As she stepped into the room, Janie caught the whiff of burned meat on the air, despite the extractor fans working harder than normal. It was maybe lucky she'd skipped breakfast. She approached the table with slightly less enthusiasm than the pathologist, and then took a step away as Doctor Sharp pulled back the sheet, her hand going up to her nose instinctively.

'Yes. Burned bodies are never much fun, and this one has the added bonus of having started to decompose. Thank the lord for the colder weather, eh?' Cadwallader switched from charming to serious in an instant, setting about his job with all the professionalism and deft speed that had no doubt kept him in the position for so long. Janie watched and listened as he noted various aspects of the body, took another step back when the scalpel came out. It wasn't really necessary to be here, and yet something compelled her to witness this.

'Death would have been fairly swift once she was set alight.' Cadwallader's words dragged Janie's attention back to the work in hand just in time for her to see the pathologist studying something that was most likely a lung.

'Swift?' she asked, then her brain caught up. 'Set alight?'

'The marks on her trachea and lungs show damage consistent with inhalation of flames. The shock would have killed her quickly. Not saying she wasn't in considerable pain, mind. She'd been given a thorough beating beforehand.'

'Beaten?' Janie took a step forward again, the better to see. Then wished she hadn't.

'Several of her ribs are broken, and there are fractures in her arms too. She's dislocated a hip, although that could have happened falling from her chair. Damage from the fire has masked the external bruising, but it's there all the same. Poor old dear was thoroughly worked over, then someone dowsed her in some kind of accelerant – my guess would be petrol – and set her on fire. I think we can rule out accidental death on this one.'

'Shit.' The word was out before Janie could stop herself, her brain too busy catching up with the ramifications of this discovery.

'Shit indeed,' Cadwallader said. 'I don't much fancy your job, my dear.'

'Have we got a clearer idea how long she'd been lying there before we found her?' Janie asked.

The pathologist looked at her in much the same way as her

old history teacher had done when she'd got the dates wrong in a test. Then he shrugged. 'There's a few indicators we can use, maggots, flies, that sort of thing. We can narrow it down further with some other tests, but as I said when we found her, I'd say she'd been lying there for a week.'

A week for the rain to wash away forensic evidence. Janie shoved her hands into her jacket pockets, felt the familiar weight of her phone. She'd come here hoping to get some more facts before writing it all up and moving on. Well, now she had those facts and more. She had a horrible feeling this case wasn't going to be so easy to solve, either. She'd not been in plain clothes long, but she'd worked enough weird cases to recognise the signs. And of course she'd worked those cases with DCI McLean, whose reputation for attracting the strange and unsettling was well deserved.

'Any news about our mutual friend the detective chief inspector?' Cadwallader asked, as if he had read her mind. It surprised Janie that he'd not mentioned him before. Or, indeed, called the man himself since they were meant to be close friends.

'Still on suspension. Professional Standards weren't at all happy with what he did over the summer. I've seen him a couple of times going into interviews, but they're dragging their feet about something.'

'I suspect that will be the wealthy and influential people he embarrassed looking to extract their pound of flesh.' Cadwallader put down the scalpel he'd been waving around and focused his full attention on her. 'Young Tony has a habit of making enemies of the most well connected.'

'I thought the Complaints were meant to be above that kind of thing.' Janie knew how foolish and naive she sounded even before the last of her words were out.

'Oh, I'm sure they are, my dear. But they'll be feeling the pressure too. Still, he's got broad shoulders. He can cope, and meantime nobody's turning the heat on you and your colleagues. You can be thankful for that.'

Janie looked away from the pathologist, her gaze sliding back to the battered and burned remains of the old woman. It hadn't occurred to her before, but the DCI must have protected the rest of the team from the fallout. She'd given the briefest of statements to Professional Standards, and that had been the last of it.

'I'm sure he'll be back soon,' she said, and hoped that she wasn't wrong. 'I have a feeling this case is going to be right up his street.'

The room swarmed with a press of uniformed bodies, the noise almost too loud for such an early hour. For a moment Janie wondered if the news about Cecily Slater had preceded her up the hill from the mortuary. But even if it had, there wouldn't have been this many officers needed or assigned, surely. No, this was something else entirely, and it made finding a senior detective to talk to almost impossible.

She edged into the room and slipped through the throng as best she could, scanning the press of bodies until she spotted the hunched form of Lofty Blane. It took a while to reach him, such was the crowd. She hadn't realised there were this many officers still assigned to the station, but then she saw several support staff in the mix. Even so, there couldn't have been anyone on shift missing. Heaven help them if there was a fire alarm.

'What's going on?' she asked once she'd managed to attract Blane's attention. Taller than most of them by at least a head, the detective constable had a way of shrinking in on himself to avoid attracting attention. It was effective, but also seemed to render him remarkably deaf sometimes, and the general noise didn't help.

'New station chief's called a meeting. Going to introduce herself.'

Janie stood on tiptoes, frowning as she stared across to the far side of the room. Without a chair for her to stand on, it was hard to see whether any senior officers were yet present.

'Could she not have done it in shifts? What if someone turns up in reception and there's nobody there to help?' What if I've just found out our fortnight-old accidental death is actually a murder and we need to get the investigation escalated as quickly as possible?

Blane merely shrugged, and before Janie could say anything more, a commotion at the front quietened down the mob. A group of senior officers had entered through the doors at the other end of the room and were pushing through the crowd towards a low podium. Janie spotted Detective Superintendent McIntyre in among the gaggle of uniformed officers, most of whom she more or less recognised. Only one was a total stranger, a tall woman wearing the uniform of a chief superintendent as if it were the highest couture. Where the other officers struggled through the crowd, she moved with catwalk elegance, gaze fixed directly ahead. Janie cursed her shortness as all but one of the group took seats at the back of the podium before she could get a good look at the new station chief's face. Her fleeting impression was of surprising youth and striking beauty. Not at all what she had been expecting from a time-served Met officer.

One of the uniformed superintendents came straight to the lectern. 'Thank you, everyone. We'll make this as brief as possible.' A Strathclyde officer, if his accent was anything to go by.

'I know it's not been easy these past few months, especially since Deputy Chief Constable Robinson retired. We've been short-staffed for far too long, especially in CID. However, that's all about to change now. I'm sure there's been plenty of gossip already, so I'll just get on with it and introduce our new station head. Chief Superintendent Elmwood comes from the Met, but I'm sure we'll not hold that against her.'

The elegant woman stepped up to the lectern, giving the superintendent who had introduced her the briefest of scowls, which Janie felt the man clearly deserved. When she turned towards the assembly, however, her face was all beaming smile. Janie would have put her in her early forties at the oldest, which made her rise through the ranks to her current position impressive. Either that or she had a painting of an ugly old hag hidden away in an attic somewhere.

'Thank you, Donald, for that delightful introduction.' The chief superintendent's accent fell strangely on Janie's ears. It wasn't the Englishness of it so much as the odd mix of posh inflection and something that sounded a bit like the actors on *EastEnders*. It put her in mind of Dick Van Dyke in *Mary Poppins* for a moment.

'I expect you're all wondering why I got this job rather than someone a bit more home grown. Well, in the light of recent events ...' The chief superintendent put heavy emphasis on those last two words, then paused for even greater effect. She had the room in total silence, which was quite an achievement, Janie had to concede.

'In the light of recent events, the chief constable thought it would be a good idea to bring in some fresh blood, as it were. Someone unconnected with Police Scotland until now.'

Another pause, and this time the quietest of murmurs rippled through the room before the chief superintendent spoke again.

'I can understand how that might put a few people's backs up. And I know I have a steep learning curve ahead of me. I aim to do my best for this station, for Edinburgh and for Police Scotland as a whole. All I ask of you is that you give me the chance to prove myself before you send me packing. I've no great desire to go back to England any time soon, as I'm sure you can all understand.'

A quiet burble of laughter echoed around the room at that,

and Janie realised the new chief superintendent had won them over with just a few well-chosen words. She could only hope the woman was as good at her job as she was at rallying the troops.

'There'll be changes over the coming weeks and months, as I'm sure you're all expecting. However, let me assure you that I won't be allowing any further reductions in the workforce here. Quite the opposite. The chief constable has already signed off on new recruitment, both in uniform and plain clothes. You'll all be informed of the changes in due course, but for now I just wanted to let you know the good news, and tell you all how excited I am to be here. Thank you.'

Spontaneous applause stuttered into life as the new chief superintendent stepped away from the lectern, something Janie couldn't ever recall for a senior management pep talk before. DC Blane leaned close as she failed to join in.

'About time we had some more detectives,' he said over the loud clap of his own massive hands. Janie merely smiled and nodded. She'd believe it when she saw it.

'Janie, have you got a minute?'

DC Harrison stopped in her tracks, causing the flow of uniformed officers to pass around her in a dark blue stream of curses and grumbles. She recognised the voice of Detective Superintendent Jayne McIntyre and knew better than to pretend she hadn't heard. And in the absence of DI Ritchie, there wasn't anyone else obvious she could take the news about Cecily Slater to anyway.

'Ma'am?' Janie pushed her way through the last of the departing officers and approached the small group still clustered at the top of the room. Closer in, she had her first clear view of the new chief superintendent, and was once again struck by her apparent youth. Her skin glowed, and her high cheekbones and thin nose gave her the chiselled look of a model rather than a senior police officer. Only her eyes, grey and piercing, hinted at something a bit more steely underneath.

'This is the detective constable I was telling you about, Gail. Harrison has worked closely with DCI McLean since moving from uniform to plain clothes – what is it? Three years back?'

Gail. Not 'Chief Superintendent' or 'ma'am', Janie couldn't help noticing. But then McIntyre had always been one for informality whenever it didn't interfere with carrying out duties.

'The Chalmers case, ma'am,' she said, after the awkward silence suggested an answer was needed. 'And yes, that would be coming up for three years now.'

'Should be making detective sergeant then, shouldn't you?' the chief superintendent asked. Janie couldn't tell whether the woman was chastising her or merely making a comment. Her accent was too English to work it out, so she went for the neutral option.

'If a DS position comes up, I'll certainly apply, ma'am. Things have been a bit busy though lately.'

The chief superintendent stared at her down that perfect nose again, saying nothing as her pale grey eyes bored through Janie's skull and into her soul. She stood her ground, and after what felt like hours but was probably only a few seconds, the chief superintendent shrugged.

'What do you make of him, then?'

For a moment Janie couldn't think who she was referring to. Then the penny dropped. 'DCI McLean? He's . . .' Put on the spot like that, she couldn't think of anything to say. The chief superintendent was quicker to respond this time.

'Impetuous? Careless? Not a team player?' There was no mistaking the tone now, English accent or not.

'I'm not sure it's very fair putting Janie on the spot like that, is it, ma'am?' McIntyre stepped in at precisely the right moment, and Janie couldn't help but notice the heavy emphasis she had put on the word 'ma'am'. A brief scowl marred the chief super-intendent's perfect features for an instant, then dissolved into a politician's smile.

'Of course, Jayne. But you know I have to review the report from Professional Standards into this summer's . . .' She paused, tilted her head like a confused dog as she searched for the right word. '. . . events.'

Janie saw the tension rise in McIntyre's body, then dissipate as the detective superintendent calmed herself. How many months now was it since that incident up on the moors? Long enough that the DCI had fully recovered from his injuries, but clearly not long enough for the people he'd upset to forget. That was his special skill, after all. Pissing off people in high places and not giving a damn about the consequences.

'You're working on an accidental death case at the moment, are you not?' The chief superintendent phrased it as a question, but it was clear to Janie that she already knew. It made a nice change, if a little unnerving, to be noticed by the high heidyins.

'I was just back from the post-mortem the now, ma'am. No' sure it was so accidental after all.' Janie gave both her superior officers a rundown of what she'd learned from the pathologist. 'I was looking for DI Ritchie, but I can pass it straight up to you if you'd prefer. I'll have the initial report done before lunchtime.'

The chief superintendent stared at her again down that long nose. Aquiline, that was the word for it. Roman, maybe. For a moment it was as if the whole world had gone silent, and Janie could feel herself withering under that gaze. And then as swiftly as it was applied, the tension disappeared, and the chief super-intendent broke into a broad smile.

'I can see why you like her, Jayne,' she said, before turning her attention back to Harrison. 'Yes, I'd like to see that report, Detective Constable. I'd also like to see your name on the list of suitable candidates for promotion. You've passed the exams, I take it?'

'I . . . Yes, ma'am.'

'Well then, acting Detective Sergeant Harrison. That report on my desk in an hour.'

5

'Explain to me again why you decided to go against procedure and enter the premises at Oakhill Farm. On your own and without any form of back-up.'

Detective Chief Inspector Tony McLean suppressed a weary sigh and shifted his position slightly, trying to find a little comfort even though the designers of the chair had carefully ensured there would be none. His hip ached where it had been broken several years before, and even though it had been months now since the events he was being asked to describe yet again, he could still feel the soreness in his muscles. Worse now the weather was turning cold and wet. Such was the joy of getting older. His ears rang, ever so slightly, with the echo of the explosion that had almost collapsed an entire cavern on his head, and the heads of several extremely wealthy individuals whose influence he could see all over this ongoing disciplinary process. Professional Standards might claim to be incorruptible, but someone was clearly leaning on them to be extra thorough this time.

'As I believe I told you before, and your colleague Inspector Williams, I had reason to believe a person's life was in immediate danger. Neither mobile phones nor the airwave network were working, so I sent Detective Constable Harrison for back-up and proceeded alone.'

'And you think that utter disregard for procedure was justified?'

McLean heard the sneer in the question; it was impossible not to. His interrogator, or maybe inquisitor was a better description, had not tried to hide his contempt from the very first interview a couple of months ago, and nothing much had changed in the intervening time.

'I rather think that's for you to decide, isn't it, Chief Inspector Crane?' He leaned back in his uncomfortable chair and quite deliberately folded his arms across his chest. At this point, McLean no longer cared whether they sacked him or not. He was satisfied that none of the junior officers involved in the case were going to get a black mark against them for what he'd done. If Police Scotland wanted to hang him out to dry, well, he could always take up gardening.

'It's precisely that attitude that's the problem, McLean. You have no respect for authority, don't give a damn about doing things the right way. You have a very poor record of attendance at senior officers' strategy meetings. Quite how you ever made it to detective chief inspector I've no idea.'

Crane's face, never exactly pale at the best of times, began to redden as he worked himself up to a crescendo. McLean had seen the performance a dozen times since the inquiry had begun, so was less worried now that the chief inspector might have a heart attack, or that his head would explode. He was a man who perhaps spent rather too much time at senior officers' strategy meetings, availing himself of the free coffee, biscuits and sand-wiches for lunch while there. Word was the chief inspector had been a rugby player in his younger years, almost but not quite making it to the national squad. If so, his rugby playing days were long gone. And like many a man active in his youth, old age had seen the muscle turn rather more to fat.

'I've never been much of an administrator. You know that.'

McLean waved a hand in the direction of the folder Chief Inspector Crane had arranged on the table in front of them like a shield wall. It was, he knew, a summary of all his failings since first joining what had been Lothian and Borders Police, the best part of a quarter century ago. Crane had brought it to all of their interviews, and never opened it once.

'Sooner or later you're going to have to come to a decision.' McLean unfolded his arms, leaned forward and laid his hands on the table in what he hoped was a gesture of conciliation. 'You know what the top brass want. Or at least the people putting the squeeze on them, anyway. My head on a plate. Maybe something suitably vindictive to go along with it. I imagine that pisses you off almost as much as my lack of respect for procedure. More, maybe, or you'd have recommended my being sacked long ago.'

Crane stared at him through eyes narrowed by the folds of spare flesh on his face. The silence sat between them like the haar that sometimes rolled off the North Sea to blanket the city for days on end. Impenetrable and smothering. McLean waited; it wasn't as if he had anything better to do. Finally the chief inspector broke.

'You're a menace, McLean.' He shook his head as he spoke. 'But your actions saved a woman's life and opened the lid on something foul and rotten that had been going on far too long. You're right. Plenty of powerful people dislike you almost as much as I do. But there's a few seem to think you're worth protecting too. Christ only knows why.'

McLean shrugged, smiled, sat back in his chair and suppressed the wince of pain as his hip protested.

'My recommendation was you be demoted to sergeant and sent on retraining, but apparently there's a shortage of detectives right now, even more so ones with decent experience in the field. Sticking you back in uniform would put people off applying for CID, I'm told. So you get to stay in plain clothes.'

Now, finally, Chief Inspector Crane opened up his folder and removed a single sheet from the top of the pile neatly stacked inside. Had it been there this whole time? Were these past months of endless interviews, debriefings, suspension from active duty, all a sham? McLean wouldn't have put it past them to be so petty.

'The new chief superintendent has also decided that filling a detective sergeant position will be much cheaper than finding a seasoned detective inspector who knows this patch. She's not so concerned about a replacement DCI having local experience, since that's really more of a managerial role anyway.' Crane's emphasis on the word 'managerial' felt like it was meant as an insult, but if so it missed its mark. He turned the sheet of paper around and slid it across the table. A letter on official Police Scotland headed paper. McLean didn't reach for it; he was fairly sure he knew what it said.

'Effective immediately, you are demoted to the rank of detective inspector, working within Specialist Crime Division and based in Edinburgh. Until such time as the post of detective chief inspector is filled, you will report to Detective Super-intendent McIntyre. You will also be required to attend a series of reorientation sessions, focusing on procedure. You can appeal this decision, should you wish, but should you choose to do so you will remain suspended without pay pending the outcome of that appeal.' Crane paused for a moment, perhaps waiting for some kind of protest, or even any kind of response at all. 'Do you wish to appeal?'

McLean leaned forward slowly, not so much to annoy the chief inspector as to avoid any further pain from his hip. He reached out and took the letter, held it up for just long enough to show that he hadn't read it, then put it back down on the table again before fixing Crane with a pleasant smile.

'No. I don't think that will be necessary,' he said.

* * *

Nobody had told him that he couldn't keep on using his old office on the third floor, so McLean let himself in then sat at his desk and stared out the glass wall at the city beyond. Someone had tidied up in his absence, and for once there was no paperwork awaiting his immediate attention. Hardly surprising given that he'd come here straight from his final meeting with DCI Crane of Professional Standards. He hadn't failed to notice that the meeting had been between the two of them, alone. No senior officers present, no witnesses to the proceedings. A simple handover of a letter and it was done. Well, there was the small matter of some annoying training sessions he'd have to endure, but it was better than sitting at home, bored. The demotion was a plus, too. He could see fewer senior officers' strategy meetings in his future, more puzzling out the strange forces that seemed to have arrayed themselves against the city.

He should probably have reported to Detective Superintendent McIntyre, maybe even checked to see if the new chief superintendent was in Edinburgh this week. Sooner or later he'd have to meet her, after all. Apart from a name – Gail Elmwood – and the fact that she had transferred to Police Scotland from the Metropolitan Police in London, he knew nothing about her at all. The only clue he had to her personality was her signature on the letter DCI Crane had handed him. McLean pulled it out of his pocket and unfolded it, not really taking in the words so much as studying that signature. Tight-packed letters, but neat. Her whole name, Gail Elmwood, spelled out in a manner that was readable at least if you knew what you were looking for. Not like McLean's own impenetrable scrawl, which usually looked like he'd succumbed to some kind of coughing fit halfway through writing it. He didn't think much of handwriting analysis, but this signature suggested a meticulous attention to detail and a desire for control. Or something like that anyway.

29

'Oh. Hello, sir. Are you back then?'

McLean glanced up at the doorway. He'd left it open, as had always been his habit. Now the unfeasibly tall figure of Detective Constable Blane blocked it almost entirely. His slumped shoulders and stooped posture might have been simply to avoid banging his head on the door frame, but like a lot of tall people, Lofty had a habit of trying to make himself look smaller whenever he had to interact with those shorter than him. Which was to say most of the time.

'So it would appear.' He folded up the letter and slipped it back into his pocket. 'Was there anything in particular you needed?'

A momentary frown of confusion crossed Blane's features, vanishing almost as soon as it had formed. 'Oh, no sir. I was on my way to find Ja— DS Harrison. Heard she was in with the chief superintendent.'

'Did you say DS Harrison?' McLean put the emphasis on the S, raising an eyebrow as he did so.

'Acting, sir. But aye.'

'I don't know. I go away for a few months and everyone gets delusions of grandeur. Good for her, though.' He stood up, then pushed his chair back in under the clean desk. Took a moment to enjoy the look of the polished wood surface. It wouldn't be long before it wasn't visible again. 'I need to see McIntyre myself. Let her know I'm back, if in a reduced capacity.'

'Umm . . . ?' Blane's confused frown returned, staying put this time.

'They bumped me down to DI, Lofty,' McLean said. 'It's meant to be a slap on the wrist, but I can't help thinking it's a blessing, really.'

The walk along the corridor to Detective Superintendent McIntyre's office took no time at all, certainly not enough for

McLean to draw out any meaningful conversation from DC Blane. Like his own office door, McIntyre's was ajar, and as the two of them approached, they could hear voices in low but urgent conversation. Blane stopped a couple of paces away, where he could neither hear what was being said nor be seen lurking.

'Should we wait, sir?'

'Probably.' McLean carried on the last metre or so, rapped his hand on the door frame and poked his head through the door. The voices stopped instantly as two people looked up at him from where they sat at the conference table. He recognised McIntyre, but the other woman was new to him.

'Tony. Speak of the devil.' McIntyre stood a little more swiftly than McLean was used to, almost as if she was shielding him from the other woman. He'd already worked out who she was, of course, so when she stood up a little more casually and turned to face him full on, he wasn't completely taken aback.

'Ah, the infamous Detective Inspector McLean. I had been hoping we'd have a chance to talk soon.'

'Ma'am.' McLean held out his hand when the chief super-intendent offered hers to shake. Her grip was cool and firm, her hand slender. Indeed, slender was a word that could be used to describe a great deal about her. Striking was another. The uniform of a senior police officer was not the most flattering of outfits, and yet she managed to make it look like the height of fashion.

'Detective . . . Inspector?' McIntyre left a slight pause between the two words, her question quite clear. McLean was grateful for the interruption as he was all too aware that he had been staring at the chief superintendent perhaps a little too hard.

'My punishment. Could have been worse.' He pulled out the letter and handed it to McIntyre by way of explanation. That she didn't know already spoke volumes.

31

'Well, you never wanted to be a DCI anyway,' she said as she handed back the letter. Then she noticed DC Blane standing in the doorway. 'Detective Constable?'

'Ah. Sorry, ma'am. I was told DS Harrison was here.' Blane shifted uncomfortably, his shoulders slumping even more as he found himself in the presence of the chief superintendent. He held up the printout he had been carrying like a votive offering. 'Forensic report from the Cecily Slater house. The scene was too badly degraded to pick up anything much.'

'Cecily Slater?' McLean asked before his brain could catch up with his mouth.

'You know her?' McIntyre asked.

'No. Not really. The name rings a bell, though. Someone my grandmother knew, back in the day. Related to the Bairnfather family, I think. But it can't be the same woman. She'd be a hundred if she was a day.'

'She was very old, sir. And the cottage is on the Bairnfather Estate.' Blane took a step into the room and offered McLean the report as if that would absolve him of any further responsibility.

'Who's SIO?' he asked, again realising as the words came out that they would best have been left unsaid. Clearly a few months away from the front line had blunted his skill at avoiding being roped into things.

'Kirsty's nominally in charge,' McIntyre said. 'But she's half a dozen other investigations on her hands already. And we lost a lot of time working on the assumption it was an accidental death. We've been playing catchup since the post-mortem. Could do with your input. It feels very much like your kind of case.'

McLean only nodded his head in acceptance; there wasn't much else he could do. He held out a hand and Blane gave him the report. The chief superintendent cast her gaze in their direction, dismissing Lofty with a 'Thank you, Detective Constable' that was both polite and unambiguous. McLean watched the giant leave, knowing full well that he had to stay. On the other hand, at least he had something to do.

'You'll be aware that I moved up from London to take this job.' The chief superintendent's words dragged McLean's attention back to her, and he found himself almost standing to attention. Something about her made him want to suck his gut in, even though it wasn't particularly prominent in the first place.

'Yes, ma'am.'

She stared at him for a long while, the gaze from her pale grey eyes uncomfortable. It wasn't that he felt she was seeing right into him, more that he simply didn't know what to say to her. He knew so little about her beyond her name, her rank, and now what she looked like. He was about to fall into the trap he so often set himself, and say something – anything – to fill the growing silence. But then she laughed and broke into a smile that seemed to light up the whole room.

'It's Tony, right?' She indicated for him to sit, taking her own seat again. McIntyre joined them at the conference table once more.

'Yes, ma'am.' McLean sounded like a scratched record, and it brought another laugh from the chief superintendent. The juxtaposition between the laughter and the uniform was unsettling.

'Please, call me Gail. Ma'am makes me sound like some kind of headmistress.'

McLean almost pointed out that her position within the organisation of Police Scotland, in charge of the largest station in the nation's capital, meant that headmistress was quite a good job description, but his sense of self-preservation was beginning to reassert itself. He nodded his understanding rather than risk repeating himself.

'That letter.' The chief superintendent pointed at the jacket pocket into which McLean had put it. 'That was one of my first official duties when I started this job. Paint hardly dry on my office door, and I've to sign a letter officially reprimanding one of my senior officers and demoting him from the rank of DCI to DI. You can imagine that's not quite what I was expecting to be doing with my time.'

Again McLean refrained from answering directly. Instead he tilted his head and nodded slowly once. It seemed to do the trick.

'There were those higher up than me, higher up than the chief constable himself, who thought you should have been given the boot, you know.'

'It doesn't surprise me,' McIntyre said, before McLean could even open his mouth. 'Tony has a knack of annoying people. In this instance three of Scotland's richest émigrés. Frankly I'd've been surprised if nobody'd tried to kick back against that.'

'Yes, well.' The chief superintendent sat up a little straighter and tugged at the front of her jacket as if it hadn't already been sitting perfectly. 'I don't like being told how to do my job like I'm some fresh-out-of-training constable, and I didn't think it would be a good start to bend to the pressure from above. Don't want to be thought of as a "yes" girl from the off.'

'I'm very glad to hear that, ma— Gail. And I'm sorry that I've brought down that kind of pressure on you before you've even got your feet under your desk, so to speak.'

That got McLean a raised eyebrow. 'I was a chief super-intendent in the Met before I came north, Tony. I think I can cope with anything Edinburgh can throw at me. Rather not have to spend all my time putting out fires you've lit, though.'

An image rose unbidden in McLean's mind then. Two young boys bored by the long summer holidays, starting a fire that spread to the moors to the south of the city and inadvertently revealed ancient and grisly secrets. The start of the whole series of events that had got him suspended in the first place.

'Do you find me amusing, Detective Inspector?' The change in Elmwood's tone was instant, snapping from friendly to drill sergeant without a pause for breath. Too late, McLean realised he must have let the ghost of a smile reach his face.

'I'm sorry, ma'am. No. It was just the phrase "putting out fires". I'm sure Detective Superintendent McIntyre can explain. Or—'

'Never mind.' The chief superintendent shook her head as she interrupted him. 'The point I'm trying to make is that you're on an official warning. As I said before, you have allies fighting your corner, Tony. They convinced me to let you stay, even if I was minded to do so anyway. Just don't make me regret that decision, OK?'

6

A chill wind blew off the Pentland Hills, shaking the high branches of the wych elms on the Meadows and tumbling dead brown leaves to the grass. Janie Harrison regretted suggesting to DC Blane that they walk over from the station, her normal stride being about half the length of his. She could have cadged a lift in a squad car, although she had to admit she missed riding in DCI McLean's Alfa Romeo. Even if there was something ever so slightly disturbing about its absurdly powerful engine under that long bonnet, its deep red leather interior.

'So how's it feel to be a detective sergeant then?' Lofty asked.

'Can't say I've noticed much difference, to be honest. Still the same amount of work to do as ever. See when we get those new DCs we've been promised, I can maybe shunt some of it on to them, aye?'

'Know what you mean. Seems daft being sent off to do this. Talking to some bloke about a harassment case, verbal abuse or something? Shouldn't that be uniform's job? I mean, I'm happy to get out of the station for a bit of fresh air, but we're short enough on detectives as it is. Should be concentrating on that poor old wifey up in the woods, shouldn't we?'

Janie shrugged, then shoved her hands into her pockets and hunched herself against the cold. 'If the chief super says jump, I

36

ask how high, OK? And besides, I get the feeling this isn't a simple case of public nuisance. You've heard of Tommy Fielding, right?'

Lofty stopped walking, which at least gave Janie a chance to catch her breath.

'The Dad's Army guy?'

'That's him. Although I'm not sure that's what he's really about.'

'How do you mean? He gets dads visiting rights when they're divorced or separated. Someone's got to fight their corner, haven't they?'

Janie took a deep breath. How to approach this delicately? Decided she couldn't be bothered. 'He's on the wrong side, aye? Defends the monsters who beat their girlfriends black and blue, gets serial rapists back out on the street when we've done everything we can to lock them up.'

'Everyone's entitled to their day in court, remember? Someone's got to defend the bad ones.'

'Aye, but they're no' supposed to enjoy it. And they're no' supposed to win.'

Blane shrugged, set off walking again so that Janie had to hurry to catch up. 'So why are we going to talk to him and no' some uniformed sergeant then?' he asked.

'Because he's on first-name terms with the chief constable is why. He's one of his golfing buddies or something. And his complaint's been passed down to our new chief super, who's keen as you like to make a good impression. End result, you and me get to tramp over to Fountainbridge for the morning, look serious while he rants at us, then do sod all about it. With a bit of luck, then we can get back to finding out who murdered that old wifey out in the hills.'

Lofty paused a moment, apparently considering this inform- ation. Then he shrugged again, said 'OK,' and set off once more in the direction of Tollcross.

★ ★ ★

They heard the noise of the crowd long before reaching the Scotston Hotel and conference centre. A group of people clustered around the side entrance, some bearing placards with such insightful comments as 'Piss Off Tommy' and 'Leave The Kids Out Of It'. Most of them were simply shouting and waving fists. And getting in the way, at least until the looming presence of DC Blane made itself felt.

Janie tucked herself in behind him, and he pushed through the demonstration as if it wasn't there. She glanced from side to side, doing her best to note faces as she went, just in case. All of them were women, as far as she could tell. They spanned all ages, from teenagers with buzzcut hairdos and multiple piercings to a couple who looked like they might be someone's great-nan and her best friend out for a day's shopping in the big toon. One face caught her attention as they reached the corner of the square. Glanced out of the corner of her eye, she thought she recognised the bright red hair, the quickest glimpse of a familiar profile. But when she turned, the figure had gone. There wasn't time to stop, let alone work her way back through the crowd for a better look. And besides, there was no way the person she thought it was would be there. She'd be down in London, surely.

'Come on, Janie. Let's get this over with.' Lofty tapped her lightly on the arm. 'Or should I call you Sarge?'

'Only if you want all the shitty assignments.' Harrison turned from the noisy crowd, still puzzled by the face she had seen, sparking a memory that couldn't be right. She shook the thoughts away. It wasn't important, unless things got out of hand and people started being arrested.

A nervous-looking day manager approached them as they entered the smart foyer of the hotel, hands clasped together as if in prayer.

'Are you the police?' he asked, only just managing to stop

himself from pronouncing it 'polis'. For all his smart suit and neat appearance, he had to work hard to keep the Muirhouse out of his accent.

'Detective Con— Sergeant Harrison. This is my colleague Detective Constable Blane.' Janie let Blane show his warrant card. 'I understand Mr Fielding has a complaint.'

'Indeed.' The manager glanced in the direction of the front door, although he looked less annoyed at the noisy protest than might be expected. Now that they were inside, it wasn't really all that noisy anyway, the front door doing an effective job of blocking much of the sound from outside. 'Please, follow me.'

He led them along a corridor and into a large conference room. By the look of things it had been set up for a presentation, with rows of seats all facing a small dais and lectern. A projector screen behind the lectern showed a slide, presumably part of the presentation. It disappeared almost before Janie could take anything in, but not before she'd seen the 'Dad's Army' logo and what looked like a pie chart claiming the vast majority of rape allegations were made up.

'The police are here, sir.' The manager approached no closer than twenty feet from the dais, announcing their presence a little more loudly than necessary. He gave Janie a strained smile as he turned away and hurried out the door. Clearly not a fan, although whether of her or the man at the lectern Janie couldn't be sure.

'About bloody time.'

Janie had never met Tommy Fielding before, but she had seen photographs and knew him by reputation. In real life he was shorter than she'd imagined, but then that was so often the way with self-important men. He wore a tailored suit that must have cost a fortune, and yet somehow he managed to look scruffy in it. Perhaps it was his scrappy, receding hair, or maybe the slight jowliness about his face. Whatever it was, it gave him the air of a man going to seed. He stepped off the dais and walked up the narrow aisle between the rows of seats to meet them, his gaze flicking only briefly on her, then focusing on DC Blane.

'Detective Sergeant Harrison,' Janie said, before Fielding could assume the male officer was the most senior. 'This is my colleague Detective Constable Blane. I understand you're having a bit of trouble with the protesters outside, sir.'

'A bit of trouble?' Fielding hardly glanced at her, and the sneer in his voice was plain enough. 'Those witches have been camped outside for days now, shouting obscenities at anyone who comes into the hotel. I'm trying to run a conference here and half my delegates have been scared off already.'

Janie doubted any of it was true, apart from the bit about running a conference. As far as she was aware, no one at the hotel had lodged a complaint so far, and the women were loud at times, but mostly peaceful. More to the point, the place where they were holding their vigil, or hurling abuse, was a public square. Moving them on would be tricky even if she wanted to, and so far Fielding had given her little reason.

'I'll go and speak to them, sir. Ask them to disperse, or at the very least to stop harassing people.' She took out her notebook and opened it to a blank page, fully intending it remain that way. 'When does your conference begin? I'm sure we can arrange for a few officers to be on hand.'

Fielding finally stopped staring at Lofty and fixed her with a glare that might have been frightening had she not faced down far worse on football match duty back in her uniform days. Nothing quite like an Old Firm derby to bring out the feral beast in a man, and Janie knew how to deal with it. She smiled sweetly, until he broke the stare.

'The conference programme starts tomorrow morning, but folk have already started arriving. Those . . .' he hooked a thumb over his shoulder in the vague direction of outside '. . . had better not cause any more trouble. The chief constable will hear of it. Mark my words, Detective Sergeant Harrison.'

The threat in naming her was about as subtle as herpes. Janie closed up her notebook and slipped it into her pocket, never once taking her eyes off the loathsome man, nor the condescending smile from her face. 'I'll be sure to bear that in mind, Mr Fielding. Now, if you'll excuse me, I think I'd better have a word with the ladies outside.'

The side entrance to the Scotston Hotel took them back out to the small square that some optimistic city planner had shoe-horned into the redevelopment strategy for the area. Perhaps in high summer it was pleasant enough to sit on the concrete benches, under the struggling plane trees, and eat a quick sandwich before heading back to the office. As autumn merged into winter, it was a grey and unforgiving expanse, all dark whinstone paving and brutally hard landscaping, what little light there was blocked out by the glass-fronted high-rise office and apartment blocks all around it. Into this forbidding space, a band of women had descended to make their protest at the event being held in the hotel.

They were an odd bunch. Janie scanned the crowd, again looking for the familiar flash of red hair, not finding it. The old grannies seemed to have left, and the whole assembly had the feel of breaking up about it, apart from a core of women who clustered around one of the concrete benches. She approached, expecting hostility, but as she neared the group, one of the women turned and smiled.

'It's Janie Harrison, isn't it? Well, this is a surprise.'

Caught on the back foot, Janie stared at the woman. She was vaguely familiar, but the name remained elusive. Taller than Janie, she carried herself with an easy elegance, and wore clothing that managed to be fashionable in a grungy kind of way, while at the same time being perfectly suited to the cold weather. It was her face that caught Janie's attention though, or more specifically her eyes. They had a strange, purple tint to them that had to be contact lenses, surely.

'I'm being unfair.' The woman held out a slender hand, wrist wrapped in bangles. 'Meghan Turner. I'm Hattie's wife. We met briefly at the dig site up in the hills this summer, I think.'

'I thought you were in Africa.' Janie took the proffered hand, feeling the warmth and strength in the other woman's grip. She was an artist, wasn't she? A sculptor? Something like that.

'Heavens, no. Hattie wanted me to go, but I've had quite enough of Africa for now. And this is so much more important.' Meghan waved at the crowd, the square, the hotel in one all-encompassing expansive gesture.

'About that.' Janie reminded herself that this was police business. 'We've had quite a few complaints, you know? And you're pushing the boundaries of breaching the peace.'

Meghan stared at her for a while, not unfriendly so much as sizing her up. 'You know what's going on in there, right?'

'A perfectly legal seminar on men's rights. Morally repugnant as it is, what Mr Fielding is doing isn't against the law. This, however . . .' Janie nodded towards the crowd, but said no more.

'Morally repugnant. I like that.' The older woman smiled.

'He called you witches. I take that as a personal insult. Still have to do my job, mind.'

Meghan's smile grew even wider, and was it just a trick of the light, or did the purple of her eyes seem to deepen? 'Oh, but we are witches, Janie. That's the whole point.'

7

'I'll no' be staying long, aye? Get myself sorted wi' a place soon as all the paperwork's done.'

Gary stands in the middle of Bazza's untidy living room and stares at the threadbare couch. He's been here a thousand times before and never really noticed what a dump it is. It smells weird too, a mixture of stale food, farts and sour, spilled beer.

'Aye, no worries, pal. You stay as long as you need.' Bazza slaps him on the shoulder, then seems to notice the few items of clothing spread over the couch. He picks them up one by one, then chucks them into the corner by the door. 'You want a beer?'

Gary doesn't answer straight away, which isn't normal for him. None of this is normal for him. He's been kipping at his ma's place since the meeting with the lawyer, but he couldn't stay there long. Too many pictures of Bella and Wee Mary, and even he could see which side she'd taken. So much for family sticking together.

He slips the strap of his kit bag off his shoulder and drops the heavy weight to the floor. Everything he owns is in that bag, or out in the works van parked outside the tower block. Can't leave it there long, mind. Bazza's place isn't the best part of town, and the last thing he needs is having to explain to the boss why he borrowed it without asking first.

'Here you go, Gary. Get that down your neck.' Bazza presses a cold tinny of Tennent's lager into his hand, the ring pull torn open. He's already taken a swig from his own can and lets out a belch as he drops into the couch and reaches for the TV remote. Gary looks around the room again, sees his future in its damp-stained walls and thin carpet. Bazza's got all the stuff that matters; big screen telly, subscription to all the sports channels, fridge full of beer and a half-decent kebab shop across the road from the tower. It's an existence, just barely.

'What was the story about you an' Trish anyways?' he asks as he self-consciously brushes at the couch seat before settling down into it. Time was him and Bazza talked about shite, got drunk together, fought with the Hibees on a Saturday night and spent Sundays on the X-Box on this very couch. That all changed when Bazza got married. And Gary hooked up with Bella not long after. Thought they'd grown up. Aye, right.

'Ach, youse know what birds are like. Promise you the earth an' suck your dick 'til they've got their feet under the table.' Bazza takes a swig of his lager, uncaring or unaware that some of it dribbles down his chin and on to his T-shirt. 'Soon as the ring's on, though? That's when they change, aye? Then it's just do this Bazza, fetch that Bazza, tidy up after yersel' Bazza. Nag nag nag.' He holds up his free hand and taps his fingers against his thumb like a naked sock puppet.

Gary takes a sip of his own beer. It's too warm and tastes like piss. 'Thought you shagged that Lisa works in Tesco, an' her best mate told some friend of hers who was in Trish's Zumba class. An' that's why she left.'

Bazza frowns, belches and thumps at his chest. 'Aye, well. Mebbe. But what's a bloke to do if his wife won't let him shag her? Plenty more fish in the sea, eh? Stupid bitch.'

The two of them fall silent for a while, sip their lukewarm, fizzy pish and stare at the telly. There's a footie match on –

there's always a footie match on – but it's two foreign teams with players whose names neither of them can pronounce. Something to look at, take the mind off how shit life's turned out for the both of them.

'It's no' right, Bazza,' Gary says eventually, the thoughts that have been sluggishly bubbling away in his head finally breaking free.

'How no'?'

'Wee Mary. I cannae even see her. No' even if she's wi' her gran. My own ma. I've tae stay away from home if . . . she's there.' Gary doesn't realise he's clenched his fist until he's crushed the can enough to spill beer on his jeans. 'Aw, fuck, man. I need tae wear these tae work. Bitch isn't even here an' she's fuckin' things up for me.'

There's another long silence while they stare at the screen. After a while Bazza gets up and fetches another couple of tins, hands one to Gary along with a cloth.

'There's a bloke I know youse should speak to.'

Gary looks at his mate without even trying to hide his scepticism. Bazza's got form for this kind of thing.

'No' like that, man. He's a lawyer or something. Runs a charity for dads who've had their kids taken away. Gets them their rights back an' stuff.'

Gary holds the can away from himself as he pops the ring pull, but this one's colder, the beer inside unshaken. There's a tiny flicker of hope in him as he speaks. The first he's felt since he signed his name on the papers the last lawyer put in front of him.

'For real?' he asks.

'Aye sure, for real. I'll gie' him a call. Set youse up like.'

'Who is he? Have I heard of him?' Gary pulls out his phone before remembering that the signal's crap in Bazza's flat, and he hasn't got the password for the Wi-Fi yet.

'Aye, mebbe. He's been on the news that many times right enough. His name's Tommy. Tommy Fielding.'

8

McLean sat at his desk, half reading the case notes for the old woman found dead in her burned out house, Cecily Slater. Not that they were any different from the last time he'd read them. A week on, and they still had nothing. Still, it was good to be back at work, and the small matter of demotion to DI suited him just fine. No more senior officers' strategy meetings, no more trips across to the Crime Campus in Gartcosh, no more wasting time briefing detective inspectors to brief detective sergeants to send detective constables off to ask questions, the answers to which were then garbled as they were passed back up the chain. He could get on with the job of puzzling out why someone would beat an old woman close to death, then douse her in petrol and set her on fire. And how nobody had noticed until she'd lain there for a week. How very few people had even known she existed at all.

He shuddered at the thought of it, reading Angus Cadwallader's terse prose in the pathology report again. For once he was glad it had been Harrison and not him attending the examination. The poor old woman had been given the works, for sure. What on earth could have possessed someone, or more likely several somebodies, to do such a thing to a ninety-year-old like Cecily Slater?

McLean frowned at the name as it appeared on the next part of the report. They had put together the basic facts, but there was no sense of the person behind them. A recluse, she'd been living in that cottage for as long as anyone could remember. She was the younger sister of the previous Lord Bairnfather, on whose family estate the cottage lay. Bairnfather Hall was a boutique hotel now, and the current lord lived in London. He'd been informed of his aunt's death, but as yet nobody had interviewed him about her. That struck McLean as odd, but a note on the file said he was currently in the US on business and would let the police know as soon as he was back. The note was almost two weeks old now.

The whole case had a lethargy to it quite out of keeping with the horror of the crime. Possibly because it hadn't been uncovered earlier; the first twenty-four hours in any investigation were crucial, and they'd long gone before anyone even knew there was a case at all. Possibly because they were so short of detectives the initial investigation had fallen to a lowly DC. McLean couldn't fault Janie Harrison's abilities, but everyone had been working on the assumption this had been a tragic accident until the post-mortem had suggested otherwise. They'd wasted so much time, lost so much invaluable forensic evidence. Now the case was going nowhere, stalled before it had even started, vital clues missed and important avenues of enquiry left unexplored. Almost two weeks since her body had been found, three since she had died, Cecily Slater deserved a lot more than she was getting.

Leafing through the actions that had been carried out so far, he found one glaring omission. An oversight, perhaps, or maybe just something that nobody had got around to yet. He picked up his phone and stared at the buttons on the console for a moment while he tried to remember how the damned thing worked. Too long out of the saddle. It would be easier just to go and find someone to ask.

It took only a few minutes to walk to the incident room, one floor down. Like the case itself, it wasn't exactly a hive of industry. A few uniformed constables sat at computer screens or talked on headsets as if they were in a call centre, but only one whiteboard had been written on so far, photographs from the scene pinned up alongside it. This whole investigation needed a kick up the arse, and he cursed himself for letting it get so bad.

McLean looked around the room until he finally spied one person not quite managing to hide behind a computer screen. Detective Sergeant Sandy Gregg knew she'd been spotted. Or maybe she'd simply been trying to finish up what she'd been doing before coming to help her DI.

'I've been reviewing the case notes, and I can't find any mention of a follow-up interview with the person who found her. Just the initial questioning at the scene. You know if that's been done yet?'

Gregg looked embarrassed. 'If it's not on the system, then my best bet is no, sir. Janie would know better, but I think she's away running errands for the new chief super.'

McLean raised a surprised eyebrow. He'd not seen much of their new boss since their first meeting. Was this Elmwood's preferred method of working, to go straight to the sergeants? Or was she grooming Harrison for greater things? Neither situation worried him much.

'Well, if you see her before I do, get her to set up an interview, can you? I think it's time we pulled everything together with this investigation, before it gets away from us.'

'I'll get right on it. Want me to send her up to your office when she comes in?'

McLean checked his watch, remembering the other reason why he'd maybe not given quite as much attention to the case as it warranted. 'No. It'll have to be tomorrow. I've got to go to a retraining session in half an hour.'

'Retraining?' DS Gregg didn't even try to keep the incredulity from her voice.

'Retraining, reorientation, whatever you want to call it. All part of my penance. Still, it could have been worse. They could have busted me down to sergeant, and then I'd be back in the CID room with the rest of you.'

It wasn't until much later that he finally managed to get some time to go over the case notes properly. Deep in concentration, McLean sensed a presence in the open doorway to his office rather than seeing anything. Looking up, he was surprised to find the new station chief standing just inside the room, her gaze taking it all in before finally coming to rest on him.

'Ma— Gail.' He scrambled to his feet. 'I didn't see you there. Is there something I can help you with?'

The chief superintendent smiled warmly, then turned and closed the door before speaking. 'Working late, Tony?'

'Catching up, mostly. I've been out of the loop almost three months and the first thing I get handed is a murder that's already two weeks old? Doesn't help that I keep getting dragged away on "reorientation" sessions.' He held his hands up and made little bunny ears in the air around the word reorientation, even though it annoyed the hell out of him when other people did it. Maybe the sessions themselves were worse.

'Boxes have to be ticked, I'm afraid. You can thank the auditors for that.' The chief superintendent walked slowly across the room, pulled a chair out from the conference table and then dragged it across to McLean's desk. Her movements weren't hurried; the word languorous sprang to mind. As if she were exhausted by the day's events, which was very possible.

'Sit, please.' She waved an elegant hand at him, and McLean settled himself back into his office chair. For some unaccountable reason he felt glad to have the solidity of his desk between him and his new boss.

'No Mrs McLean waiting patiently for you to come home?' Elmwood asked after an awkward silence.

'I'm not married.' McLean held up his hand to show the absence of any rings. Something like surprise flitted briefly across the chief superintendent's face before she smiled broadly.

'A man like you? I'd have thought they'd be queueing round the block.'

'I have a partner. She's in Africa at the moment, though. Part of a team of forensic archaeologists working on mass graves in Rwanda. She flew out a few weeks back.'

'So you're all alone. That must be . . . lonely.' Elmwood stared at him with her piercing grey eyes and McLean began to understand what the mouse feels like as the owl screeches in from the night sky.

'Was there something you wanted?' he asked, keen to get whatever this was over with. The chief superintendent didn't answer straight away, but instead stared at him, the lightest of frowns furrowing her brow as if she were trying to find the right words.

'You've been a detective here, what? Twenty years now?'

McLean nodded his head once. 'Something like that. I don't want to think about it too much, really.'

The chief superintendent's face lit up with a smile at his joke. 'We all get older, Tony. But unlike most, you've been happy to stick at what you do best, right?' She didn't wait for him to answer. 'I've been doing a bit of background reading of my own, and I know you didn't want to be promoted to DCI. All that nasty business with Forrester and his son. Quick thinking in a crisis, but you got bumped up to where you didn't want to be.'

'Well, I got this office out of it, so it's not all bad.'

Another one of those smiles. The chief superintendent had a

way of making you feel like her entire concentration was focused on you, McLean noticed. It should have been pleasant, but he found it deeply unsettling.

'It's a nice office. Good view, I'm told. When it's not dark before six. It's handy too. Just along the corridor from my own.'

Was there a note of flirtation in her voice? McLean didn't want to read so much into it. She wasn't that long in the job, and he knew very little about her past life in the Met. She wore no rings either, so no Mr Elmwood anywhere in the mix. Too focused on the job to ever settle down? That wasn't his problem. The chief constable wouldn't have chosen just anybody for the post. At least he hoped so.

'Is that useful? I mean, we have phones.' He gestured at the heavy plastic console on his desk.

The chief superintendent's smile was more shark-like this time, her teeth startlingly white and straight. 'Of course. But I need to know I've got an ally here, Tony. Someone I can trust. It's not easy coming into a new station, a new country even. Yes, I've done my homework, and I've a good team of officers working with me. But I need someone to bounce ideas off, someone to run things by before I make a fool of myself in front of the police authority or heaven forbid the Minister.'

McLean couldn't help thinking the speech was too well rehearsed to be entirely sincere. He also wasn't quite sure he wanted such a role. But he wasn't so stupid as to think he could say no.

'I'm sure I'd be happy to give advice if you feel the need for it,' he said, hearing the sound of his own grave being dug with each word. The chief superintendent's smile broadened into a wide grin as she stood up in a graceful, fluid motion.

'Splendid. I knew we'd get along fine.'

And without another word, she strode out of the room,

51

leaving the empty chair behind like some kind of territorial marker.

'Looks like it's just you and me again.'

McLean placed his briefcase on the kitchen table, following up with the bag of takeaway curry he'd picked up on the way home. It was later than he'd have liked, but Mrs McCutcheon's cat never seemed to mind. A sure sign that winter was not far off, she had taken up her habitual place in front of the Aga. Reasonably confident the cat wouldn't help herself to his supper, McLean went through to the hall and leafed through the day's post. There wasn't much, but a hastily scribbled postcard with a picture on the front of the hills behind Kigali reminded him of the last time Emma had gone travelling. He hoped she'd be home before Christmas, not away for two years again.

He had finished half of his curry and put the rest away for the next day, much to the horrified indignation of Mrs McCutcheon's cat, and was pouring himself a second beer when he heard a noise outside. Headlights swept the darkness through the window, the sound of car tyres crunching on the gravel of the drive. McLean went to the front door, opening it just in time to see the departing rear lights of a taxi and the large, bulky shape of his unexpected visitor.

'Rose. This is a surprise. Come in, please.'

Madame Rose, fortune teller, Tarot reader, antiquarian book-seller and purveyor of occult curios, smiled broadly as she stepped into the hall. She had dressed for cold weather, wrapped in a coat that a Russian Tsar might have worn through a Saint Petersburg winter, even though she'd presumably come all the way from her home in Leith comfortably warm inside the taxi.

'Tony. It's been too long.'

Now that she mentioned it, McLean realised it was true. He couldn't remember when he'd last spoken to the medium. Had it been the winter, and all that trouble with the refugees? He shook away the thought as he took her coat, marvelling at the weight of the thing, then led her through to the library.

'Emma out?' Rose asked, after she'd settled herself on to the sofa.

'In a manner of speaking. She's gone to Africa to help identify bodies in a mass grave.'

Madame Rose raised one perfectly sculpted eyebrow, then gave the lightest of shrugs. 'As long as she's happy.'

'From the emails and texts, I'd say so. It was a bit of a godsend Professor Turner showing up when she did. Em needed a change of scene.'

'Professor Turner?' Madame Rose tilted her head slightly, as if shaking loose a memory. 'Oh yes, the forensic archaeologist. She was a student of your grandmother's, I seem to recall. I didn't know she was back in Edinburgh. And you, Tony. Have you been busy?'

The question came as something of a surprise. McLean was used to Madame Rose knowing everything, and yet the way she asked seemed entirely genuine.

'Actually I've been on enforced leave for the best part of three months. There was a bit of a mess in the summer. You might have seen it on the news?'

'I must confess, like dear Emma I have been away travelling myself. Only just got back to the city today. I've been catching up with a few important people and you are quite high up on that list.'

'That might explain why you never warned me about the band of cannibals hiding out in the Moorfoot Hills then.' McLean explained about the case, enjoying the look of surprise on the medium's face. It wasn't often he caught her off guard.

'The Brotherhood of the Rose Well? I thought they had all died out a long time ago. A footnote in the arcane histories.

Nothing more.' She paused a moment, eyes unfocused, before coming back to herself with a small shudder. 'How strange.'

'And you?' McLean asked to the silence that followed. 'Your travels went well? Did you go anywhere interesting?'

Madame Rose smiled at that. 'Oh, Tony. Everywhere I go is interesting. How could it not be, with me there? But yes, my travels went well. Alas, I return to a city that is . . . less happy.'

'How so? I mean, I've been out of the loop a bit, but I'm sure I'd have heard.'

Madame Rose shook her head slowly. 'Not the sort of thing Police Scotland would be expected to deal with. At least, not directly. The fallout? Well, I have a horrible feeling that will come soon enough.'

McLean pushed down his frustration at the medium. She had a habit of skirting around the subject, couching her words and generally being annoyingly enigmatic.

'Anything more solid than vague hints?' he asked.

'Oh, Tony. You wouldn't believe me if I told you, and I know it annoys you when I speak of dark forces and the balance of things. It is out of kilter all the same, though, whether you believe it or not. Something has upset the natural order. I fear it will be up to us to put it right. Again.'

'I'd love to help, really. But I'm only just finding my way back into the new order at work. I'm no longer a DCI. Still a cat slave, though.' McLean nodded at the creature as Mrs McCutcheon's cat wandered into the room. She walked straight up to Rose, tail held high, then sat in a most un-catlike way and stared at the medium. The silence held for what was probably only a few seconds, but felt like hours. Almost as if the two of them were communicating in some telepathic manner. Rose was the one to break the moment.

'I have a feeling you'll be busy soon enough, Tony. With the job that is. Cat slave is for life, I'm afraid.' Rose pressed her large hands to her knees and levered herself to her feet. 'Well, it's been lovely seeing you again, but I've other folk to get round before the night is out, so I'd best be getting on.'

'Can I not get you something first? Tea perhaps?' He turned to the bookcase and the secret compartment where all the good whisky hid. 'Something stronger?'

Madame Rose shook her head slightly. 'Perhaps another time. I hear you have some fifty-year-old Ardbeg in there. I could tell you a story or two about the head distiller who made that dram.'

Mrs McCutcheon's cat stood up abruptly. Tail high, and twitching a little this time, she sauntered out of the room and Madame Rose followed as if she was being led. The cat stopped at the front door, clearly expecting McLean to do the menial work. He helped the medium back into her heavy winter coat and handed her the fur-lined hat that had gone with it.

'It's good to be back,' she said as she took it from him. 'And good to see you're safe. Give Emma my love when you speak to her later.'

When he opened the door to let her out, a different taxi was already waiting. McLean helped Madame Rose into the back, then watched her leave, wondering all the while how she managed to pull off her little magic stage show. Back in the kitchen he retrieved his beer and picked up his phone from the table. He'd been planning on making the call, but Rose couldn't have known that, surely?

He tapped the screen, then raised the phone to his ear, listening to the oddly foreign tones as the call spanned continents. Finally it was answered, a slightly weary voice too far away.

'Hey, Tony.'

'Hey, Em. How's it going?'

9

Gary knows he's out of his depth when a lad a bit younger than him comes up and offers to take his coat. Sure, the hotel's posh in that old-fashioned way that makes him feel uncomfortable, but it makes him wonder how much money this Tommy Fielding's going to charge for his services, too. The last lawyer wasn't cheap, and he cost Gary his daughter as well as the fee.

He goes through to the bar feeling slightly naked now that he's shed his outer skin. Fair play, the young lad hid his sneer at the cheap nylon parka, but Gary knows he sticks out here. Everyone's wearing suits, even some of the women. He's never backed down from a fight in his life, but this place gives him the heebie-jeebies. The urge to turn tail and flee is strong; he'd even consider leaving the parka behind.

'You must be Gary.'

The voice takes him by surprise, as much that someone who isn't being paid to serve customers here might talk to him as that they know his name. He turns to see one of the suited men not more than a couple of paces away from him. Taller by half a head, thinning hair and the beginnings of a paunch even his expensive suit can't hide. He looks like the sort of lawyer you'd find defending the villain in a movie. Slick. That's the word.

'Mr Fielding?'

'Call me Tommy, please.' The suited man holds out a hand, and after a moment Gary takes it. The shake is firm, Fielding's other hand coming around to clasp Gary's elbow in that over-familiar way posh folk have. Only he's not posh, not really. There's an edge to his accent that's working class, even if the man has made a lot of effort to hide it.

'Tommy, aye.' Gary retrieves his hand, resists the urge to wipe it on his jeans. Fielding's handshake was firm, but his palm is damp with sweat. 'Baz— Barry said he'd spoken to you.'

'Poor old Bazza.' Fielding shakes his head. 'But we're here to talk about you, not him. Here, let me buy you a drink.'

Gary's confused as he follows Fielding to the bar. He doesn't act like a lawyer, and when was the last time one of those offered to pay for anything? True, this might be softening him up before the kill, but it doesn't feel like that. They take their drinks – a pint of posh lager for Gary, a double malt ruined by being poured over ice for Fielding – and sit down in a cosy alcove away from the hubbub. Not that the bar's all that busy, mind. The prices they charge it's hardly surprising.

'So. Bazza tells me you've lost access to your daughter. Mary, isn't it?'

Gary's halfway through a mouthful of lager when Fielding says this, and swallows it badly. 'You done your homework,' he says, choking on the words.

'Not really, no.' Fielding shakes his head slowly, a thin smile on his lips. 'It's just a story I've heard all too often. There you are, trying to be the best father you can for your wee girl, and then all of a sudden it's all taken away. Just like that.' He snaps his fingers, the noise of it cracking in the air like a bone breaking.

'Aye, well. It's no—'

'It exactly is, Gary. And don't let them tell you otherwise.' Fielding's leaning in close now, eyes alive. 'Let me guess. Lawyer came to you with an ultimatum. Give up all rights, or she presses charges and you go to jail, right?'

'I—'

'They didn't give you time to think about it, did they, Gary? Just shoved the paper in front of you and bullied you into signing on the dotted line. Next thing you know, you're on the street, no one to turn to, and no hope of ever seeing your daughter again.'

'Well—'

'That's how they operate, Gary. How they get away with it. The court system is loaded against people like you and me.'

'I— you?' Gary finally manages to get a word in.

'My boy. Jim. He's almost twenty now, can you believe that? His mother tried to take him away. Succeeded for a while, but I fought back, right? Took it all the way to the Supreme Court. Learned a fair bit about how the system works against us while I was at it.'

'And did you . . . ?'

'Win?' Fielding picks up his glass and stares at the melting ice cubes for a moment before answering. 'Aye. After a fashion. I got my visiting rights back. It was a hollow victory, though. She'd poisoned his mind against me. The lies she told that I've only found out recently, now he's grown.'

Gary reckons there's more to it than that, but he doesn't say anything. His head's still reeling from the cascade of events. How a simple slap has ended up with him here, talking about Supreme Courts and visiting rights and Christ only knows what else. Fielding swirls the remains of the whisky around for a moment before knocking it back, ice cubes clattering against his teeth. When he puts the glass down again, he fixes Gary with a determined stare.

'You want to get your wee girl back, right? Want to be able to visit her whenever you choose, even if she's living with . . .'

Fielding pauses as if the words 'her mother' are too hard to say. Gary knows the feeling.

'Is that even possible?'

Fielding picks up his glass, stares at it and then over at the bar. 'Trust me, Gary. Anything's possible if you put your mind to it.'

10

A heavy dampness hung in the air, somewhere between fog and rain, it played havoc with the automatic sensor for his windscreen wipers as McLean drove west out of the city on the Balerno road. He'd not been this way for a while, but nothing much seemed to have changed. A marked difference from most of the other arterial roads, where ribbon development was spreading from the city like a metastasising cancer.

Beside him in the passenger seat, Detective Sergeant Harrison stared at her phone, occasionally tapping the screen as she used its navigation app to try and find the address they were looking for. Mains of Bairnfather Farm hadn't shown up on the system built into the Alfa Romeo for some unaccountable reason. Perhaps because the whole area was a maze of single-track roads that seemed to be taking you in the right direction but ended at a locked gate into a field full of contented cows or another impenetrable stand of trees. McLean feared for the underside of his car as he backed his way out of the turn into a muddy farmyard and finally drew up outside a squat but sturdy stone-built house.

'What's the farmer's name again?' he asked.

'Uist, sir. Tam Uist. We took a statement off him on the day, but I don't think anyone's spoken to him since. It was all a bit muddled when we first got the call. Nobody senior available to take charge, so we did the best we could. Thought we were just dealing with an accidental death, too, so there wasn't much of a sense of urgency.'

'Well, if Professional Standards hadn't drawn out their inquiry for so long, maybe I'd have been on hand to help. It would still probably have been the same though. Best we can do is make up for lost time, eh?'

An inquisitive and noisy pair of Patterdale Terriers came racing around the corner of the building as McLean and Harrison climbed out of the car. They weren't unfriendly, but their muddy paws and tendency to jump up in excitement meant McLean would be needing a clean pair of trousers soon. A sharp whistle had the two dogs turn as one and race away, meeting the man who must have been their owner as he appeared from the back door.

'You'd be the polis, then?' As he approached them, McLean saw he was wearing the farmer's standard uniform of grease-stained green John Deere overalls and heavy Rigger boots. He had a rag that was so dirty it could only smear the grime on his hands into a thin layer rather than clean any of it off.

'Mr Uist?' McLean asked.

'Tam Uist, aye.'

'Detective Inspector McLean. This is my colleague Detective Sergeant Harrison. I understand you were the one who found Cecily Slater's body, at the cottage in the woods.'

A sad frown creased the farmer's face, his shoulders slumping as he let his hands drop. McLean was glad he'd not offered one to shake.

'Aye, terrible business that. Poor Mistress Cecily. She was a grand old woman.' He paused for a moment, then seemed to remember himself. 'Come on in the house. I'll get Margaret to put the kettle on.'

* * *

Margaret turned out to be a small, sturdy woman to Tam Uist's thin and wiry frame. McLean was put in mind of the old nursery rhyme about Jack Spratt and his wife and their strange dietary foibles, but he kept that to himself as they were bade to sit at the kitchen table.

'I spoke to one of the constables on the day,' Tam said as he emerged from the utility room at the back of the house, drying his now much cleaner hands. 'Big tall fellow. Told him all I knew then.'

'This is more of a follow-up conversation, Mr Uist,' McLean said. 'We're trying to get as much background information on the old lady as possible. I understand you visited her about once a week?'

The farmer pulled out one of the chairs and sat down as his wife busied herself at the cooker. 'Only since the old bridge fell down. 'Fore that I'd sometimes see her every couple days if there was something needing done, or maybe not for a month if she wanted left alone.'

'Was that common? For her to want to be left alone?'

Uist paused a moment before answering, partly to gather his thoughts, but mostly because his wife placed three mugs of tea down in front of them all, along with a plate piled with biscuits. She didn't join them at the table but remained in the room. At first glance she appeared to be busying herself with cooking, but McLean knew someone wanting to eavesdrop on a conversation when he saw them.

'I can't rightly remember a time Mistress Cecily didn't live in that cottage. I was born here, grew up here. I've been farming this land all my life, and she's always been there.'

McLean studied the farmer's face. He had that weathered texture to his skin, his close-cropped hair flecked with grey, but he was probably only just past forty. Possibly younger.

Farming could turn you old before your time.

'But she's always kept herself to herself, is that what you're saying?'

'Aye. Back when I was a lad, everyone said she was a witch an' she'd curse us if we crossed her.' Uist took a bite out of his biscuit, a mouthful of tea, then carried on speaking as he chewed and swallowed. 'Sounds daft now I'm older, but I believed it back then. We all did.'

'All?'

'Aye. This is the home farm, but there's a half dozen others that are part of the Bairnfather Estate. Then there's the hall itself. That's a hotel now, but it's still got groundskeepers, maintenance men. Must be a hundred or more cottages and houses all told. Families growing up here. Everyone knew Mistress Cecily wasn't to be disturbed. But as she got older, well, she asked every now and then. A bit of help in the garden, something needing fixed in the house. Then when the bridge collapsed a couple of months back, the only way in and out was over the old ford. Wouldn't even trust a Land Rover to it, so I took stuff to her in the tractor.'

'But only once a week.'

'Aye, like I said. If she didn't need something doing, she liked to be left alone.'

'You say she's always lived in that cottage. Since you can remember, anyway. Do you know if she has any family nearby?'

Uist cocked his head slightly, an expression on his face as if he thought McLean daft for asking. 'Maybe no' nearby. Least not all the time. But there's Lord Bairnfather himself.'

'I understand he lives in London. To be honest, I'm surprised he's not come back here yet. We informed him over a fortnight ago.'

'Well that's Reggie down to a T now, isn't it?' Margaret Uist bustled over with a cloth, wiping the mess her husband had left on the tabletop from eating biscuits.

'How do you mean?' McLean asked.

'Mistress Cecily never cared for the titles and the privilege and all. She hated the hall, though she loved her wee cottage. She never said much about it, mind, but I got the feeling the family had done her wrong. Many years ago.'

'Did she not get on with her nephew then? Do you know how he felt about her?'

'Can't remember the last time I spoke to Lord Reginald,' Tam Uist said, as if that explained everything. 'Most of my business is with Charlie.'

'Charlie?' McLean felt acute embarrassment in asking. He should have been far better briefed before coming to this interview.

'Charlie McPherson. He's the estate manager. Lord Reggie's right-hand man.'

'We spoke to him on the day, sir,' Harrison interrupted before McLean could say anything more. 'Should have been a transcript of the interview in the file. Not that he could add much to what Mr Uist here told us.'

'Of course.' McLean finished his tea, carefully placing the mug back down once he was done. 'Mr McPherson's next on our list of people to speak to again. I'm afraid what we took for a tragic accident at the start is beginning to look like something a bit more serious.'

Margaret Uist let out a little gasp, her hand reaching for her throat. 'Oh my word. You think somebody . . . did for her?'

Before McLean could answer, the farmer had crossed the room and taken his wife in his arms. A head and more shorter than him, she melted into his embrace.

'I'm very sorry to be the bearer of such bad tidings, Mrs Uist.' McLean turned his attention to her husband. 'Mr Uist, I would appreciate it if you kept this information to yourselves for now. We will find out what happened to Cecily Slater, I can assure you. But it's easier for us to carry out our investigations if people aren't speculating about what might have happened.'

11

'ow. This is a bit posh, isn't it?'

DS Harrison leaned forward over the steering wheel, the better to peer out the windscreen at the approaching mansion. McLean sat in the passenger seat, happy to be driven for a change, even if it was only the short distance from the farm. Harrison liked driving the Alfa, he knew, and she did it well. None of the other junior officers dared even try, declining whenever he suggested it to them. It was probably for the best.

'Ostentatious is the word you're looking for, I'd say.' He watched the building appear to grow in size as they came ever closer. No doubt whoever had designed the grounds surrounding Bairnfather Hall had intended it to work that way, the mature woodland on either side of the drive easing gently away to reveal more and more of a massive sandstone edifice. That it had all been the residence of just one family seemed rather obscene, and its current use as a hotel for the kind of people who didn't blink at spending a five-figure sum on a bed for the night wasn't much better.

A half-dozen needlessly expensive cars were parked on a vast gravel circle in front of the main entrance. McLean's Alfa wasn't cheap, but it might as well have been an old banger in comparison. He should probably have run it through a carwash, or maybe taken a bucket and rag to it himself whilst he'd been suspended, sitting at home and mostly twiddling his thumbs. Instead he'd neglected the poor thing, and its black paint was more road grime grey, reflected in the dazzling polish of the gleaming, and spectacularly ugly, Rolls-Royce SUV Harrison parked next to.

It would be easy to forget that Edinburgh city centre was less than a half-hour's drive away. Set in gently undulating parkland, surrounded by distant woodlands and sheltered by the rising slopes of the Pentland Hills, the hall felt like it belonged in a different era, or perhaps another dimension. That, of course, was what the punters paid for, and only the occasional plane climbing into the air from Turnhouse and the omnipresent dull roar of the M8 spoiled the otherwise perfect calm.

They climbed a set of elegant stone steps to the front entrance and a hall almost as large as McLean's entire house. A low mutter of voices escaped from a room off to the left, but before McLean could investigate, a young man in an immaculate tailcoat approached the two of them.

'Good afternoon, sir, ma'am.' He bowed, minimally. 'Welcome to Bairnfather Hall. Might I be of assistance?'

McLean ignored him, allowing Harrison the honours. She dug her warrant card out and presented it to the doorman. 'Detective Sergeant Harrison. This is Detective Chief Inspector McLean. I wonder if we might have a word with Mr McPherson?'

To his credit, the doorman didn't miss a beat. Nor did he bother inspecting Harrison's warrant card. With another of those minimalist bows, he turned. 'If you would like to follow me.' And without waiting to see if they would, he set off across the hall. McLean offered Harrison a raised eyebrow, which earned him a scowl. Promotion had boosted her confidence, and it had also made her less respectful of his rank.

'You do know it's only Detective Inspector now, not Chief,' he said, quietly enough that their guide wouldn't hear.

'Aye, sir. But this place . . .' Harrison shrugged. 'Seems like it needs someone a bit more senior?'

He had to admit she had a point. They followed the doorman, trekking across vast acres of polished marble floor. The entrance hall, or grand hall or whatever the hell it was called, rose up to a glass cupola high overhead. It wasn't that impressive by the standards of modern engineering, but given it had been built in an age when sophisticated construction involved placing stones on top of other stones, it was quite breathtaking. Something about knowing it had been built with sweat and muscle, rather than computers and heavy machinery, lent it a solidity McLean didn't get from the enormous conference centres, shopping malls and business hotels that had been popping up in the city in recent years. Bairnfather Hall had the benefit of a couple of centuries of not falling down, too. That helped.

'If you could wait here a moment, I'll just see if I can find Mr McPherson for you.' The doorman had stopped by a door that was a good six feet taller than it needed to be, and surrounded by an architrave that must have taken months to carve. McLean checked his watch while they waited, Harrison doing something with her phone. He was surprised she could get a signal behind all this stone.

'Charlie McPherson. How can I help you?'

A man not much older than the one who'd led them to this point had appeared at the door as if by magic. He was dressed a little less formally, his double-breasted suit and shiny, slicked back hair giving him the air of a fifties used car salesman rather than manager of such an exclusive hotel and vast estate. His proffered hand was aimed at McLean, even though Harrison stood a little closer.

'Cecily Slater,' McLean said as he shook that hand. McPherson's grip was loose, warm and sweaty, but there was no mistaking the twitch as he heard the name. He looked from

McLean to Harrison, then back again, his faux-helpful smile falling to an expression of resigned weariness. He pointed at another over-large door a fair distance away.

'Why don't we go to my office.'

Charlie McPherson's office was the most opulent McLean had seen in many a year. He wasn't sure what the room had been originally, back when Bairnfather Hall had been a private residence. It might have been Lord Bairnfather's study, or possibly a ladies' withdrawing room. Like the rest of the building, it was larger than anyone could possibly need, with a high ceiling decorated with ornate plasterwork. Two tall windows looked out on to the formal gardens to the rear of the house, and from there to the woods that climbed up the northern flank of the Pentland Hills. Between them, McPherson carried out his business from a massive antique desk, but he led McLean and Harrison to a long table incongruously blocking an Adam fireplace. Despite there being no fire in the grate, the room was comfortably warm.

'Coffee?' McPherson asked as he poured from a glass jug he'd removed from under a catering-style filter machine. McLean nodded, and soon enough the three of them were seated around one corner of the table.

'Lady Cecily.' McPherson gave his head the most minimal of shakes. 'What a terrible business.'

'Lady Cecily. Yes.' McLean put his emphasis on the title. 'I have to admit that we weren't initially aware of her . . . lineage? I knew she was part of the family, but I thought maybe a distant cousin. Not Lord Bairnfather's aunt.'

McPherson raised an eyebrow. 'I'm surprised. Lady Cecily Slater, daughter of the ninth Lord Bairnfather.' He pointed to a portrait hanging on the wall not far from the fireplace. 'That's him there. Sir Reginald Archibald Slater before he inherited the title.'

'And yet she lived in the gamekeeper's cottage?' Harrison asked the question before McLean could voice it himself.

'She's . . . She was quite a character. Could have had a nice townhouse, even her own suite here in the hotel for that matter. Sir Reginald does. That's the current Lord Bairnfather, named for his grandfather.' McPherson shook his head a bit more effusively now. 'But no, she insisted on that cottage. She used to say it was where she was born, and it was where she was going to die. That seems rather prophetic now.'

McLean took a sip of his coffee, pleasantly surprised at how good it was. 'Did you see her much?'

McPherson tilted his head like a confused dog, eyes going out of focus as he read some calendar in his brain. 'Lady Cecily? No. Can't remember the last time she came to the hotel. She didn't go anywhere. Hips were pretty much shot to pieces, and she didn't trust doctors enough to let them give her new ones.'

'So, you're telling me she lived alone in that cottage, cut off from the world. Quite literally, given the state of the track and the bridge. Ninety years old and nobody did anything about it?'

'I . . . That is . . .' McPherson squirmed in his chair like he needed to be excused. 'She's . . . was . . . very forthright, you see. And her nephew, the current Lord Bairnfather, he always defers to her.'

McLean thought it odd, perhaps even verging on careless, but it matched what the farmer, Tam Uist had said. And he'd known old women like he imagined Cecily Slater to be. His grandmother had been one of them. Self-destructively independent.

'Ms . . . Lady Cecily lay undetected for the best part of a week before the farmer found her. It seems strange to me that nobody noticed the fire. You don't recall anyone mentioning the smell of burning? Somebody must have noticed something, surely?'

'Believe me, Inspector. I've asked all the staff and nobody remembers anything. The gamekeeper's cottage is a couple of miles away, in that direction.' McPherson pointed at the fireplace. 'First we knew anything was amiss was when your constable came round. I was told it was a tragic accident. Has that changed?'

McLean ignored the question. 'Going back over the past few weeks. Can you remember a group of people coming here, maybe drinking at the bar? Not the usual crowd or guests at the hotel?'

McPherson gave McLean that confused dog look again, only this time his gaze remained clear. 'We don't have a usual crowd, Chief Inspector. This isn't that kind of hotel. People don't come out here for a drink on the way home from work. We cater for very high-end weddings, wealthy industrialists and celebrities who don't want to be disturbed. The most you'll find in our bar is a few of the hotel guests having a drink before going to bed. I told all of this to Constable Stringer. Did he not pass any of it on to you?'

'He did,' McLean lied. Well, not exactly lied. DC Stringer's interview transcripts would have been logged and filed and were probably in a report somewhere on his desk. It wasn't the same as being there when the questions were asked, seeing the face of the person doing the answering. McPherson was a little too ingratiating, and his slicked back hair and vintage suit were trying too hard, but he didn't come across as someone being deliberately unhelpful or obstructive. He didn't even seem to be anxious that a police presence might upset the guests at his hotel, which was perhaps a little suspicious. There was nothing more to be learned here though, of that McLean was sure.

'I'm sorry if it feels like we're going over old ground, Mr McPherson. Sometimes a key detail gets overlooked; an insignificant thing turns out to be important after all. Policing is all about the little things. Much like running a hotel, I'd think.' He stood up, and beside him Harrison hurriedly finished scribbling her notes. McPherson accompanied them to the office door but stopped himself from escorting them to the exit. McLean was glad he didn't offer a damp hand to shake again.

'Thank you for your time.' He made to turn away, then stopped. 'Oh, one other thing. Lord Bairnfather is your boss, you said?'

'That's right.'

'Have you spoken to him recently? About his aunt?'

McPherson's head drooped low. 'The same morning your constable came around. It was not a happy conversation.'

'Where is he now?'

'Your constable— oh, Lord Bairnfather.' McPherson checked his watch, which McLean thought was probably unnecessary. 'Somewhere over the Pacific, I expect. He was in Tokyo when I called him, had some crucial meetings in America on his way home. He'll come straight here as soon as he lands in the UK. He was most distraught.'

And yet he's taken his time coming home, not let it interfere with his business.

'Does he own all this?' McLean raised both hands to indicate the hotel.

'Well, the hall and estate are in trust, but in essence yes. One of his companies runs the hotel business.'

'And the gamekeeper's cottage? That's part of the estate.'

'Correct. Lady Cecily was also a beneficiary of the trust. Her right to live there was part of her inheritance.'

McLean said nothing more. He nodded his thanks, then turned and walked away across the great hall.

12

Apart from the damp and cold, it would have been a nice walk from Bairnfather Hall to the gamekeeper's cottage, had the bridge not collapsed and the recent rain made the river too deep to ford. There was no sign of Tam Uist and his tractor either, so they took the car instead. Driving around to the forestry tracks and walking up through the woods took almost three quarters of an hour. Climbing the path through trees dripping with condensed fog left them both soaked, although Harrison's coat appeared to be a lot more water repellent than McLean's. He turned up his collar to try and stop the water going down the back of his neck, with little success. By the time he stepped into the clearing, McLean was ready to give the whole thing up as a bad job.

'What do you suppose will happen to the place?' Harrison asked as they approached the ruined cottage. Rain had washed away some of the soot and taken with it any smell of charred wood and burned carpet. The props holding up the ceiling inside had been joined now by some rusty old scaffolding around the most collapsed corner of the building, but it seemed a half-hearted effort at best.

'I imagine they'll most likely demolish it and build something new on the plot. Unless it's a listed building, in which case they'll probably try to get out of having to rebuild it.'

'It's not listed,' Harrison said. 'Lofty checked already. Part of the background search on Slater. Lady Cecily, I should say.'

'I rather think she wanted to leave all that behind, don't you? Why else live in a run-down old place like this?' McLean walked slowly around the building, not quite sure what it was he was looking for but certain he would know it when he saw it. Only the crime scene tape remained to suggest anything more un-toward than a house fire had happened.

'What are we looking for?' Harrison echoed his thoughts. She'd taken a few paces in the other direction from him, as if to skirt around the ruins to the back door along the path worn by countless recent visitors. Now she stood uncertain, since he'd not followed her.

'Anything that was missed before. Some better clue as to who she was, and why someone would want to kill her. Too much to hope forensics missed a hidden security camera.' He'd meant it as a joke, but Harrison's face suggested she'd taken it seriously. He shooed her off in the direction she'd been going. 'You go that way, I'll meet you at the door.'

The side of the house was taken up by an overgrown vegetable and fruit garden. Once-tidy gravel paths linked a series of raised beds, but the weeds were reclaiming it all. McLean didn't know much about gardening, but he managed to identify some cater-pillar ravaged cabbages and what he suspected might have been brussels sprouts in among the grass and thistles, although they were purple rather than the green things he'd hated so much at boarding school. A couple of the tall sprout shoots had been broken in half, and the more he looked around, the more he saw evidence of careless feet trampling the ground. Had forensics been over this part of the scene? Stupid question, really. Of course they would have, but a week after the event when the rains would have washed any useful evidence away.

An old wooden lean-to shed had been built on to the gable wall of the house on this side. Protected from the fire by thick stone walls, it had remained unscathed. In it, McLean knew from the forensic report, were gardening tools, a potting bench beneath a window that looked out on to the garden, an elderly wind-up radio tuned to Radio 4. The details had all been meticulously logged. He didn't remember any reference to the little cat-flap cut into the base of the shed door itself. Maybe because the door had been open then and now it was closed.

He opened it, stepped inside. There was something about the quietness of the place that calmed him. It reminded him of the ramshackle shed in his own garden. Not as it was now, but as it had been when he'd been a boy. Back when it had been the domain of Bill Bradford the gardener. Many was the time McLean had ended up in there, watching as the old man patiently dibbed seeds into pots of fresh compost, or rolled his horrible-smelling cigarettes. Like that shed, this one was a place of old tin boxes, neatly stacked terracotta pots, hand tools and bundles of bamboo stakes. The workbench under the window had been cleared, but time and lack of use had covered it in dust, spider-webs and the husks of half-eaten insects. This wasn't a place often visited.

A series of shelves on the opposite wall held ancient boxes of fertiliser, fish, blood and bone, more tools of the gardener's trade. No slug pellets, poisons or weedkillers as far as he could see, but there on the bottom shelf was an empty food bowl, and beside it a bag of cat food. A pile of old hessian sacks bore a dent in the shape and size of a cat. When he ran his fingers over the surface, they came away with a few short black hairs stuck to them.

'Thought you were going inside, sir.'

The voice startled him, and McLean almost banged his head on the upper shelves as he stood up in a hurry. Harrison stared at him from the doorway, her expression one of concern.

'Anyone know what happened to the cat?' he asked. Harrison's face was answer enough.

'What cat?'

McLean pointed at the bowl, the food, the makeshift bed, but Harrison was already pulling out her phone. She stepped away from the shed, either for a better signal or because the conversation with the incident room was likely to be embarrassing. He took another look around the shed, but saw nothing of interest, nothing that suggested it might be a clue as to why someone would come here in the night, beat an old woman to within an inch of her death, then finish the job with petrol and a match.

'No mention of a cat in any of the reports, sir,' Harrison said as he stepped out into the garden a moment later. McLean carefully closed and latched the shed door. He looked out across the abandoned vegetable patch, then up past the trees to the slate-grey sky overhead. Fat raindrops started to fall as if they'd been waiting for his upturned face. He turned away, pulling up the collar on his jacket against a sudden chill.

'Come on. Let's go have a look inside.'

A smell of damp pervaded the interior of the house as McLean stepped in through the front door. Instinctively, he reached out and took hold of the nearest steel prop, checking it was still firmly holding up the first floor before ducking under the lintel and into the narrow hall. The room where Cecily Slater had died was at the front of the house, he knew, but that was also where the worst of the collapse had happened. No point going in there, so he turned left and stepped into the kitchen.

In many ways it reminded him of his own kitchen, even if it was considerably smaller and the range cooker appeared to run on wood rather than expensive heating oil like his Aga. Marginally more environmentally friendly, maybe. The cupboards were of a similar vintage, handmade by some long-forgotten carpenter and far removed from the sleek designs he had seen in some of the glossy magazines Emma occasionally left casually open around the place. Twin green lines stained the deep Belfast sink, the marks of years of drips from a pair of ancient brass taps. McLean would have bet good money the pipes feeding them were made of lead.

He resisted the urge to bend down and look, instead going through the cupboards one by one. It was exactly as he might have expected to find in the kitchen of a lone old woman who had lived here for many years. A few pots and pans; chipped plates and cracked cups from a set that once had been both elegant and expensive; some sad-looking vegetables that had probably been past their best even before the fire; packets of dried pasta, beans, rice and enough oats to sink a battleship. Drawers yielded cutlery, cooking utensils, the sort of bric-a-brac that got put somewhere in case it might be useful someday. But then didn't everyone have a useful drawer? He certainly did; it was the first place he ever looked for anything, even if it was rarely the last.

'Find anything?' Harrison asked as she appeared in the doorway. McLean went to shut the final drawer, but something caught his eye. A length of shiny red ribbon glowed as if someone had shone a torchlight on it. He reached out and picked it up, finding that it was tied around an old iron key.

'Not exactly.' He held up the ribbon and watched the key twist under its own weight. 'I don't suppose we know what this is for?'

Harrison's shrug was answer enough, but McLean kept a hold of the ribbon and key as he pushed the drawer closed and went back out into the hall. The rainclouds had cast a gloom over the clearing, and what little light there was struggled to illuminate the hall. Even so, he could see there would be no going upstairs. A jumble of half-burned rafters and crumbled plaster blocked the way on to what might once have been a landing.

'From what I'm told, she didn't use the upstairs, sir.' Harrison correctly read his gaze and pointed to a couple of doors on the opposite side of the hall to the kitchen. 'There's a bedroom to the front there, and the bathroom's next door.'

McLean looked in both of them, but it was obvious the forensics team had been there before him. He caught sight of fingerprint dusting powder here and there, and all the toiletries and brushes had been moved to one end of the dressing table in the bedroom. He stood for a while, trying to imagine a ninety-year-old lady living here on her own, searching for an idea of who Cecily Slater had been, but there was nothing of her in the place. Or at least nothing he could sense.

It was only as he stepped out of the bedroom back into the hall that he noticed the cupboard under the stairs. It was locked, but the keyhole was much the same size as the key he'd found in the kitchen drawer, and when he slotted it in and turned it, the lock clicked and the door swung open. Too dark to see much, but he pulled out a pen torch and clicked it on, scanning the light over the interior.

A mop and bucket, an elderly vacuum cleaner, its flex that brittle fabric material he remembered from his childhood, two dustpans and brushes hanging from hooks on the back of the door; the little cupboard contained exactly what McLean would have expected it to. There was even a shelf with little pots of shoe polish, Brasso and a neat pile of folded polishing cloths. Wedged in under the stair, he saw an old hazel broom, hand-made, its handle shiny with decades of use. He reached in and picked it up, feeling a substantial weight to the thing. A good balance, too.

'Wow, that's a proper witches' broom, right enough. Reckon you could play Quidditch with that.' Harrison stared at the broom, her mouth slightly open as if it were something far less mundane than a tool for sweeping floors.

'Quidditch?' McLean asked, even though he knew what she was talking about.

'You know, sir. Harry Potter?'

'Here you go then, Hermione. Take it outside for a spin.' He thrust the broom at her. Startled, Harrison took it in one hand. He thought she would underestimate its weight, let it fall to the floor. He had, after all. But the moment she touched it, her hand jerked upwards a little, then steadied. She swung the handle around until she held it in both hands, but drew the line at straddling it, which was just as well. He might have tolerated that from a constable, but never a sergeant.

Turning back to the cupboard, McLean saw what looked like an old shoebox lying on the ground under the lowest stair tread. It had been hidden behind the broom, no doubt forgotten many years before. He crouched, leaned in and fetched it out, seeing as he did so that it was tied up with the same red ribbon as the key. The top of the box was thick with dust, but he could make out handwriting underneath it. He carried the box to the porch, blowing away the dust as best he could. Outside, the rain had strengthened, coming down in stair rods. What was it the Welsh said? Old ladies and sticks? He looked back at Harrison holding her broomstick, then past her to the room where the old lady had died.

'What is it?' the detective sergeant asked, although whether she meant the box or his sudden change in expression he had no idea. He wiped away the last of the dust from the box and peered at the writing on the top again. A single word, written in neat ink that had faded over time.

'Burntwoods?' Harrison asked as she leaned over his shoulder for a look. 'What's Burntwoods?'

'I have no idea,' McLean said. Outside the falling rain had begun to roar as it hit the ground and the surrounding trees. 'But it looks like we're stuck here for a while, so we might as well have a look.'

13

They took the box back to the kitchen, the only place in the house that had a couple of chairs. Judging by the state of the table, the forensic team had been making use of the facilities while they were here, although McLean wasn't sure how they'd managed to boil a kettle. The range had a cold, dead feel to it, and the electricity had been cut off when the collapsing back wall had snapped the overhead cable bringing power to the house.

'Could really do with a little more light,' McLean said as he carefully untied the red ribbon and took the lid off the box. Rain clattered against the window, and the sky had turned almost black. Harrison dug into her pocket and pulled out her phone, tapping at the screen until the flash on the back lit up. The pale yellow light wasn't much, but it was better than nothing.

'There you go, sir. Hope it doesn't kill the battery.'

McLean grunted his thanks, then turned his attention once more to the box. Inside lay a collection of papers, photographs, letters written in neat copperplate handwriting, a few ancient invoices and some yellowing newspaper cuttings. He picked up a postcard showing a sepia print image of the seafront at Carnoustie, at least that was what it said it was. Flipping it over, he saw that it had been addressed to C. Slater, the address not Bairnfather Estate, but Burntwoods in Angus. No post code, and the stamp would have excited many a collector – this card had been sent sometime before the Second World War, when Cecily Slater would have been a young girl.

'Can you read that? My eyes can't cope.' McLean held the card up for Harrison to see, relieved that she, too, had to squint to make out the message written in faded ink. He could kid himself he didn't need spectacles for a little while yet.

'Not sure, sir. Looks like "Came to . . ." something "you but could not . . ." something.' She held her phone up to the card, snapped a picture of it, then pinched and zoomed to enlarge the text. 'Ah, that's better. "Came to visit you but could not enter the place. Seems my kind are not allowed. Trust you are being treated well by the witches and that you will soon be able to come home. Father and I both miss you terribly. Your ever loving brother, Archie." Well, that's as clear as mud. Witches?'

McLean took the card back and stared at the handwriting again. Without the benefit of modern technology, he still couldn't make out much of what it said, but there was something about that one word that stood out. He ran his finger lightly over the text, feeling for any irregularities, perhaps a sign that something had been erased or altered. A full forensic examination would be more revealing, but he didn't think it would be a good use of their scarce resources. There was nothing particularly odd about the postcard other than its message, and that might simply have been the way two siblings spoke to each other back when the card had been written. Eighty years ago, give or take. If it was a clue to anything, it was a very cold one.

'Archie would presumably be Sir Archibald Slater, Tenth Lord Bairnfather.' Harrison was peering at her phone again, which meant the torch light wasn't shining in a particularly helpful direction. McLean was beginning to wonder whether there was any point to searching through this box at all, apart from killing some time until the rain eased off.

'According to Wikipedia, he was born in 1925 and died in 1984. Speculation is it was AIDS, although the family denied it and the rumours he was gay. The current Lord Bairnfather's his son, so perhaps he swung both ways.'

'You know half of the stuff on the internet's made up, right?' McLean leafed idly through some of the photographs. There were family pictures, black and white and awkwardly posed. A few showed Bairnfather Hall in an earlier era, a massive coach and horses pulled up in front of the grand entrance. A couple were portraits of young women, perhaps Cecily herself. And tucked almost at random in among the others were a series of pictures of a stately home that made Bairnfather Hall look small by comparison. Granted, McLean wasn't exactly an expert on the nation's country mansions, but he didn't recognise this one at all. The photographs were all black and white, or shades of sepia yellow, and nothing in them suggested any kind of modernity. Perhaps, like many of those places, this one had been demolished when it became too big and too expensive to run.

'Aye, I know that, sir. Wikipedia's a good enough place to start, mind. And there's a lot of stuff here about the Bairnfathers I didn't know.'

'Did you know much? I only knew the name, and mostly because of the hotel rather than the family. There was some function I was meant to go to a couple of years back. Meet the politicians and their paymasters kind of thing. Don't think anybody noticed I wasn't there.' Idly, McLean flipped over the last photograph of the mansion. None of the others had been written on, but this one had a brief description in soft pencil. Burntwoods – July 1949. He held it up for Harrison to see. 'You know anything about this place?'

'Burntwoods?' The detective sergeant leaned in close to look at the image. 'Doesn't ring any bells. Big old place, isn't it? How on earth could anyone afford to build places like that? Why on earth would they?'

McLean glanced at the window, aware that the rattle of rain had ceased. The light appeared brighter, as if the heavy clouds had passed over. Time to make a run for the car; he didn't think they'd find anything more in this cottage.

'The why of it would be showing off, same as men have always done. See how successful I am. My house is bigger than yours.' He stood up, put everything back in the box and closed the lid, then tucked it under his jacket to keep it as dry as possible. 'As to how they could afford to, well a lot of these places were built by rich merchants looking to do something with all their new-found wealth. And most of that wealth came from trade between Glasgow, Africa and the New World.'

Harrison had put her phone away and was zipping up her jacket, better equipped for this outing than McLean. Her expression was one he had come to recognise as her not knowing what he was talking about but unsure whether she should be asking for clarification.

'Slaves and sugar, Sergeant. These mansions might have been built by Scottish stonemasons, but they worked on the backs of African slaves and Europe's sweet tooth.'

It didn't really matter that the rain had stopped and the clouds begun to part. They still got soaked walking from the old game-keeper's cottage back through the trees and down to where McLean's Alfa Romeo was parked. Fat drops of water fell from the branches, and the tips of the pine needles glistened with it. Impossible to avoid brushing up against wetness with every step. McLean had the shoebox tucked under his jacket to try and protect it as much as possible; everything else was thoroughly rinsed.

'Knew I should have worn a hat,' Harrison complained as she

peeled off her coat and shook it. McLean popped open the boot of the car and placed the box alongside the stout walking boots he'd forgotten to put on before heading up to the cottage. His raincoat and woolly hat might have been useful too, although it was a bit late now.

'Let's just get back to the station. I'll ask a constable to have a more thorough look at that box, but my best guess is it's a red herring. Reckon we'll get further following the money, which means we really need to speak with the current Lord Bairnfather. Given my past history with the rich and famous, that should be fun.'

Harrison gave him a look that was half knowing, half incredulous. 'You think he'd have anything to do with this?'

'Maybe not him directly. Families can be weird that way though, and rich families tend to be the worst. I don't know what the set-up with the hotel is, how the Bairnfather Estate trust works. Could be any number of reasons why one beneficiary might want to get rid of another, great-aunt or no.'

'I'll get Lofty to look into it. He's the best when it comes to numbers.' Harrison folded her coat neatly and placed it in the boot so it wouldn't stain the leather seats. 'You want me to drive, sir?'

McLean handed her the keys, not quite sure when it was he'd decided he preferred being chauffeured to driving himself. Perhaps it was the car, with its ridiculously over-powered engine. He found himself unaccountably yearning for the simplicity of his old GTV. Or maybe he was yearning for the past it represented.

Shaking his head at the stray thought, he closed the boot and walked round to the passenger door. Inside, the car was warm and dry, the seat welcome after being on his feet for a while. He pulled the door closed, strapped on the seat belt, and only then noticed that Harrison hadn't climbed in behind the wheel.

She'd opened the door, just a crack, and then stopped.

'You're letting the cold air in, Sergeant,' he said, half joking. Harrison didn't respond, so he craned his neck forward to see where she was looking, then followed her gaze to a point a few yards off, beside the path that climbed up from the forestry track to the clearing. And then he saw it, sitting still as a statue, staring with that intense gaze that went right through to your soul. A black cat. Not large like Mrs McCutcheon's cat, who had grown portly on an exercise regime that consisted mainly of sleeping in front of the Aga. It had sheltered as best it could from the rain under a frond of bracken, but even so its coat was slick with wet. As he watched, it lifted a front paw, licked it, and then wiped its face a couple of times.

Not quite knowing why he did so, McLean unclasped his seat belt and opened the car door. As if it had been waiting for his invitation, the cat stopped cleaning itself, stood up and trotted over. It had the decency to shake the worst of the water off its back, then leapt gracefully into his lap. He held out a suspicious hand, but the cat only nudged it once, marking him with its scent, before curling up into a neat black ball.

'Umm . . .' Harrison peered in through the now fully open driver's side door, her uncertainty as evident as McLean's own.

'It's not the first time this has happened to me,' McLean said. 'Guess we'll need to stop off at a vet on the way back to the station.'

14

'**B**oss wants to see you, Gaz.'
Big John's words are the last thing he needs to hear. He's only just got in, still bleary eyed and sore from another sleepless night on Bazza's couch. Gary knows he can't stay there much longer, but finding anywhere in this city's a nightmare these days. When did it all get so expensive? And the council couldn't give two fucks he's been kicked out of his own home. Still got to pay the rent, mind. Fucking child support for a kid he's not even allowed to see any more.

'He say what it was about?' Gary thumps the corner of his locker with the heel of his hand to get the door opened. Who needs a padlock when the fucking thing's almost welded itself shut? Cheap piece of foreign shit.

'No' Stevie. He's away up at the new site. It's Sheila in charge now.'

As if Gary's day couldn't get any worse. He pulls the door open, shoves his bag inside on top of the pile of hi-vis gear and his steel-capped boots, then slams the door hard shut again.

'Fuckin' marvellous. What genius puts a woman in charge of a site like this, aye?' He's not expecting an answer, and doesn't get one. As Big John trudges off towards the building site, Gary rolls the stiffness out of his shoulders, runs a hand through his hair and heads for the admin block.

They've been on this site a couple of years now, and everyone knows the project's winding up. The heavy concrete work for the foundations and main structure is done. Now it's the turn of the sparkies and plumbers, the glass boys and those mad bastards who do the tiling. Detail work to make the new St James's Centre all shiny for the public. Gary doesn't do detail. Rebar, concrete pumps and hard graft, that's his thing.

'Come in.' The voice from the other side of the frosted glass door is all wrong when Gary knocks. He's known Stevie Tanner the best part of a decade now, since he started work out of school. They've been on the same jobs that whole time, so how come Stevie's away and Gary's still here? He knows he's not the sharpest pencil in the box, but he's not stupid either. With a sigh, he pushes open the door.

Sheila's sitting at Stevie's desk. She's old. At least forty, with a face like she's sucking a lemon while someone pulls her hair. Not that she's got much of that, mind. Cut short on top, shaved around the sides. She reminds Gary of those uppity lesbian bitches camped outside the hotel where he met Mr Fielding.

'Ah, Mr Tomlinson. You're here. Have a seat.' Sheila's voice is never friendly, but now it's colder than the wind coming in off the Forth. Gary sees the chair, set up in front of the desk, and knows exactly what's coming. He's still too craven to refuse her command though, even if he hates himself for it.

'As you know, Mr Tomlinson, the main structural work on this site is all completed now. Barring a few corrections, and the addition to the basement levels that team four are working on, there's no more concrete pouring work to do.'

Get on with it, you bitch, Gary wants to say. He can't though. He's struck dumb by the dawning realisation of what's happening.

'We've moved a few workers to other sites, but there's not as much building work going on at the moment, so we're having to restructure our workforce. To that end, I've been tasked with carrying out performance appraisals of all staff.' She's had her hands folded on the desk in front of her, and now he sees they've been partially covering a thin folder. His name is printed across the top. Fuck.

'I'm afraid your score is at the bottom of the list, considerably below the average. We can't afford to carry any baggage in these straitened times, Mr Tomlinson, so I am afraid we can no longer offer you employment here.'

Her words are all strange. Gobbledegook. He can't see properly. 'The fuck?'

'There's no need for that kind of language, Mr Tomlinson. You will receive a generous severance package and a reference that's frankly better than you deserve, judging by your appraisal score.' Now Sheila opens the folder, takes out a sheet of paper from the top, swivels it around and pushes it across the desk towards him.

'You . . . You're firing me?' Gary's mind, never the fastest, is struggling as if it were wading through recently poured concrete.

'We're ceasing your employment, yes. Effective immediately. Don't worry though, you'll get a month's pay regardless.'

'I . . . whut?' Gary's still wading through concrete, but now his anger's beginning to burn. Before he's even managed to stand though, the office door has opened and two of the site security guards are directly behind him. He knows them, Ted Sillars and Mac Henderson. He's drunk with them on a Friday evening, swapped dirty jokes. Fuck, he's even seen Mac a few times in the stands at Tynecastle. But now they're all business. Don't even look embarrassed about it, the fuckers.

'Thank you for being so understanding, Mr Tomlinson.' Sheila stands up, the thin folder clasped in her hands like a shield. 'You can collect your personal belongings from your locker, and then these two gentlemen will escort you to the gates.' She sticks out her hand, and for a mad moment he thinks she wants him to shake it. Then she nods at his chest and the lanyard hanging around his neck. 'Your security pass, please.'

And just like that, he's fired.

Interlude

A cold wind blows in across the Tay, bringing with it the smell of burning wood from the salmon smokers and the silty tang of the mudflats. High clouds hide a weak sun, and out across the water the port of Dundee can be seen as a smudge of dirty air blurring the Sidlaw hills. There will be rain later on, she knows. A storm from the North Sea to make life yet more miserable for these people. She won't be around to see it, although there is scant comfort in that knowledge.

'Agnes Carter. You have been found guilty this day of the foul practice of witchcraft. Your sentence as decreed by King James himself is that you be burned at the stake. Do you renounce your evil, reject the worship of the devil and take the Lord into your heart?'

The man's a fool, but he's a dangerous fool. Head addled with power and a little learning. He understands nothing, and yet she's the one tied to a pole, surrounded by wood dowsed in oil. The smell of it makes her senses spin. Easy enough to just do as he says, but then if she'd been that kind of person she'd never be in this situation in the first place.

'Will it do me any good?' she asks. 'If I sing praise to the Lord, will you cut me down and send me on my way, sir?'

He startles at her voice, perhaps not expecting anything from her, perhaps thinking she will rant and rail, curse him in strange tongues. How many women has he executed now? Him and his like, travelling the land, sowing discord and mistrust, finding small grievances and building them into stories of horror these superstitious folk accept without question. Gullible people, so easily swayed and controlled. They blame her for their misfortune even though they've brought it on themselves. Will they stop and wonder, once she's gone and nothing has changed, that they might not have been wrong about her? She doubts that very much.

'The Lord is forgiveness.' The witchfinder steps towards her pyre, one hand clutching his leather bound bible. With the other he draws his sword from its scabbard, and she can see well enough how sharp he has honed its edge. 'Recant your sins and I will send you to him swiftly.'

'Not much of a choice then, is it.'

She is trying her best to keep the fear and panic from her voice, but even she can hear the tremble. They will kill her here, and it will be painful. There is nothing she can do about that though. No one is going to ride to her rescue, and even if she were to escape the ropes that bind her to this stake, the mob would rip her apart before she could take more than a dozen paces. They have gathered with the morning, their numbers growing until it is clear nobody tends the livestock or tills the fields for miles around. The forge will go cold, the loaves in the bakery fail to prove, and the blacksmith and baker both will blame her. The farmers will blame her for the weather and the fishermen for their poor catches. Same as they have blamed her for every little thing that has gone wrong in their lives even as they have turned to her for help with their ailments.

'Well, do you recant, witch?'

She looks at the man in surprise. Had she really forgotten he was here? She has let her mind wander too soon. It would be easy enough to sing his song, take an easy death, quick and clean. Except that she no more believes in his mercy than she does his intelligence. This is a show for the people, not an exercise in leniency for her. He wants to extract a confession and repentance from her so that he can show them he is in charge, doing the Lord's work. And the king's. Well, they will all be disappointed this day.

She fixes him with a stare that would stop a rampaging bull. 'A plague upon you, and all of your kind. I cannot recant that which I have never done, and neither will anything I say change your blinkered mind.'

He recoils as if her words sting. Good. She wants him to remember this day. May it haunt him for what remains of his short and miserable life. He says nothing, but sheathes his sword and then beckons for the torch. For one slow breath she thinks he is going to prolong the moment, perhaps give her one more chance to play his game. But instead he merely shrugs before setting the pyre alight.

15

McLean was on his way to his office, carrying his canteen spoils of freshly brewed coffee and still warm chocolate muffin, when he heard his name being called. He stopped walking, took two steps back until he could see in through the open door to where Detective Sergeant Sandy Gregg stood, one hand clasped over the mouthpiece of her desk phone as if the mute button had never been invented.

'Were you wanting me?' he asked.

'Aye, sorry to shout, sir, only I saw you passing and thought you'd want to know about this.'

McLean doubted that. Unless it was news that someone had handed themselves in with a signed confession and hard evidence they'd murdered Cecily Slater. Chance would be a fine thing.

'Well?'

'There's a dead body. Basement flat in Meadowbank. First officer on the scene called it in as – and I quote – "bloody weird".'

'Weird how?'

'Something about the body being almost burned away, but no real damage to the room? To be honest, sir, he wasn't making a whole lot of sense.'

McLean dragged his gaze away from the telephone handset. Gregg must have been about to call someone, rather than having them on hold while she spoke to him. Maybe it'd been him she was going to call. 'Who's the officer?'

'Sergeant Gatford, sir. Which is why I thought I'd bring it to your attention. Don's usually steady, even if he should have retired years ago. He sounded fair spooked on the phone. Said it was the sort of thing you'd know how to deal with.' Gregg put the emphasis on the pronoun, just in case McLean missed the point.

'You got an address?'

Gregg finally put the handset back on its cradle and peeled a Post-it note from the stack sitting beside the phone, then stuck it to the side of his coffee mug. At least her handwriting was neat. She held up a hand before McLean could get his next question in.

'Tied up with stuff at the moment, sir. And I've a case review with DI Ritchie starting in ten minutes.'

McLean looked around the CID room, remembering a time when it had bustled with detectives. Now most of the desks were empty, but not all of them. A lone figure near the back was trying to hide behind his monitor, but there was no way someone so tall could shrink enough not to be seen.

'You busy, Constable?' he asked as DC Blane gave up the fight and sat straight.

'Nothing that can't wait, sir.'

'OK then. Sort out a pool car and I'll meet you downstairs in five minutes.' He looked at the coffee and muffin. Still fresh and warm. He'd been hoping to savour them while getting up to speed on what needed doing today. Best laid plans and all that. 'Better make it ten.'

Tucked in under the shadow of Meadowbank Stadium, the tenements of Cambusnethan Street were in the main tidy, although they might also have been described as tired. A century and more of Auld Reekie's smoke had blackened the stone facades, and the mixture of old-fashioned sash windows and more modern uPVC replacements marked out the different ownership of the individual flats as clearly as any signpost. It wasn't hard to find the address they were looking for; a stream of white boiler-suited forensic technicians were ferrying equipment from a pair of battered vans, past a police cordon and in through a gap in the railings where they disappeared down into a basement. McLean was glad he'd parked on Lower London Road and walked the rest of the way. No one was going to drive down the length of the street any time soon.

'You got the message then, sir. Good.' Police Sergeant Don Gatford met them at the cordon tape with a smile that was a mixture of relief and nervousness. McLean hadn't worked directly with the man for many years, but he was a solid and reliable officer.

'What have you got for me, Don? The message said weird.'

'Aye, and I don't think I can describe it. Dead body, burned, but there's no sign of a fire in the room.'

'You think they were killed elsewhere and brought here?'

Gatford shrugged his shoulders, gave a tiny shake of his head. 'I don't think so, sir. Best if you see for yourself.'

'Do we know who it is?'

'Aye, sir.' Gatford looked relieved to be back on familiar territory. He pulled out his notebook and leafed through the pages until he found the details. 'Mr Stephen Whitaker. Lives alone, neighbours don't see much of him, don't really know anything about him, but then he lives in the basement with its own entrance, so it's no' like he's chatting wi' folk in the hallway.'

'Who found him?'

'That was a neighbour. Old wifey lives on the ground floor, above his flat. Went to complain about the smell and found him . . . well, you'll see. Pathologist's down there just now if you're wanting to talk to him.'

McLean turned to DC Blane, a full head taller than both him and PS Gatford. Most Edinburgh tenements had high ceilings, but not in the basement flats. 'Why don't you two go and get a statement from the neighbour, OK? I'll see if I can find a boiler suit that fits, and go see what all the fuss is about.'

The smell had been foul ever since he had begun the climb down the stone steps outside, a horrible fug of burned meat and rancid fat that brought to mind bad house fires and worse barbecues. As he stepped through the door, McLean gagged at the reek of it, so powerful it was almost impossible to breathe.

Nothing about the basement flat was big, and the front room was no exception. The back wall was taken up by the most minimalist of galley kitchens; a sink, single electric ring cooker and microwave. Shoved against the side wall, a narrow table was covered in empty pizza and kebab boxes, half-crushed beer cans and other detritus. A single wooden chair had been pushed underneath the table, and the only other place to sit beside the floor was an elderly armchair next to the window. It hadn't been put there to make the most of the view, which was made up entirely of rubbish that had blown or been thrown into the gulley between the pavement and the tenement.

'I had a feeling you'd be along soon. Tell me what you think about this, then.'

McLean had been concentrating on the peripheral details and somehow had managed to miss the white boiler-suited figure of the city pathologist. There was no sign of his assistant, which was just as well since there was barely room for the both of them.

'No Doctor Sharp?'

'Alas, no. Tracy's gone to help Tom MacPhail with another

case on the other side of town. They told me this was a house fire, so I thought I'd be safe enough coming on my own. Wasn't exactly expecting this.'

McLean edged closer until he could see the figure sitting in the chair. As he did so, he noticed a pair of discarded work boots placed in front of a low table. A laptop computer sat open and facing the chair, as if whoever had been sitting in it had been watching something on the screen. Given that there was no telly in the tiny living room, this was most likely the case.

Other details came to him as he scanned the scene. The chair was upholstered in some dirty brown cloth material, clearly treated with fire retardant as it hadn't burned much. Directly above it, a greasy black smear of soot looked like the kind of mark a candle makes when placed under a shelf without thought. Only this spot was much larger than any candle could leave. Something lay on the arms of the chair, and then, as McLean took another step closer, it all resolved into a horrific whole.

'Dear God. What happened to him?'

Stephen Whitaker had not discarded his work boots when he had sat down to watch something on his laptop computer. He was still wearing them. The misshapen somethings lying on the arms of the chair were, in fact, his arms, hands clenched around the soft fabric as if he was hanging on for dear life. If that had been the case, it hadn't worked, as he was very dead. That was, if he was indeed Stephen Whitaker. Apart from short stumps of legs and shorter stumps of forearms, there wasn't really much of him left to identify.

'I really don't know, Tony. It looks like spontaneous human combustion, but in all my years in the job I've never encountered an actual case of it. Never had a colleague mention they'd seen it either. I'd thought it was just an urban myth. Something from the *Fortean Times*.' Cadwallader waved an open hand at the blackened and grisly remains. 'Not real.'

'Could it have been staged?' McLean knew the answer before he even asked the question, but it needed to be voiced anyway.

'That's your department. And the forensics team. I'd say no, though. Everything about the body points to it being burned here. I just don't understand how it can be like this, but no damage anywhere else in the room.'

McLean crouched down to peer under the chair. A dark circle of burning matched the one on the ceiling above, as if a bolt of pure energy had descended from on high, spearing through Mr Whitaker on its way down into the earth. That couldn't be what had happened, of course. Otherwise the neighbour who'd called it in would have had a different story to tell.

'You'll let me know when the PM's going to be?' He backed away from the burned remains, taking one last look at the minimalist living room.

'Of course. Probably won't take long, though. There's not much of him left to examine.'

McLean found DC Blane back out on the street, chatting with Amanda Parsons, the senior forensic technician who also happened to be DS Harrison's flatmate. Of Sergeant Gatford there was no sign, but a fresh-faced uniformed PC had taken over manning the cordon, so it was possible the old copper had sloped off for a cup of tea.

'You get anything useful from the neighbour?' he asked after he'd struggled out of the white overalls. The air was cool in the shade of the tenements, a brisk wind blowing in off the Forth and thankfully taking the stench of burned meat away with it. Down in the basement had been stifling, but now the damp sweat on his back and neck made him shiver.

'Not much, sir. Seems Whitaker kept to himself most of the time. He's not been living here long, either. Only moved in a couple of months ago. According to Mrs Collings there.' Blane nodded his head at the front window of the ground-floor flat, where an old lady stood and stared out at the proceedings. She caught his eye and gave him a cheery wave. 'As she tells it, Mr Whitaker's marriage was on the rocks and he'd moved out of the family home.'

'Do we have the address?'

'Not yet, sir. I've asked Jay— DC Stringer to run it down. And where he worked, too. Mrs Collings thought he had something to do with the new construction up at St James.'

'OK. Keep digging. I want a full profile by shift end.'

DC Blane nodded and pulled out his airwave set. McLean knew the constable was a better detective in front of a computer than out in the field, but there were a few more things to cover before they could head back to the station.

'Anything to report yet?' he asked Parsons. Her face mask hung around her neck, and she had pulled back the hood attached to her protective overalls, wayward blond hair fluttering in the breeze.

'We only just got here, Tony. I mean, Detective Chief Inspector, sir.' Parsons pulled herself to attention, but stopped short of snapping an insolent salute.

'It's just detective inspector, Manda. Didn't Janie tell you?' McLean didn't wait for an answer to that. 'And I meant first impressions. Is it going to be a hard scene to process? Do you think you might find anything to explain what happened?'

'Umm . . . you went in and saw the body, right? Or what's left of it, anyway. I've been doing this job almost six years and I've never seen anything like that. I don't even know where to start.' Despite her complaint, Parsons began to count on her fingers. 'I mean, there's no obvious sign of any accelerant, nothing to suggest how the fire even started. From what I remember of training, you need a fierce old heat to burn a human body, and yet a stack of girlie mags on a table just a few feet away didn't catch fire. The pages weren't even crisped, more's the pity. The ceiling should have burned through and set the whole tenement alight, but nobody even noticed there was a problem until Mrs Collings there couldn't put up with the stink any more. It makes absolutely no sense at all.'

'Angus reckons it could be spontaneous human combustion.'

Parsons ran a gloved hand through her hair, perhaps forgetting where she had been and what she had been doing there. When she spoke, the sarcasm was as marked as it was uncharacteristic. 'Really? I guess all his many years of experience haven't been completely wasted then. Human? Tick. Combustion? Tick again. Spontaneous?' She said no more.

'OK. I get the picture. I'll leave you to it, shall I?'

'Unless you've a good idea for getting him out of there in one piece.'

McLean didn't, so he left Parsons to her job and walked back to his car. DC Blane was hunched beside it, airwave to one ear, finger in the other as he tried to hear whatever was being said at the other end. The wind had picked up now and was whistling down the narrow street, accelerated by the tall buildings on either side. McLean unlocked the car and climbed in, thinking Blane would do the same to get away from the noise, but he'd started the engine and cranked up the heater before the detective constable joined him.

'That was control, sir. They've been on to the council. Got another address for Whitaker. I'm guessing that's the family home he moved out of. He's still on the register for council tax there, but there's another person registered at the address too, Miranda Whitaker. Must be his wife?' Blane had the good sense to make it a question.

'Don't guess, find out.' McLean checked his mirror and then indicated before pulling out of the parking space. 'Then you and Harrison can go have a chat with her.'

16

Up the hill towards Liberton from the Cameron Toll shopping centre and Inch Park, the housing estate was a twisty mess of cul-de-sacs and circles designed to confound even the most well-developed sense of direction. It had been built long before the advent of Sat-Nav, and Janie Harrison could only imagine that the planners involved had suffered miserable childhoods. It didn't help that all the houses looked the same, making it almost impossible to tell whether they had been down any particular drive once or half a dozen times.

'Not the most inspiring of places,' she said as she leaned over the steering wheel and peered out through the windscreen. The pool car she'd managed to grab wasn't as nice as the boss's Alfa, but it was a lot quieter. One of the new additions to the fleet, a boxy little Nissan, it ran on electricity and was surprisingly fun to drive. It seemed to have a decent range too, if the numbers on the screen built into the dashboard were anything to go by. How long it would last when a forgetful constable left it parked up overnight without plugging it in was something they would no doubt find out soon enough.

'Doesn't look much, no. But these houses are a lot bigger than the shoeboxes they're throwing up nowadays. Friends of mine rented one when they were at Uni.' DC Blane had pushed the passenger seat so far back he was practically looking out the rear window.

'You've been here before then?' Janie asked, as she indicated to turn down yet another street with no obvious street sign.

'Not for a while. But I crashed a couple of times. It's fine and handy for the King's Buildings.'

Janie tried to keep the exasperation out of her voice. 'So you know your way around then, Lofty, so how the hell do we get to Cairn Close?'

Blane sat up a little straighter, his head brushing the roof lining. 'Sorry. Thought you knew where you were going.' He pointed to an opening between two houses that might have been a road. 'It's up there.'

Janie muttered under her breath, but followed the directions, and soon enough they were sliding into a parking space in front of an anonymous semi-detached house. Much like the others in the close, it was harled in grey-brown pebble-dash render, with dark brown frames to the windows and a matching front door. If the estate's planners had intended the houses to have front gardens, that wish had long since given way to two-car family lifestyle. Number Twelve was fronted by an uneven patch of tarmac with dead weed poking through plentiful cracks. An elderly Volvo estate had been backed in tight to the wall that marked the boundary between the two halves of the semi-detached house. Judging by the patina of dirt, the faded paintwork and the flat tyre, it hadn't moved anywhere recently. Janie pointed at the number plate. 'Run that when we get back to the station, aye?'

Lofty nodded, pulled out his notebook and was in the process of writing when the front door opened wide. A woman not much older than Harrison herself stood in the doorway, a small child apparently welded to her hip.

'What youse want? If you're here to sell Jesus, I'm no' buying.'

'Detective Sergeant Harrison.' Janie held up her warrant card with one hand and pointed at Lofty with the thumb of her other. 'My colleague, Detective Constable Blane. Would you be Miranda Whitaker?'

The woman took a step forward so that she could see the card. Janie gave her all the time she needed to read it. They were bearing bad news of a sort, nothing to be gained from antagonising her.

'Aye,' she said, after a moment.

'Could we possibly come in?'

The inside of the house lived up to the low expectations of the exterior, although Lofty had been right about the generous size of the rooms. Miranda led them through a hallway that would have been wide had it not been for the baby buggy and other detritus cluttering up the space. Open-tread stairs in a dark stained bare wood climbed up to the first floor, and someone had made a makeshift gate at the bottom to stop the toddler exploring. It reminded Janie of her gran's house. All very chic and fashionable in the seventies perhaps, but not exactly practical for modern living.

'Will this take long? Only I've tae get Senga down soon or she'll be a right pain later on.' Miranda hefted the child to her other side. Janie wasn't much of the mothering type, but even she thought the little girl looked a bit dopey. Wide eyes stared at nothing in particular, and she sucked continuously on a rubber teat. Maybe she'd just had a feed.

'How old is she?' It seemed the thing to ask, even if Janie didn't think it would pertain much to their investigation.

'Eighteen months, good as. Been out twice as long as she was in.' Miranda smiled at her own joke, then turned serious again. 'Come on through and sit down. Youse wanting a coffee?'

Tempting though it was, Janie declined. They went through into a slightly less cluttered living room that looked like it hadn't been redecorated in fifty years. Lofty sat first, no doubt aware that his size could be intimidating. Janie waited for Miranda to settle with her child into a large armchair, then perched on the arm of the sofa so her head was at the same height as her colleague.

'Your child's father, Stephen. You're separated now, yes?'

Miranda joggled young Senga on her knee, the child no more animated than a doll. 'Steve? What's that bastard done now?'

'There was a fire at his tenement last night. I'm sorry, but he didn't survive.'

The silence that fell on the room lasted a long time. Somewhere a clock ticked, and the soft shush shush shush of Miranda's foot on the carpet was the only other sound. She didn't look shocked, or even sad. Something else entirely spread its slow way across her face.

'He's dead?' she asked eventually. Then without waiting for an answer added: 'Well thank fuck for that.'

As responses went, it wasn't quite the one Janie was expecting. She'd done more than enough death knocks in her time, and the responses were usually much the same. Shock, surprise, denial, anger. She'd never encountered relief before, at least not worn so openly.

'Did he suffer?' Miranda asked, then shook her head. 'Doesn't matter, really. He's dead and that's the end of it. Thank fuck.'

'How long has it been since you separated?' Janie asked.

'Not long enough. Four months? Maybe five? Still waiting on the divorce to come through, but at least he's out of the house.' Miranda paused a moment, then her face lit up. 'Guess I won't be needing the divorce after all. Won't be a trial either.'

'Trial?' Janie glanced across at Blane, who was doing his best to be unobtrusive. He shook his head and shrugged, no more clued up than she was. That was unlike him.

The brightness disappeared, replaced by anger. 'You don't know?'

'I . . . No. I'm sorry. It only happened this morning.'

'Unbelievable.' Miranda shook her head slowly for a moment, then stared straight at Harrison. 'I caught him abusing our wee girl. Playing with her like she was . . . and she was barely three months . . .' Her face screwed up in utter disgust. 'Oh, he tried to deny it, but then I found stuff on his computer. That's when I called you lot. You should've locked him up and thrown away the key, but that fucker of a lawyer pops up and the next thing he's got bail. At least they stopped him coming round here, but . . .'

She stopped speaking, partly because she appeared to have run out of words, partly because the child had finally picked up on her mother's agitation and begun to sob. Not the full-throated *someone's trying to kill me* wail that Janie associated with small infants, but distress nonetheless.

'Hey, hey, little one. Daddy won't hurt you ever again, my sweetheart.' Miranda hugged her daughter close, one hand gently stroking the infant's wispy hair. In moments the child had calmed.

Janie stood up, one hand going to her pocket. She pulled out a card, aware that it still identified her as Detective Constable Harrison. It didn't matter, the numbers were the same. 'I'm sorry. We should have known about Mr Whitaker's . . . situation before we came here. I'd offer my condolences, but I don't think you'd want them. If you need anything else though, give me a call.'

She slid the card on to the coffee table. DC Blane was already through the door and into the hallway.

'We'll see ourselves out, Mrs Whitaker. Thank you for your time.'

Janie was halfway to the door before the woman spoke.

'It's Miss Keegan. There's no Mrs Whitaker any more.'

★ ★ ★

'Well that was a bit bloody embarrassing.'

Janie sat in the passenger seat this time, staring out at the identikit houses as DC Blane drove slowly away from Miranda Keegan's address.

'Sorry, Janie. I should have done a proper background on him.'

'Don't sweat it, we all make mistakes. Still embarrassing, finding out from her like that.'

'Do you think it makes a difference to the case?' Blane hunched over the steering wheel, elbows out at awkward angles as he tried to fit into a space not built with him in mind. Janie should have offered to drive, but he'd insisted it was his turn.

'What do you mean? Do I think she somehow torched her ex?' She shook her head. 'No. She was genuinely surprised to hear he was dead. Elated, sure, but surprised.'

'We'll still have to get her in for an interview. Look into her background.'

'Like we looked into her husband's?'

'Aye, well. Like I said. Sorry about that.'

'She didn't strike me as the vengeful type. Not the way you said her husband died.'

'I didn't see it, but from what the forensics team said, it was weird. Like he'd burned from the inside out, and the fire had barely touched anything else. Don't see how anyone could do that, even if they were angry.'

'Well she was certainly that. But you're right. The way he died, Whitaker. That doesn't square with vengeful wife. She'd have stabbed him in the bath or poisoned his food or something. What happened to him is too . . .'

'Complicated?' Blane offered.

'I was going to say bizarre, but that too.'

Janie stared out the side window at the passing tenements as they sped their quiet, electric way around the Cameron Toll roundabout and on to Dalkeith Road. She could see things getting more and more complicated with each new revelation.

'I'll run a proper background on Whitaker soon as we get back to the station.'

'Aye, Lofty. You said. Don't fret about it. Mistakes get made.'

Crammed in behind the wheel, the detective constable already looked uncomfortable, but Janie thought she saw an added level. Something more than physical was paining Blane. 'What's up, Lofty? You've been acting weird for weeks now.'

'It's nothing. Tired, I guess. Meg's overdue already but she's been nippy sweetie for months now. Sooner the wee one's born the better . . .' He tailed off, clearly as uncomfortable talking about it as he was squashed into a space designed for someone a foot shorter than him.

'Oh God, Lofty. I'm sorry. I'd forgotten. Is she very late?'

'Coming up on a fortnight. They're going to induce her if she doesn't start soon. I was told it got difficult once the wain was born, but see these past few months . . .'

'You'll be away on the paternity soon, then?' Janie voiced it as a question, even though she knew the answer.

Blane shrugged, causing the car to swerve dangerously towards the oncoming traffic before he pulled it back into the right lane. 'Thought about putting it off, given how short-staffed we are. But there's some new DCs arrived now so I don't feel so bad.'

'Just have to hope they shape up. Who knows? We might even get a new DCI too. Place could be awash wi' detectives.' Janie stared at the lines of squad cars as they pulled into the station car park, noticed DI McLean's black Alfa Romeo squeezed in between two armoured Transits. Brave or foolhardy, she couldn't really decide. 'Seriously though, Lofty. Is it any surprise we make mistakes like that, given how few of us have been here to do the work? Anyone calls you out for missing that Whitaker was out on bail and on the register? You let me know and I'll give them a piece of my mind.'

17

Gary sits at the front of the room, impressed by the number of people who have come to see Tommy Fielding speak. There must be over a hundred, maybe more. He's surprised to see a few women in the crowd too. Why would they want to come along to this? Are they press? And why would Tommy let them listen to him? Surely they're the enemy.

'Take Jim here.'

Mr Fielding's standing behind a modern glass lectern, and he points with an open hand towards a man sitting not far from Gary. Jim shuffles nervously in his seat, clearly unhappy at being picked out from the crowd.

'Jim was happily married for eleven years. He's got two kids, Fiona and Esme. Twins, but not identical, is that right?' Fielding waits for the man to nod before continuing. 'Jim thought everything was fine in his life. Good job, beautiful wife, kids doing well at one of the top schools in the city. Then he comes home one day and the house is empty. Well, I say empty. There was a letter on the kitchen counter, from his wife, telling him she wanted a divorce and had taken Fiona and Esme away.'

A murmur of outrage ripples around the room, people shifting in their seats as the terrible tale begins to unfold. Gary takes another look at unhappy Jim. He's perhaps mid-forties, short-cropped hair going grey at the temples and receding completely from the shiny top of his head. He wears narrow-framed specs and his jacket's one of those expensive designer jobs that Gary thinks looks shit but knows costs more than he earns in a month. Earned in a month, fuck it. When he even had a job. Jim's shoes look expensive too, even if he is wearing a faded pair of jeans like half the men in the room.

'Jim's wife claimed he'd been molesting his daughters.'

Gary's still looking at the man as Fielding lets slip this new nugget of information, and he sees Jim stiffen visibly, as if he's been prodded with a sharp stick. Well, fair enough. Gary reckons he'd feel the same, having his dirty laundry aired in this room.

'She has no evidence, of course. Because there's no truth in the allegation. Just her say against his. The judge, though? She . . .' And here Fielding pauses for maximum effect. '. . . she took Jim's wife's side. Granted her the divorce and custody of the children. Jim was denied visiting rights pending an invest-igation into the allegations. That was two years ago and he hasn't seen them since.'

The murmur of outrage grows, rumbling around the room like a drunk man in a pub. Gary looks over his shoulder, sees some of the women glance nervously at each other, the environ-ment suddenly turned more hostile than perhaps they were expecting. Well, it was their choice to come, only their fault if they get hurt.

'Jim's not the only one here today who's been cheated. His is a tragic, terrible injustice, but we've all of us suffered at the hands of our so-called courts.' Fielding is working himself up now, fuelled by the simmering anger in the crowd. It's intoxicating stuff, Gary has to admit. The man knows how to work an audience. If he's half as good in court then Bella's in for a shock. Well, she will be if he can come up with the cash to pay the lawyer.

'You've all come to hear me tell you how to fight back, right? You want to know how to get justice in a system rigged against us.'

A murmur of agreement works its way around the room, but as Gary looks back towards the rear, he hears other noises too. It sounds like voices chanting, and he remembers the crowd outside the hotel as he came in. Protesters, making out that Fielding was some kind of monster, woman hater, Christ only knew what. A moment later, and the double doors into the room burst open, the noise suddenly painful as a gang of them rush in, screaming.

Gary's on his feet before he knows it. Who the fuck do these people think they are? Breaking in here, accusing him and the others of all kinds of sick filth. They look like lesbians, all short-cropped messy hair, baggy clothes and piercings. As if they weren't ugly enough as it is. He's facing up to them, spoiling for a fight. Ready to clock one as she strides towards Fielding at the podium.

'Crawl back under your rock, you disgusting paedo.' She points an accusing finger at him, even as a security guard grabs her around the waist and pulls her away. She shrugs him off, face almost as red as her ugly, stubble-shaved hair. Her anger's contagious, stoking Gary's own, and he moves to intercept her before she can get to the lawyer. He starts to raise his fist, soon put her in her place, but a hand grabs his wrist.

'Not now, Gary. Not here.'

The voice is pitched low, almost a growl, and with enough menace in it that it penetrates the red mist beginning to descend, blows it away. Gary turns swiftly to find Fielding standing close, almost too close. Their eyes lock for a moment, and then the lawyer lets go of his wrist, jerks his head towards the podium.

'Come on. Leave security to the pros. We can get out this way.'

Gary follows Fielding through a small door at the back of the stage, into another room. Half a dozen men are there already, including Jim, the one whose wife accused him of molesting his daughters. They're a bit shaken, but more angry than afraid, ready for a fight. Fair enough, it was only a bunch of ugly dykes who could do with being given a hard lesson in manners, after all. As one, they turn to see who's come in.

'Lads, I'd like you all to meet Gary.' Fielding makes introductions, although Gary isn't sure he'll remember many of the names. Jim, sure. He's easy enough to recognise. The others all look alike, as if they all buy their clothes from the same shop, or maybe subscribe to the same gym. He can see they're better off than him, maybe a bit higher up the social ladder too. None of them seem to look down on him, though.

'What's going on out there, Tommy?' one of them asks.

'Just a few bitches getting uppity, Christopher. No need to worry about it. Security'll deal with it, and I had a word with the polis. They'll treat this lot a bit more seriously now.'

Gary notices that word, polis. The inflection of it jars with Fielding's otherwise polished accent. It feels more like the way Bazza would speak than a posh lawyer. But then Fielding's not really posh, is he?

'Reckon it's safe to go back out there?' one of the other men asks, earning stares from his comrades. He goes a little red in the face as he realises what he's said, what he's admitted to. 'I didn't mean it that way. Just don't want to get in the way of the security men, right?'

There's a moment's silence, which is as much an answer to the question as any. Then Fielding slaps the man on the back. 'It's OK, Don. We all know what you meant. Sounds like they're done in there anyways. Shame about the meeting, though. I thought it was going well before those witches broke in.'

'Witches?' Gary asks, earning himself a puzzled look from the others.

'All women are witches, Gary. Thought you'd know that. Of all people.' Fielding puts a fatherly arm around his shoulder and steers him towards the door. 'Come on, you lot. Let's go get a beer, shall we?'

18

'You paid a visit to that fathers' rights bloke, didn't you?'

Detective Sergeant Janie Harrison looked up from her desk to see who had spoken, saw the duty sergeant standing in the doorway. 'Aye, what of it?'

'We've just had a report of a disturbance. Bunch of protesters broke into the meeting and started screaming at everyone there, apparently.'

Janie sat up straighter, resisting the urge to glance at the clock on the wall. She'd been filling the time to shift end going over the Cecily Slater case notes for perhaps the thousandth time, but now she could see both that and an early night slipping from her grasp.

'Who's attending?' she asked.

'Uniforms out of Torphichen Street mostly. It's a bit of a mess, way I hear it. You know what these angry feminists can be like.' The duty sergeant's brain caught up with his mouth and he shrugged away his embarrassment. 'No offence.'

Janie wondered how it would go down if she told him that actually yes, there was considerable offence. Reg was a time-served sergeant, close to retirement, old school and very much set in his ways. She might have been the same rank as him now, and as a detective sergeant the senior officer in the room, but given she'd only been a detective sergeant for a few weeks, it was a point she thought best let go.

'Who's in charge over there?' She picked up her phone and notebook, both lying on the desk beside her keyboard.

'Kenny Stephen, I think. No' really something plain clothes need to be involved in, but I thought you'd want to know. Seeing as you were there before.'

He was right. There was no need for her to get involved at all. The hotel wasn't far from her flat though, or at least it was a good deal closer than the station. And it wasn't all that long until shift end.

'I'll just pop over and see what's happening all the same. It's on the way home, and chances are Fielding will be bending the ear of anyone he can find. Better to be one step ahead, aye?'

The duty sergeant raised an eyebrow but said nothing more as Janie gathered the rest of her things together and turned off her computer. He stood aside to let her leave the room, and only then did she remember her manners, or rather that it was always a good idea to be nice to the duty sergeant, however misogynistic he might be.

'Thanks for the tip-off, Reg. I owe you one,' she said, but hurried away before he could make good on her offer.

By the time Janie reached the hotel, there was nothing left but a pair of squad cars parked on a double yellow line. A uniformed constable stood a few paces from the front door, chatting with Detective Constable Blane. With his back to her, Lofty didn't notice she was there until she tapped him on the arm.

'What the—?' He whirled around in surprise, almost clocking her on the side of the head. 'Jesus, Janie. What're you doing creeping up on me like that?'

'You got my message then?' she said, to cover her alarm. It was one thing to know the detective constable hadn't meant her any harm, quite another to still feel the rush of air on her face as a hand not much smaller than her head brushed past it with millimetres to spare.

'Aye. Was heading home, but I figured this must be important. Davey here was telling me they've got it all under control, mind.' Lofty waved his dangerous hand at the uniformed constable, and Janie recognised one of her old colleagues hiding under his hat and cold weather gear.

'Hey, Janie. How's it goin'? Hear you made sergeant now so I s'pose I should call you ma'am.'

'Funny, Dave. How about you just let me know what happened.'

'Well, you know that bloke Tommy Fielding's here, right? Giving talks about men's rights and all that stuff?'

'Aye, Davey. I spoke with him a while back. And the protesters outside. Seemed peaceful enough, if a bit loud and smelly. I don't need the full story, just where you came in.'

'We got a call from hotel security maybe an hour, hour and a half ago? Some of the protesters had managed to get in through a fire door round the back. Fielding was talking to a group of maybe a hundred or so in the main conference room when they all burst in and started screaming.'

'Screaming?'

'Aye, that's what it was. They didn't do anything violent. Didn't break furniture or try to hurt anyone, like. They were just wailing at the top of their lungs. Proper banshee stuff, y'know? Security dragged them out best they could, but it ruined the event.'

'My heart bleeds for them. Where are the protesters now?'

'Some of them got away. Some the security guys threw out. Most of them had dispersed by the time we got here, but there's a half-dozen had somehow managed to barricade themselves in a smaller function room. They've been taken off to your nick, seeing as ours doesn't have enough holding cells any more.'

'Ah well, I guess that'll keep Reg happy. Suppose I'd better go and speak to Mr Fielding again. Then I can go home and have a shower to wash the dirt off.'

'He's no' that bad,' the constable said.

'Aye he is. Worse. He's the reason women can't go out on their own after dark. He's the reason we have to think twice about what we wear and who we talk to. It's people like him putting stupid ideas into young men's heads that means I spend half of my life interviewing victims of domestic violence and lying when I tell them we'll keep them safe.' Janie walked off before she lost her temper, or had to hear any reply, only stopping when she reached the front door and saw Lofty wasn't following. 'Come on, then,' she shouted. Eventually the detective constable nodded goodbye to his friend and followed her inside.

'Was that really necessary, Janie?' he asked once they'd stepped into the reception area.

'Was what necessary?'

'Chewing wee Davey's ear off like that. And what you said about Fielding. He's the injured party here, remember?'

Janie stopped herself from shaking her head. This wasn't the time or place to get into an argument with a colleague she had a lot of respect for, even if on this particular point he was as wrong as wrong could be.

'Let's just get this over with, shall we?' She went to the reception desk and showed her warrant card. Before she could even ask, the receptionist pointed to a door across the hall.

'Mr Fielding's in the Walter Scott bar at the moment.'

Janie thanked the man, then led Lofty in the direction they'd been pointed. The Walter Scott bar was much like any posh hotel bar, quieter than most pubs and with an interior design that leaned rather too heavily on shiny red leather and polished wood for her tastes. Standing in the doorway, she didn't have time to scan the whole room before an angry voice piped up from a table of people off to one side.

'Detective Sergeant Harrison. It's about bloody time someone showed up.'

What was it the boss said to do in situations like this? A silent count to ten, wasn't it? Janie curled her hands into loose fists as she let the numbers grow, then turned slowly to meet her accuser, fake smile plastered across her face.

'Mr Fielding. I'm so sorry your event was disrupted. I gather nobody was hurt?' A slight inflection at the end of the sentence made it a question, even though she knew the answer. It was more an invitation to the man to talk, which he clearly needed to do. Or at least rant.

'It's a disgrace. You should have moved them on when I asked you to. None of this would have happened if you'd just done your job.'

Janie only half heard what the man had to say. She was too busy looking at the group of men who were sitting with him. She didn't immediately recognise any of them, but they all seemed cast from the same mould. Middle-aged, fairly well-to-do, well groomed and yet somehow greasy. Or was that just her prejudices getting the better of her? Only one of the men seemed out of place. A bit younger than the rest, rougher around the edges. He caught her eye and then looked away like a guilty suspect.

'I can assure you we take the matter most seriously, Mr Fielding. I will speak with hotel security and find out how the protesters got in. As I'm sure you're well aware though, whilst they were outside and not causing an actual public nuisance, there wasn't much we could do about them.'

She knew it wasn't going to mollify him, and she wasn't disappointed. Perhaps it had been a mistake coming here; better to have sent a male officer. Maybe even Lofty on his own, although Janie knew that Fielding would have taken it as an insult to be dealt with by a mere constable.

'Preposterous.' He mangled the word, something of his true nature fighting through the false posh Edinburgh accent he affected most of the time. 'I'll see the ones who broke in prosecuted. Mark my words. They'll do time for this.'

Janie found herself clenching her fists even tighter, started mentally counting to ten again. To her surprise, and relief, Lofty stepped in before she could say anything she might regret later.

'Did any of the women say anything, sir?' He had his notebook out, and even though Janie could see he'd not written anything down, it was an effective prop. Fielding clearly liked being called sir too.

'The redhead called me a paedophile, which is gross slander, I'll have you know. The rest of them were just screaming like witches. Horrible racket, wasn't it, lads?' Fielding finally turned to his companions. Janie noticed that none of them looked too happy about being dragged into the conversation, with the exception of the younger man. Maybe he had less of a reputation to lose, or maybe he hadn't yet understood what his being associated with Fielding might mean.

'It was like they were zombies or something. Ken that movie wi' the pod people? Had Spock from *Star Trek* in it, aye? The first Spock, ken? No' that new chappie. What's it called?'

'*Invasion of the Body Snatchers*?' Janie had to admit she was impressed the man would know about an old movie like that. He seemed more the football and beer type. Then again, it was never a good idea to judge a person solely by their appearance. Or even the company they kept.

'Aye, that's the one. See that fella at the end, how he kind of points and screams? That's what they was like in there.' The young man nodded his head in the direction of the conference room. His companions looked embarrassed to be seen out with him, but he seemed to be warming to his theme.

'Would you be prepared to make a statement, Mr . . . ?' Janie let the question hang, hopeful that the young man might give her his name. Fielding had other plans, however.

'I'm sure there'll be time for that later. When you've pressed charges against the miscreants.'

'You're a lawyer, Mr Fielding, so I'm sure you understand how these things work. My job is to collect evidence and build a case before charges can be brought. If you'd like to give me a list of the names of everyone who attended this evening's meeting, I can take statements from them all. This is, after all, a very serious breach of the peace.'

Something close to anger flitted across Fielding's face. Janie could feel the change in the atmosphere, too. Almost as if his temperature had spiked and was heating the air between them. And was it her imagination, or had the bar suddenly gone very quiet?

'I'll expect to be kept informed of developments, Detective Sergeant Harrison.' Fielding put heavy emphasis on Janie's surname in a ham-fisted attempt to intimidate her. He knew who she was, it said, and he'd make sure she'd pay if he didn't get what he wanted. She merely stared at him, even though what she really wanted to do was punch him in the face. A con-descending smile, a silent count of ten. That's what the boss would do. She'd only got as far as seven when Fielding broke.

'Come on, lads. Let's go find somewhere a bit more private, aye?'

Janie stepped aside as the group all stood to leave. Most left unfinished drinks, but the young man with the better than average knowledge of seventies cinema quickly downed the remains of his pint before joining them. She gave him a little nod as he hurried to join the others, and he smiled back nervously. In moments they were gone.

'Well, that went OK, wouldn't you say, Lofty?'

DC Blane looked down at her as if she was mad. 'You know he's going to make a formal complaint, right? And he's mates wi' the chief constable?'

Janie wiped her forehead, surprised to find a slight dampness there. 'Aye, I do. And he probably will. Just hope it hits the right desk. I was kind of getting used to being a sergeant.'

19

All Detective Sergeant Janie Harrison wanted to do was go home, have a long, hot shower to wash away the dirty feeling that talking to Tommy Fielding had left on her skin, and then collapse in front of the telly with a takeaway curry. She knew if she did that though, the report-writing and paperwork would be waiting for her in the morning. They were already scheduled for an early briefing and case review on Cecily Slater, and there was a report for the Procurator Fiscal to be prepared regarding Steve Whitaker too, so with a weary sigh she cadged a lift from a passing squad car and headed back to the station.

Late shift had settled in by the time she arrived, which meant that hopefully the canteen wouldn't be too busy. She needed coffee, and possibly chocolate, if she was going to get the paper-work squared away in less than an hour. Passing the corridor that led to the holding cells, she heard something that wasn't so much a commotion as . . . singing? Never one to ignore the siren call of curiosity, she changed course and went to see who had such a fine voice.

The custody sergeant sat at his desk in the room where people were processed before being detained. Mostly the cells were filled with drunk and disorderly young men, and if they sang at all it was generally football chants and out of key. The song Janie

could hear was pitch perfect and quite haunting, although the echo from the cells meant she couldn't quite make out any of the actual words.

'What's going on, Tam?' she asked. 'Someone arrest a choir outing?'

'I should be so lucky. It's those bloody women from the protest. Soon as we asked them to stop screaming, they started singing instead. Can't say it's not an improvement, but I'd rather they just shut up altogether.'

'The protest?' Janie peered down at the sergeant's desk, trying to see the names written on the register. 'Who've you got, then? I'm just back from trying to calm down the aggrieved Mr Fielding.'

'Rather you than me. He's a right bastard that one. Heard he plays golf with the chief constable.'

'Aye, so people keep telling me.'

'You'll be wanting a look at this then, I guess.' The sergeant turned the register around and lifted the top, blank page so that Janie could see the names beneath. She picked up the clipboard, leafing through the pages. Six women, varying ages.

'What's going to happen to them?'

'The usual. They'll get a caution and then sent on their way. If they turn up at the hotel again, then we'll maybe arrange a wee visit to the Sheriff Court.'

Janie went to put the clipboard back down again, then the last name registered a vague memory. 'Isobel DeVilliers? Where have I heard that name before?'

'Oh Christ, her.' The sergeant rolled his eyes. 'What a temper, aye? Rest of them are peaceful as anything you like, but her? I'd lay odds on her being back here within the day. Bloody English.'

'Ah, come on, Tam. What's it the First Minister said? If you want to make Scotland your home, you're welcome?'

The custody sergeant half shrugged, half shook his head. 'She's a posh one, too. They're always the worst. Think they've more to prove. Aye, she tries to hide it wi' her swearing and those rubbish clothes, but you can tell good breeding a mile off.'

DeVilliers. Janie was sure she knew the name. And then in a cascade of memories, she did. It explained the fleeting glimpse she'd caught at the protest the first time she'd been there, too. Not the person she'd thought it was, but her younger sister. Half-sister. Someone who had every right in the world to be angry, particularly at men like Tommy Fielding.

'You processed these yet?' Janie waved the clipboard about.

'No' just the noo.' The custody sergeant narrowed his eyes at her. 'Why?'

'If I was to take this one . . .' Janie gently unclipped the sheet with Isobel DeVilliers' details on it from the small pile '. . . off you. That'd be one less for you to worry about. The awkward one and all. And I'd owe you, right?'

The sergeant narrowed his eyes even further, his bushy eyebrows merging into one. 'You'll take her away? An' you'll make sure she doesnae go breaching the peace again?'

'Guide's honour,' Janie said, hoping he wouldn't know she'd never been a Guide, and that Isobel DeVilliers would take advice from someone she didn't know. She waved the sheet of paper gently while the custody sergeant made up his mind. In the end it didn't take long.

'Aye, OK.' He stood up, fetching a set of keys from a chain on his belt. 'An' if you can get that other lassie to pipe down, I'll see about letting the rest of them out too.'

Seeing her led out of the corridor where the cells were and told to sit in one of the uncomfortable plastic chairs lined up along the far wall, Janie was struck by just how much Isobel DeVilliers looked like a younger, angrier version of Con Fairchild. She had the same nose, same cheekbones, her vivid red hair cut spiky short, eyes blazing with righteous fury. She wore the standard uniform of the street protester: overlarge cotton khaki jacket sewn with a few unidentifiable badges, baggy black cotton joggers worn more for warmth than style. The bead bangles looped around her wrists were a slight nod to hippy culture, although the effect was somewhat ruined by the custody sergeant having taken the laces out of her Doc Marten boots. Tam told her to wait, then he turned to Janie, winked, and left the room. DeVilliers slouched in the plastic chair, legs spread wide like a teenage boy on the underground, head tilted back and gently thud, thud, thudding against the wall behind her. She paid Janie no heed whatsoever. Being detained clearly didn't scare her, which suggested it wasn't a new experience.

'Isobel DeVilliers?' Janie asked, beginning to regret the course of action she'd committed herself to. The young woman barely reacted, tilting her head forward just enough to get a glimpse of her before leaning it back against the wall again.

'You don't look like a lawyer,' she said.

'That's because I'm not. Detective Sergeant Janie Harrison.' Janie crossed the room, resisting the urge to kick Isobel's legs together, and sat down in the chair beside her. 'I worked a case with your sister earlier in the year.'

A slight exaggeration, but it got the result she was hoping for. DeVilliers sat up straight, pulled her jacket down where the lapels had ridden up her neck, brought her legs in together and started paying attention.

'Con's my half-sister,' she said, and even her accent was the same.

'Half-sister, sister. It's no matter. She's my friend, so I'm helping her out. By helping you out, Isobel.'

'It's Izzy. Only my dad calls me Isobel. My real dad, that is.'

'Well, Izzy. I'm sure he'll be proud of you getting yourself locked up in a police cell. Isn't he some kind of justice of the peace or something? Be a bit embarrassing for him, his youngest arrested. I dare say Con won't be too happy either.'

Izzy's eyes narrowed. 'You've told her?'

'Is that the first thing you think of? Really? I'd have thought you'd be more worried about spending time behind bars for public order offences. Could be time in jail for what you did.'

Izzy folded her hands across her chest, upper lip twitching as she tried to suppress a sneer. 'You lot would do that, would you? Lock us up while trash like Fielding are free to spout their hate and get paid for it?'

Janie rubbed at her nose, feeling the oncoming itch that heralded her allergic reaction. It might have been something Izzy was wearing, but the girl didn't look like she'd had a bath or shower in days, let alone shoved on some aggressive deodorant. Far more likely the custody sergeant was a fan of Lynx body spray.

'No. Us lot wouldn't. Between you and me,' she leaned in a little closer, lowered her voice, 'I'd be happy to see Fielding and his little band of half men run out of town. Your noisy protest outside his hotel's not exactly making that easy.'

'It's not my protest. I'm just there to help. What he does is wrong, you know?'

Janie stood up, sniffed back the sudden runniness in her nose. 'I know. Come on.'

Izzy looked at her, confusion wiping away the anger. 'With you?'

'Well, unless you want to stay here. Reckon the custody sergeant will be back soon, get you processed and charged. Into a cell until you can be taken to the Sheriff Court.' Janie made a show of checking her watch. 'It's late now, so that'll be tomorrow.'

'Fuck that.' Izzy was on her feet and halfway to the door

before she seemed to notice her boots were loose. 'Any chance of getting my laces back?'

Janie caught up with her, opened the door and ushered her out. 'Probably best we pick you up some new ones, eh? I'm chancing my luck enough as it is.'

20

The group of officers sitting around the conference table was much smaller than McLean would have liked for a murder investigation team. Detective Constables Stringer and Blane sat at the far end, DS Harrison and DS Gregg on either side of them. He'd hoped to entice DI Ritchie, and possibly even Detective Superintendent McIntyre into the case review meeting, but both were apparently on the other side of the country. Instead, Ritchie had sent along two of the new intake of detective constables, both looking a bit shell-shocked, and terribly young. Had he been like that, when he'd first made the move to plain clothes? Barely needing to shave of a morning? Probably.

Not that either of these two needed to shave. Jessica Bryant had come through the fast track, not long out of university. Her colleague, Cassandra Mitchell, had transferred in to SCD from Traffic. McLean hoped they survived being thrown in at the deep end.

'OK then. I think that's everyone who's coming.' He cast a glance at the open office door, even though he knew nobody else was going to walk through it any time soon. 'Let's get down to business. Cecily Slater. This case is going nowhere fast.'

Harrison spoke into the awkward silence that followed. 'It doesn't help much that she was dead for a week before anyone found her, sir. And everyone thought it was just a house fire, too. So we weren't exactly searching for clues from the off.'

'I know. And I'm not looking to lay blame anywhere. But we need to get a grip on things. Forensics haven't turned up anything useful, there's no CCTV in the woods, more's the pity, and the only potential witness we've got is a cat who's keen on eating but less so on talking.' That got a murmur of laughter that died away as quickly as it deserved.

'What we do have is a ninety-year-old reclusive woman who was viciously beaten, then doused in petrol and set on fire. That's not something you do because you've been disturbed while burgling a house. That's an act of hatred and rage, which suggests a killer who knew the victim.'

'Suggests they were looking for her, too,' DC Stringer added. 'I mean, they knew where she lived and set out to get her. Nobody's going to stumble on that place by accident. Especially not with the bridge collapsed. That would mean they planned it, so we need to ask why? And why now?'

'Who stands to gain from her death?' The question came from DC Mitchell, which at least showed some initiative.

'That's a question I'd hoped we'd have answers to by now, really,' McLean said. 'The cottage is part of the Bairnfather Estate, which I understand is largely held in trust. We need to tug on that string a bit harder, find out how it's run. Carefully though. Lord Bairnfather's a rich and powerful man who'll no doubt complain if we poke our noses in where he thinks they don't belong.'

'Is that not up to us to decide, sir?' Mitchell asked.

'It is indeed. And since we've nothing else, I reckon we'll have to follow the money. Think that's your area of expertise, Lofty?'

The tall detective constable tilted his head in weary acknowledgement. 'Aye, sir. I'll get on that. Could maybe do with some help with the Whitaker case if I'm to concentrate on Slater, mind.'

'Whitaker?' McLean took an embarrassing moment to recognise the name. 'Oh, the burned body in the basement. That was next on the agenda, actually. Where are we with that? Is it looking suspicious, or just weird?'

'No' sure, sir. Post-mortem's not 'til later this afternoon. We've done some background on him though.'

'Executive summary?' McLean asked, ever hopeful. Blane looked across at Harrison, who had already produced a sheaf of papers. Fresh from the printer, if the slight whiff of ozone when she shuffled them was anything to go by.

'Steven Whitaker. Thirty-two years old. Married to Miranda, with whom he has— had a daughter, Senga Jane, aged eighteen months. Whitaker was investigated just over six months ago after his wife claimed that he had abused his daughter. His laptop was found to contain several hundred indecent images, mostly of pre-pubescent and very young adolescent girls being forced to perform sexual acts.'

'How the hell didn't we know this as soon as his name and address came through Control?' McLean asked. 'He should have been on the register, shouldn't he?'

'Hasn't made it to court yet, so it's all still under review. Whitaker's defence claims his wife planted the images on the laptop, and since she has access to it that can't be ruled out. There's only her word he abused their daughter, too. No medical evidence, apparently. She got an interim order keeping him away from the child, and was in the process of suing him for divorce. He'd been charged on the laptop, but the case is complicated. Word is the PF was thinking about dropping it altogether, but in the meantime he was to keep away from wife and daughter.'

'Hence living in a pokey wee basement flat in Meadowbank.'

McLean stared sightlessly at the closely typed sheets of paper in his hand. 'We know where he worked?'

'Aye. He was an electrical engineer, working on the St James site. The new hotel.'

'A sparky?' McLean pictured the burned remains. Could something electrical have done that? A question for the pathologist. 'How about his last movements?'

'According to the neighbour, he didn't have people round to the flat,' Blane chipped in. 'She said she wasn't sure, but she thought he got in about eleven the night he died. She's a nosey old woman, mind, so I reckon she'll be pretty accurate on that. Told me the smell woke her up, and she went down to complain about it at six in the morning. She saw what was left of him through the window. Control logged her call at ten past six, so that makes sense.'

'OK. So Stephen Whitaker somehow managed to burn himself to death without setting the tenement, his room or even the chair he was sitting in on fire.' McLean massaged his temples. He'd known this was going to be one of those awkward cases from the moment he'd seen the body, but what they'd found out so far only made it worse. 'When's the PM?'

DC Blane glanced at his watch. 'Half three, sir. You want me to go?'

McLean was tempted, but shook his head. 'No, you get on with Cecily Slater's financials. DC Mitchell, Cassandra? You help him. The rest of you keep working on her profile for any possible motive. We need to focus our attention on her, at least until we know whether Whitaker's death was accidental or not. I'll go and see if Angus can explain how a man can just spontaneously burst into flames.'

Despite the state-of-the-art air conditioning system in the city mortuary, McLean could smell the stench of burned flesh before he even entered the examination theatre. Angus was waiting for him, scrubs on and gloved up. Beside him, his assistant Doctor Sharp busied herself with the instruments of torture. A third figure sat on a stool a few paces away and waved as McLean entered. Doctor MacPhail had started to go grey since the last time they'd met, no doubt the strain of working alongside a man like Cadwallader.

'Late as ever, Tony. I was about to start without you.'

'I almost didn't come. Wasn't sure there was much left for you to examine.' McLean reached a point well away from the examination table, but close enough that he could observe, then stopped. The body lay under a white sheet, and he could see from the way it hung that large parts were missing.

'Oh ye of little faith,' Cadwallader muttered, then turned his attention to the job in hand. Doctor Sharp rolled back the sheet to reveal the dead man's head and a portion of his chest. It was impossible to make out much of Steve Whitaker's features, as the fire had burned away most of his skin. Black chunks of charred muscle clung to bone in a manner horribly reminiscent of flame-grilled meat. McLean fought back the bile that rose in his throat at the thought. He'd attended far more post-mortem examinations in his career than he cared to think about; it was a long time since one had made him feel like being sick.

'Subject is male, approximately one hundred and eighty centimetres tall. Hard to give an exact figure as a large section of his torso appears to have been burned away.' Cadwallader worked his way around the body, peering close every so often, taking samples and handing them to Doctor Sharp to label for later analysis. It wasn't possible to open him up, since the fire had already done that, so McLean was at least spared that unpleasantness.

'Thighs have been badly scorched on the front, but the damage from burning does not appear to extend down below the knees. Subject was found in a seated position and this would suggest that the fire occurred while he was sitting down.'

'What could have done this, Angus? You'd need some fierce heat, surely?' McLean inched a little closer as he asked the question, drawn in by a morbid fascination at the damage done.

'I'm really not sure, Tony. There's a few things that might do it. Phosphorous, perhaps. Magnesium. Some kind of incendiary weapon. We'll screen for residues when we analyse the samples, of course, but . . .' Cadwallader shrugged. 'He'd have to have swallowed the damned stuff to end up like this, and even then it would have taken his head off first.'

McLean clenched at the image, took a step back. Despite the chill air in the mortuary, sweat beaded in his armpits and dripped uncomfortably down his side.

'The hands are interesting, see?' Cadwallader addressed these words to Doctor MacPhail, which was something of a relief. McLean watched as the two pathologists leaned over one of the forearms that were laid out in their correct place anatomically alongside the remains of the body. That they weren't still attached was made evident when Cadwallader picked up the arm and turned it over to inspect the palm of the hand.

'Again, no sign of burning here, which is strange. You'd think if he'd dropped something on his lap that caught fire, he'd grab at it, try to get it off. You'd expect extensive burning to the fingertips and palms. The only damage here is some abrasion of the skin and a tear in one fingernail.' Cadwallader put the arm back down again, held up his own hand and formed it into a claw. 'He was gripping the arms of the chair so hard he almost broke his fingers. Of course, that could have been muscle contraction due to the fire. He may have already been dead at that point.'

'Could he have, I don't know, accidentally set himself alight while drunk? We found some booze in his room, but you'd have to be pretty hammered to . . .' McLean waved a hand at the body.

'That's actually my working hypothesis. Did a little reading on the subject last night. Not Dickens, in case you were wondering. Some more scholarly works on the subject. If your man here had been, as you put it, hammered before he came home, carried on drinking until he was in a stupor, he might well have set himself alight with a cigarette or something. It happens, although the damage isn't usually this localised.'

'But there's no glaringly obvious sign of foul play, I take it.' McLean wasn't sure whether he wanted the answer to be yes or no. If this was nothing but an unfortunate accident, they could get on with all the other work that needed doing. It felt wrong to be looking for the easy way out, though. Regardless of the things he'd heard about Steve Whitaker, the man deserved his death to be properly investigated.

'We'll know more once the chemical analysis is done, although given the state of him I doubt anything will be conclusive.' Cadwallader shook his head slowly. 'No, if you want evidence of foul play, I think you'll have to look elsewhere.'

21

He's never been one for drinking during the day, but then in almost ten years since he last walked out through the school gates, Gary's never been out of a job either, so he's hardly had the opportunity. He's worked hard, played hard, lived his life. Until a month ago, it was all going well. He had a partner, a kid, a home. The city was booming, new buildings going up all over the place. No shortage of work for a strong man who didn't mind getting his hands dirty. How the fuck did it all fall apart so quickly?

'Heard you were in a spot of bother, Gary.'

A figure slides on to the stool beside him, elbows on the bar. Gary's slow to respond. He's not had that much to drink really, just enough to take the edge off his anger. Or maybe stoke it. When he does look round he almost falls off his seat, slopping beer on to his hand in surprise.

'Mr Fielding?'

'Tommy, please. I heard from your mate Bazza they let you go at the building site. You should have said, back at the meeting.'

'I didnae think . . . No' wi those women screaming an' all.' And there was the small matter of not knowing how he was going to pay the lawyer, if he didn't have a job.

'Not good. Not good at all.' Fielding shakes his head a couple of times, then the barman arrives. 'I'll have a double scotch. On ice. You wanting another, Gary?'

Gary looks at his pint, still three quarters full, and only the third to go with his burger and chips for lunch. 'Ta, but no. Should probably lay off a bit. 'S no good for your health, aye?'

'Everything in moderation, my friend.' Fielding nods to the barman to indicate he's only needing the one drink. 'Including moderation.'

'What brings you to this end of town then?' Gary asks once the lawyer's got his whisky. Gary's never been one for spirits. Too fiery, and he tends to get a bit violent after one too many drams. Christ, he'd had a couple with Baz the night he'd slapped Bella, but she was asking for that, the cow. Yapping on and on about how she was the only one doing any work around there when she didn't even have a job. The cheek of it.

'Actually, I was looking for you.'

That gets his full attention. 'For me? Why?'

'Because you've been fucked over, Gary. First your child taken from you, then your house. Now you're out of a job. I heard it was that Sheila Manley woman did the firing. Not the first time she's been brought in by senior management to "make strategic adjustments to the payroll".' Fielding makes little rabbit ears with his fingers as he speaks, which only confuses Gary more.

'Eh?'

'She's a professional firer, Gary. That's her job. Telling people like you that they're no longer needed, and ten years of service to the company means fuck all. Christ, I bet she didn't even offer you a decent severance.'

'I got a month's pay. That's no' bad.'

Fielding shakes his head slowly. 'Gary, that's awful. You should have had at least a month's pay for every year you worked

135

there. And a couple of months' extra as a goodwill gesture. Tell me you didn't sign the forms, aye?'

Gary's confused. He'd signed forms. Thought he was getting a good deal. Fuck, had they stiffed him even worse than he'd thought? He'd fucking kill that bitch if he ever saw her again. He'd—

A hand on his arm. The lightest of touches. He looks down, then follows the hand, up the arm to Fielding's face. It's like the lawyer can read his thoughts.

'Anger's good, Gary. But only if it's properly focused. I can help you do that. Help you get what's rightly yours.'

Gary's rage disappears almost as swiftly as it had come, and now it's replaced by booze-tinged self-loathing. 'I can't afford a lawyer. Couldn't before, when it was my wee girl I was fightin' for. But now? It's hopeless. If I cannae get another job, what am I goin' to do?'

Fielding takes his hand away. He clasps his whisky glass and rolls it slowly from side to side, leaving a wet smear of condensation on the bar top.

'Do you know what pro bono means?'

Of course Gary doesn't. 'Isn't he the singer in that old Irish band?'

That gets a smile from the lawyer. 'No, it means I work for free. Literally *pro bono publicum* means "for the public good", but we won't quibble.'

'Nah, now you're taking the piss.' Gary laughs, swigs from his beer. 'Lawyers never work for free.'

'You're right. We don't. But we don't always charge money, either. There's things you can help me with, Gary. Things I think you'd want to do anyway. And if you help me, then I can help you get your old life back. At least, those bits of it you actually want back.'

Gary's still two and a half pints down, but his head's beginning to clear now it's got something to work on other than moping. He doesn't know what to make of Fielding, but he's not going to turn down an offer of help. He raises his glass towards the lawyer. 'Aye, sure.'

Fielding raises his own glass, leans forward and clinks it against the pint. 'To a better future, where we're not constantly being ordered around by women. A world without witches.'

It's an odd thing to say, but it makes sense too. Gary grins, feeling better than he has in days. 'A world wi'out witches. Aye. I'll drink tae that.'

22

'What's this I hear about you bringing a cat in for questioning, Tony?'

McLean looked up from his desk to see the unexpected figure of the new chief superintendent standing in his open doorway. Half a day spent wading through paperwork, staff allocations and case reviews written in prose so dry it might catch fire in the sunlight, any distraction was welcome. Acting on instinct, he stood up and was halfway across the room before her words sunk in.

'I . . . Who on earth told you that?'

'Ah, so you don't deny it then.'

'Well, there was a cat. I'll give you that much, ma'am. I don't think it's going to be answering many questions though, and I didn't bring it in. Just picked it up and took it to the vet for a check-up. Hoped it might be chipped so we could find out who owned it, but no such luck. It's too tame to be feral, so my best guess is it belonged to the dead woman, Cecily Slater.'

McLean realised that he was babbling, wondered why. The look on the chief superintendent's face was one of barely suppressed laughter, the faintest of lines wrinkling from the corners of her eyes in a genuine smile. It made a welcome change from the fake camaraderie of the previous station chief.

'Please, Tony. Call me Gail. "Ma'am" makes me feel as old as my grandma.'

McLean shrugged, indicated with his outstretched hand that they have a seat at the conference table across the room. 'Was there something you wanted?' he asked. 'I can just about manage coffee.'

That got him another smile, albeit brief. 'I'm fine, thanks. Try not to drink the stuff after lunchtime.'

McLean pulled out two chairs, letting the chief superintendent sit before he did the same. He supposed technically it was after lunchtime now, although he'd not managed to eat anything since breakfast.

'How are things progressing with the Cecily Slater case?' the chief superintendent asked.

'More slowly than I'd like. I wish I'd been there at the start of the investigation. Seem to be going over a lot of old ground, finding out things that we should have known much sooner.'

'Like the fact that she's part of the Bairnfather dynasty, yes.' The chief superintendent's smile faded a little as she said this, the wrinkles around her eyes deepening.

'You've heard that, then.'

'I had a phone call. Someone who really should know better and could just as easily have called you, or Jayne. I think they were trying to make a point, and that pisses me off.'

'Now you know why I never wanted to be a DCI. It's bad enough trying to carry out an investigation when there's hardly any evidence. We don't need people telling us to be careful about upsetting rich folk.'

'Nevertheless, we do need to be careful. And you especially. Your reputation on that front isn't exactly . . . stellar.'

McLean opened his mouth to protest, then his brain caught up with him. She had a point. He didn't like it when people misused their power and privilege to avoid the consequences of their actions, and he really didn't like it when they put unnecessary obstacles in his way in an attempt to protect reputations that weren't worth a damn anyway. He closed his mouth before saying so, though. Elmwood had already put her neck on the block reinstating him; he owed her at least a little understanding.

'Good. I see you get my point,' she said, and the smile returned. Only this time there was an altogether more predatory look to it. 'And to that end, there's something I need you to do for me.'

It sounded a touch ominous, and something of that must have shown on his face. The chief superintendent gave a short, mocking laugh. 'Oh, it's nothing like that, Tony. Dear me, no. But I do need you to represent Police Scotland, and particularly Edinburgh CID at various functions going forward.'

'Functions?' McLean tried to keep the horror out of his voice, but might have failed.

'Don't worry. I'm not sending you in to meet the Freemasons alone or anything like that.' The chief superintendent held her hands up in a gesture of mock surrender. 'There are a number of liaison committees, statutory bodies and the like. And we have a need for representation at charity events, local business forums – you know. Functions.'

McLean said nothing. There was nothing he could think of to say.

'There's a kind of unofficial rota among the senior officers. If an invitation comes in and the CC doesn't like the look of it, he passes it down to me and the other chief superintendents. We pass it on to each other or anyone else we think might be suitable. Sometimes we'll double up if necessary. That's where you come in.'

'Me?' McLean finally managed to gather his wits. 'But I'm just a DI.'

Elmwood's smile reminded him of a nature documentary about sharks he'd seen in the months of his suspension from active duties, broad and threatening and containing far too many teeth.

'Yes, you're only a DI in rank, Tony. But you're time-served. One of our most experienced detectives. And more than that, people have heard of you. They want to meet you. And that takes the pressure off.'

There was something more to it than that, he could tell. Even if he wasn't quite sure what. It made sense too, in a mad, twisted kind of way. If he was the centre of attention at whatever function it was the chief superintendent had in mind, then all the talk would be about the sensational horror of the cases he'd investigated, and none of it would be about the need for budget cuts, or complaints about too many Strathclyde officers getting free with their stop and search powers when they were shipped across to Edinburgh to walk the beat.

'Do you have any particular function in mind?' He stopped himself from adding 'ma'am' at the end, and there was no way he was going to call the chief superintendent 'Gail'.

'I knew you'd understand.' She reached out and patted him gently on the arm, and McLean felt horribly like a small boy being admonished by matron. Except that this matron was much the same age as him, and he wasn't a small boy. Why did she make him feel so uncomfortable?

'Where's the cat now?' Elmwood asked as she stood up. It took McLean a moment to understand the question, coming as it did so far from the left of field. He was slow to stand, almost tipping his chair over in the process.

'The cat,' she continued. 'The one you were bringing in for interrogation? Or taking to the vet's or whatever? I presume it's off to the local shelter for rehoming now.'

'I . . .' And now McLean felt unaccountably awkward again.

'Actually, it's at my place. Seemed easiest in the long run, and it's not as if I've a lack of space.'

That brought another smile, few teeth this time but predatory all the same. 'That's what I like about you, Tony. You attend to the little things, the seemingly unimportant details. Keep up the good work.'

Then she strode from the room and was gone.

McLean stared at the open office door for long minutes after the chief superintendent had left, unable to quite parse what had happened. On the face of it, he was being roped into more of the police liaison work he had studiously avoided over the course of his career. Part of him understood that it was necessary to meet the politicians and community bigwigs who had a vested interest in the way Police Scotland ran. Part of him even understood that these kinds of meetings usually took the form of social events, dinners, charity fundraisers and the like. What he couldn't understand was why he needed to be involved. It was the kind of thing management did, and that meant uniformed officers of superintendent rank and above. Not some recently demoted detective inspector in the unglamorous world of Edinburgh CID. Elmwood's excuse that he was, to put it bluntly, famous, held some water. And he was part of the city's old guard, however much he disliked the idea. It was still a nuisance he could have done without.

Shaking his head at the stupidity of it all, he turned back to the conference table. As he slid his and the chief superintendent's chairs back into line with all the others, he noticed the box that he and Harrison had found in Cecily Slater's cupboard. He'd put it on the table, intending to go through it more carefully once he'd finished sorting out all the overtime sheets for the week. It would probably have been quicker simply to hand the whole thing over to one of the new DCs to leaf through, except that they were all busy, and the box didn't seem to be particularly relevant to the investigation. McLean didn't quite know why he was drawn to it. There wasn't much chance they'd find a clue in among the ancient papers, but they called to him all the same.

He picked up the box, looking around almost guiltily as he saw the word written on the lid again. Burntwoods. A big old house somewhere near Carnoustie in Angus. He wanted to look it up, but there was too much work to do. Leaving the box on the table was no good; it would continue to sing its siren song and soon enough he'd give in. So he tucked it under one arm and strode out of the room.

A few uniformed officers offered greetings or nodded politely as he tramped down the stairs from the third floor to the basement. It always surprised McLean how much the atmosphere of the station changed as he descended from the ugly concrete building thrown up in the eighties and into the older, arched-stone levels of the Victorian station that had stood on this site before. Why they hadn't dug everything up and started from scratch, he'd never been able to find out. Not that he'd tried all that hard. It remained one of life's little mysteries.

The Cold Case Unit had its centre of operations in what had once either been an evidence locker or a drunk tank, depending on which grizzled old sergeant you asked. Quite probably it had been both, but now it was little more than a file store with a few desks shoehorned into whatever available space could be found. The only natural light in the room came from a lightwell at one end that opened up on to the car park at the rear of the building. At the other end, ex-Detective Superintendent Charles Duguid's desk sat empty.

McLean glanced quickly at his watch, surprised to find that it was, indeed, late enough for Dagwood to have gone home. As far as he was aware, the CCU weren't deep into any particular case at the moment, but were working their slow and methodical way through an altogether far too long list of unsolved murders.

'You just missed him.' A familiar voice piped up from the shadows, and moments later Grumpy Bob stepped into the light, clasping a thick archive file in both hands. He shuffled over to his desk and gave the file a theatrical blow across its surface, as if to remove dust, before dropping it down on to the desktop.

'Afternoon, Bob. Didn't realise you were back already.'

Grumpy Bob lowered himself into his seat with a gentle 'oof' noise, much like the one McLean found himself making whenever he bent down to pick something up off the floor these days.

'I've been back the better part of two months, Tony. Not as if I had anything much better to do, and this . . .' he held up the dusty folder '. . . beats sitting at home watching the telly until it's time to go to the pub.'

'Guess I'm the one who's been out of the loop, then. You settling in here OK?'

'My natural element. And I can pretty much keep my own hours. Dagwood's not so bad a boss now he's not having to balance budgets and deal with too many idiots. As retirements go, it's worked out fine.' Grumpy Bob dropped the folder, leaned back in his chair, put his hands behind his head and his feet up on the desk. Then he seemed to notice the box tucked under McLean's arm. 'Except when people bring me unexpected gifts.'

'This? I don't know what you mean.' McLean placed the box on Grumpy Bob's desk as the ex-detective sergeant removed his feet from the suspiciously clean surface and leaned forward for a better look.

'Burntwoods. Why does that name ring a bell?' He pulled the lid off and lifted out a handful of papers from inside.

'Big old house outside Arbroath or Carnoustie or somewhere. Don't think it's there any more, but for some reason or other our murder victim, Cecily Slater, spent time there as a child. Found that in her house.'

'The fire in the woods? Aye, heard about that. Not a nice way to go.' Grumpy Bob pulled a grubby pair of reading spectacles out of his breast pocket and slid them on before leafing slowly through the papers. He stopped when he reached the first black and white photograph of the mansion, let out a low whistle.

'It's probably nothing to do with the case at all. Just something the old lady kept as a memento of childhood. I can't really justify giving it to the team to research, but . . .'

'You thought I might have some time on my hands?' Grumpy Bob arched an eyebrow, then grinned. 'Aye, I'll have a look through it all. It'll cost you, mind.'

'How does a pint up front sound? More when I see the work.'

Grumpy Bob was on his feet more swiftly than a man half his age. 'Sounds like a fine excuse to get out of this gloomy basement.'

Interlude

S he is asleep when they break down the door, still groggy as they pull her from her bed. Too dazed to understand what is happening, she is hauled outside without a fight. Not that she would have been able to do much to these strong, young labourers.

The light dazzles her, coming so soon after the darkness of her tiny cottage. But she can see the crowd gathered on the scrubby grass. She knows these people, they are her neighbours. She has helped them out over the years, attended at the births of more than a few. Is that not Murdo McKenzie there, with his wife Bethan? It was only last week she sent him that salve for the boils on his leg. Perhaps that is why he won't meet her eye.

'Kathrine Black.'

The words are not a question. She turns her head and sees the man standing a few paces off. She does not know his name, but his black clothes and dour face leave her in no doubt as to who he is.

'You stand accused of the practice of witchcraft. That you did consort with the devil and cast curses upon your kinfolk. Confess your sin, repent your evil ways and God will welcome you back into his embrace.'

The young men turn her around so that she can face the man,

but before she can respond they force her to the ground. She kicks out, catching one of her captors a blow to the chest, but he barely grunts before grabbing her leg once more. Out of nowhere, a hand catches her a blow to the head and the world dims around her for a while.

'Lay not your hand upon her, brother,' the man says. 'It is not for us to force the devil from her. By her own word will she condemn or save herself.'

They pin her to the ground, arms and legs outstretched, and all she can do is shake her head as two more men bring a stout wooden board into view. She has only enough time to see that it is her own front door before it is placed on top of her. Head forced to one side, she sees the mud-spattered riding boots of the dark man as he approaches, hears his words muffled by the planks.

'How do you plead, witch? Guilty or no'?'

The cruelty in his voice is laced with an edge of glee. She cannot answer. Nothing she might say would ever satisfy the likes of him. He seeks not justice for any wrongdoing, nor salvation for her soul. He wants only power for himself.

'Nothing?' he asks, crouched down close to her. Then his voice fades as he stands, turns, addresses someone else. 'The rocks. A little weight will loosen her tongue.'

She grunts as the first rock pushes the door down onto her. Sharp stones in the ground stab into her back. A second rock cracks the dry wood, its weight making it almost impossible for her to breathe.

'Confess, Kathrine. Repent and you will be with God.'

The third stone drives the air from her in a short, whistling gasp. She cannot draw another in. Panic plucks at her like night terrors, but there is nothing she can do. Even the strong men at her arms and legs need no longer hold her; she has no strength left, no life.

'Not one word of contrition? Then may you rot in hell.' The man's voice is distant now, the terrors receding as the darkness comes to take her. The people from the village, folk she has known all their lives, stand silent witness to her death.

Their silence is one final mockery, a dreadful mimicry of her own affliction, and here at the last she hates them all for being so weak, so craven, so superstitious. She would curse them if she could, but such was beyond her even before they crushed her with rocks. For even had she air to speak, she could not form the words. Malformed tongue and crooked neck, she has been mute since the day she was born.

23

Early morning, and McLean sat at his desk, squinting at the screen of his laptop. The sun streaming in low through the window that formed one entire wall of the room made it almost impossible to see the words of the email. Sadly, he knew that wouldn't wash as an excuse. He'd realised that it would only be a matter of time before the first of the chief superintendent's invitations came in, but had hoped he'd be given more than a few hours' notice. A function at the North British Hotel wasn't exactly onerous, but that same evening? Had to be a mistake, surely. He couldn't be expected to jump so quickly, not even if the station chief commanded it.

Frustrated, he picked up the desk phone and after a couple of abortive attempts managed to find the right number. The chief superintendent herself didn't answer, of course. She had secretaries for that. In some ways that made things easier.

'Chief Superintendent Elmwood's office. Helen speaking.'

Helen. McLean tried to picture the woman. Short, mid-fifties, dark hair going chaotically grey, nice smile. 'Hi Helen, it's Tony McLean here. About the chief superintendent's email. I wonder if I could—'

'Ah yes, the Safe Streets Committee. Gail was particularly

149

keen you join her as the representative of Specialist Crime Division.'

'But it's this evening.'

'That's right. Seven o'clock sharp. Gail will meet you there.'

'I . . . But . . . Wait. She's going to this thing anyway? Why do I need to be there?'

'As I understand it, Detective Inspector, there's always a representative from plain clothes at these functions. The chief superintendent is attending because she feels the need to engage with the community as much as possible. You know how it is, surely? She's come up from England and that can put people's backs up a little. Helps to have a local on hand to smooth the waves, as it were.'

'Could I possibly have a word with her? I had . . .' He was going to lie and say plans, but before he could get the word out, Helen had interrupted him again.

'I'm afraid she's over at Gartcosh in meetings all day. You could try her mobile, but I suspect it will be switched off. You know how annoyed the chief constable gets when he's interrupted.'

Bloody marvellous. McLean rubbed at his forehead as if that would make the inevitable easier to accept. It didn't really help.

'Seven o'clock, Detective Inspector. It shouldn't last more than a couple of hours.' Helen's voice was cheery but insistent, and he was beginning to reconsider the merits of her smile. Before he could say anything more however, she had hung up, leaving him with a quiet hissing on the now dead line.

He sat there, head in hand, phone to his ear, for what felt like an age but was probably only a few tens of seconds before a light knock at the open door distracted him. For a moment he wondered whether it was Helen come down the corridor to apologise for her rude behaviour, but instead he was greeted by a worried smile from Detective Sergeant Harrison.

'Morning, sir. Hope this isn't a bad time?' She put a light inflection at the end of the sentence as if she meant it as a question, or had turned Australian.

'Nothing I can't cope with.' McLean put the phone receiver back in its cradle. 'Morning, Janie. This about the building site accident you texted me about at crack of sparrow?'

'Aye, sir. Didn't know whether to call you out or just let you know. Decided I could handle it for now, but you might want to have a look for yourself. It's . . . weird.'

'Weird?' He tried to keep the exasperation out of his voice. There'd been too much weird about recently and the last thing he needed was even more. 'Remind me where it was again?'

'Up Liberton Brae. You know, the new apartment block?'

McLean did. It was an eyesore, but then so was the building he was sitting in. 'How bad?'

'One dead. Name of Don Purefoy. He's . . . was the sales rep for the development. Nobody's really sure why he was out on site last night, but the poor sod got crushed by a rockfall. One of those big steel mesh things filled with boulders?'

'Gabions?'

'Aye, that's the word. Seems one of them failed, spilled out all the rocks just as Purefoy was walking past. Talk about bad timing.'

'And you suspect it's more than just an accident?'

'Well that's the thing. I've spoken to site security and the head engineer. They can't see how it can be deliberate, and looking at it I can see what they mean. Guy was just in the wrong place at the wrong time. And these were big rocks, see?' Harrison held her hands wide enough to explain how they might easily have killed a man.

'But you don't like the smell of it, right?'

'I guess it all just looked too neat. The way it happened. When they found him he was on his back, arms wide. Huge boulder on

151

his chest, a couple more either side of him. But somehow the
rockfall managed to miss his head.' A slight shudder ran through
Harrison's frame. 'And there was no blood, no shattered bone.
You'd think it'd be like a car crash, but no. Looked more like that
one big rock had been placed on top of him. Only there's no way
it could have.'

McLean rubbed at his face, finding a rough patch on his
jawline the morning's hurried shave had missed. He'd be a right
mess come the evening. Ah well, that's what happened when you
sprang surprises on him, and the sooner the chief superintendent
worked that out, the better.

'We'll need a report for the PF anyway, so might as well get
started on that. I take it Health and Safety are investigating too?'

'Arrived just as I was leaving, sir. As did the pathologist.'
Harrison checked her watch. 'Body should be at the mortuary by
now. They had to bring in heavy machinery to move the boulder
first.'

McLean took a moment to gather his wits. They needed
another investigation like a hole in the head, but he was prepared
to trust Harrison's instinct on this. If she thought something was
amiss, then he wasn't about to stop her finding out what, and
how. It's what he would have done, regardless of whatever his
superior officers told him.

'OK, Janie. Gather up as much intel on the dead man as you
can. We can decide how to proceed once the post-mortem's
done.' He stood up, shrugged the stiffness out of his shoulders
and came to join her at the door. 'Now if you'll excuse me, I
need to go see someone in the basement.'

The noise and bustle decreased to almost nothing as McLean
descended into the bowels of the earth, a welcome silent calm
falling over him with each step downwards. How much nicer it
would be if he could leave all the office politics and unnecessary

bureaucracy behind, find himself a permanent desk in the Cold Case Unit. Spend his time poring over dusty archives and chasing down long-forgotten clues.

'The Detective Inspector returns. There goes my morning.' Ex-Detective Superintendent Charles Duguid looked up from whatever he'd been reading, slowly taking off his spectacles like some disappointed teacher as McLean stepped into the room. Maybe working live cases upstairs wasn't so bad after all.

'Grumpy Bob not in?' he asked, scanning the empty desks.

'Detective Sergeant Laird has gone off in search of decent coffee.' Duguid picked up his mobile phone, glanced at the screen, then put it back down again. Presumably checking the time, since there was no chance of a signal surrounded by so much stone and so deep underground. 'He's a creature of habit, so I reckon he'll be another five minutes. Was there anything in particular you wanted him for? Only he's meant to be sorting out the witness statements for a hit and run in 'ninety-five we never got to the bottom of.'

'Just something peripheral to the old lady we found dead out in the woods on the Bairnfather Estate. He might not have had time to look at it yet if you've got him working something else.'

Duguid polished his spectacles with a red spotted handkerchief for a moment, his expression impossible to read as ever. 'Heard about them knocking you back to DI. I'm guessing you're not too upset about that.'

'Means I can pass the paperwork further up the line. Spend more time actually trying to solve cases rather than telling other folk what to do, then telling them again when they do it wrong.'

'Ha. As if you'd ever delegate anything important, McLean.' Duguid leaned to one side and retrieved something from the floor. When he placed it on his desk, McLean recognised the box he'd found under the stairs in Cecily Slater's cottage.

'Grumpy Bob, on the other hand, has no such qualms.' The

ex-detective superintendent lifted the lid off and took out the top few items. McLean stepped forward for a better look as Duguid laid them out on the desktop. There were a couple of photographs of the house, one black and white, one colour; a series of letters written in neat but tiny handwriting; some newspaper cuttings, their paper yellow and brittle with age; and a small leather-bound diary with the date 1943 tooled in gold on the cover.

'It tells an intriguing tale.' Duguid picked up the black and white photograph. It wasn't one McLean had seen in his cursory look through the box, but now he studied it he could see that the house was only a background feature. The foreground consisted of a group photograph, slightly blurred, of perhaps fifty girls lined up in rows. They varied in age considerably, the youngest sitting cross-legged at the front, the oldest on chairs directly behind them and a third row of teenagers standing at the back.

'Burntwoods was a boarding school?' McLean took the photograph and held it close, peering at the faces as if he might somehow recognise a young Cecily Slater even if the focus meant most of the features were blurred.

'Not exactly, no. It belonged to a lady called Mirriam Downham. You'll remember the Downham Trust?'

It took him a moment to make the connection, coming as it did rather out of context. 'The shelter for abused women?' McLean thought back to the last time he'd worked with Vice, or the Sexual Crimes Unit if he was being formal. The Downham Trust had been occasionally helpful in getting sex workers away from violent and manipulative pimps, battered women away from their abusive husbands and boyfriends. They ran a women's refuge south of the city, one of many dotted around the whole of the UK.

'That's part of what they do, and apparently it all began at Burntwoods. From this photograph it's clear that they took in children as well, gave them some kind of formal education.

154

According to this, though . . .' Duguid fished out one of the newspaper cuttings '. . . the house burned down in 1930 and was never rebuilt.'

'Really – 1930? But this photograph.' McLean looked at it again, trying to find any clue that it had been taken in the forties, when Cecily Slater was supposed to have been there. Turning it over, he saw the neatly inked words 'Burntwoods – Summer 1943' in a stamped box that included the name of the firm of photographers, Carnegie and Sons, Dundee.

'That's a mystery in itself, although there's no date on that newspaper clipping so it's possible they rebuilt after all. Certain, I'd say, given the other photograph.' Duguid passed it over, and McLean saw the house in colour this time, albeit faded like the few pictures he had of his parents. Like those, this one seemed to have been taken by an amateur, and it showed a young woman posing in the foreground. It was difficult to be certain, but he'd have put her age in the mid-twenties. He flipped the picture over to see the words 'Cecily – August 1956' written in heavy pencil.

'Cecily Slater would have been what . . . twenty-five then, so that makes sense. I expect she went back to see someone, maybe? What about that?' McLean pointed at the diary.

'That?' Duguid picked up the slim notebook and flipped through the pages, then handed it to McLean. 'I've neither the time nor the inclination to read the daily outpourings of a twelve-year-old girl. Bob's had a wee look, but the writing's tiny and it's hard to make much sense of any of it. Some's written in a kind of code, too. There's more in the box here. Every year from 'thirty-eight to 'forty-six. They're all Cecily Slater's, and they all have Burntwoods written in the front cover as the address.'

'Eight years. And she was still going back ten years later. She must have had some attachment to the place. Might explain why she preferred to live alone, out in the woods. Never married or had kids. All the locals thought she was a witch.'

'You think she was abused? As a child?'

McLean shrugged. 'It's possible. Maybe I'll ask Lord Bairnfather when I interview him.'

Duguid grinned, not something McLean could ever recall having seen before.

'Now that's one interview I'd like to sit in on.'

24

'Where the hell have you been, Tony? We've been looking for you everywhere.'

Detective Superintendent Jayne McIntyre stood outside the door to McLean's office as he approached along the corridor, somewhat giving the lie to her claim. Hands on hips like a fishwife, the glare she cast in his direction was more than enough warning for him not to point that out.

'Down in the basement talking to Dagwood. CCU's still my responsibility, as far as I'm aware. I asked Grumpy Bob to do some digging in the archives for me. Stuff we found out at Cecily Slater's cottage.'

McIntyre narrowed her eyes. 'Trying to shift the investigation costs on to another budget? If I didn't know better, I'd say you were starting to learn how the system works.'

'That wasn't . . .' McLean started, then stopped as he realised he wasn't going to win that argument. He led the way into his office. 'Doesn't matter. It's fascinating stuff, but probably irrelevant. There's bugger all forensics, so we're digging for motive. That's why I had Grumpy Bob looking into the archives. Trouble is, she was such a recluse it's hard to imagine her pissing off anyone. Not enough to do what they did to her, at least. I'm hoping her nephew might be able to shed some light, but

I'm not holding out much hope. He's not hardly rushed home at the news.'

'That's what I was hoping to talk to you about, actually. I wanted to catch you before you spoke to Lord Bairnfather. It's only right you interview him, since you're Senior Investigating Officer and he'd take offence if anyone of a lower rank did it. He's aware that this is a murder investigation now, too. Just remember he's rich and powerful and has the ear of many an influential politician. Your kind of person, Tony.' McIntyre smiled wearily at the joke. 'Oh, and he went to university with the chief constable. Apparently they were both in the Archery Club together, although I understand golf's more their thing these days.'

Which would explain why McIntyre was looking for him and not, for instance, Detective Constable Stringer to pass the message on. The chief constable had spoken to her directly. Always bloody politics.

'What do you want to do about this morning's unexplained death?' McLean asked before McIntyre could warn him to tread carefully. She looked slightly taken aback at the sudden change of subject, but rallied swiftly.

'The site's closed for now, I take it?'

'Health and Safety have got it locked down while they investigate. Sandy Gregg's co-ordinating with them.'

'Good. She's a safe pair of hands. Keep on top of it, at least until we've got the pathology report. Might get some of those new DCs to review any CCTV footage they can lay their hands on, too.'

McLean nodded. It was what he'd been going to do anyway. 'It's odd though, don't you think? Two mysterious deaths in quick succession.'

'You can't possibly think there's any link between the two, can you?' McIntyre grimaced as if the mere thought of it were painful.

McLean shrugged. 'Apart from the fact they're both dead, no. But you know me and coincidences. Something doesn't feel right. I need to work out what, and how.'

'There's no point my trying to stop you from ploughing your own furrow, Tony, so I won't even try. But please keep an eye on the budgets while you're at it, eh? And I don't mean ask Grumpy Bob to do all the work for you.' McIntyre walked to the door, but stopped before stepping out into the corridor. 'Oh, and don't forget the Safe Streets Committee function this evening. Gail's very keen to get to know all the local civic dignitaries.'

McLean had been trying to forget about it, and might even have faced the wrath of the new chief superintendent by not turning up and instead coming up with some lame excuse like investigating the murder of a ninety-year-old woman. That McIntyre was reminding him meant that it would be much harder to duck out of the invitation.

'Is it really that important I have to drop everything and try to be sociable?'

'It is, Tony. Gail fought your corner with Professional Standards even though she knew nothing about you. The least you can do is pay her back by being helpful.'

McLean suppressed the protest he wanted to make, taking a moment to formulate his argument against the deputy chief constable's request. But before he could come up with anything coherent, McIntyre had gone.

The pool car smelled like someone had been using it for a stakeout for the best part of a week, and hadn't bothered to give it a clean once they were done with it. McLean had suggested they take his Alfa, but DS Harrison had been nowhere to be seen, and DC Blane wasn't all that keen on driving it. He said nothing for the first ten minutes of the journey, concentrating

159

on negotiating the traffic snarled up at Tollcross. McLean was happy for the chance to gather his thoughts and try to put some kind of order on the tumble of events that had made up the day so far.

'Did you attend the building site scene with Harrison this morning?' he asked, as they moved slowly past another, different housing development. Edinburgh seemed full of them, every last inch of space being pressed into creating yet more tiny apartments.

'No, sir. Heard about it though. Sounded nasty. Poor bugger just walking along and bam!' Blane hit the steering wheel with the heel of one hand, causing the car to swerve.

'It's possibly a bit more complicated than that.' McLean explained what Harrison had told him about the scene and the unlikely manner in which the accident appeared to have happened. Blane said nothing for a while, weaving the car through a complicated series of back streets towards the old Kilmarnock road, presumably in some misguided attempt to avoid the worst of the traffic. McLean would have gone straight to the bypass and round, but he knew better than to suggest it.

'That's going to make our workload a bit of a nightmare, isn't it?' the detective constable observed. Blane had originally trained as an accountant, McLean remembered. How like him to cut through all the horror of a man being slowly and painfully crushed to death, and focus instead on the logistics. He wasn't wrong, though.

'We'll manage. Hopefully. The new batch of DCs will help, even if we'll need to keep an eye on them for a while. Talk about in at the deep end. Three suspicious deaths to investigate, one a full murder inquiry. Not exactly what I'd want my first week in the job.'

'You think they're linked, all three deaths?' Blane echoed McIntyre's words earlier. McLean had considered it, but couldn't find a way to make it work. Too little information, for one thing.

'I don't know. No reason to think the two men are linked to Slater. Hopefully Janie will come up with some useful information on Purefoy. You've done the background on Whitaker, right?'

For once, Blane kept his eyes on the road as he replied. 'Yes, sir. Not that there's much to it. He started off as an unskilled labourer straight out of school at seventeen. Got his training on the job and then a diploma at night school. Same firm all the way, so I guess they saw something in him and took the time to nurture it. Not many firms would do that.'

Something about the way Blane spoke made McLean think it was personal. He said nothing though. If the detective constable wanted to talk about it, there were better times and places to do that than driving across the city on the way to conducting an interview with a recently bereaved member of the aristocracy.

'He married Miranda Keegan five years ago. Janie – DS Harrison – and I interviewed her the day we found his remains. She wasn't exactly upset to hear he'd died. Not that I think she was responsible, mind, but it was a bit cold. Claims she found him abusing their wee daughter.'

'I saw the briefing notes, aye.' McLean stared ahead as they left the twenty mile an hour zone and Blane accelerated swiftly to forty. 'That's why he was living in that pokey wee basement, right?'

Blane's hands tensed on the wheel, the car shimmying in the road before he got whatever was going on with him back under control.

'She was suing him for divorce. Hadn't been finalised, but the interim ruling meant he couldn't see his bairn and he had to move out of the family home. Only reason he wasn't in jail was because he had a good lawyer on his side. That's why he was living in that shithole. Sir.'

McLean noticed that last 'sir'. Along with DC Blane's ill-concealed agitation at the perceived injustice. It jarred with the image he'd formed of the detective constable.

'Who was the lawyer?' he asked, unsure what else to say.

'Tommy Fielding.'

'What? The men's rights guy? Weren't you and Harrison looking into him?'

Blane turned his head to look at McLean, something in the detective constable's face he hadn't seen before. Was it anger?

'We weren't looking into him, sir. We were responding to a complaint he made about a demonstration outside the hotel where he's been holding his seminars. A bunch of protesters broke in and disrupted one of his meetings the other night, so I think his complaint's fairly justified. Nobody seems to want to take him seriously though. Certainly not Janie. It's almost like she's made her mind up about him and won't be budged. I thought we were meant to be all about facts, sir.'

So that was what had been eating him. McLean nodded, in the hope that if he appeared to be agreeing then Blane would concentrate on the road again. It seemed to work.

'I'll have a word with Harrison,' he said, which seemed to mollify Blane a little.

'Sorry, sir. I didn't mean to speak out of turn. It just . . .' He didn't finish the sentence, simply letting whatever it was go unsaid. McLean let it go. If the big man wanted to talk about it, he'd find his time. Meanwhile they had more pressing business to attend to.

'No need to apologise, Lofty. I'd much rather my officers came to me when they had a problem than let it fester and affect their work. Now, let's see if we can't find out a bit more about Cecily Slater, aye? We can worry about Tommy Fielding another day.'

★ ★ ★

A squall of rain splattered across the windscreen as they parked up, Bairnfather Hall looking suitably Gothic against a backdrop of moorland and slate-grey sky. McLean hurried to the front door, Blane taking his time to lock the car but still catching up with him by the time he'd got there. Inside, they were greeted by a different flunky, who had clearly been warned they were coming. He escorted them to a vast and elegant room at the front of the building, all wood panelling and leather armchairs. Two fireplaces burned merrily, and opposite them the tiniest of bars looked almost like an afterthought.

'I will inform His Lordship of your arrival, sirs. In the meantime, can I offer you something to drink?'

McLean eyed the bar. There were no beer pulls or anything you might associate with a pub in the city. Shelves on the wall behind it held some interesting bottles of whisky. Too early for that, though, and he imagined paying for a dram here would make your eyes water far more than the alcohol.

'A coffee would be nice. You want anything, Detective Constable?'

Blane only shook his head, so the flunky gave them the most minimal of bows then turned and left. McLean had hardly enough time to scan the room and take a seat before a smartly dressed waiter appeared with a tray containing cafetiere, jug of milk, tiny bowl of sugar, elegant china cup and, best of all, a generous plate of chocolate biscuits. He set about them with all the gusto of a hungry man, pausing only to pour himself some fine-smelling coffee.

'You're missing a treat, you know?' he said to Blane, who still hadn't sat down but instead was looking around the room as if he expected to be attacked at any moment. 'Is there something wrong?'

'Sorry, sir. Just I had a lot to get done. Being kept waiting by someone referred to by a bloke in a penguin suit as "His

Lordship" wasn't how I thought I'd be spending the afternoon.'

That wasn't what was really wrong, McLean knew, but it did well enough for the detective constable. An obvious hook to hang his growing irritation upon. Now wasn't the time to find out what was really going on, although their conversation in the car on the way over suggested it might be something to do with Harrison, and quite possibly her promotion despite her being younger than him. Add it to the list of things to deal with when there was time.

'Detective Inspector McLean? A pleasure to meet you.'

Wrapped up in his musings about DC Blane, McLean was startled by the words. He looked up to see a balding man in an ill-fitting suit approaching from the open doorway. He wasn't exactly fat, but had an air about him of having gone to seed. His florid face spoke of a long and happy association with alcohol, but his smile was genuine as he held out a hand to be shook.

'Lord Bairnfather,' McLean felt a grip both firm and surprisingly soft, like being squeezed by a bag full of warm jelly.

'This is my colleague Detective Constable Blane,' he said, and Bairnfather looked up, then up again.

'My, you're a big one.' He let out a nervous chuckle, a weirdly feminine sound coming from his jowly, masculine face. 'I see they've brought you coffee. Good. Shall we have a seat and get on with this, then?'

25

McLean had been going to say that it would be better if they conducted the interview in private, but as he looked around the room he realised that they were the only people there. Even the bar staff had left, silent and efficient, with no sign of any order having been given. With a little shrug, he indicated that it would be acceptable, then waited for Bairnfather to take a seat before sitting down himself. DC Blane sat a little further from the table, and took out his notebook. He hadn't said a word, not even responding to Bairnfather's observation about his height. Not a fan of the aristocracy, then.

'First off, Lord Bairnfather, I'd like to offer my condolences. It must have been a terrible shock to find out that your aunt had passed away.'

Bairnfather's face slumped. There was no other way to describe the way his genial smile fell into a grimace, taking his cheeks and chins with it. His whole body seemed to sink in on itself as if he'd been overinflated and someone had pricked him with a pin.

'Poor dear Sissy,' he said with a sigh. 'Who'd have thought.'

'When was the last time you saw her?' McLean asked.

'Saw her? A month or two back, I suppose? I don't come up here as much as I used to. So much going on in London. All around the world, in fact. I was in Tokyo when I got the news.'

'Did you visit her at the cottage, or did she come here?' Through the corner of his eye, McLean could see Blane taking notes, his expression one of deep irritation. Or maybe that was what he looked like when he was concentrating.

'The cottage? Heavens, no. Haven't been there since I was a boy. It's . . .' Bairnfather paused a moment, his jowls wobbling ever so slightly as he shook the thought away. 'No. Sissy would come up to the hotel whenever I was in town, and we'd have a meal together. Other than that I didn't have much to do with her.'

'You're both beneficiaries of the Bairnfather Trust, I understand.'

'The trust?' Bairnfather looked momentarily confused by the question. 'Yes, I suppose so. I don't really gain much from it. I mean, there's an income, of course, and I've a suite of rooms here at the house. But as I said, I spend most of my time in London these days, and my business interests bring in far more.'

'It would have been the bulk of Lady Cecily's income though, wouldn't it? And the cottage was her home?'

'Oh, she wouldn't have liked being called Lady Cecily. No, no, no.' Bairnfather shook his head with studied emphasis. 'As I understand it, she lived very frugally. Didn't have a car, or even a mobile if you can believe that. She always loved the old game-keeper's cottage though. I've not been to see it yet. Is it badly damaged? I understand it was set on fire.'

'What will you do with it now?' McLean left Bairnfather's question deliberately unanswered.

'Do with it? Why, rebuild it, of course. If we can. It was special to her, and that needs to be preserved.'

'Why was it special to her, do you know? Surely growing up in a house like this would have been far more of an adventure.'

McLean raised both hands towards the ornate plasterwork on the ceiling a good twenty feet above them.

'Oh, Sissy hated this house. At least, I always assumed it was the house she hated. But it might have been Grandpa, of course. Her father.'

'Why did she hate her father?'

'Is this really relevant to her death, Inspector? I mean, Grandpa died when I was twelve. Hate to admit it, but that was a bit more than fifty years ago. That's old history, unlikely to be of any relevance, wouldn't you say?'

McLean hesitated before answering, aware that he'd allowed his curiosity to get away from him. 'I'm sorry, Lord Bairnfather. I have to confess that we've not managed to find much in the way of forensic evidence to help identify who might have killed your aunt. That's why I'm trying to ascertain a motive, and for that I need to get to know her. You're right though, her child-hood's unlikely to be relevant. Can you think of anyone who might have wanted her dead? Any enemies she might have had?'

That brought the ghost of a smile back to Bairnfather's face, but it lasted only a moment before the weary slump dragged his features down again. 'She was ninety years old, Inspector. I've no doubt she'd pissed off a fair few folk in her life. Sissy could be difficult at times. But if anyone wanted her dead, they'd have been as well waiting a year or two. She didn't have long left. Told me as much the last time we dined together.'

'Was she unwell?'

'Frail would be the word I'd use. She was still as sharp as a pin, mentally. But her joints had all but seized up with arthritis and she struggled to move around. I suggested she might want to move somewhere a little less remote. It didn't have to be the hotel, we could have found her a place in the city. But she was adamant. Wouldn't be moved out of that cottage unless it was in a box.'

'Have you any idea why she was so . . .' McLean searched for the right word '. . . attached to the place?'

Another slight smile passed briefly across Bairnfather's face as he recalled some cherished memory. 'Ah now, there's a story, Inspector. You'll understand this was long before my time, of course. Sissy was born in 1931, you see. She was my grandpa's second child. My father was almost ten years older than her, and there was a whiff of scandal about the whole thing. My grandmother, Lady Maude, had been estranged from him for a while by then. They lived in separate wings of the house and never attended social functions together.'

The mention of social functions reminded McLean of his engagement that evening with the chief superintendent. He managed to suppress the urge to check his watch. They still had plenty of time.

'You think maybe she wasn't his child?'

'I really don't know. Grandma never admitted anything, but she had her own coterie of friends, and I think my grandpa was happy enough to pursue his own interests. She'd given him what he wanted, after all, an heir to keep the Bairnfather name alive. Anything else was fair game, as far as he was concerned. Perhaps with the emphasis on game.'

'Sounds a bit Lady Chatterley to me,' DC Blane said, reminding both McLean and Lord Bairnfather of his existence. So quietly had he been sitting off to one side taking notes, he'd almost managed to become invisible. An impressive feat for such a large man.

'Quite, Constable.' If Bairnfather was upset at the insinuation, he didn't show it. 'There was a gamekeeper in the cottage at that time, and Grandma was noted for spending far more time with the workers on the estate than with those of her own social standing. I couldn't say whether the gamekeeper was Sissy's father. It's possible, although I always thought she looked a lot like my grandpa but without the violent temper. She certainly had the Bairnfather nose.'

'So why the whiff of scandal then?' McLean asked.

'Well, she was visiting the gamekeeper's cottage when she went into labour, you see. For whatever reason, I have no idea. But they decided it would be unwise to move her, so Sissy was born there, in the front room if the stories are to be believed.'

A little shiver ran down McLean's spine at that. Like someone was walking on his grave, as his own grandmother had been fond of saying. There was a horrible symmetry to the old woman dying in the same room in which she had been born.

'I suppose that might account for her reluctance to leave,' he said.

'It put a strain on my grandparents' relationship too. Grandpa never really took to Sissy, but then he wasn't all that keen on any women who answered back. Thought she should have found herself a nice duke or earl and got herself married, but she wasn't interested.'

'Not interested in marriage, or not interested in men at all?'

Bairnfather cocked his head to one side at that question, something of a knowing look in his eyes. 'I'm really not sure, Inspector. Some people aren't interested in either. Not the way I suspect you're meaning, at least.'

'You were fond of her, though. And she of you?'

'More so than my own parents. I was never anything but a disappointment to them, even if I've made the estate profitable and saved the hall from going the way of so many of Scotland's historic buildings.' Bairnfather looked at his watch, the first sign that he wasn't completely happy with the interview. Time to wrap things up then, at least for now.

'I won't keep you much longer,' McLean said. 'But there was just one thing. Does the name Burntwoods mean anything to you?'

For the tiniest of instants, Bairnfather went very still. It was the smallest of tells, but McLean had been trained to see things like that.

'Burntwoods? No, I don't think so. Should it?'

'Not particularly. It was just something we came across when doing background checks on your aunt. Ancient history and probably not important.' McLean stood up, Blane rapidly doing the same. It took Lord Bairnfather a little longer to get to his feet, the look on his face slightly more worried now than when he had first entered the room.

'I'll be here for a while, I expect. Sorting funeral arrangements, the trust, all that. Please keep me up to speed on developments, Inspector.'

'I will, sir. And if I have any other questions, I'll let you know. Thank you for agreeing to see us.'

Bairnfather nodded once at McLean, once at Blane, not offering a hand to be shaken this time. Then he turned and walked out of the room.

No sooner had Lord Bairnfather left than a pair of waiters reappeared, one heading to the bar, the other collecting the coffee tray.

'Come on then, let's get out of here before they bring us a bill.' McLean set off for the front entrance, the detective constable following on behind. He waited until they were both in the car before speaking again.

'What did you make of all that, then? Particularly the last bit.'

Blane started the engine, checked his mirror even though there was nothing but grass and trees behind them, and pulled away from the parking space. 'For someone who professed to care more for his aunt than his parents, he seemed remarkably relaxed about her having been beaten and burned to death. And

170

I've no idea what Burntwoods is, but he knows and doesn't want to talk about it.'

It occurred to McLean then that Blane wouldn't know about the house near Dundee, or anything else that had come from the box he and Harrison had found at the gamekeeper's cottage. 'Cecily Slater spent most of her childhood at Burntwoods. There's not much information about the place, but we think it was possibly some kind of refuge.' As he said the words, he recalled the old insane asylum at Rosskettle, south of the city. It had been part of NHS Scotland by the time it was closed, but long before that it had been a privately run hospice. An insane asylum, yes, but also somewhere wealthy families sent their problem children to prevent them becoming a social embarrassment. Could Burntwoods have been something similar before the war? It didn't quite square with the somewhat sketchy history of the place Duguid had given him, but it might be worth pursuing.

'Something tells me that Lord Bairnfather knows she was sent there and why,' McLean continued. 'He wasn't particularly embarrassed about her possibly being illegitimate, maybe even the daughter of one of the estate workers. He was almost proud about her having been born in that cottage. And yet he didn't want us to know about the place she was sent to when she was a child.'

'To be honest, sir, I thought he was making the whole thing up.'

'Everything?' McLean asked.

'Aye, well. Maybe not everything. But he came across as . . . I don't know. Insincere?' Blane waited for a car to pass the end of the hotel drive, then pulled out on to the main road, his swift acceleration making the tyres chirp in protest.

McLean went over the conversation in his head. It was true Lord Bairnfather had been keener than most to share old family gossip, but he had seemed genuinely saddened by his aunt's death. In that restrained, undemonstrative way that was beaten into you at the worst private schools.

'I think you're perhaps being a bit hard on the man. Not everybody wails and gnashes their teeth when a relative dies, you know. Not in public, anyway.'

The detective constable glanced in McLean's direction, the car drifting slightly towards the roadside as he did so.

'But I asked for your opinion, and I'm grateful for it, honestly,' he said hurriedly, nodding his head at the windscreen and an oncoming bend. Blane seemed to get the message, correcting their course a little aggressively.

'I just expected him to be, I don't know, a bit angrier?' the detective constable said after a few moments' concentrating on negotiating the corner. 'If it was my aunt was killed like that, I'd be screaming blue murder at us to find her killer. He's only turned up today and she's been dead for weeks.'

Put like that, McLean had to admit that Blane had a point. On the plus side, it seemed unlikely that Bairnfather would be making a complaint to the chief constable about their behaviour. At least, not yet. But they hadn't gathered as much information about Cecily Slater as he'd hoped.

'You're right, Lofty. But we need to tread carefully with Lord Bairnfather.' McLean heard the unspoken deference to power in his words. 'Not that he deserves kid gloves more than anyone else, but he can make our jobs difficult if he wants to.'

'Aye, sir. Private law. That's what privilege means, doesn't it? One rule for them an' another for us?'

'If he's guilty of anything, I'll find it, Lofty. I don't do favours for friends of the chief constable, especially not where murder is involved. But we need to be subtle about it. Follow the money, of course. We need to find out everything we can about the Bairnfather Trust and Cecily Slater's financial interests, but we mustn't let Lord Bairnfather know that's what we're doing. And we need to look into Burntwoods too.'

'You think it's really relevant, sir? I mean, it was a very long time ago.'

'And yet she kept mementoes of it for her whole life. And it spooked her nephew when we mentioned it. Someone who, as you've pointed out already, is not exactly prone to emotional outbursts.'

Another few moments of silence as the road roared along underneath them. 'I'll add it to the list of actions, sir.' Blane was clearly trying to keep the exasperation out of his voice, but not entirely successfully.

'Cheer up, Constable. It's got to be better than accountancy, aye?'

Blane nodded his head slightly in agreement, but the fact he didn't say anything suggested to McLean that perhaps the detective constable was having second thoughts about that.

26

A light shower of rain dampened the shoulders of his jacket as McLean stepped out of the taxi and crossed the road to the North British Hotel. The massive building loomed over Waverley Station, solid and immovable. It wasn't his favourite place to visit, for the very reason he was entering it now. This was where functions happened, where he was supposed to be polite and sociable, to mingle and make small talk when all he really wanted to do was sit alone with his thoughts.

An elderly gentleman in the uniform of a concierge directed him through to the main ballroom. McLean checked his watch as he walked along the wide corridor, hoping he wasn't too late. He didn't want to be here, but neither did he want to get on the wrong side of the new chief superintendent.

'Ah, Tony. You're here. Excellent timing.'

The voice came from behind him, and as he turned he almost did a double take. Elmwood came down the corridor like a catwalk model, elegant and effortless. She wore her police uniform, with all the unnecessary shiny bits associated with her rank, but somehow she managed to make it look almost glamorous. She'd let down her hair from the tight bun she wore at work, and as she came closer he caught a whiff of expensive perfume. Her whole stance was different, as if this were some fun social event and not important police business. He was glad he'd asked Lofty Blane to drop him at home so he could shower and change before coming out, but even so he felt dowdy and unclean in Elmwood's presence.

'Ma— Gail,' he corrected himself. 'I thought this was a meeting of the Safe Streets Committee.'

Elmwood smiled, white teeth flashing behind lipstick just the tasteful side of gaudy. 'Meeting is such a utilitarian word. Yes, we're meeting people. But there isn't an agenda. I don't need you to take minutes. Someone'll give a short presentation, I'm sure, and then it's all about getting to know who's who. Mostly I think everyone wants to meet me, since I suspect they all know each other already. Shall we?'

She indicated the room, and for a horrified moment McLean thought she wanted him to take her arm. Instead he strode to the door and opened it for her.

'Come on, Tony. Let's get something to drink. You do drink, don't you? Christ, I need one. These functions are always a lot easier with a little alcohol to lubricate proceedings.'

McLean looked around the vast ballroom, echoing to the sound of a few dozen voices. Chairs had been lined up in front of a small podium with a lectern on it and a projector screen behind. A couple of liveried hotel staff stood at a table lined with champagne flutes. Outside, the last light of the day had fled, leaving only an orange glow diffracted by the rain on the tall windows.

'Do you have anything soft?' he asked, as a waiter appeared, holding a tray laden with champagne. 'I'm driving,' he added by way of pathetic excuse.

'Rookie error, Tony.' Elmwood leaned past him to take a glass, tipping half of the champagne down her throat in a most unladylike way. 'Grab one and hold it for me. Might as well make yourself useful, eh?'

He did as he was told, as the chief superintendent drained her first glass and took up another.

'Christ, I needed that,' she said, as she led him over towards the podium and a small group of people. 'A whole day stuck in a stuffy office over at the Crime Campus, listening to boring old farts going on about five-year projections and budget management. I can see why you never wanted to give up being a detective.'

McLean opened his mouth to say something, but closed it again as the chief superintendent began to speak over him.

'And what bloody idiot came up with the name "Crime Campus", eh? Makes it sound like some kind of training ground for crooks. Mind you, seeing some of your colleagues that's maybe not far off the mark.'

He was spared the need to make any comment on this by the arrival of the chairman of the Safe Streets Committee, a man called Alan Forbes. McLean only knew these two facts because the man introduced himself. As he scanned the growing crowd, he saw very few faces he recognised, and none he could put an actual name to. If his presence here was meant to be a means of introducing the chief superintendent to the great and good of Edinburgh, then they'd picked the wrong man.

'Well, well, well. If it isn't Tony McLean. Of all the people I expected to bump into here, you were most certainly not on my list.'

Ice water dripped down his back as he heard the voice. He didn't need to turn to know who was speaking. There was only one person whose simple existence put his teeth on edge.

'Mrs Saifre.' He spoke the words before facing her. 'What brings you to town? I wouldn't have thought safe streets were a high priority for you.'

McLean had to remind himself that the woman standing in front of him was in her sixties at least. She looked not a day over thirty-five, face immaculately made up, raven-black hair worn long so that it waved past her shoulders. Her black cocktail dress suited her perfectly, but the whole effect was ruined by the hint of irritation in her eyes.

'Jane Louise, please, Tony. Mr Saifre died a very long time ago. Tragic, really. And it's the Dee Foundation that is concerned with safe streets. Most of my work these days is in the charity sector. Had you not noticed?'

McLean had noticed. The Dee Foundation seemed to be everywhere these days, putting resources into things that government should but didn't. If he hadn't had run-ins with her in the past, he might even have fallen for Mrs Saifre's saintly behaviour, but he had and he wouldn't.

'Ah, Tony. There you are.' Another female voice behind him reminded McLean that he wasn't at the function alone. Mrs Saifre's perfectly drawn eyebrow arched as she looked past him to greet the chief superintendent. Then she focused back on him with the kind of smile a bleeding diver might see on the face of a great white shark.

'Mrs Saifre, this is Gail Elmwood, our new chief superintendent. Gail, this is Mrs Saifre. She's . . .' McLean ran out of steam. He could hardly say 'the devil incarnate', even if that was what he thought of the woman.

'Pleased to meet you, Mrs Saifre.' Elmwood held out a hand to be shook.

'Tony's such a tease. I don't really go by Mrs Saifre these days. It's Jane Louise.'

Watching the chief superintendent's face, McLean could see the cogs turning as she put the pieces together. How many glasses of Dee Foundation champagne had she downed?

'Jane Louise Dee?' The chief superintendent rounded on McLean, her drink spilling on his jacket with the motion. She slapped him lightly on the arm with her free hand in a manner far too familiar for his liking. 'Tony, why didn't you tell me?' She turned her attention back to Mrs Saifre again, this time managing to keep the much-diminished liquid in her glass. 'I was so hoping to meet you tonight. Can't say what a pleasure it is. The Dee Foundation's work with young offenders is held up as a shining example down in the Met.'

'Is it now?' Mrs Saifre had a different smile for the chief superintendent, but McLean wasn't entirely sure it was any better than the shark. He dabbed at the damp patch on his jacket with what had been a clean handkerchief as the two women fell into a conversation from which he was excluded. At any other time he might have taken offence, but for some reason he didn't mind. He was about to make his excuses to them both and flee, when he felt his phone vibrate in his pocket. He pulled it out and stared at the text on the screen, a message from DS Gregg.

Urgent we locate you. Please call control or phone me direct. Incident at Tollcross. Hope you're not involved.

He was just about to text back asking what she was on about, when the chief superintendent spoke to him. 'It's about to start, Tony. You coming with us?'

'Something's come up.' He held up the phone and gave her an apologetic shrug. Beside her, Mrs Saifre's stare was as inscrutable as a wall.

'Go on, then. I'll catch up with you later.'

McLean would have thanked her for the dismissal, but she'd already turned away. Not one to look a gift horse in the mouth, he fled the room.

'What's going on, Sergeant?'

McLean held his phone tight to one ear, straining to hear over the noise. He'd called DS Gregg as soon as he'd left the ballroom, and then walked down the corridor straight into an entrance foyer seemingly full of loud, chattering tourists.

'Oh, thank Christ you're OK, sir. I thought you were dead.' DS Gregg's voice sounded almost like it was breaking.

'Dead? How? I'm at the North British with the chief superintendent.' He didn't add that being dead would probably have been preferable, especially once he'd discovered it was a Dee Foundation event. Gregg's worried tone suggested she was being serious.

'Report just came in ten minutes ago. Bad car accident at Tollcross. Officers at the scene said the driver was killed instantly, and the index is . . . well, it's your car, sir.'

McLean frowned, even though there was nobody around to see him. 'But my car's parked in the station car park.' At least it had been when he and DC Blane had left for Bairnfather Hall in a pool car. 'That place is meant to be safer than Fort Knox.'

'Aye, about that.' Her initial worry gone, now DS Gregg sounded embarrassed. 'Duty sergeant's doing his nut in. Got half the station going over the CCTV, but as far as we can work out, some wee scrote just walked through the back gate, climbed into your car and drove off like he had the keys. Whole thing done in less than twenty seconds. Nobody saw him, and everyone assumed you'd gone home.'

McLean shoved his hand in his pocket and felt the familiar weight of the key fob. He had a spare, but that was in a drawer at home, wasn't it? 'Who was driving? Do we know?'

'Not yet, sir. Still waiting on confirmation from the officers attending.'

'Where exactly did it happen?' He could look it up as soon as he was off the phone, of course. Chances were there'd be news feeds and camera-phone footage on social media already. Bloody marvellous.

'Corner of Lauriston Place and Tollcross. Apparently the car was going like the clappers, spun into a shop window. Lucky nobody else was hurt, to be honest.'

'OK. Thanks for letting me know, Sandy. Not a lot I can do about it right now, so I'd better head back into the meeting. Copy me in on the RTA reports, would you? And any update on how the little bugger stole my car from under the noses of a few hundred police officers too.' McLean hung up before DS Gregg could say any more, then turned back towards the double doors that opened on to the ballroom. He didn't really have to go back in there, did he? Fate had given him a cast-iron excuse to leave. Even the chief superintendent couldn't get too upset with him for running off after what had just happened, surely?

But then he had left her with Mrs Saifre, and that was never a good idea.

'You going in?'

McLean startled at the voice, unaware that someone else had approached the ballroom doors. He turned to see a man walking towards him with the slightly harried posture of someone who knows they're late for something important. As he came closer, McLean recognised him and reconsidered the whole doing a runner thing. Strange to think his name had come up in conversation only a few hours earlier in the day.

'Mr Fielding. Surprised to see you here.'

The lawyer looked at McLean more closely for a moment when he heard his name. Recognition came more slowly for him, which was something of a compliment.

'Detective Chief Inspector McLean, is it not?'

'Just Detective Inspector.' McLean reached out and opened the door. Beyond it, the noise suggested any presentation was already over and the serious hobnobbing had begun.

'Demoted and forced to attend a Safe Streets Committee event. You must have seriously blotted your copybook.'

'Our new chief superintendent needed someone to introduce

her to the great and good of the city. Your guess is as good as mine as to why she chose me.'

Fielding had been about to step into the room, but he paused, blocking the doorway. 'She? They put a woman in charge?'

Something about the way the lawyer said the word 'woman' immediately put McLean's back up. He'd met Fielding before, and heard all about him. Knew he specialised in fathers' rights cases and defending wife beaters. What was his little organisation called? Dad's Army or somesuch. Surprising he hadn't been sued for that, less so that the man himself was so instantly dislikable. What he was doing here was anyone's guess.

'I can introduce you, if you'd like. That's what I'm here for, after all.'

Fielding stared at McLean for a moment longer than was polite, then shook his head. 'That won't be necessary. I'm here to see one person only.' Without another word he stepped into the room and began moving through the crowd.

McLean stood in the doorway a moment longer, aware that as yet he'd not been spotted by anyone. Idle curiosity had him scanning the people, looking to see who it was that Tommy Fielding had arranged to meet. It wasn't important though, and the sight of the chief superintendent and Mrs Saifre laughing at some shared joke reminded him of just how little he wanted to be here. Stepping back into the corridor, he closed the doors and set off in search of a taxi to take him home. Elmwood was a grown woman, a chief superintendent. She could look after herself.

27

The major incident room hummed quietly, but not through any great activity on the part of the team at work. Earlier it had been flies buzzing against the window, but now that it was dark outside they'd given up and the task of making an irritating noise had been handed over to the dying fluorescent lights sunk into the false ceiling. Over in the far corner by the water cooler one was flickering and blinking in a manner that made Janie glad she wasn't an epileptic. Or particularly susceptible to migraines. It was making her tetchy all the same.

'Has anyone been on to maintenance about that bloody light?' she asked as she cut and pasted a chunk of useless information from one window to another, putting together a background report on the man whose dead body she had seen first thing that morning.

Mr Donald Purefoy had not led the most interesting of lives, his only brush with the law a half a dozen speeding tickets spread over just enough time that he never quite lost his licence. He'd been briefly married, two kids, divorced for a couple of years now. Janie had spoken briefly with Katie English, the ex-Mrs Purefoy, who hadn't exactly been upset by the news. Neither had she seen Purefoy in over a year, since moving to Aberystwyth to lecture at the university. Katie had doubted she'd make the trip up for any funeral, or that the children would even notice the further absence of their father. Yet another sad tale that left Janie wondering why people bothered hitching up in the first place.

Frustrated, it took her a while to notice that nobody had answered her question. True, she hadn't been expecting anyone to actually do anything about the lights; that was something she'd have to sort out in the morning herself. A non-committal grunt from Jay at the desk opposite might have been nice, though. Only, when she looked up, DC Stringer was nowhere to be seen. Neither was anyone else for that matter. She pulled out the earbuds that didn't actually block out any noise, but did stop people from bothering her unnecessarily, stood up and glanced around the room. Empty.

'Where the hell is everyone?'

It struck her as she walked around the unmanned desks that asking such a question in the circumstances was a bit stupid. She pulled out her phone, swiped the screen to see if anyone had messaged her. There was nothing, but the numbers at the top told her it was past shift end. The night shift should have been in by now, though, so that didn't explain why the room was empty.

Outside, the corridor looked like something from a horror movie. Nobody in sight, another pair of fluorescent lights blinking and buzzing at the far end. Janie was almost spooked, but then a familiar face rounded the corner.

'You heard the news?' Constable Amy McKay had come up through training with her, but stuck to uniform when Janie had made the switch to CID. Plain Amy, the other recruits had called her, which was unfair. But then coppers could be cruel.

'What news?' A slight shiver of worry ran through her at the possibilities. Something bad enough to empty the incident room, but not bad enough anyone would interrupt her.

'The Detective Inspector. His car. There's been a horrible crash up at Tollcross.'

The shiver turned to an icy block in the pit of her stomach. 'DI McLean?' she asked, although none of the other DIs would have been described by the car they drove. The car she had, in a roundabout way, helped him buy. 'Is he OK?'

'Paramedics are trying to save the driver, but he went through the windscreen. It's a miracle no pedestrians were hurt.'

Janie's mind raced. And then something occurred to her. 'I thought the DI was at that Safe Streets do with the chief super-intendent this evening.' She pulled out her phone and checked the time again. 'Why would he be driving through Tollcross? You sure it's his car?'

Amy shook her head, looked at Janie as if she was daft. 'Someone nicked it, see? Right out of the car park here. Duty sergeant's spitting blood. Got half the station looking at CCTV and the other half being questioned about what they might have seen.'

'So he wasn't driving it, then?' Janie struggled to keep up.

'Who?'

'DI McLean, Amy. He wasn't driving the car when it crashed? He wasn't anywhere near it?'

'Far as I know.'

'Has anyone told him?' She didn't much fancy the task herself.

'The sergeant's giving him a call, but you know what he's like for answering his phone, aye?'

Janie gave her a weak smile. 'Aye, you're right enough there. Thanks, Amy.'

She went back to the major incident room, logged into her computer again, and searched for any information on the crash. There wasn't much logged on the system, but a quick Google search brought up the news fast enough. There was no denying it was the boss's car, although from what she could see in the shaky camera-phone footage, it wasn't going to be his car for much longer. Christ, it must have been going at some speed.

Janie picked up her phone, tapped the screen until the number came up, then hovered her thumb over the call icon. It had been instinct to get in touch, but did she need to really? It wasn't as if there was anything she could do right now, and by the morning they'd have more information to go on.

She switched the phone off, slipped it into her pocket, then logged out of the computer and grabbed her coat from the back of her chair. Some of the night shift were beginning to filter into the room now, Sandy Gregg bringing everyone up to speed. Not that there was a lot for them to do. Most of the chatter seemed to be about the DI's car anyway.

Janie slipped away unnoticed, let herself out the back door and walked through the car park to the road. Glancing up, she saw the CCTV cameras covering every inch of parking space and marvelled at the balls of a thief who could stride in as bold as brass and steal the nicest car in the place. Cheeky sod. Not that it had done him much good.

A light squall of rain kicked up out of nowhere as she made the walk to Nicolson Street for a bus. Janie pulled her collar up, wishing she'd brought a hat. Winter was coming, as that mad telly series Manda went on about kept saying. Still, it would be nice to get home to the flat, have a bite to eat and curl up on the sofa for some mindless viewing. If she could get her mind to switch off for a moment, that was.

She was so wrapped up in her thoughts, Janie almost didn't notice the footsteps behind her. They weren't heavy or threatening, but they were coming closer. Not quite a run. She shoved her hand deep into her pocket, made a fist around her bunch of keys. Not tonight. Not any night. She didn't need this shit.

Whirling around at the last moment, she pulled her hand out of her pocket, swinging down and back in readiness to land a punch. The figure hurrying towards her wasn't a mugger though. Quite the opposite. She looked like someone had attacked her already. And she was familiar.

'Janie? Janie Harrison? Thank fuck for that.' The young woman's English accent was the final clue.

'Izzy?' Janie shoved her keys back in her pocket and went to grab the young woman before she fell down. 'What the fuck happened to you?'

The Southsider wasn't Janie's favourite pub, but it had the benefit of being close. She led Izzy inside, a wave of warm air washing over them and bringing with it the familiar pub smell of stale beer and body odour.

'You look like you need a stiff drink,' she said, as she guided the young woman to a seat in the corner, miraculously free of punters at this early stage of the night's drinking. 'Sit there and I'll get you something, aye?'

Izzy did as she was told, but didn't say what she wanted. Janie went to the bar and ordered two glasses of wine. Whisky might have been better, but it was still a bit early for that, and the pay rise that came with her promotion wouldn't hit her bank until the end of the month. It occurred to her as she carried the glasses back to the table that Izzy – Isobel DeVilliers – was probably one of the richest people in the country. Hadn't she inherited a share of her dad's billions?

'There you go. Get that down you. Should settle your nerves.'

Izzy seemed to be coming back to her senses now, the shock of whatever had happened beginning to wear off. In the poor light of the pub, she looked a mess. Of course, she'd looked a mess the first time Janie had seen her – wasn't that part of the whole hippy chick grunge look? – but Janie was fairly sure that didn't include scrapes and bruises on the face and hands, and certainly not a cracked and swollen lip.

'Thanks,' she said, then winced as she tried to take a sip of her wine. She paused for a moment before going for it again, taking a decent gulp this time and grimacing as she swallowed. 'Ugh, maybe not. What is that?'

'You're welcome.' Janie ignored the comment and took a sip from her own glass. It was horribly sour, but the alcohol would numb her tastebuds soon enough. 'So tell me. What happened to you?'

Izzy shuddered slightly, then pulled herself together. 'There were two of them,' she said, after another gulp of the foul wine had disappeared down her throat. 'Jumped me as I was walking up the Royal Mile. I'd been down at Holyrood trying to get a chance to speak with someone about that bloody man, Fielding.'

As she spoke, Janie studied the young woman's face, trying to get an idea of her injuries. She was bruised, shaken, but also angry, which suggested any physical harm was superficial.

'Did you get a look at them?' she asked.

'They had their faces covered with those stupid bandana things.' Izzy shook her head. 'One of them's got at least three broken fingers and I'm pretty sure I broke his nose. The other's going to need surgery on his right knee. Oh, and he's probably got a ruptured testicle too.'

Something about the way she said it, her delivery perfectly deadpan, utterly serious, made Janie burst out laughing.

'I meant it,' Izzy said, a faint hint of annoyance in her voice.

'Sorry.' Janie pulled herself together, chugged back too much of the wine to help give her a little time. 'It's just . . . I don't know. Maybe because that's what I've wanted to do to Fielding every time I've been in the same room as the wee scrote.'

'Scrote?' Izzy's puzzled frown lasted for a few seconds, then realisation dawned. 'Ah. Apt.'

'Seriously though, Izzy. You really inflicted serious injury on them? Your attackers? You fought back?'

'Of course I did. I'm not going to let any man push me around like that. They had it coming.'

Janie heard the defensiveness in the young woman's voice, back-pedalled as quickly as she could. 'Not trying to suggest you should have done anything different. Honest. They deserved it, like you say. I meant you seemed, I don't know, frightened when you caught up with me out on the street. And your injuries . . .' She raised a hand tentatively towards Izzy's face, but didn't touch her.

'Like I said, they jumped me. Stupid, really. I should have been paying more attention, but I was that pissed off with the bloody politicians refusing to see me. If I'd been thinking straight those two would never have got anywhere near.' Izzy clenched her hands into tight fists, the grazes on her knuckles beginning to ooze a little fresh blood. 'I legged it while they were down. Knew the police station you worked out of was close by and hoped you'd still be at work. Saw you just leaving, didn't I? Had to run to catch you up.'

Janie reached into her pocket and pulled out her trusty notebook. Most policing was done with electronic PDAs these days, but technically she was off duty, and the batteries were always flat when you most needed them not to be. Flicking forward to an empty page, she opened it up on the table.

'These two men who attacked you. I know you said you couldn't identify them, but can you give me a few more details?'

'Yeah, I guess so. Don't know if it'll be easy to press charges, mind you. Men like that . . .' Izzy tailed off, her eyes going to a faraway place Janie couldn't even imagine. She took another swig of her wine to fill the silence, and something of the motion must have brought the young woman back to the here and now.

'Maybe not. But if you can give us a detailed description of the injuries you inflicted, then that might be interesting if any of Fielding's associates turn up limping, or with a bandaged hand, wouldn't you say?'

Izzy's face brightened at the thought. 'That would be something, wouldn't it? Yes. That's a great idea.'

It took the best part of an hour, going back and forth over the details. Janie knew that she should really have walked Izzy back to the station, lodged a formal incident report and taken a statement from her there. But she also knew the connection with Fielding was entirely conjecture, and that an attempted attack on a young woman wouldn't get the full attention it deserved. If they'd found her body in one of the narrow closes off the Royal Mile, then there would have been a full investigation, but Izzy had escaped relatively unharmed. Any search for her assailants would be cursory at best.

'Where are you staying at the moment?' Janie asked as they picked at the remains of their fourth packet of crisps and second glass of wine. As she'd expected, once you'd had one, the next didn't taste so bad. Or, indeed, of anything much at all. Still, she was aware that the time was marching on, her night in front of the telly disappearing rapidly.

'That's the thing. I was staying with Con's friend, Rose? You know her?'

'Aye, I know Rose. You want me to arrange someone to take you back there?'

'Christ, no. I don't think I can bear to stay in that house any longer. It's too weird. She's too weird. And all those cats, always watching you. Swear they're all reporting back to her the whole time.'

Janie wanted to laugh again, except that everything Izzy said was true.

'Do you not think she'll worry, if you're not there?'

'Nah. I left a note. Half expect to see one of the cats sitting on a wall outside keeping an eye on me anyway. Told her I'd find digs somewhere else, but that was before all this happened.' Izzy indicated the notebook, the wine, the packets of crisps. 'I'm not really in a position to turn up at the North British and get myself a room for the night.'

'Really? I thought you were loaded. What with . . .' Janie left the sentence unfinished, suddenly embarrassed.

'I wish.' Izzy didn't seem to have taken offence at the statement. 'Maybe someday. Right now all the DeVilliers money is locked down tight in all manner of legal cases. Charlotte, my half-sister, she's doing her best to sort it all out, and she's way better at it than I'd have ever believed possible. Mum's moved in with Con's dad, which is all kinds of awkward, let me tell you. Long and short of it is I used to be a trust fund kid in a posh private school and now I've barely two beans to rub together.'

Far from being upset by it, Janie could see that Izzy was happy at the freedom not being one of the country's wealthy elite brought to her. Perhaps it was the folly of youth, although she wasn't that much younger than Janie. Not really. If you squinted. Maybe it was the certain knowledge that she'd be rich again soon enough. Whatever it was, she didn't seem bitter about it, which given all the things that had happened in her life showed a remarkably wise head on those young shoulders. Christ, she was beginning to sound like her mum.

'Don't suppose you know anywhere I can crash?' Izzy asked. 'Sure I'll find somewhere tomorrow, but it's getting kind of late now.'

For a moment Janie thought about the boss, with his big old house and all its spare rooms. He'd put up waifs and strays before. She'd almost reached for her phone to give him a call, but then she remembered what had happened to his car. He'd either be out dealing with that, or home and pissed off. She'd check in with him tomorrow.

'Come on then.' She made up her mind as she stood and reached for her coat. 'It's only a couch in the living room, but you can crash at my place for the night.'

28

Early morning, and McLean drove Emma's little Renault ZOE to the station. He'd thought long and hard about taking it, since she'd not had the car long before heading off with Professor Turner to Africa. For the past few weeks it had been sat by the old coachhouse, plugged into its own special charging point. He only hoped Emma wouldn't be upset with him when she got back, but it was either that or a lot of taxis.

He took the long way to the station, pretending that it was so that he could view the crash site on the way. After the deep-throated V6 growl and twitchy throttle of the Alfa, the electric Renault was noticeably quiet. It was surprisingly comfortable too, and being small was much easier to navigate through the snarled up roads around Tollcross.

The Alfa had been removed from the shop front it had demolished, no doubt taken away to the forensics labs out by the airport. Would Manda Parsons be the one to examine the wreckage? Even if she wasn't assigned the job, she'd probably barge her way into it anyway. Poor Manda, she'd been begging him for a ride in the car since he'd got it. That wasn't going to happen now.

A horn blaring behind him dragged McLean's attention back to the here and now. He glanced briefly in his mirror, contemplating trying to memorise the number plate of the offending car, then moved off as swiftly as he could. The route took him over the Meadows, and he couldn't help but glance up at the trees as he passed the entrance to Jawbone Walk. No dead bodies in them this time, but the leaves were beginning to pile up on the grass beneath them now. Winter wasn't far off.

A chain had been hung across the normally open gap, and a uniformed constable greeted him at the entrance to the station car park. He held up an unnecessary hand, indicating for McLean to stop, while simultaneously mouthing something into the collar microphone of his Airwave set. Probably reading off the number plate before letting him in, although that smacked somewhat of horses and stable doors. He found the button to wind down the window, then held up his warrant card for the young lad to see.

'Sorry, sir. Didn't recognise the car,' the constable said, then promptly turned a curious shade of red. 'I . . . Umm . . . That is, of course . . .'

'No need to apologise. Can I come in, though?'

'Yes, sir. Of course, sir.' The constable scurried away to unclip the chain, and McLean drove silently in. He considered taking the same space where his Alfa had been the day before, then remembered what car he was driving. Since acquiring an electric pool car, the station had installed a single electric vehicle charging point. Usually it had a petrol squad car parked in front of it, but today of all days it was free. He parked, then spent a frustrating ten minutes trying to work out how to plug the car in before realising it was almost fully charged anyway. Still, it wasted a little more time before his inevitable dressing-down from the chief superintendent.

Tempted though he was to go straight to his office and hide, McLean had already seen the angry text summoning him before the headmistress. Elmwood might have looked like she was enjoying herself when he'd left the Safe Streets Committee event the previous evening, but he was well aware that he was meant to be her second. His excuse for bailing was sound, but that didn't necessarily mean she would accept it.

The chief superintendent's office door was closed, Helen sitting at her desk outside, typing up some notes. She looked up and smiled as he approached. 'Go on in, Tony. She's expecting you.'

'Is it bad?' McLean asked.

'I have no idea. She's not an easy one to read, that one.'

'Wish me luck then.' He knocked lightly, then opened the door and stepped inside.

The chief superintendent sat at her impressively large desk, head down as she studied some report that was clearly of great interest. McLean closed the door behind him and walked across the room towards her. He'd only made it a couple of feet before she spoke.

'A bit casual, waltzing into work this late, isn't it? Almost lunchtime.' The chief superintendent looked up at him, her face inscrutable. A totally different character to the one he'd met in the North British Hotel the night before. McLean knew better than to look at the clock on the wall, even as he also knew it wasn't yet eight o'clock in the morning.

'I swung past the crash scene on my way in. Hadn't appreciated just how bad the traffic would be.'

'Your car. I heard. That would be why you slunk off and left me with that Saifre woman last night, I take it?'

McLean nodded. 'Did you get on OK?' He meant at the event as a whole, but the chief superintendent took it to mean something else entirely.

'She's very pushy, that one. Said a lot of nice things about you, though. If I didn't know better I'd think she was a little jealous you were my plus one and not hers.'

McLean hadn't been aware that he was anyone's plus one, and

the casual way the chief superintendent used the term put him on edge.

'I'd be careful around her if I were you. She has a way of making you indebted to her, then calling in those debts at the least convenient time.'

The chief superintendent cocked her head to one side as if unsure what to make of this. Then she shrugged away the thought with a little 'hmph' noise, reached for her phone and picked it up. On the other side of the door, McLean could hear the secretary answer.

'Helen, tell the driver we'll be leaving in ten minutes. And can you let Gartcosh know our ETA. Ta.' She hung up and looked straight at McLean. 'You can tell me everything about Jane Louise Dee she didn't tell me herself on the way to the Crime Campus. Meet me downstairs at the back door in ten.'

'I . . .' McLean started to speak, then realised he had nothing to say that wouldn't have been a whiny complaint. The chief superintendent was ready with her answer anyway.

'Kirsty's got the major incident room under control for now. Your team are chasing down leads as best they can. There's nothing you can do to help them. And there's a detective inspector from the NCA who's very interested in talking to you about last night.' She stood up as she spoke, straightened her uniform and grabbed a heavy black leather case from beside the desk. Hefting it up, she swung it in his direction. 'Here, you can carry this for me. Ten minutes. Downstairs. Now if you'll excuse me, I need a piss.'

McLean understood why the chief superintendent might need a driver. She was a busy woman and her job involved endless meetings, pre-meeting discussions and long-winded telephone conversations. At any moment she might be called by the first minister or any of a dozen cabinet ministers, committee First

Minister MSPs, Police Authority members, the Procurator Fiscal's office – the list was endless. She couldn't be expected to drive herself and waste valuable conversation time. What he couldn't understand was why she needed two constables to accompany her, although as he settled into the back seat and she squeezed in alongside him rather closer than was strictly necessary, he began to have an inkling of an idea.

At least it wasn't a limo, with a motorised partition to cut off the passengers from the chauffeur. Anything said or done on their trip across the central belt to Gartcosh was going to be witnessed by two uniformed officers. That didn't really make him feel any better about it, and he still couldn't understand quite why he was being dragged along. It couldn't be that obvious, could it?

He spent the first twenty minutes or so of the journey texting various members of the investigation team, pulling together what few advances had happened over the course of the morning. Which was to say none at all. DS Harrison wasn't answering her phone, which was unlike her but not enough to be a worry, and DC Blane had called in to say his wife was being induced that day. Small things, easily managed, but he would much rather have been in the incident room reviewing their lack of progress and discussing different avenues of approach than driving ever further west and away from the city.

'So then, Tony. How would you feel about having a more active role in the liaison team between Specialist Crime and the chief constable's office?'

Might as well ask him how he felt about having his leg cut off without anaesthetic, but McLean was all too aware that he was trapped here in this moving metal box, with the deputy chief constable sitting uncomfortably close, her expensive scent making the air difficult to breathe. And she was his boss. His boss's boss, if he was being correct about things. She could make his life hell if she wanted to, although the more he thought about it, she was doing a good job of that already.

'Are you sure that would be a good use of my skill set?' he asked. 'There's plenty other more senior officers in Specialist Crime who'd be much better at the job.'

'Really?' The chief superintendent didn't try to hide the disbelief in her voice. 'Can you name any?'

'Well, there's Jayne McIntyre for a start. She really should be doing that job, shouldn't she? And I know for a fact Jo Dexter would be happy to move out of Vice if there were an opportunity. That's not a job you want to get stuck doing for long, and she's been in it years now. Kirsty Ritchie's got a much better head for the bureaucracy than me, too.' McLean silently cursed himself for potentially throwing any one of his colleagues under the bus, but in truth any of them would be better for the job than him, and if there was a promotion in the mix then maybe they'd even forgive him.

'Hmm. I'm not sure any of them really fit my criteria.'

McLean was about to ask her what her criteria were, even though he suspected he already knew. He was saved by her phone ringing, a different tone to the one he'd heard before. Whoever it was, they were clearly important enough to have to answer.

'Dammit. What now?' she muttered under her breath, then hitched a smile on to her face that McLean could tell wasn't intended for him. 'I have to take this.'

She tapped the screen, lifted the phone to her ear. 'Minister. How nice to hear from you,' spoken with all the sincerity of a politician.

He leaned back into his seat, stared out the window and watched the motorway verge speed past as he tuned out a very one-sided conversation. Whichever minister it was clearly had a lot to say, and for that McLean was extremely grateful.

29

Janie tiptoed through the living room in her socks, trying not to make a sound as she gathered all her things for the day. On the couch, buried deep under a mound of spare duvet and blankets, Izzy DeVilliers snored like someone who'd drunk rather too much of Manda's special Russian vodka the night before. Poor girl was going to have a head like an Orange Day parade when she woke up, but she only had herself to blame. Well, herself and Manda, maybe. Janie was glad she'd stopped after the first shot glass.

It occurred to her as she stooped to lace up her boots that she wasn't entirely sure Izzy was old enough to drink. She'd have to check the record sheet from her arrest at the hotel. Except that she'd persuaded the duty sergeant to lose the paperwork when she'd first heard Con's little sister was in the cells. That might come back to bite her if she wasn't careful.

At least Manda had the day off too, another reason why the two of them had got stuck into the vodka. Janie left them to their slumbers, let herself out and hurried down the tenement stairs.

Outside, the air hung wet with a smir of rain. That annoying stage between fog and downpour that somehow managed to soak you through without you noticing. She hurried to the bus stop, pleased to have timed it perfectly for once, and was soon back in the warm.

On the bus, she pulled out her notebook and flipped through to the pages where she'd taken down Izzy's description of her attackers the night before. Well, not so much of her attackers as the injuries she'd inflicted on them. A broken nose could be easily explained, and there were probably hundreds seen by A and E on any given night. Likewise, broken fingers were probably ten a penny. A ruptured testicle was a rather more esoteric injury, and the kind of damage that a well-placed kick to the knee could inflict would almost certainly both need medical attention and be remembered by whichever doctor administered it.

By the time the bus pulled up at the stop closest to the police station, Janie had called in several favours, and now there was nothing she could do but wait for her various contacts to get back to her. She wasn't entirely sure why she was doing this. Not while in the middle of a murder investigation and looking into two other suspicious deaths. There was the connection with Fielding, of course. That was how she'd justify it if it ever came back to her. She couldn't see DI McLean being upset, but Ritchie was a bit more of a stickler for the rules. And McIntyre might act like everyone's mum, but she could be sharp as a paper cut if she wanted to be. Janie had seen her tear strips off enough constables, sergeants and even inspectors to know better than to cross the detective superintendent.

The major incident room was quiet when she let herself in, only a few of the night shift still hanging around to pass on the little information that had dribbled in overnight. Most of the talk was about DI McLean's car, and how someone had managed to steal it from right underneath their noses. Reg, the duty sergeant when it had happened, was chewing up the furniture and shouting at anyone unfortunate enough to cross his path, as if it were his fault entirely that it had happened. Janie was glad she'd missed him when she came in.

She logged in to one of the terminals. Working through the routine emails didn't take long, even if she wasn't kidding herself there'd be more to deal with soon enough. DI Ritchie would be calling the morning briefing in a few minutes, and Janie glanced at her phone hoping something might have come through. Still no reply. She logged off the computer and stood up, scanning the room for the familiar figure and not seeing it anywhere. That was strange. It wasn't as if he could easily hide.

'You seen Lofty?' she asked of a uniformed constable as he scuttled past, clutching a load of folders to his chest.

'Phoned in to say his wife's being induced today,' came the answer, and then the uniform was gone. A little curt for a constable addressing a sergeant, but she let it go. She should have remembered about Lofty's wife. He'd been unusually surly recently – he must have been worrying about her. Having a break during paternity leave might do him good.

Her phone rang as she watched DI Ritchie stride into the room, followed by a gaggle of detective constables. About time they had some new blood in the place, even if what they really needed was experienced officers. She checked the caller, one of her friends who worked at the Royal Infirmary.

'Hey, Ali. You got my text then?'

'Aye, Janie. Wondered about that. You're not usually one to miss a chance for a chat. This all a bit hush hush?'

Alison Perry had been one of her closest friends at school, but their careers had taken different paths since and they only met up occasionally now. An A and E nurse, she could be a useful source of information sometimes, and a dreadful gossip the rest.

'I was on the bus. Didn't want to upset any of the other passengers.'

'Fair enough. Can you tell me what this is all about then?

200

Only I think I might have dealt with your two miscreants last night.'

Janie looked up at the clock, then over at the crowd gathering for the morning briefing. Sandy Gregg was there, so they had at least one detective sergeant to cover. If she slipped out now before anyone noticed, she could always catch up later.

'You at work now?'

'Aye. Shift's no' over for another hour. Then I'm away to my bed.'

'OK, Ali. Can't tell you on the phone, but I'll be over in about a half an hour. Buy you breakfast.'

The squad car she'd cadged a lift from dropped Janie at the main entrance to the Royal Infirmary forty minutes after she'd snuck unnoticed out of the morning briefing. She'd sent a quick text to DI Ritchie and Sandy Gregg whilst en route, hoping she wasn't volunteered for some unpleasant duty or shift in her absence. If her hunch paid off, it would be worth it.

She found Alison getting herself ready to leave A and E at the end of what had clearly been a long night. Janie hung around until the clock swung to the hour, then followed her old school friend to the staff canteen and bought her a coffee.

'Probably shouldn't have this,' Alison said as she sipped her latte. 'Going home and straight to bed, and I don't need anything keeping me awake.'

'Bad night, was it?'

'Ach, I've had worse. It just never ends, though. Especially now the nights are long and dark and it's getting cold. Folk are just accidents waiting to happen.' Alison took another sip from her mug, put it carefully down on the table and rubbed at her eyes with the heels of her hands. 'You didn't come here to talk about me though, did you? It was the bloke with the ruptured testicle and the wrenched knee, right?'

'The same. And if he had a friend with a broken nose and fingers, I owe you big time.'

'Might take you up on that.' Alison reached into the pocket of her nurse's uniform and pulled out a thin sheaf of printed A4 sheets, placed them face down on the table and slid them over as if she were in some spy movie and any moment now James Bond was going to walk in and sweep her off her feet. He could do worse, Janie thought. Ali had always been pretty, even if the exhaustion on her face was doing its best to hide the fact.

'That's technically confidential information, so you didn't get it from me. Two men, I'd say late thirties, early forties? Came in around ten last night. I didn't deal with them myself, that was Cara. She says they told her they'd been drinking, slipped on the steps at the top of Fleshmarket Close, and tumbled down them together. It's plausible. Happens more often than you'd think. One bloke loses his footing, grabs at his mate for support, the two of them end up at the bottom with broken bones.'

'So they might have been telling the truth then?' Janie asked. Fleshmarket Close wasn't so far from the place where Izzy said she'd been attacked, but it wouldn't have been much fun getting there with a ruptured testicle and blown out knee.

'It's possible. Cara reckoned they were hiding something, though. They said they'd been drinking, but they didn't seem all that drunk. Not like the usual evening crowd we get to patch up. And the one with the injured bollock? That's not something I'd associate with falling down the stairs. That's a Saturday night brawl kind of injury. Come to think of it, so's a busted knee.'

'Well, if they're who I think they are, they were both taken out by a teenage girl not a lot taller than me. They thought she was an easy target.'

It was perhaps a measure of how tired Alison must have been that she barely raised an eyebrow at this. 'Well good for her. Friend of yours, I take it?'

Janie considered the question for a while before answering. She hardly knew Izzy DeVilliers, and yet the young woman was crashed on her couch right now. There was something about her Janie couldn't help but admire. 'Aye. I reckon so.'

30

McLean had been to the Crime Campus at Gartcosh a couple of times since its opening, but it wasn't somewhere he felt the need to visit often. It was too far from his usual stomping grounds, for one thing, and it represented a very different approach to policing from the one he was accustomed to. Then again, crime had evolved in directions nobody could have even dreamed of when he had still been a beat constable. The internet had barely been a thing back then, and yet now maybe half of the crime they dealt with was directly linked to the web. Even everyday criminals used smartphones and encrypted emails, and the old boundaries between countries had all but dissolved away.

A case in point was the theft to order of high-end cars, as he was finding out at far greater length than he would have cared to know. Detective Inspector Maurice Ackerley of the National Crime Agency was part of a team tracking down a gang who operated throughout the UK and Europe, sourcing expensive and exotic machinery.

'Your car would have been in a container and on its way to Africa or China before you'd even noticed it was gone,' he said, as they stood in an incident room that looked more like the starship *Enterprise* than somewhere organised crime was investigated.

Banks of computer equipment lined the walls, far more modern than anything McLean's team had access to, and in one corner a massive screen showed an electronic map of the greater Glasgow area.

'It has a tracker in it.' McLean knew this was what Ackerley wanted him to say; he wasn't an idiot after all. The DI came across as extremely proud of his technical facilities.

'Ah, but those are easily traced and disabled. And I've no doubt you thought your Alfa Romeo was well protected by its alarm and immobiliser, and yet they proved no more of a problem to overcome than the lock.'

McLean tried to ignore the hint of triumph in Ackerley's voice, as if the DI was impressed with the ingenuity of the thieves. Almost as if he respected them. He glanced across to where the chief superintendent was standing by the door, and tried not to smile at her raised eyebrow and ever so slightly rude hand gesture.

'That much would seem obvious,' he said. 'Along with the fact that the wee toerag who stole the car might have had all the technology he wanted, but he still didn't know how to drive.'

Ackerley's animated excitement evaporated in an instant, his whole body slumping like a teenager asked to take the rubbish out. 'That's what doesn't add up,' he said. 'I mean, don't get me wrong. Alfa Romeo Giulia Quadrifoglio. That's not your average policeman's ride. Five hundred horsepower through the rear wheels?' He made a little 'poof' noise and flicked the fingers of both hands open to indicate an explosion. 'Plenty of them parked backwards in hedges when they first came out. But these guys . . .' and now he turned towards the big screen, even though it didn't show anything that might indicate the gang stealing expensive cars to order. 'They know how to drive, Tony. They're some of the best. They don't show off. They steal the car, then get it as quickly and safely to their lock-up as possible.'

'Well this one obviously hadn't read the script. You know who he is? Was? Whatever.'

Ackerley tapped his keyboard. The big screen changed to a profile page, and finally McLean got a look at the man who had stolen his car.

James 'Jimmy' McAllister had been twenty-six years old when he died. Average height, a skinny sixty-five kilos, he had the pasty white complexion of a north Edinburgh housing estate and a surprisingly clean criminal record. He'd been cautioned a couple of times as a youth, both for joyriding offences, and then from his eighteenth birthday until the day of his death he appeared not to have put a foot wrong. He appeared not to have had a job either, or paid any tax. And yet his address was one of the modern apartments in Fountainbridge. Not somewhere you'd live if you were eking out your dole money.

'That's pretty close to where he crashed,' McLean said, all too aware that he was stating the obvious. 'Do we know where he was going? Not home, I take it.'

Ackerley tapped his keyboard again, and the screen changed to an Edinburgh street map. A red line from McLean's police station to the point of the accident took an odd, circuitous route first north, then west, and finally south again.

'That's what we can't work out. From the reports we've had, and the CCTV we've managed to collate, he came roaring up the Lothian Road from the Princes Street end. But if he'd been heading from your station car park to Tollcross, he'd have gone across the Meadows. It's a stupid route the way he went. Makes no sense.'

'And I had to come all the way here to be told that?' McLean spread the question between Ackerley and the chief super-intendent. 'Could you not just have phoned? Or maybe sent me a copy of the report?'

'Well, I was hoping you could answer a few questions about

your daily use of the car, where it's parked at night, that sort of thing. We need to work out how McAllister knew where to find it.' Ackerley's tone was one of mild confusion rather than annoyance, which made things worse as far as McLean was concerned.

'I don't know if you're aware, Detective Inspector, but I'm currently SIO on a murder investigation and my team is looking into two other suspicious deaths that will probably turn out to have also been murders. We're short-staffed enough as it is, without my being dragged across the country to deal with this. The theft of my car is quite low on my list of priorities right now.'

Ackerley looked across the room at the chief superintendent, who shrugged unhelpfully. This really wasn't how policing was supposed to be done.

'OK.' McLean conceded defeat. He was stuck here anyway, might as well make the best of it. 'I'll answer your questions as best I can. But I'd like something in return, if it's not too much to ask?'

'Name it,' the NCA man said, which was perhaps a little foolish of him.

'Your vast database of stuff.' McLean waved a hand at the big screen. 'I'd like you to run a name through it, see what pops up.'

'Shouldn't be a problem.' Ackerley stepped up to the keyboard again, flexing his fingers like he was expecting a fight. 'What's the name?'

'Slater. Lady Cecily Slater.'

'You didn't need to be quite so hard on Maurice, you know. The NCA can be very helpful when you're nice to them.'

Much later, and McLean sat next to the deputy chief constable as they drove back to Edinburgh, wondering how he was going to catch up with a wasted day. He'd climbed into the back when they were finally ready to leave the Crime Campus, thinking that the same two constables would be in the front seats as before. To his annoyance, only the driver reappeared, and now he eyed up the front passenger seat with deep longing. Anything to get away from the too-close proximity of Gail Elmwood.

'Everything we did today could have been done in an email,' he said. 'There was really no need for me to travel halfway across the country for any of it.'

'And would you have dealt with that email straight away? Or would it have lain unread in your inbox for a fortnight?'

McLean didn't want to admit that she had a point there. 'A phone call, then. Or sending a constable over with some questions. Instead I'm stuck in a car in traffic when I should be . . .' He stopped speaking, aware that he'd been about to say 'out there investigating a murder'. That would have left him open to the accusation that as SIO he should most certainly not have been 'out there', but back at the incident room co-ordinating his sergeants and constables to go 'out there' and do the job their pay grade demanded. And which they had no doubt spent the whole day doing. Without him.

'You did OK out of it though, didn't you?' The chief superintendent nodded towards the brown folder McLean held on his lap like some kind of protective ward. It contained a printout of everything the NCA database had spewed out for him about both Cecily Slater and her nephew, the eleventh Lord Bairnfather. Ackerley had even promised to send more over if he turned anything up about the Bairnfather Trust and the hotel, although he'd admitted there was nothing on their radar he was aware of.

'Again, if I'd needed it I could have emailed them or picked up the phone. I only asked face-to-face because I was already there.'

'Relax, Tony. You can't be fighting crime all the time. You have to let others deal with all the details, sort and sift the information they bring to you. Delegate, in other words.' The chief superintendent took her own advice literally, loosening her collar and leaning back in her seat as if she were a vacuous celebrity in a stretch limo on the way home from some gaudy awards ceremony, and not one of the most senior police officers in the country, on duty.

'With respect, Gail, that's not the way I work. That's not the way murder investigations work either, especially not ones like this, where there's no obvious motive and no forensic evidence.'

The chief superintendent reached out and placed a hand on his knee, just briefly. More the lightest of pats than anything else, but McLean did his best to hide the flinch at her touch. He was still trying to give her the benefit of the doubt, but it was hard to ignore the evidence, especially when he'd been trained to notice such things. The deputy chief constable was a welcome change from her predecessor in many ways, but at least McLean had understood Teflon Steve.

'Why is it that whenever someone begins a sentence "with respect" it's actually the complete opposite that they mean?'

'Probably because it's considered rude to be frank.' McLean focused his attention on the chief superintendent where before he had been doing his best to avoid her gaze. The expression on her face didn't fill him with great joy. This was a game for her, he could see, and right now he was doing exactly what she wanted him to.

'I'd be horrified if I thought my officers were holding back on me, Tony. Be frank. I won't be upset.'

OK. If that was how she wanted to play it. 'You've never been a detective, have you, ma'am?' He posed it as a question, even though he already knew the answer. Neither did he give her time to speak before he carried on. 'I know we can have a bit of a reputation for being difficult, us plain clothes coppers. We don't keep an eye on the budgets as much as you'd like, I'm sure. And we've a tendency to get a bit fixated sometimes. It's part of the training. So you can imagine how anything that distracts us from the task in hand can be a bit annoying. Especially if there's no obvious good reason for it. Like today's trip and last night's so-called function.'

Something like irritation flickered across the chief super-intendent's face then, but she kept it well hidden. For a while there was nothing but the roar of tyres on road and the whistle of wind around the car's wing mirrors. Then she hitched a smile on to her face that would have done a politician proud.

'I can sort of see your point, Tony. Really, I can. But you hit the nail on the head right there. Specialist Crime has a tendency to think of budgets as a distant second priority, if it thinks of them at all. But we live in a world of finite resources, sadly. Cuts are everywhere, and they're only going to get worse.' And now she leaned in close, her hand back on his knee but not lightly this time. 'And that's why I need you by my side. So I can fight off the accountants and the Police Authority when they come demanding we keep chipping away at the costs. I need someone who's been at the coal face to remind them that it's not pounds and pence, but people's lives.'

It was a good speech, he had to admit. Even if it was all bollocks. McLean held the chief superintendent's stare for a moment longer, then looked pointedly down at her hand. She followed his gaze and a moment later removed it, sliding away to sit more comfortably in her seat with the faintest flicker of a smile playing across her lips.

'Think about it, Tony. You and me, we could do great things together.'

McLean let his head tip back and stared at the cloth lining the roof of the car. He didn't need his years of experience to hear the unspoken threat. Sure, they could do great things together, but she could also make his life hell if he continued to spurn her advances.

31

'What exactly are we here for, Janie?'

Detective Sergeant Harrison sat in the driver's seat of the pool car and watched the house across the street. Beside her, Detective Constable Jay Stringer wasn't exactly fidgeting like a bored child, but it came close. They'd been parked up for half an hour now, and he either needed to go to the toilet or had actual ants in his pants.

'This, according to our records, is the house of Christopher Allan,' Janie said.

'Aye, I know that. An' I know you want to talk to him. So why are we sitting here staring at the place and not chapping on his door?'

It wasn't a bad question, although Janie didn't feel she needed to answer it straight away. Instead she posed her own question. 'What do you make of it? The house?'

'The house? How?'

Stringer's comment wasn't particularly helpful, but it was also accurate. Christopher Allan, it appeared, lived in a nondescript semi-detached bungalow on the outskirts of Colinton where it bumped up against Dreghorn to the south. A row of near-identical pebble-dash harled bungalows arced in a shallow curve towards the main road. Each of the buildings had a short stretch of front garden, many of which had been paved over to provide off-street parking. Judging by the cars, it was a relatively affluent area. More expensive than a detective sergeant's salary might stretch to, certainly.

'It's not exactly the kind of place you'd expect a mugger to live, is it?' she said.

'Not a street mugger, no,' Stringer conceded. 'Maybe a banker though, and they're a bit like muggers, when you stop and think about it.'

Janie smiled at that. Jay wasn't bad company. A lot less surly than Lofty Blane these days, for sure. She hoped he wouldn't get into trouble when someone higher up the command chain found out what she was doing here. Unless, of course, what she was doing here went well, in which case they'd probably get away with it.

'So this is where your man lives? With the broken bollocks?'

Janie was about to explain what a ruptured testicle actually was, wondering all the while how a man might not know that when she did. Before she could speak, the front door opened and a woman stepped out. From a distance she appeared to be in her late thirties, maybe early forties, although it was difficult to tell given her long raincoat and wide-brimmed hat. She didn't look back as she set off up the street towards Colinton Village, and neither did she notice the two detectives sitting in their unmarked car as she walked past. Janie watched her in the mirror until she reached the end of the road and disappeared around the corner.

'Come on, then.'

She climbed out of the car, waited for Stringer to do the same, then locked it. Together they approached the house, Stringer stepping to one side of the door as Janie reached out and rang the doorbell. Inside the house it chimed a cheery ding-dong that echoed away to silence.

'You want me to go round the back?' Stringer asked.

'He's got a blown knee and a ruptured testicle, Jay. He's not going to leg it anywhere.' Janie rang the doorbell again, and this time as the ding-dong faded away she saw movement in the textured glass sidelight. She waited patiently as a person moved very slowly across the hall and unlocked the door.

'If you're trying to bring me good news from the Lord, forget it.'

'We're not Jehovah's Witnesses, don't worry,' Janie said in her friendliest voice. 'Would you be Christopher Allan, by any chance?'

Leaning on the door frame for support, the man glowered at her. Like the woman who had recently left, he was perhaps pushing forty. He was dressed in baggy jogging pants and a hoodie, face sporting a day's worth of stubble, hair tousled as if he'd not showered recently. Bloodshot eyes suggested he'd not slept much recently either.

'Who wants to know?'

'Detective Sergeant Harrison.' Janie held up her warrant card just long enough for him not to be able to focus on it properly. 'And this is my colleague Detective Constable Stringer. Might we have a word, Mr Allan? It's about the accident you had last night.'

She could see the thoughts play themselves across his face as plainly as if they'd been written in a little bubble above his head. Fear widened his eyes and the colour drained from his cheeks. Unable to run, and certainly in no position to put up any kind of fight, he was trapped and he knew it. His gaze slipped briefly past Janie towards the street beyond, but the woman wasn't coming back any time soon. When he finally resigned himself to the situation, it was almost as if a weight had been lifted off his shoulders.

'Aye, you'd best come in then.'

★ ★ ★

213

The inside of Christopher Allan's house wasn't much more inspiring than the outside. It didn't appear to have been redecorated since it had been built, sometime in the fifties if Janie was any judge. When he opened the door fully to let them in, she saw that Allan was walking with the aid of a single crutch, and the leg of his jogging bottoms on that side had been neatly cut open so that the brace on his knee could fit. He led them at a snail's pace to a pleasant living room at the back of the house, French windows opening up on to a long, thin garden with a half-decent view of the Pentland Hills.

'My sister was just here.' He lowered himself into an armchair with much effort and a great deal of grimacing. Even once he had settled he didn't look particularly comfortable.

'That's OK. It's you I wanted to talk to. About the accident.'

'It's just that I'd offer tea or coffee, but it takes me a while to move.'

'We're fine, thanks.' Janie perched herself on the edge of the sofa and took out her notebook. 'Unless you're wanting one yourself? I'm sure Constable Stringer can find the kitchen.'

That seemed to cheer Allan up no end. 'You sure? I'd love a coffee then. Milk, no sugar. Kitchen's that way.' He twisted as he pointed towards the front of the house, then winced as the motion sent a spasm of pain through his groin.

'I'll no' be long,' Stringer said. 'You wanting one, ma'am?'

Janie suppressed the laugh that would have spoiled the mood. 'Aye, go on, Constable. Same for me.'

She watched him go, then turned her attention back to the injured man. 'We'll not keep you long, Mr Allan. I can see you're in quite some discomfort there.'

Allan squirmed like a little boy who's wet himself. 'Aye. They've given me some painkillers right enough. But they don't seem to do anything.'

'As I understand it you fell down the steps at Fleshmarket

Close. Got a bit tangled up with your mate . . .' Janie left the sentence unfinished, hoping Allan would fill the gap and not being disappointed.

'Brian, aye. Brian Galloway. We'd been having a few drinks in the Malt Shovel, see? Maybe one too many. Cannae remember if I tripped an' grabbed him or he tripped an' grabbed me. All I know is one moment we was at the top of the steps moaning about life, an' the next we were at the bottom covered in blood.'

'It's been wet lately, so I guess the steps were slippy, right enough.' Janie flipped a page in her notebook, even though so far she'd not written anything down. 'So, you and Brian. You go drinking together often?'

A ghost of alarm flickered across Allan's face at the question, as if he wasn't sure how relevant it might be. 'Aye, mebbe once every week or two. Have a blether about the old days. We've known each other since we were bairns. You know how it is.'

Janie didn't, but then she was considerably younger than Allan. She glanced around the room as he spoke, taking in the details that showed what kind of life he lived. It was tidy, but perhaps not clean, and there weren't many personal touches. One corner of the room was dedicated to the god of big screen telly, complete with Blu-ray player, Xbox and a jumble of cables. The shelves behind it were full of games and discs, no books to be seen anywhere. On the other side of the room, the original fireplace had been boarded up, one of those electric fires made to look like a fake wood-burner in front of it.

'Do you always go to the city centre? The Malt Shovel?' Janie stood up and walked over to the mantelpiece as she asked the question. There were two photographs in cheap wooden frames sitting on the dusty surface. One showed a younger Allan, his arms around two young boys who must surely have been his sons. The other showed a slightly older Allan being presented with something by an old man with a heavy gold chain of office draped around his neck.

'Aye, usually. I work in the Old Town, an' it's no' as if we've much to go home to, either of us.'

'Your boys?' Janie asked, indicating the photograph.

'Wi' their mother in Australia. I tried to stop her taking them, but the courts—' Allan's words cut off abruptly as DC Stringer re-entered the room bearing two mugs of coffee.

'That must be very hard. Not being able to see them often.' Stringer handed Allan his coffee with a sympathetic smile.

'Hardly even get to speak to them these days. I can video call, but that's not much good if their mother's filling their heads wi' all kinds of shite about me so's they don't want to talk to me any more.'

Janie could hear the anger in Allan's voice, but it was a tired, old anger, beaten down by harsh reality. What could he do, after all, if his children were on the other side of the world? If their mother had turned them against him? But then again, why had she left him, and why had the courts let her take the children so far away? She shook the questions away. Not relevant, but then this entire visit was not relevant. And skating on thin ice.

'Are you likely to want to take this up with the council, Mr Allan?' she asked, waving her hand at his leg to explain the sudden change of subject. He stiffened, as if suddenly realising what was happening to him.

'That why you're here? To gather evidence? Make out me an' Brian were so pished we've only ourselves to blame?'

'Far from it. The incident was logged, so we have to follow it up. Paperwork, you know? It's the bane of our lives.'

From the narrowing of Allan's eyes, Janie knew that she'd blown it. Of course there had been no incident logged; there'd been no incident to log. She put her untouched coffee down on the side table and stood up swiftly. At least Allan wasn't able to do the same.

'We'll not trouble you any more, Mr Allan. I can see you're in a lot of pain. We'll see ourselves out, aye?'

'Can we get on to the court records, find out what grounds there were for Mr Allan's divorce? I'd like to know who represented him. I've a suspicion I already do, though.'

Janie drove slowly along Morningside Road, mentally kicking herself for not taking the bypass and coming back into town at Burdiehouse. Traffic backed up Bruntsfield Place all the way from Tollcross, the aftermath of the previous evening's car crash combined with yet more roadworks. In the passenger seat beside her, Stringer pulled out his PDA and started tapping at the screen. Not that he'd be able to access the information she wanted on it, but he could get someone else back at the station to make a start.

'What was all that about, though?' he asked after he'd finished and they'd moved another couple of hundred metres closer to their destination. It would have been far quicker to walk.

'To be honest, I was making most of it up as I went along. Much like he was, too.'

'What do you mean?'

'You don't think he really ruptured a bollock and blew out his knee falling down the steps at Fleshmarket Close, do you?'

Stringer paused a moment, head tilted slightly in thought. 'I've seen folk do worse when they've had a skinful.'

'OK then. Why were the two of them walking down the close anyway? If they'd been drinking at the Malt Shovel and were looking for a cab, they'd have walked down Coburn Street to the taxi rank outside Waverley Station. No, the whole falling-down-the-stairs thing's nothing but a cock and bull story to cover up what really happened to them.'

'And you know what that was?'

'I have an inkling.' The traffic started to move again, the lights for once working in their favour. 'Need to speak to his friend, Brian Galloway. Only, I reckon poor Christopher there will have been on the phone to him soon as we left. Getting their stories straight and all that.'

'You seem to be forgetting he's the one with the injuries, Janie. Bad enough losing his kids like that, but now he's going to be off work for a month. Probably won't ever be able to walk properly again.'

'He got those injuries when him and his pal tried to assault a teenage girl, Jay. More fool them for not knowing she was trained in self-defence and harbouring a great deal of anger towards all men.'

Stringer opened his mouth to say something to that, but clearly couldn't think of anything. He stared at her, gaping, for a good twenty seconds.

'Careful you don't swallow a fly,' Janie said, and he closed it with a hollow clunk. Moments later her phone rang, DI Ritchie's name appearing on the dashboard screen. She tapped the button to accept the call on hands free but didn't even have time to say hello before the detective inspector started shouting.

'Where are you, Janie? And what the hell are you up to?'

'Ma'am? I'm on my way back to the station now.'

'Don't you "ma'am" me. I've just fielded a call from a weasel lawyer by the name of Tommy Fielding, asking why you're harassing one of his clients.'

The pieces, so close to fitting together, all began to click in Janie's mind. 'I think harassing is a bit strong. We went round to see if he was OK. Poor chap took a nasty tumble yesterday. Sustained some serious injuries.'

The line went quiet for a while, although the screen on the dashboard assured Janie that DI Ritchie hadn't hung up. By the time she spoke again, they were being waved into the car park by the poor uniformed constable who'd been landed with the job of manning the chain stretched across the gateway.

'You've been working with Tony McLean far too long, Detective Sergeant.' Ritchie's tone was terse, but perhaps not as annoyed as it could have been. Janie knew better than to make any response. She didn't think she'd get such a soft dressing-down from Detective Superintendent McIntyre.

'Find me as soon as you get in. I want to know everything you've been doing. And I want to know why.'

Janie started to say 'Just parking, I'll be there in a minute', but before she could even open her mouth, Ritchie had hung up.

32

'What do you know about witches, Gary?'

It's not a bar he'd come to normally, even if it's not that far from his scabby bedsit. The beer's way too pricey for one thing, and the punters are all office types in smart suits. For some reason Fielding seems to like it though, and since he's generous when it comes to the drinks, who's Gary to complain? All the same, the question catches him off guard.

'Witches?'

'Aye. Witches. What do you know about them?'

'What? Pointy hats an' long hook noses an' stuff? Black cats and flying around the place on broomsticks?'

Fielding's face isn't easy to read most of the time, but Gary's not had much to drink yet and he can see the smirk. Bazza's the same when he thinks he knows better than Gary. Trouble is, he's usually right but they end up fighting about it anyways.

'That's the myth, of course. The fairy-tale witch. The old crone who might well heal you one day and curse you to death the next. That's not what I'm talking about here.'

Gary doesn't say anything. Fielding invited him here, paid for his beer. Least he can do is hear the man out, aye?

'The thing about myths though, Gary, is that they're usually founded in truth. Even if that truth gets bent out of shape a little with time.'

The smirk's gone from Fielding's face now, his expression entirely serious. Is it Gary's imagination, or is there something different about his eyes, too? They seem to be glowing a dark red colour, but when he looks over his shoulder to see where the light is, there's nothing to match. Brakes from a passing car reflected through the window. Aye, that'll be it.

'Those women camped outside the hotel the other day, remember? You think they might have been witches?'

Gary can't stop staring at Fielding's eyes. 'I . . . I dunno. I mean, they was acting pretty strange.'

'What about the ones who broke into the conference room?'

The memory sparks in Gary's mind as clearly as if it were happening right in front of him. The redhead woman. Not much more than a girl really. Shouting abuse at him and Fielding as if they were the monsters, not her and her mad screaming friends. There'd been something about her, hadn't there? Something more than unreasonable rage.

'Aye. Thought they were on somethin' right enough.'

'Oh, it's much worse than that, Gary. Those women weren't high on any drug. No. They were high on their own magic. They've sold their souls to the devil, Gary. Given their bodies to him. And in return he has gifted them a power few understand.' Fielding shakes his head slowly, and Gary can't help but notice that the red glow doesn't slide from his eyes as they move. It's almost as unnerving as the topic of conversation. Is this what he was called here for? To be told women were witches? Well, he knew that already. Kind of.

'You mean, like spells an' stuff? Making youse sick or bringing bad luck on you?'

Fielding tilts his head, the smile back but encouraging this time. 'Well I don't see you having much luck recently, Gary. Why do you suppose that is?'

'I . . .' He starts to speak, but can't think what to say. It makes sense, after a fashion. 'Bella? She's no . . . Surely?'

'It's not necessarily her, Gary. Could be a friend of hers practises the dark arts. But this is the thing.' Fielding leans forward, that gleam in his eyes like there's a fire deep in his brain. 'Witches aren't all old crones with hairy warts and pointed hats. They walk among us unseen. Bear our children then take them from us. Sack us from the jobs we've done well all our working lives. Make screeching demands for equal rights when they've lived off the back of our hard labour since Eve first tempted Adam.'

'But how—?'

'Do we find them?' Fielding interrupts, although that is just one of the many questions Gary wants to ask. 'They're easy enough to see once you know the signs. It's dealing with them that's more tricky. Would you like to know how to do that, Gary? How to get back what was taken from you by all those women? All those witches?'

'I . . . I just want things to go back to how they were, ken?'

'That's all any of us want. But what are you prepared to do to get your wish? What sacrifice would you make?'

Gary drags his gaze away from Fielding's face, looks around the posh bar. The men here are all confident, wealthy, in charge. The few women look at their partners the way Bella used to look at him, back when they first met. They know their place, as they should. There's a natural order to things, but outside these walls it's out of kilter. If Fielding is offering him a chance to put that right, then who is he to turn it down?

'What did you have in mind?'

Interlude

Grey clouds scud across a lowering sky, the wind whipping waves from the Forth, white horses dancing under wheeling gulls. In the distance, scarce visible through the haze, the lion's head of Arthur's Seat rises over Edinburgh and the king who is the source of her misfortune.

'Elizabeth Simson. You have been accused of consorting with demons. By your foul practice of witchcraft have you brought famine and pestilence to this land.'

They stand at the end of the long stone pier, sober men all dressed in black. Behind them, closer to shore and the derelict fishermen's cottages, a crowd has gathered for the show. Not much entertainment to be had in these parts. Not much joy since the crops began to fail and the nets came up empty.

'It is not too late for your soul to be saved. Confess to the sin of witchcraft, repent and throw yourself upon God's mercy.'

She stares out across the waves, doing her best to ignore the men behind her. Her time has come, she knows. The God of her tormentors has mercy only for the men who worship him. He has no time for women at all.

'Do you confess your sins? Willingly and here before these witnesses?'

Finally, she turns and faces the crowd, enjoying the

momentary flinch on some faces, the involuntary step back as if she is some fearsome beast and not a tired old woman. What harm could she possibly do them? They have tied her with stout rope, hung heavy weights about her. She can do nothing but stare, and sneer.

'And should I confess to a crime I have not committed, is that not yet a sin?'

'Very well. If you will not confess, then it shall be for God himself to decide.'

Their leader, the puffed up laird, nods to his two deputies. They step forward, uncertain at first but with growing conviction as they are not struck down. They guide her to the edge, and she looks down at the choppy water. It is not deep here, but it is deep enough.

'You will be dead before the year is out, Master Thackray.' She smiles as the words fall upon superstitious ears. They will take it as a curse, even though it is not. He has the marks on his skin where he has scratched himself, the tiny red spots mostly hidden by his white ruff collar. The ague is not a pleasant way to die, and that gives her some small comfort as she faces her own, swifter end.

'Foul sorceress, your soul will burn in hell.' He nods to the two men, and they shove her hard.

It is a short fall to the water. The stones drag her under, and swiftly to the bottom. She panics then, even though she had promised herself she would not. A lifetime of study, of helping these poor, ignorant people, means that she knows all too well how long it takes for a person to drown. Her end will not be long, though it will certainly feel it.

She holds her breath as if it was the most precious thing. The water is cold, sapping away the last of her strength as the light slowly fades to nothing. The panic lessens. She can feel herself slipping away, the blessed release almost upon her.

And then the rope pulls tight, dragging her back upwards. She breaks the surface in an explosion of noise, sucks in air that never tasted so sweet. They haul her limp body back up onto the pier, dump her unceremoniously at the feet of the magistrate. She has no strength to stand, so he crouches down to look her in the eye.

'Do you confess, Bessie Simson? Will you repent of your sins and accept God into your heart?'

She can see the hope in his eyes. He means to kill her whatever she says, but if she gives him what he wants then he will go home with his conscience clear. So it ever was. So it ever will be.

The weight of her soaked dress drags her down, the ropes around her and the rocks tied to her legs. And yet she struggles to swaying feet. Her throat is raw, her voice husky and ominous as she stares first at the laird, then at all the others who have come to witness her execution.

'With my dying breath I curse thee,' she says, and falls back into the sea's embrace.

33

The tinny electronic beep of his phone woke him from restless sleep. McLean rolled over, remembering a couple of seconds too late that Emma was on another continent. In the time it took him to reach for the handset, his mind went through the alarm at her not being there, through the relief that she hadn't stormed out on him after yet another row, and on to the realisation that he wouldn't see her again for weeks, maybe months. Last time they'd spoken, she'd sounded exhausted but excited at the discoveries they were making and the new skills she was learning. Had something happened to spoil that?

'Hello?' He did his best to keep the yawn out of his voice, and hoped that whoever was at the other end of the line couldn't hear the noise of him rubbing sleep from his eyes.

'Morning, sir. Sorry to call so early.' Not Emma, but the unmistakable voice of Detective Sergeant Sandy Gregg. McLean pulled the phone from his ear for long enough to see that it was past six in the morning. Had he forgotten to set his alarm?

'It's not a problem, Sandy. What's up?' He swung his legs out from under the duvet, shivering slightly at the chill in the room. Approaching winter had overtaken the elderly and inefficient central heating system in the house, it would seem. Either that or he'd forgotten to switch it on yet.

'Report's just come in of a dead body. House over Fountain-bridge way.' She rattled off an address, and McLean's mind wandered back to his meeting with the NCA detective, Ackerley. The bawbag who'd nicked his car had lived in Fountainbridge, but then so did a lot of other folk. Probably just a coincidence.

'Any idea why CID need to get involved?' He stared out the window at the darkness that was just beginning to melt away. The nights were fair drawing in now, mornings coming later and later. Soon he'd be leaving for work and coming home in the dark.

'Not CID, sir. You in particular. Word came in from the chief superintendent's office, apparently.'

'That's a bit irregular, isn't it?' The question was out before he realised he'd spoken it. 'Sorry, Sandy. That's unfair. I know you're just the messenger. Send me the details and I'll head straight there from home.'

He hung up, put his phone down on the bedside table and wandered into the bathroom. By the time he was showered, dressed and ready to go, the name and address had arrived in a text. Little else to go on, which was strange. In the kitchen, Mrs McCutcheon's cat looked up at him from her spot in front of the Aga. The other cat was nowhere to be seen, but when McLean pulled out a chair, it shot off in surprise. He was about to put the kettle on and see if the bread wasn't too spotty for toasting when his phone buzzed the arrival of another text.

Thx for taking this case. Swift report would mean a lot to me. Update as soon as you get in. Gail.

He stared at the screen for a long time. He didn't have the chief superintendent's personal number in his address book, so his phone hadn't tagged who the text was from. Plain enough to see from the message, though, and again highly irregular.

McLean slid the handset back into his pocket, considering his options. He could go to the station, gather what information he could about this mysterious dead man beyond his name, address and the fact he was somehow connected to the deputy chief constable. Or he could go straight to that address and assess the situation for himself. Report back to Elmwood as requested, and maybe she'd stop picking on him as company for all her social engagements. Chance would be a fine thing, but if he dragged his feet over it she'd make his life even more miserable.

He grabbed his coat and Emma's keys, took one last look at the kitchen and decided breakfast could wait.

'Looks like you two are on your own for the day,' he said to the cats, now both curled up in front of the Aga. 'Don't do anything I wouldn't do.'

Once again, McLean was thankful for Emma's little Renault as he manoeuvred the car into a parking space his old Alfa would have fitted into about as well as the shop window that had killed it. He showed his warrant card to the uniformed constable guarding the front entrance to a nondescript modern terraced house. It was still early enough that there weren't too many people about, lights on in the other houses suggesting that, unlike him, normal people were having breakfast before heading out to work.

'Pathologist's not long here, sir.' The constable stood aside to let him in through the already open door. McLean nodded his thanks and stepped inside.

A narrow hallway didn't so much greet him as crowd his senses. McLean was no great student of architecture, but he was fairly sure whoever had designed this house hadn't been either. It had quite clearly been built with a price in mind, and a low one at that. At least for the developer. Given the way house prices were going in the city these days, and the location of this particular terrace, the house was worth considerably more than the constable guarding it would be able to afford.

An open flight of stairs climbed to the first floor, the hallway continuing past it to a pair of doors. Immediately to his left, another door stood open, revealing a depressingly small living room. Like many of its kind, it was dominated by an overly large flat-screen television, which served only to make the space feel even smaller than it really was. As did the handful of people clustered around an armchair whose back was to the door. McLean recognised Tom MacPhail. Standing a little further back, clearly uncertain what she should be doing or why she was even there, one of the new intake of detective constables watched nervously. The relief on her face as she saw him enter was palpable, if mixed with a certain trepidation.

'DC Mitchell, isn't it?' McLean said as the constable edged around the room to greet him. She was much the same height as him, but bent her head and rounded her shoulders to make herself smaller in a manner that reminded him of Lofty Blane. Her dark skin and short, almost shaven, black hair marked her out both in the room and back at the station, where faces tended to be either pasty white or sunburned angry red.

'Yes, sir. Cassandra,' she helpfully reminded him. 'Although people call me Cass.'

'As long as they believe you when you tell them what the future holds.'

The uncertain look returned, which suggested to McLean nobody had taught her Greek mythology. Something for another day, perhaps. He turned his attention to the pathologist, bent over as he peered at something in the chair.

'OK if I come in, Tom?'

'If you think you can fit,' MacPhail said. 'Shouldn't be long here, mind you.'

McLean inched a little more into the room. From where he

stood he could see the top of a man's head, thinning hair beginning to go grey. A hand lay on the arm of the chair, its fingers taped up with white gauze and a splint to keep them straight. The sight of it sent a little shiver of worry through him, and he stepped carefully around the pathologist until he could see the man full on.

The thinning hair had been neatly trimmed at the front, framing a face that had seen battle fairly recently. Dark black bruises bulged under each of his staring eyes, yellowing at the edges. The bridge of his nose bore a cut from where it had been broken, the scab almost black. Along with the strapped-up fingers, it was obvious he'd been in a fight, but something about the face seemed oddly familiar.

'We know who he is?' he asked.

'Name's Brian Galloway, sir.' DC Mitchell pulled out a notebook but didn't open it. 'His mother found him like that when she popped round an hour ago.'

An hour was good going for the pathologist to be out already. This Brian Galloway must have been important, or well connected. That might explain Elmwood's interest. The name didn't ring any bells, though.

'Is she still here? The mother?'

'Aye, sir. In the kitchen. Caitlin's with her. PC Wells, that is.'

'Thanks. I'll go and have a word with her in a moment. Why don't you have a look round the place. See if anything looks unusual.'

The detective constable nodded her understanding and edged out of the room. McLean turned his attention to the pathologist, crouching down to be on the same level as him. 'What's the story then?'

'He's dead.'

'That much I can see. Any idea what killed him?'

MacPhail shifted slightly, reaching a gloved hand in to gently manipulate the man's damaged hand. 'I only just got here, Tony. Give me a chance, eh? It wasn't these injuries, for sure. They're recent, but not life-threatening. Might possibly be a reaction to whatever painkillers they gave him. I'll need to get him back to the mortuary to be sure.'

'Do you think it might be . . . ?' McLean was going to ask if it was suspicious, wondering why it was that he'd been called out to this scene if the death was most likely accidental. The look on the pathologist's face persuaded him not to. 'I'll go and talk to the mother,' he said instead, then levered himself back upright with only a minimum of groaning.

'You do that, Tony. I'll let you know what I find out as soon as I find it out, OK?'

34

If he'd thought the living room small, it was palatial compared to the tiny kitchen at the back of the house. That same inexperienced designer responsible for the whole street must have worked hard to fit everything in, but at least the single window allowed for a bit of natural daylight. Most of the space that wasn't designer kitchen units was taken up by a table and four chairs, what an estate agent would optimistically call a dining area, no doubt. Two women sat at the table in silence as he entered, one young, one old. Only the young one moved, springing to her feet as she saw him.

'Detective Inspector, sir.'

McLean hadn't been sure whether he knew Police Constable Wells by sight, although he was sure he'd heard her name before. He was relieved to see that he did recognise her. She'd been part of the team that had searched the woods south of the city that summer, turning up one key piece of evidence that had helped crack open that case. He'd been put on suspension for months for solving it, of course, but that wasn't her fault.

The old woman moved more slowly. She'd been staring at her coffee mug – still full, McLean saw – but now she turned her head to fix her gaze on him. It was hard to see any similarity between her and the dead man, but then he'd been sporting black eyes and a broken nose.

'Mrs Galloway? I'm Detective Inspector McLean.' He considered holding out his hand to shake, even though the woman only stared at him, mouth very slightly open. Her hands twisted in her lap as if she had arthritis in her fingers and was stretching them against the cold, but it was warm in the kitchen.

'I'm very sorry for your loss,' he said, after a moment's awkward silence. 'Do you feel up to answering a few questions?'

It took a while, and obvious effort, but slowly Mrs Galloway pulled herself back together. She took in a deep breath, held it for a few seconds, then let it out in a long, heartfelt sigh.

'I suppose so. Gets it over and done with.'

McLean pulled out the chair recently vacated by Constable Wells, and with a brief nod in her direction, settled himself into it. He was tempted to help himself to her coffee, but reckoned that might be a step too far.

'This is your son Brian's house, is it not? He lives here alone?'

Mrs Galloway breathed out heavily through her nose in a minimalist humourless laugh. 'As if there's room for anyone else.' She sat up a little straighter. 'Aye, this is his place. Not quite as luxurious as he was used to, but times change, eh?'

McLean had the nasty feeling he wasn't getting something that should have been obvious. 'Did he only move in here recently, then?' he asked.

Something of a smile crept across the old woman's face. She took hold of her mug, but didn't lift it to drink. 'You've no idea who he is, have you, Inspector?' As much a statement as a question, although she didn't wait long enough for him to answer. 'Brian Galloway? Frontman for the Idle Lunatics?'

It still didn't mean anything to him, but the context helped McLean guess. 'I'm not familiar with their music,' he admitted.

'Aye, well. Guess you're maybe a bit old for them, though you don't look it.' Mrs Galloway shook her head, as if remembering something. 'I guess that'll put a spanner in the works of their reunion tour, mind. Poor old Brian. He was looking forward to getting back on the road.'

'You were here very early this morning, Mrs Galloway,' he said, in an attempt to get the interview back on track. 'Was that normal?'

'Heavens, no. I kept away from this place since the day he moved in. Lizzie was right to kick him out. He got exactly what he deserved.' She paused a moment, her words catching up with her. 'Except perhaps this.'

'I'm sorry, Mrs Galloway. Who's Lizzie?'

'Dear me, Inspector. You don't read the tabloids, it would appear.' Mrs Galloway finally took a drink from her mug, then grimaced slightly at the taste. 'Lizzie was Brian's wife, until about eighteen months ago when the divorce came through. She got the house in Barnton, the kids, most of his money. But that's what happens when you have sex with the babysitter.'

'I have to admit, I wasn't aware of any of this, Mrs Galloway. However, it was, as you say, eighteen months ago. If we could perhaps come back to this morning?'

'Aye, well. I've not had much to do with him since the divorce. He was always such an angry child, angry when he grew up too. I was happy enough to let him get on with his life. But he had a nasty accident, broke his nose and some of the fingers on his right hand. He called me asking for help, and, well, I'm his mother. Couldn't really say no now, could I?'

'When did you last see him?' McLean asked. 'Before this morning, I mean.'

'Yesterday evening. Around six, I guess. I came round to help him with a few things. Oh, you'd think he'd been paralysed from the neck down, the fuss he made. It's just a busted nose and some broken fingers. But I got him cleaned up, took his dirty washing home to deal with. When I left he was in that same chair, watching the telly and waiting for his takeaway pizza to arrive.' Mrs Galloway gave another heavy sigh as the full enormity of what had happened began to sink in through the shock. 'When I came in this morning I thought he'd fallen asleep in that chair. Only he hadn't, had he? Fallen asleep.'

The old woman fell silent after that, and McLean felt no need to intrude any further on her grief. It was clear that she'd not seen eye to eye with her son for a while, but in his experience that usually made things worse, bringing guilt into the equation when it didn't really belong there.

'I'll go and see how they're getting on.' He stood up, then indicated the PC. 'Constable Wells will stay with you until Family Liaison get here. They'll arrange to take you home.'

Mrs Galloway had gone back to staring blankly at the wall, her hands cupped around her still full coffee mug. At the last moment, she looked up swiftly.

'Do you think this is suspicious? Was my boy murdered, Inspector?'

There was an odd tone of hope in the question, something McLean had heard many times before. Grief was easier to deal with if served with a side order of outrage. Far better for a mother that there be a reason for her son's death than that it simply be his time come before hers.

'I don't think so, Mrs Galloway, no. It's unexpected though, and the pathologist will be able to confirm things one way or the other. I'm just here because these things have to be looked into.' He reached into his pocket and drew out a business card, slid it on to the table. 'That's got my contact details on it. Call me at any time if you have a question, or if you remember something you think might be important. I'll be in touch soon.'

★ ★ ★

The front room was a lot busier when McLean reached it a few moments later. Tom MacPhail and his assistant stood in the corner by the TV, making as much room as possible for a couple of paramedics and a stretcher, already laid out with a black body bag. The pathologist noticed him standing in the doorway and beckoned him in.

'Ah, Tony. Good. We're ready to move him, if you're OK with that?'

McLean shrugged. 'It's your call, Tom. Have you worked out what killed him yet?'

MacPhail indicated to the paramedics to carry on, and they eased the body out of the chair. Brian Galloway had been dead long enough for rigor mortis to set in, which made getting him into the body bag an interesting task. Maybe it would have been better to get Mrs Galloway out of the house and on her way first; she must surely be able to hear all the noise from the kitchen.

'It's a bit of a puzzle, actually.' The pathologist stepped around the struggling paramedics and joined McLean in the hall, both of them squeezing against the far wall so MacPhail's assistant could leave with the heavy bag of instruments. DC Mitchell picked that moment to come down the stairs, but hung back when she saw there was no room.

'Not natural causes then,' McLean said.

'What are natural causes though, Tony? Your man in there had suffered a recent head trauma, and also fractures to some of his fingers. I'm told he fell down the steps at Fleshmarket Close, although his superficial injuries don't really square up with that account.'

'Have you been talking to DS Harrison?' DC Mitchell asked.

MacPhail raised a surprised eyebrow, McLean too. 'No. Should I have been?'

'I heard she'd been asking questions about that incident. DI

Ritchie wasn't too happy about it. If this is the same man . . .'
Mitchell left the sentence unfinished.

'We'll need to follow that up.' McLean added questioning the
detective sergeant to his list of immediate actions. 'Are you saying
his injuries might have been fatal?'

'I doubt it was the injuries. I've not found out what painkillers
he was prescribed yet. There wasn't anything close by him, so
they'll probably be upstairs in the bathroom. It's possible he had
a reaction to them, but that doesn't explain the way he seems to
have died. That's the real puzzle, see?'

McLean didn't, because the pathologist hadn't told him
yet. MacPhail could be like that, he remembered. So could
Cadwallader for that matter. It must have been something they
were taught at pathologist school.

'How did he die then?'

'I'll not be able to confirm it until I've got him on the
examination table at the mortuary, but he shows distinct signs of
severe hypoxia. And yet I couldn't find any obstruction in his
throat and there's no sign on his neck of strangulation. He didn't
choke on anything, but something stopped him from breathing.
Almost as if he drowned, only without any water.'

'Find anything interesting, Constable?' McLean asked, once the
mortal remains of Brian Galloway had been manhandled out of
the narrow hallway and into the ambulance blocking the street
outside. DC Mitchell paused before answering, as Mrs Galloway
was escorted from the kitchen by PC Wells and another uniformed constable who must have been the family liaison officer.

'Not a lot, sir. Don't think he'd been living here long by
the look of things. Seems kind of, I don't know, impersonal?
There's no pictures on the walls, no bookshelves or books. Two
bedrooms upstairs, but one of them's so full of boxes you can
hardly get in.'

'His mother said he was recently divorced.' McLean thought back to the conversation. 'Well, eighteen months ago. You'd think he'd have settled in a bit more. Put a bit of a stamp on the place.'

'Unless he's only just moved in. He's unpacked some clothes, mind you. Pretty wild costumes.'

'Sort of thing a rock star might wear on stage?' McLean asked.

'Yeah, I guess.' Mitchell narrowed her eyes in thought. 'Was he? A rock star?'

'Apparently so. Lead singer of some band called the Idle Lunatics.'

From narrow slits to wide in surprise in an instant. 'Mad Bastard? That was Mad Bastard? No way.'

So apparently it was only McLean who had never heard of them. 'The same.'

'Christ, but he's loaded, isn't he? Their last album went double platinum. Heard they were rehearsing for a reunion tour.' Mitchell's face, excited for a moment, now fell. 'Shit. Don't suppose that'll happen now. Can't have the Idle Lunatics without Mad Bastard.'

'I'll take your word for it. What's the story about him falling down the steps at Fleshmarket Close?'

Mitchell looked a little uncomfortable at being asked. 'Something Janie was looking into. Apparently two drunk blokes fell down the steps, got themselves banged up pretty badly. Heard one ruptured a bollock and blew out his knee. DI Ritchie told her to leave it alone, concentrate on the Slater case. It was only when I saw the injuries there it clicked this must be the other one. Christ, Mad Bastard. Just like him to get so drunk.'

McLean suspected there was more to it than that, but he could take it up with Harrison when he got into the station. 'You find any drugs upstairs?' he asked, then added 'prescription or illegal'.

'Nothing illegal, which is a bit disappointing now I know who he is.' Mitchell pulled a clear plastic evidence bag from her pocket, inside which was a half-flattened cardboard box with a couple of layers of blister-packed pills still in it. 'Found these though. Prescription mark's from the Royal Infirmary. Pretty strong painkillers.'

McLean glanced out the open front door, where the ambulance was still parked. 'OK. See if the pathologist's still here and give them to him. Otherwise, make sure they go with the body.'

Mitchell nodded, then hurried off, passing PC Wells on the steps outside. McLean climbed the stairs to give the constable room on her way back to the kitchen, and was half tempted to go and have a look around the first floor anyway. No, it was a waste of time, and what was the point in asking Mitchell to do it if he then went and did it again himself? Wasn't that what everyone was telling him not to do?

PC Wells was washing up the mugs when McLean stepped into the tiny kitchen once more.

'Thanks for staying with her,' he said, as she dried them up and put them in a cupboard. What would become of them now?

'Poor woman. That must have been some shock coming in and finding her son dead like that.'

'You get anything else from her? Apart from what we spoke about?'

'Not much, sir. She was putting on a brave face, but, well, I've seen folk do that before and she was definitely shocked by the whole thing. Doesn't help that she seems to have rowed with him recently, either. I think she took her daughter-in-law's side in the divorce.'

Something niggled at the back of his mind when Wells mentioned the divorce. A conversation with someone else, perhaps. Another broken marriage? McLean shook his head slightly. It would come to him if it was important.

'OK then. I think we're done here for now. You've got keys?'

Wells shoved a hand in her pocket and brought out a keyring. 'I was even given a lesson in how to set the alarm.'

'Lock it all up then. We'll have to wait and see what the pathologist has to say.'

35

The station car park bustled with activity as McLean claimed the parking spot in front of the car charging point again. He considered plugging Emma's Renault in, but the screen on the dashboard told him it was still almost fully charged, so he didn't bother. If anyone else needed electricity, they could always ask him to move. It reminded him that he needed to get something to replace the Alfa. Another one, perhaps? Or would he gracefully admit his age and visit the Jaguar dealership where Professor Turner had bought hers? Something to worry about when he wasn't chasing down murderers and suspicious deaths. It wasn't as if Emma was going to need her Renault any time soon, after all.

His stomach rumbled as he put his foot on the first step inside the station, reminding him that breakfast hadn't happened yet. Turning away from the climb to the third floor, McLean made a beeline for the canteen. Armed with a large mug of coffee and a couple of bacon baps, heavy on the brown sauce, he retreated to a table in the corner and the hope of a few minutes of peace to gather his thoughts. Fate had other ideas.

'That doesn't look particularly healthy, Tony. Mind if I join you?'

Detective Superintendent Jayne McIntyre didn't wait for

permission. She pulled out a chair and dropped herself into it with a weary 'oof' noise. Halfway through the first of his bacon baps, McLean couldn't say anything until he had finished chewing and swallowed.

'You're in early, Jayne.'

'As, I see, are you. Breakfast not good enough at home these days?'

McLean shrugged. 'There wasn't time. I've already been out running errands for her ladyship.'

McIntyre raised an eyebrow, then picked up McLean's mug and took a sip of his coffee. 'You be careful now. Gail's a good person to have fighting your corner, but I've seen what she can do when the shoe's on the other foot. If you'll excuse me mixing my metaphors.'

'She asked me to go and check out an unexplained death.' McLean told McIntyre of his early morning wake-up call and subsequent trip to Fountainbridge. 'I have to assume that she and this Galloway bloke have history. How else did she know about it before pretty much anyone else? And why does everything have to be done on the hurry up? The guy had a heart attack, or a bad reaction to his painkillers. There's no suggestion of foul play.'

'And instead of going up to the third floor to tell her all that in person, you're down here eating bacon baps.' McIntyre helped herself to more of McLean's coffee. He could see her eyeing up the second bap too, and he edged the plate away from her in an overtly possessive manner.

'I'll go and report to her soon as I've had my breakfast.' He tried to keep the exasperation out of his voice. 'I don't quite share your admiration for her, though. Something about her puts me on edge. Her chumminess, maybe.' Or the hand on his knee in the car driving back from Gartcosh, the casual, almost joking referral to him as her 'plus one'.

'She's finding her feet, Tony. Not been in the job long and she's already got half of the Police Authority eating out of her hand. Plus she got us half a dozen new DCs we've needed for ages. She's unorthodox, I'll grant you that much. But so are you, and I seem to remember you get results.'

'And suspended, and demoted.'

'You never wanted to be a DCI.'

'It's the principle of the thing, though.' He paused long enough to take another bite of bacon bap, wash it down with coffee. 'Sorry. I'm just a bit cranky before breakfast.'

'No wonder Emma's running away to Africa.'

'Run away. She's been gone a few weeks now. Communication's been a bit sporadic, but all seems to be well so far.'

McIntyre eyed the coffee, then looked across at the canteen serving counter, no doubt trying to decide whether she should get her own mug or continue stealing McLean's. 'How goes your murder investigation, anyway? Last I heard it was a bit bogged down.'

'A bit is being kind. The whole thing's going nowhere. We've drawn a blank on forensics, CCTV in the area's non-existent, the victim was a recluse with very little social interaction, so we can't even find a motive. Unless we can come up with something to suggest the Bairnfather Trust wanted her out of the cottage so it could redevelop the land, we've basically got nothing.'

'Is that even likely?' McIntyre asked.

'Not really, no. It doesn't track right. If someone wanted the site, they could just have torched the house without killing the old girl. Or they could have simply moved her out. Not as if she'd be able to put up much of a fight. She'd have been looked after well for the rest of her days. Probably a suite in the hotel, or a care home in the city. Money doesn't seem to be a problem for Lord Bairnfather, so it's not that.' McLean took a swig of coffee, marshalling the few facts he'd managed to unearth into some kind of order. 'If I had to guess, I'd say it was a hate crime. It has all the hallmarks. They beat her black and blue before setting her on fire, after all. I just can't work out why someone would hate a ninety-year-old woman living all alone and hardly ever inter-acting with society. Why her, and why then?'

'Well, not to put a dampener on things, but you'll need to come up with something fairly soon. I'm getting a fair bit of pressure to wind the whole thing up. Stick it in a cold case file and move on.'

McLean took the last bite of bacon bap, nodded his under-standing as he chewed and swallowed. 'Thought that might be the case. Not that I like it much. Poor old girl deserves better.'

McIntyre pushed back her chair and stood up. 'Aye, I know, Tony. But we do what we can and we have to be realistic about when to stop.'

'And if Lord Bairnfather isn't happy about it? He's well connected, you know, might kick up a stink if he thinks his sainted aunt's being swept under the rug. If you'll excuse me mixing my metaphors.'

McIntyre smiled at the joke. 'Touché, Tony. But you can leave the smoothing of ruffled feathers to Gail. It's what she's best at. Which reminds me. Aren't you meant to be reporting in to her about now?'

The way to the chief superintendent's office took him past the major incident room, so McLean felt he could be forgiven for letting himself in and checking on the lack of progress before delivering his report on Galloway. A quick scan of the room revealed that DC Stringer and DS Harrison were head to head like thieves in the far corner. Possibly hearing the door close, or some sixth sense kicking in, they both stopped whatever it was they had been doing and turned to face him.

'Morning, sir,' Harrison said, a moment before Stringer could get his greeting in. 'Heard you were at an unexplained death in Fountainbridge. Anything unusual?'

'I take it your interest means there's no progress on the Cecily Slater case?'

Harrison had the decency to look sheepish. 'Not as such, sir. We've extended the archive search, but the most recent mention of her name I've found is a newspaper report about her brother's funeral in 1984, so we're pretty much stumped for useful background information. Can't find much motive in the financials, either. She didn't care about money, and the only beneficiary of her will's already rolling in it. Gains nothing from her death.'

Nothing he hadn't already known. McLean considered Detective Superintendent McIntyre's words to him in the canteen, and the thoughts they had provoked. 'Let's go further back in her life then. See if we can't wring something out of the Burntwoods angle. Only, don't spend too long chasing it down.'

'They're closing the case?' Harrison asked. So cynical for one so young.

'Murder cases are never closed, you know that. They just get sidelined by other work and quietly slip down to the basement.'

'Seems a bit early though, doesn't it? We've barely scratched the surface of this one.'

'I know. And I'll fight our corner as long as I can. But unless we get a substantial lead from somewhere soon, we're only going round in circles.'

McLean could see that the two detectives weren't happy about it, and the quiet that had descended on the room suggested none of the other officers working the case were either. A quick look at the whiteboard wall reminded him of the messy corpse that had been left behind by whoever had taken out their anger on Cecily Slater. He wanted to find that person, or persons, and put them away. He wanted justice for the old woman so that she could rest in peace. So that he could rest in peace, more like. And yet sometimes you had to know when to let go.

'One other thing, Janie,' he said, as the detective sergeant began to turn away. She immediately snapped her attention back to him.

'Sir?'

'I hear you were looking into an incident in the Old Town a few days back. Two drunkards falling down some steps and doing themselves damage.'

Harrison wasn't good at putting on an innocent face, but she gave it her best shot. 'Aye, sir. Wasn't really anything much. Just following up a complaint for a friend. Kir— DI Ritchie told me to drop it, so I did.'

McLean knew there was a great deal more to the story than that; Kirsty had bent his ear at great length about his corrupting influence. 'You spoke to one of the men, yes?'

'Christopher Allan, sir. He confirmed the story about the accident. Nasty injuries, though.'

'The other one. Was his name Brian Galloway, by any chance? Lives in Fountainbridge?'

'Aye, sir. Downfield Street . . .' Harrison's voice trailed away, her mouth staying open as the implications caught up with her.

'Well there's no point in trying to talk to him any more. He's dead. Possibly a bad reaction to his painkillers, but we won't know until the post-mortem's done. Of course it's equally possible that he died of the injuries inflicted on him when he accidentally fell down the steps of Fleshmarket Close. If that is indeed what happened.'

'Oh.' Harrison joined the dots.

'This friend of yours with the complaint. What was that about, and where are they now?'

'I . . . Umm . . . She's at mine and Manda's place. She crashed there the night of the attack. I sort of said it was OK for her to stay a while if she wanted.'

'That's very decent of you.'

'Aye, well she was staying with Madame Rose, but she said the house was doing her head in. That's why—'

'Rose?' McLean interrupted. 'How does she know Rose? Who is this friend of yours?'

Harrison paused a moment before answering, and McLean could see the thoughts tumbling across her face. There shouldn't have been any harm in him knowing the name. Even if it turned out Galloway's injuries had proved the ultimate cause of his death, he was on record as saying he got them falling down steps in a drunken stupor. No point in trying to prosecute anyone for that other than himself. And yet something was bothering Harrison.

'I need background on Galloway for the Procurator Fiscal. If you want me to keep your friend's name out of that, Janie, I'll need a good reason why. Better than Rose, for sure.'

'Her name's Izzy. Isobel DeVilliers.'

Well, that was a better reason.

'She's Con Fairchild's half-sister, sir. You remember, that nastiness with the evangelists back in the spring?'

'I'm aware of who she is. What's she doing in Edinburgh?'

'Well she was part of the crowd protesting against Tommy Fielding. I'm guessing that's why he set a couple of his goons on her. Pity they didn't know she could more than look out for herself.'

McLean sighed and pinched the bridge of his nose in the hope that it would all go away. It didn't.

'Detective Sergeant,' he began, then realised that the entire room was listening in avidly. 'Can we discuss this in my office?' He gestured towards the door at the exact moment that it opened and the chief superintendent stepped in, closely followed by DI

Ritchie. Elmwood had a scowl on her face that morphed into a broad smile the moment she saw him. Not a *hello old friend* smile, though. This was more of an *I've got you now* grin of triumph.

'There you are, Tony. I was beginning to wonder where you'd got to.' She patted Ritchie on the shoulder in the manner of a schoolmistress sending the admonished pupil back to her seat in the class, then turned her attention fully on him. 'Come on then. I think you owe me a report?'

36

'What exactly is your relationship with Brian Galloway, ma'am?'

McLean stood in front of the chief superintendent's desk, much as he had done many times before over the long years of his career. This had been Duguid's office once, then Detective Chief Superintendent Brooks had taken it over. That was before all the restructuring of Police Scotland had ended up with a deputy chief constable being assigned this station as their centre of operations, and of course the first onc had nabbed the best room in the building.

'That's not really any of your business, Tony.' Elmwood had sat on the business side of the desk the moment they had both entered the room, tidying up a couple of open folders McLean wasn't at all interested in sneaking a look at. Now she stood up, smoothed her uniform. 'Why don't we sit down and discuss this like grown-ups, eh?'

She indicated the corner of the room, where a couple of comfortable chairs and a sofa were arranged around a low table. Behind them a shelf unit held a more expensive coffee machine than the one McLean had inherited with his office. As he sat down, Elmwood busied herself with it, not having bothered to ask him if he wanted a cup. It would have been a stupid question, of course. But she wasn't to know that.

'Milk?' The chief superintendent bent to a small fridge wedged under the counter, and McLean was reminded uncomfortably of some of the more risqué films he'd rented as a teenager. The woman wasn't exactly subtle, although she was better at dialogue than the actresses in police uniforms he'd seen on those old VHS tapes.

'There you go.' She handed him a cup. McLean took it, ignoring the touch of her finger on his hand. He'd chosen one of the chairs to sit in, and Elmwood looked at him slightly askance for a moment before seating herself on the sofa opposite.

'Well, this is all very nice, isn't it?' she said after a moment, and McLean began to reappraise her skill with dialogue. 'So tell me what you saw at Brian Galloway's place.'

The chief superintendent didn't seem overly upset at the death of someone she knew, so that suggested they hadn't been close friends. There was a connection, though, and that in itself should have excluded her from having anything to do with the investigation. Even if it turned out Galloway's death was entirely natural.

'I spoke to his mother,' McLean said, watching Elmwood's face for any hint of a reaction. 'She was the one who found him and called it in. She said he'd not been living in that house long. The state of the place backed that up. It wasn't what you'd call a home.'

'What about Galloway himself? I take it the pathologist saw him?'

McLean nodded. 'He'll schedule the PM as soon as possible, but his initial thoughts were something interfered with Galloway's breathing. No signs of strangulation, though, so his best guess is some allergic reaction. He was on painkillers, you know? He'd broken his nose and several of his fingers.'

Elmwood seemed unsurprised by this knowledge, which set

McLean's internal alarms to a gentle ringing. It hadn't been that long since Galloway had either fallen down the stairs as he'd claimed, or been soundly beaten by a young woman still in her teens. The former incident had been logged and filed away as needing no further investigation; the latter was knowledge not shared among a great many people. And yet the chief super-intendent knew.

'How did you find out about his death, ma'am?' McLean tried again.

'You really have to stop calling me that, Tony.' Elmwood smiled that predatory smile at him. 'Even Kirsty calls me Gail.'

McLean put down his coffee cup, still as full as when the chief superintendent had handed it to him. He stood up, edged around the low table. 'I'll be going now, ma'am. Please don't ask me to run errands for you when I'm in the middle of a murder investigation again.'

He didn't make it as far as the door before she called out, but he had gone further than he expected.

'Detective Inspector McLean. I expect my officers to obey orders when they are given. Now come back here and report.'

He fought against clenching his fists, began a quick, silent count to ten in his head, made it as far as five before turning swiftly to face the chief superintendent. The smug expression on her face only made things worse, which he knew perfectly well was why she had pasted it there.

'With all due respect, Chief Superintendent, I am a detective inspector with over twenty years' experience. A detective con-stable could have – should have – been despatched to that scene to make a preliminary examination. That order should have come from Control, not from one of my detective sergeants on instruction from you. And there was no reason to do everything so swiftly. It's not like he was going anywhere. So I'll ask you again. How did you know about Galloway's death?

Who brought it to your attention and why?'

'Are you angry with me, Tony?' Elmwood actually fluttered her eyelashes at him, which wasn't a good idea when he'd been up way too early and only had the one coffee.

'This is a waste of time, ma'am. I'll email you a report once the post-mortem's done.'

McLean had his hand on the door handle before the chief superintendent spoke again. 'Detective Sergeant Harrison shows a lot of promise, wouldn't you say?'

He grasped the cold metal but didn't turn the handle. It was easy enough to see the threat for what it was. The chief super-intendent knew she had no power over him; he could walk out of this office, down the stairs, get into Emma's car and never come back. They could sack him, even find a way to deny him his pension, and it wouldn't make a difference other than being petty. But Harrison was at the bottom of the ladder, just begin-ning to climb. She had a bright future ahead of her, and Elmwood would crush it if he didn't do exactly what she told him to. Damn her, and damn all the bloody politicians getting in the way of just doing the job properly.

McLean slowly released his grip on the door handle, let his shoulders slump in an overly theatrical show of defeat. Let her think she'd won – she had, after all. This time.

'Galloway died of asphyxiation, most likely due to a reaction to prescription painkillers. There's nothing to suggest his death was anything other than an unfortunate accident. Despite his rock and roll background, we didn't find any evidence he'd been supplementing his medication with something illegal, so you needn't worry yourself on that score. I'll have the post-mortem results by tomorrow at the latest, and a report for the PF by the end of the same day. It will, of course, come to you first. Is that OK, ma'am?'

Elmwood stared at him for long seconds, her face unreadable, but not friendly. Finally she nodded, once, and with the minimum of movement possible. It was enough for McLean. With an even more minimal nod of his own, he turned and left.

His meeting with the chief superintendent still weighing on his mind, McLean strode back to his office and slumped into his chair. The reports and paperwork piled around his desk were things he needed to attend to, but it was hard to focus on anything. Not when he knew that woman was only a few tens of metres away.

He should have seen the game she was playing from their first meeting. Looking back, it was painfully obvious, and yet also unbelievable. He'd been grateful to her for cutting through the Gordian knot of internal investigations, Professional Standards hearings and all the political pressure being brought to bear to punish him for the Anya Renfrew case. The demotion had been meaningless; a small pay cut he of all people would barely notice, and a big drop in responsibility when it came to strategising and forward planning. No wonder he'd ignored the warning signs; Gail Elmwood had ridden in like a knight in shining armour to rescue him.

And now she was calling in the favour, since he was clearly not going to respond to her incessant flirting with him.

Frustrated, he pulled the nearest folder to him and flipped it open. For a moment he couldn't recall the details of the case, but then it started to fall back into place. The estate agent, Don Purefoy. Crushed to death by a rockfall on his building site. The post-mortem report confirmed that he'd died from asphyxiation due to the weight of boulders pinning him to the ground. His ribs had been cracked, but otherwise his body had been left remarkably unscathed. The few photographs in the report made that abundantly clear, as Purefoy's head showed no signs of damage whatsoever. There had been no obvious sign of foul play, but it was clear from Angus's terse prose that he considered the circumstances unusual. DS Harrison had conducted preliminary interviews with the two people who had found the body, and she had compiled this report on his death for the Procurator Fiscal. Which reminded him he needed to have words with the detective sergeant, both a ticking off and a warning to tread very carefully where the chief superintendent was concerned. He reached for his phone, about to call her, when something else caught his eye.

Putting the report to one side, he flicked through the piles on his desk until he found another one. Steve Whitaker, spontaneous human combustion victim. The photographs in the report reminded him of the scene itself, and he could almost smell the burned flesh. Again, Angus had been cautious with his post-mortem results, although this time it was more obvious why. It was possible, given the right combination of circumstances, for a body's subcutaneous fat to act a bit like the wax in a candle. That was the best available explanation for the extremely uncommon but certainly real phenomenon. His best bet, and the conclusion of the report, was that Whitaker had fallen asleep drunk and managed to set himself on fire in such a way that only his torso burned. Not his head, lower legs, arms or indeed the chair in which he had been sitting. Crucially, there were no obvious signs of foul play. Same as with Purefoy, and now with Brian Galloway.

There had to be a connection between all three men. His gut told him there was. He just needed to look at them all the right way. Or maybe get a fresh pair of eyes to look at them for him.

Gathering up the two reports, McLean left his office and went in search of a spare detective. There was no sign of either DI Ritchie or Detective Superintendent McIntyre, which probably meant they were both in important meetings somewhere. DC Stringer and DS Gregg were both on their phones when he stuck his head into the Cecily Slater incident room, so he ducked out again before either of them noticed. He briefly considered going across to the offices of the Sexual Crimes Unit and speaking to DCI Dexter, but this wasn't really connected to her line of work, and Vice was usually even more busy than Specialist Crime. He could see if anyone was in the Cold Case Unit down in the basement, but he'd leaned on them too much already.

In the end, McLean's feet took him to the CID room and its mess of desks assigned to the detective constables and sergeants in his own division. For a long time the room had felt like a classroom the day after term's ended, but now it was beginning to fill up again. There weren't any actual detectives there; that would have been too much to hope for. But the once-empty desks now bore evidence of occupation. Elmwood had promised them new DCs, and McLean had even met a couple of them. They were too new to be any use to him right now, though. He needed someone with a few miles under their belt.

'You looking for anyone in particular, sir?'

Hidden away at the back of the room, her body obscured by a large flat-screen computer monitor, McLean hadn't noticed DS Harrison until she stood up. He didn't want to admit that he'd been looking for her in particular, but there weren't any other officers who knew all the cases. And he needed to warn her about the chief superintendent's threat, of course.

'Actually, yes. It was something you said before we were interrupted earlier.' McLean glanced around the empty CID room. Tempting though it was to speak in there, it was almost inevitable they would be interrupted. Likewise heading down to the canteen. And if he took Harrison up to his office, who knew what the gossips would make of it. Damn, but he hated how things like that got in the way of doing the job. 'You busy right now?'

Harrison looked at him like he was mad or something. 'Are

you kidding, sir? I'm always busy. Nothing that can't wait a while though.'

'Well see if you can't find us a pool car and meet me downstairs in ten minutes. I've got to go and speak to Mrs Galloway about her husband. You can tell me all about Isobel DeVilliers on the way there.'

'Izzy?' Harrison's voice hitched up a half-octave. 'What do you—?'

'Not here, Janie. Sort out a car and meet me downstairs. I need to go and see Grumpy Bob first.'

37

The temperature rarely changed down in the basement where the CCU hid its offices, and in the height of summer it was a welcome relief from the sweltering heat of the glass-walled offices upstairs. Now that autumn was on the turn, the cool seemed somehow chilly, seeping into McLean's bones. It must have been seeping into Grumpy Bob's bones too, as the ex-detective sergeant sat at his desk with a small heater blowing away underneath. When he noticed McLean at the door, he rubbed his hands together and blew on them theatrically.

'You should've retired to Florida if you wanted to keep warm in your old age, Bob.' He stepped fully into the room, noticing as he did that there was no sign of Ex-Detective Superintendent Duguid.

'Florida? Aye, I went there once with Mrs Bob. Before she decided she'd had enough of me. Too much sun for a man of my delicate complexion.' Grumpy Bob closed the folder he'd been reading, took off his spectacles and slid them into the breast pocket of his jacket. 'Heard you were getting sweet-talked by our new chief superintendent. You want to be careful there. She's trouble if you ask me.'

'Funny you should mention that, Bob. I was coming to much the same conclusion myself.' McLean crossed the room, pulled up a chair and sat opposite the detective sergeant. 'She's manip- ulative and doesn't like being told no. Which is fine when she's going up against the politicians for an increase in our budgets, less so when she wants me to follow her around wherever she goes, like a wee spaniel or something.'

'You've tried, I take it? Telling her no.'

'Just this very morning.' McLean recounted the events, starting with his rude awakening before dawn, and ending with the chief superintendent's veiled threat to his team. Grumpy Bob listened carefully, as was his way. When McLean had finished, the ex-detective sergeant got up slowly, walked across the room to where a coffee machine sat on top of a short filing cabinet, and poured out a single mug.

'I'd offer you one, but I get the feeling you're only here to ask a favour.'

'You know me too well.'

Grumpy Bob returned to his desk, sat down. 'So what are you going to do about her?'

McLean considered for a moment before answering. 'That depends very much on what she's trying to hide.'

'And I suppose you want me to find out what that is, aye?'

'To be honest, Bob, I'm surprised you don't know already. There's not much happens in this station behind your back.'

'I'll take that as a compliment, even though I'm not sure it is one. But I have to admit I've not found out much about our new leader as yet. No one's got a bad word to say about her so far, but that's probably because she's not been here long enough to put too many folks' backs up. And she's shaken some more money out of the budgets, which goes a long way to gaining an officer's deep and abiding loyalty, in my experience.'

McLean slumped in his seat. 'Maybe it's just me she's got her eyes on, then. I could do without the attention, mind.'

'That bad?'

'Worse. We're in the middle of a murder investigation, three more suspicious deaths on top of that, and she drags me over to Gartcosh with her so she's not lonely in the car. And that Safe Streets Committee event. That was a bloody joke. If I'd been home like I was meant to be, my car wouldn't have been in the station car park to get nicked, either.'

'Aye, shame about that car. It was a bit flash, but much more comfortable than the old one.'

'Maybe it's nothing,' McLean continued. 'Like you say, she's new in the job, still finding her feet. And she's more pleasing on the eye than Call-me-Stevie. He never put his hand on my knee, though.'

Grumpy Bob almost spat out his coffee as he tried and failed to suppress a laugh. 'Oh dear. She's really not got any idea, has she?' He turned serious again. 'But that's a problem I can see blowing up out of all proportion. Needs nipping in the bud, right enough.'

McLean stood up and returned the chair to the desk he'd found it under. 'Have a chat with that infamous network of old retired detectives I've heard so much about, eh? There must be something the chief superintendent would rather wasn't common knowledge. Not that I'd ever go public with anything, but she doesn't need to know that.'

'About earlier, sir. I'm sorry. I was out of line. I should have told you the moment Izzy came to me.'

DS Harrison had entirely failed to secure a pool car for the journey, and now she sat in the passenger seat of Emma's little Renault ZOE. They'd driven in silence for about five minutes before she'd broken. Not that McLean had been trying to sweat her out; more he couldn't work out how to begin.

'Why didn't you?' It was the question that had been bothering him since he'd found out.

'It's . . . complicated?'

'Well we've got at least ten minutes.' He waved a hand at the windscreen, beyond which traffic choked the road in an unmoving smog of exhaust fumes. 'Try me.'

'You know how I said Izzy was one of the protesters at Tommy Fielding's conference?'

McLean nodded, fairly sure he already knew where this was going.

'Well, she was actually one of the half dozen who broke into the hotel and got themselves arrested.'

McLean hadn't been involved in that, but he'd read the daily station briefing email. 'I thought there were only five of them. And they were let go with a caution.'

'Exactly. I found out Izzy was in a holding cell and sort of persuaded Tam to forget she'd ever been in there?'

'Persuaded?' McLean knew the custody sergeant of old. Not exactly one to give out favours, unless he'd mellowed as he approached retirement. 'No, I don't think I want to know.'

'It's nothing like that, sir. Honestly.' Harrison shook her head. 'I could have told him what Izzy had been through, but I thought she'd rather not have that mentioned. You know about that, aye? Her step-father, Roger DeVilliers?'

'Not the full details. She was abused, though, I know that much.'

'He sexually assaulted her from the age of six, sir. He shared her with his sick friends, and when she tried to run away he used his money and influence to track her down. It's amazing she's not a total gibbering wreck. I don't think I'd have survived if something like that had happened to me.'

McLean risked a sideways glance at the detective sergeant. There was an anger in her voice he wasn't used to hearing, even if it was entirely justified.

'That would explain how she was able to defend herself. How

she managed to inflict quite so much damage on her attackers.'

'Actually I think she learned that at her posh boarding school. Wish they'd taught us that sort of thing at Broxburn Academy.'

'All the same. What you did was wrong, you know?' McLean pre-empted the inevitable, interrupting Harrison before she could answer him. 'And yes, I do get that it's a bit rich coming from me of all people. But someone's got to point it out. Helping a friend's sister out with the duty sergeant is one thing, but tracking down her attackers? Taking a detective constable with you to interview one of them? Who sanctioned that? Nobody, because there wasn't a complaint filed, no official investigation, no paper trail. And now one of those attackers is dead, circumstances as yet unexplained. This could all come back to bite you big time, Janie.'

'I . . .' Harrison started to say, then fell silent.

'Look, I know why you did it. I'd most likely have done exactly the same myself. This isn't a formal warning or a dressing-down. It's a *be careful*. If what you've found out about Galloway proves useful to any of our ongoing investigations, there won't be any problems. I can see to that. But you need to be aware that the chief superintendent is very interested in him, and as yet I've no idea why.'

'The chief superintendent?' Harrison's voice went up a squeaky octave in surprise. 'But how would she even know about him?'

'That's a mystery I'd very much like to get to the bottom of. And trust me, I'm working on it. There's something else that's been bothering me, though. What you said about Galloway and the other man.'

'Christopher Allan?'

'Aye, him. You said they'd been sent by Tommy Fielding to shut the DeVilliers girl up. What was it you called them? His goons? Are you sure it was him?'

'Why else would they do that?'

McLean glanced at the Sat-Nav, unhelpfully suggesting he take a turn down a street currently closed for roadworks. 'Young women get attacked all the time, Janie. You know that as well as I do. It seems a bit . . . far-fetched? I know Fielding's not a nice person, but getting people to beat up a young woman? He's one of the city's top lawyers, you know. You start throwing around accusations and he'll end your career before you can even log off your shift.'

'So what? You think they were just trying to rape her, then? Nothing else?' Harrison's tone was a warning.

'I don't know. That's the whole problem. But Galloway's dead, his death is unusual, and someone brought it to the attention of our new chief superintendent. She got me to take over the investigation so that she can keep an eye on things, keep it under control. I need to know why, and who tipped her off. Throwing Tommy Fielding into the mix just makes things more complicated than they already are.'

They fell silent for a few minutes, the unnerving quiet of the car only adding to McLean's unease. There was too much going on, too many half-connections and coincidences. And all the while it was distracting him from the investigation into Cecily Slater's murder, her killers slipping ever further out of reach.

'What if Fielding knows her, sir?' Harrison said out of nowhere. 'The chief super, that is. What if he was the one tipped her off about Galloway? Asked her to keep it quiet so nothing comes back to him?'

McLean shook his head slowly. He could see their destination a hundred metres up the road now, checked his mirror, indicated and began to slow. 'You'll be telling me he killed Cecily Slater next. Let's stop speculating and start trying to find out some actual facts, eh?'

38

Brian Galloway's former house was not as big as McLean's own home on the other side of the city, but it was still a sizeable mansion by anyone's reckoning. Late Victorian, if his scant knowledge of architecture was anything to go by, it was well maintained, but had a gaudiness about it that jarred. By the time he'd parked and he and Harrison had climbed out of the car and taken all this in, the front door was open and a woman stood on the step. Tall and thin, her long blond hair snaked in an elegant braid over one shoulder and down almost to her hip. She wore a zip-up hoodie over a plain white T-shirt and those jeans that look like they're ancient and frayed but most likely came out of the wrapping like that. She stared at him almost frowning as she approached, but she'd let him in the security gate so he assumed that she was short-sighted and had lost her spectacles.

'Detective Inspector McLean?' Her voice had a slight American drawl to it, but the intonation was pure Edinburgh. As she spoke, her gaze slid past him to the car, and she broke into a smile. 'Oh, you drive a ZOE. Snap!'

'It's my partner's, actually. I'm only borrowing it. Yes, I'm DI McLean. My colleague DS Harrison.' He pulled out his warrant card and held it up, but the woman didn't bother looking at it. 'You're Elizabeth Carter? Mr Galloway's ex-wife?'

The smile scrunched into a frown at the mention of the name, but it was short-lived. 'Lizzie. Yes. Brian was my husband. And as the father of my children I should probably be a bit more sad that he's dead.' She paused a moment, rubbed at her arms as if only then realising how cold it was. 'Why don't you both come in, then? Brian's mum's here with the kids. I'll put the kettle on.'

They followed Lizzie Carter into the house, through a large hallway and out to a spacious and modern kitchen at the rear. Through a set of folding glass doors, a large glass structure covered a swimming pool, with a tidy patio area at the nearest end. The noise of splashing and excited childish shouting echoed through the doorway, bringing with it a sharp tang of chlorinated water.

'So then. What do you want to talk to me about?' Carter had her back to them as she talked. She worked her way methodically through various cupboards, bringing out teapot, tea, milk, biscuits and setting them all out before turning.

'When was the last time you spoke to Mr Galloway?'

Carter tilted her head to one side, her long plait of hair dangling further to the floor like Rapunzel. 'Let me see. Couple of weeks ago? Could be a month, actually. He wanted to see the boys.' She nodded her head towards the open door and the pool beyond.

'And did he? See them, that is?' Harrison asked.

'Christ, no. Wouldn't let that bastard anywhere near them after what he did.'

The kettle clicked, and Carter turned away to deal with the making of tea. McLean let the silence grow as she went through the motions. There was no need to rush, and so far she was being unusually helpful. He'd not eaten in a while either, and didn't want to jeopardise his chances with a substantial plate of biscuits. After a protracted ritual, Carter put everything on to a tray and lifted it up.

'Come on. Let's take this out to the poolside. Irene's watching

the boys, but after . . . this morning, she could probably do with
a bit more adult company.'

They stepped from the dry warmth of the kitchen into the
steam of the pool house. McLean didn't want to think how much
it cost to keep that pool heated, but it was clearly a source of
great enjoyment to the two young boys dive-bombing into the
far end before scrambling out and doing it again.

'Detective Inspector, we meet again.' Old Mrs Galloway sat at
a cast-iron table far enough from the pool to avoid getting
accidentally splashed, but close enough that she could keep an
eye on her grandsons at play. She half rose, but McLean indicated
she should stay seated before introducing Harrison.

'I have to admit I wasn't expecting to see you here, Mrs
Galloway. I hope the family liaison officer was able to help.'

'Oh yes, thank you. Nice young lady. Took me home in
a panda car and then brought me here. I don't think what
happened this morning's sunk in yet, if I'm being honest. I
expect the shock will hit eventually. Helps to have the boys here.
And Lizzie, of course.'

'How old are they?' Harrison nodded towards the dive-
bombing. Carter answered as she poured tea.

'Jamie's eight and his brother Edward's ten. We've not told
them about their father yet, but they've never really asked about
him since the divorce.'

'He didn't get visiting rights?'

'He should have gone to jail for what he did.'

McLean was surprised by the sudden anger in Carter's voice.
'I'm afraid I don't quite understand. As I heard it, he cheated on
you, which is certainly grounds for divorce. But jail?'

'Cheated on me? You make it sound so quaint, Detective
Inspector. You know Brian was a rock star, right? Mad Bastard,
lead singer of the Idle Lunatics. Scotland's answer to Oasis.'
Carter spoke in a kind of sing-song voice as she recounted the

potted biography. 'Cheating on me was part of the deal. He was away on tour for months at a time. Groupies throwing themselves at him. Hell, I was one of them, right at the start of it all. I knew about the cheating. But Jenny? The babysitter? She was only thirteen when he raped her. Right here in this very house.'

McLean had taken the opportunity of Carter's monologue to sneak a biscuit off the plate. Now it was poised halfway to his mouth. It might have only been a few hours since he'd been sent to the tiny house in Fountainbridge, but one of the first things he'd got the team to do was run Galloway's name through the system. After the mess with Whitaker it had seemed prudent. There'd been a few brushes with the law over the years, but it was all the sort of thing you might expect a rock star to do, and the most recent caution was for possession of marijuana over ten years ago.

'We don't have a record of that offence,' he said. By the look on both Carter and Mrs Galloway's faces, it wasn't perhaps the best response.

'Have you any idea how difficult it is to make a rape charge stick?' Carter asked, not angrily but certainly aggressively.

'I do. I'm sorry. I didn't mean to—'

'It was a stitch-up from the start. Brian got himself some fancy lawyer who somehow managed to smooth the whole thing over. I was presented with an ultimatum. Divorce, the kids and the house. Plus a substantial payment to her if I persuaded Jenny to withdraw the allegations.' Carter's hands rested on the table, either side of her teacup, and she clenched them into tight fists as she spoke. 'I didn't give a damn about divorce or the house. But he was threatening to take my children away. I made a deal, but only if he agreed to keep away. No visiting rights. It wasn't until after I'd signed the papers that I found out Jenny wasn't the first. Who knows if she was the last?'

Mrs Galloway spoke into the silence that fell. 'Like I told you before, Detective Inspector. Brian was an angry child, and an angrier man. He never could keep a control of his passions or his anger for long. That might have made him a good artist, I don't know. But it made him a bad man. Maybe I could have done better by him. I tried my best.'

McLean let the words sink in, aware of both women watching him uncomfortably closely. A scream punctured the moment, followed by a loud splash as one of the boys managed a spectacular dive bomb on his brother. He could only hope the two of them turned out better than their father.

'Does the name Gail Elmwood mean anything to you?'

Both women looked blank. Carter shook her head slowly. 'No. Doesn't ring a bell.'

So much for that link. McLean opened his mouth to ask the next obvious question, but Harrison beat him to it.

'You said Mr Galloway got himself a fancy lawyer who stitched up this whole deal.' She raised both hands to indicate the house and all it represented.

'Aye, that's right.'

'You don't remember his name, do you?'

'Don't think I'll ever forget it. Horrible slimy man. Made me feel dirty the way he looked at me.' Carter almost shivered as she spoke. 'Fielding, he was called. Tommy Fielding.'

DS Harrison kept her comments to herself until they were once more in the car and driving back to the station, for which McLean was grateful. He could see that she was pleased with herself, and no doubt wanted to call him out on his earlier scepticism about the link between Galloway and Fielding. It didn't change the fact that she'd stepped over the line.

'I know it's a bit speculative, sir. But am I the only one beginning to see a pattern here?'

'You are? How?'

'Well, see how Galloway's wife divorced him, kept the house and the kids, aye?'

'And he stayed out of prison thanks to Tommy Fielding.'

'Aye, but that's not what I'm on about. That chappie Steve Whitaker? That lad who burned himself to death? Seems his wife divorced him not so long ago, took the kid with her, no visiting rights. Same with Purefoy at the building site.' Harrison waved her hand in the direction of Liberton Brae. 'He had two wee boys, but his wife got sick of him playing away from home. And there was Christopher Allan too, now I think about it. You know? The guy Izzy kicked in the nuts so hard he'll probably always walk with a limp now. His wife divorced him and took the kids to Australia.'

'What? You think Fielding defended them all? Doesn't say much for his skills as a lawyer if they all lost.'

Harrison shrugged. 'Fair point. But like you said, Galloway could have lost way more. What if the same was true for the others? What if they all owe Fielding? What if they all have a grudge against women?'

McLean tapped his fingers against the steering wheel in thought. 'Allan and Galloway both claimed they'd fallen down the stairs, but you reckon your friend beat the crap out of them, right?'

'Aye, sir. Izzy was very clear about the damage she inflicted, and those two both ended up at A and E with those injuries not more than an hour or so later.'

'And she claims they were put on to her by Tommy Fielding because she disrupted his conference?'

'Reckon there's maybe a wee bit more to it than that, but she was trying to lobby one of the MSPs at Holyrood about Fielding's men's rights activist organisation. Something about getting its funding cut or de-platforming it or whatever. That's why she was in that part of town.'

McLean negotiated a roundabout, then floored the throttle as the road opened up ahead of him. No great surge of power pinned him into the seat, and the noise was more washing machine spin cycle than roar of untamed Italian horses.

'I need to speak to her, to Izzy. Soon as possible.'

Harrison reached for her phone. 'I can give her a call. Ask her to come to the station.'

McLean shook his head. 'No. Best keep this unofficial for now.'

'Well, she's staying at my place right now, but I can bring her over to yours after work if that's better.'

McLean considered it, then remembered the state he'd left the kitchen in that morning. Not that it really mattered. Izzy DeVilliers was a teenager after all. 'Where did you say she was staying before she came to you? With Madame Rose?'

'With Rose, aye.'

'OK. There's still plenty to get done before your shift ends. Give Izzy a call and ask her to meet us at Rose's place. Eight o'clock should be fine.'

39

As he pulled it out of his pocket and tossed it on to his desk, McLean's phone buzzed and its screen lit up. For a moment he thought he might have broken it, then he saw the name on the screen indicating an incoming call. He was sorely tempted to let it go to voicemail, but he knew some nettles were best grasped straight away. Before it could ring off, he grabbed the handset up again.

'Afternoon, Jo. It's been a while. I take it this isn't a social call.'

McLean was only half joking about it having been a while. Jo Dalgliesh, sometime reporter for the *Edinburgh Tribune*, although more freelance these days, had been all over his story in the summer, thwarting all attempts by the high heidyins to hush the whole thing up and hope nobody noticed. He had fed her a few choice details on the understanding she kept his name out of it as much as possible, and fair play to her, she'd stuck to the deal so well this was the first time they'd spoken in months.

'You driving? Only I heard that posh car of yours got nicked and then parked in a shop window. That's got to be embarrassing for Police Scotland, hasn't it?'

'That what you wanted to talk about? My stolen car? Only, I'm not exactly in the loop on that investigation.'

'No, no. You're still trying to find out who killed that old wifey up at Bairnfather, aren't you? Heard that wasn't going so well. What's it been? A month? Two? Shouldn't you have arrested someone by now?'

McLean had known Jo Dalgliesh a long time, and the fire of hatred towards her that had burned for years had more or less extinguished itself. She had her uses, and was on balance one of the more reliable and less back-stabbing of the journalists he'd dealt with in recent years. There were times, however, when she reminded him of why she had been such a thorn in his side for so long, even if she had saved his life from a homicidal maniac with a very sharp knife once.

'Cut to the chase, will you, Dalgliesh? I'm a busy man.'

'Aye, well. Fair enough. We're all busy these days. And being the busy kind, I heard on the grapevine that you attended an unexplained death this morning. Over Fountainbridge way.'

'We're not viewing it as suspicious, if that's what you're after. Can't really comment until the post-mortem's done.'

'So you can't deny or confirm that the deceased in question is Brian "Mad Bastard" Galloway then?'

Sometimes he wondered why Dalgliesh bothered calling him. She'd not have asked the question if she hadn't already known the answer, and so this was either a bid to get a little extra inside knowledge, or her annoying way of letting him know the story was about to hit the papers and other news media. He was surprised it hadn't already. Social media usually knew what was going on long before the police did.

'There'll be an official announcement soon enough. But since next of kin have been informed, I guess I can confirm it.'

'Rumour has it he overdosed and died in his armchair. Staring out the window at the wreck of his life.'

'We haven't found any evidence of anything stronger than a prescription painkiller. The exact cause of death won't be known until they've carried out the post-mortem. I expect that'll be tomorrow, after which there'll be a full press release for you lot to spin however you want.'

'Is that a note of sarcasm I hear in your voice, Tony?'

'Not really, Jo. I know how you operate. This is celebrity gossip, not news. You need to put as much lip gloss on it as you can, right?'

A moment's pause as the barb sunk deep. 'Anyone ever tell you how much of a cynic you are?'

'It may have been mentioned a few times. Mostly by you.' McLean knew the conversation was coming to a close if Dalgliesh was resorting to old insults. He was relieved at the thought of dismissing her from his mind, whilst oddly grateful to her for reminding him that the press would have more interest in Galloway's death than they might in Don Purefoy or Steve Whitaker. Or Cecily Slater for that matter. He was about to say goodbye and hang up, when a thought occurred to him.

'You're looking for an angle on Galloway, right?'

'Is the Pope Catholic? Aye, of course I'm looking for an angle. Not that you'd ever give me much.'

McLean ignored the insult. 'Well maybe I can point you somewhere. It's nothing I actually know, so don't come crying to me if it doesn't pan out. But let me give you two names to add to Mad Bastard.'

'Hang on. Let me get a pen. Need to write this down. A lasting memento of the one time Tony McLean was helpful.'

'Very funny, Dalgliesh. Two names. That's all I've got. The rest you'll have to find out for yourself.'

'Go on then. The suspense is killing me.'

'Tommy Fielding. Gail Elmwood.'

Another silence, longer this time. McLean glanced around the office, saw the door wide open on to the corridor that led a short distance to his superior's office. This wasn't how he liked to work, but she was forcing his hand.

'Gail new chief superintendent Elmwood?' Dalgliesh's voice was husky and McLean pictured her drawing on her vape.

'And Tommy Dad's Army Fielding. Yes. Like I said, might be nothing, and you didn't get it from me if it turns out to be something. I wouldn't mind a heads-up, though.'

'Aye. Sure. I'd better be off then. Speak later, Tony.'

McLean opened his mouth to say 'bye', but the line was dead.

Perhaps to try and atone for his conversation with Dalgliesh, McLean spent the rest of the afternoon diligently working his way through the paperwork that had begun swamping his desk. Every few minutes he'd pause and glance at the door, but no one came in. No one even walked past, as far as he could tell. Chances were that the chief superintendent was away at Gartcosh anyway, and nobody had heard him mention her name and Fielding's to one of the city's more persistent muckraking journalists.

Finally it was time to head to the major incident room to catch up on the day's lack of progress in the Cecily Slater case. He closed his office door behind him as he left, confident there'd be more work waiting for him the next day.

DS Harrison and DC Stringer were busy at one of the workstations when McLean entered the incident room. Harrison's sixth sense must have kicked in, as she looked up almost immediately. He crossed the room to join the two of them, not failing to notice how quiet everything was. Little point in having a briefing when there was no measurable progress.

'I'm guessing we've nothing more on Cecily Slater,' McLean said. 'You dig up anything useful on our two dead men yet?'

Harrison glanced back at the screen. 'Not a lot, sir. Plenty of calls made and messages left, but it's not easy finding the right people to speak to. Whitaker's wife confirmed Fielding was his lawyer for the divorce. She reckoned they were maybe planning an appeal or something, too.'

'Remind me what the grounds were for that one?'

'She found child abuse photos on his computer, caught him doing something to his own daughter. Never got the full story of what, and I don't really want to know. The only reason he wasn't locked up was because Fielding managed to argue she could have planted the images herself. And the accusation of abuse was his word against hers. Still enough to deny him access, though.'

McLean compared Harrison's words with what they'd learned about Galloway earlier. The parallels were striking. 'What about the estate agent, Purefoy?'

'Still trying to track down the full details, sir.' Harrison shook her head slowly. 'Divorced two years ago. Lost access to his kids. Ex-wife claimed he'd been mentally abusing her for years. Jay spoke to his current girlfriend who wasn't exactly sad he'd died. Said, and I quote, "He could be lovely at times, but he also scared the crap out of me." She also said she sometimes worried he'd hunt her down and kill her if she ever left him.'

McLean recalled the post-mortem report, Cadwallader's veiled suspicions. 'Could she have killed him?' he asked.

'She wasn't in town when it happened,' Stringer said. 'Not sure she could have done something like that anyway. She's a tiny thing.'

'What about Fielding? He have any connection to Purefoy?'

'Nothing we've managed to establish so far.' Harrison finally noticed she was fiddling with her phone, held it up and stared at the blank screen. 'I'm still waiting on a couple of calls, but Fielding wasn't involved in Purefoy's divorce. There was one thing, though.'

'Aye?'

'It was about Izzy DeVilliers, see? I was at the hotel not long after she and her fellow protesters were arrested. We had a complaint from Fielding. Me and Lofty landed the short straw of going to placate him.' Harrison looked down at her phone again, but only to avoid McLean's gaze this time. 'That might have had something to do with why I did my best to get Izzy off. I'd have done the same for the rest of them if I could, but I heard the charges were dropped anyway.'

'Is this going somewhere?' McLean asked.

Harrison's head jerked up as if she'd been poked. 'Sorry, sir. Aye. It was when we were at the hotel being lectured by Fielding. Fair made my skin crawl to be in the same room as him. Breathing the same air. Euch.' She shuddered. 'But he was with a bunch of blokes who'd been at his conference or whatever the hell it was he was doing. A seminar? I don't know. Anyway, I didn't really pay that much attention to them at the time. But when I saw Purefoy at the building site? See, I was sure I'd seen him somewhere before, and recently. It'd been bugging me for days and then going over his file just now it suddenly clicked. He was there, at the hotel, with Fielding and a bunch of others.'

McLean was about to ask whether or not Harrison was sure, but he stopped himself. She was a trained detective, and good at it. She noticed things, remembered people. 'We'll need some kind of corroboration,' he said.

'I've asked the hotel if they've still got CCTV from the event. You never know, might get lucky.'

'What are you thinking then? With these connections to Fielding.'

'That's what I can't work out, sir. These three deaths are weird but not obviously murder. Galloway's probably overdosed on his painkillers, Whitaker dropped a fag in his lap when he was pished, and Purefoy just got unlucky.'

'You don't believe that any more than I do.'

'No, you're right. It stinks something rotten. We going to do something about it?'

'Not sure what we can, right now. Keep on the hotel for that footage. Maybe see if you can get hold of a guest list for the conference. If Galloway and Whitaker were there too, then I'll take it up higher, see if McIntyre reckons it's worth looking into. Meantime we need to concentrate on Cecily Slater, right?' McLean waved a hand at the general lack of busyness in the room. He was only half joking when he added, 'And if you can find a link between her and Fielding, then we're all set.'

40

It had been a while since McLean had visited Madame Rose at her house on Leith Walk. It wasn't as if he had been consciously avoiding her, or at least that was what he told himself. He didn't mind her company, if in small doses. But more often than not he preferred solitude to being swept into her powerful orbit.

The house seemed unchanged, much as it had probably been unchanged in over a century. A parking space became available opposite her front gate as he pulled into the street and approached it. No charging stations here, but Emma's little Renault still had enough electricity in it to take him to Fife, should madness possess him. Plenty to get home later.

As he crossed the small courtyard and climbed the stone steps to the door, he felt a cold stare on his neck. Turning, he saw a black cat sitting on the wall, motionless as a statue until it realised it had been seen, at which point it started to lick a nonchalant paw. When he turned back, the door was already open.

'Tony, how lovely to see you. Do come in, come in.' Madame Rose beckoned him inside. McLean allowed himself to be led through the large hall and then up the stairs to the first floor. The last time he'd been in the living room here it had been to see an old gypsy woman and a young Syrian refugee. He briefly wondered what had become of them. Good things, he hoped.

'Settle yourself in, why don't you? I'll see about some tea.' Rose barely did more than open the living room door before hurrying off, leaving McLean to his own devices.

The room was large, with an extravagantly high ceiling, but like everywhere else in Madame Rose's house, it was cluttered with a bizarre collection of what he could only describe as stuff. Her business card described her as a fortune teller and tarot reader, but also a dealer in occult curios, and this was clearly where most of them ended up being stored until some equally eccentric buyer could be found for them. Glass-fronted book-cases lined three walls, some filled with books, others with things McLean had no ready name for. At least the middle of the room was only filled with overlarge furniture. Two figures sat on a sofa with their backs to him; a third emerged from the depths of a large, leather, wing-backed chair that had been angled towards the fire.

'Tony. Wondered when you were going to show up.' Unexpected, but not unwelcome, Amanda Parsons came up and gave him a hug. By the time she released him, the other two people had stood up to greet him too. One he'd been working with until quite late in the day already, which meant the other one must be Izzy DeVilliers.

McLean hadn't really known what to expect, but the woman who stared at him through narrowed eyes was not it. She was young, he knew. Not yet nineteen if the dossier he'd scanned was up to date. A child of the twenty-first century. And yet those eyes had seen far more than her short life should have allowed. She was dressed in a mess of loose-fitting casual gear that made her look like a refugee from the Greenham Common protest camps. Her hair was a vivid shade of red, and if she'd paid to have it cut she should probably be looking for a refund. He guessed she'd probably done it herself with the first pair of kitchen scissors she'd managed to get her hands on. Either that or she'd shaved her head a month past and was now letting it grow out. The only thing missing from her uniform was any sign of tattoos, which was hardly surprising given how little of her skin was uncovered. Neither did she have any piercings, which was the thing he found most surprising. A nose stud seemed to be almost compulsory these days.

'Izzy, this is the boss. Detective Inspector McLean.' Harrison confirmed his suspicion of her identity, not that there had been any uncertainty.

'Ms DeVilliers. Thank you for agreeing to meet.' He held out a hand to shake, but she made no move to reciprocate so he let it drop back down again.

'Tea, anyone? Or would you prefer something a little stronger?' Madame Rose bustled in through the door at precisely the right moment to defuse the awkwardness. Izzy's intense and uncomfortable stare slid off McLean like a bucket of cold water and latched on to the medium. Its unfriendliness softened a little, but didn't disappear entirely.

'I'm driving, so tea's fine for me, thanks,' McLean said. Madame Rose stepped past him, carrying an enormous tray laden with teapot, cups, a jug of milk, bowl of sugar, plate heaped high with home-baked biscuits, and an enormous chocolate cake. Despite what must have been a considerable weight, she hefted the whole thing with little obvious effort, weaving an intricate path through the furniture until she reached a suitably clear table and set the tray down.

'Tea it is, then.' Madame Rose smiled at everyone in the room, quite deliberately choosing to ignore the tension boiling off Izzy. 'Let's all sit down and have a nice wee chat.'

It didn't take McLean long to realise that he was the problem. Izzy sat on the smaller of the two sofas, close to DC Harrison, her entire posture defensive. Manda Parsons had retreated back to her comfortable armchair by the fire, leaving him and Madame Rose the larger sofa. He'd tried a little small talk to reduce the tension, but that clearly wasn't going to work on the young woman. Having heard her story from others, he could understand why.

'Did Janie explain why I wanted to talk to you?' he asked, after his comments on the Edinburgh music scene had been met with stony silence. Harrison started to open her mouth to reply, but stopped herself just in time.

'Something about the two twats who tried to jump me on the Royal Mile?' Izzy smiled at the memory, an improvement over her habitual scowl, albeit short-lived.

'You reckon they'd been sent by Tommy Fielding. Why did you think that?'

'Duh. Because nobody else would try and drag me into a side street for a laugh, would they?'

McLean noticed she said 'side street' and not 'close'. Izzy's accent was English, and while she was trying to sound like she'd lived her life on the wrong side of the tracks, the posh slipped through occasionally.

'Did they say anything when they grabbed you?'

'Don't really remember, do I? Too busy fighting for my life.'

'Seems you made quite a good accounting for yourself. The way I hear it, Christopher Allan will likely always walk with a limp, and the other one, Brian Galloway? Well, he won't be walking anywhere ever again.'

Izzy tensed at the insinuation she might have been responsible for his death, and McLean mentally kicked himself for being knocked off course by her attitude. Had this been a formal interview at the station, he would have been much better prepared and the setting would have kept him on track.

'I'm not accusing you of anything other than defending

yourself. There's no suggestion that Galloway's death had anything to do with his injuries. Of the two of them, he had the least damage. Although I'd have thought the broken fingers would have made the reunion tour a bit tricky.'

That got Izzy's attention, so clearly Harrison hadn't told her everything. 'Reunion tour?' she asked.

'Aye, did you not know? Brian Galloway was lead singer in a band called the Idle Lunatics. You're probably a bit young to remember them.'

'Idle . . . ?' Izzy's eyes widened. 'That was Mad Bastard? No fucking way.'

'Isobel, dear.' Madame Rose sat up straighter as the young woman swore. Izzy half shrugged by way of apology.

'For real? I got jumped by an ageing rock star? That's so cool.'

McLean could think of other words to describe it, but he decided not to say so. 'Putting that to one side, there's nothing that happened that directly links them to Fielding, right?'

Izzy's eyes narrowed again, her lips pursing. McLean could see the angry tirade coming, raised both hands to stop it before it could start.

'I'm not trying to defend him, Izzy. Quite the opposite. But I need facts, not conjecture, however well founded it is.'

That seemed to mollify her, at least a little. She crossed her arms and hunched forward like a sulking teenager. Which, McLean supposed, was what she was.

'OK. Perhaps we can go back a bit further. You were part of the group of women who started protesting outside the Scotston Hotel a while back, right?'

Izzy waggled her head from side to side a little. 'Part of's maybe a bit strong. I only went to give my old roomie Jen a bit of moral support. Edinburgh's a nicer place to be than London these days and I'm trying to get a place at the uni.'

As far as McLean was aware, and judging by the number of

fresh-faced young students wandering around the city centre gawping at the sights, the new year had already started. He let it go for now. Izzy didn't really have to justify why she was in town.

'How did you find out about Fielding, then? Did this . . . Jen call you?'

'Christ, what planet are you living on? Janie said you were a bit old-fashioned, but I had no idea.'

McLean couldn't help looking at Harrison, as she was sitting on the sofa right beside Izzy. She wouldn't meet his eye. On the other hand, it was probably fair comment.

'OK, so you know about Fielding because he's a misogynist creep who runs fathers' rights campaigns and regularly defends men accused of all manner of horrible crimes against women. That close?'

'Not even by a whisker. You make him sound like some kind of naughty schoolboy when he's responsible for most of the far right radicalisation of the past decade. You think he's just a sexist pig, but he's far worse than that. White supremacist trash. He's a domestic terrorist in a smart suit. Part of a group of people systematically undermining our society, and people like you let him.'

Put like that, McLean could understand why Izzy didn't trust him. But her allegations went a lot further than what he knew of Tommy Fielding, tipping over into the realms of fantasy, perhaps.

'What makes you think he's that much of an extremist?'

Izzy rolled her eyes and slumped back into the sofa. 'Oh, come on. Please. You don't know about his online hate mobs? His gangs of enforcers? He even calls himself a modern-age Witch Finder General, for fuck's sake. That's his user ID, Witch-finder underscore General.'

Madame Rose tutted gently under her breath at the coarse language, but McLean was more concerned with the allegations. 'Are we talking about the same man here? Tommy Fielding, QC.

One of the country's leading lawyers specialising in divorce and family law?'

'Is there an echo in here?' Izzy threw her hands up. 'Course I'm talking about him. That's his pretty face for the papers. Dig a little deeper into 8kun and some of the dark web forums, why don't you? Haven't you got a department of teenagers who sniff all this alt-right shit out for you? He's literal slime. Incel-king. I'd throw away my boots if I stepped in him by accident.'

'You have evidence of this?' McLean knew it was the wrong thing to say even before the question slipped out.

'Sure. He's that open about it you've arrested him already and broken up his entire organisation. Oh, hang on. No. You're too busy arresting us when we try to do something about him and his kind.'

'You were let go with a caution, but I take your point. The problem is, for all you say Fielding's a nasty piece of work who sets grown men on to young women who cross him, we don't have any actual evidence to arrest him.' McLean leaned forward, resting his forearms on his legs in an attempt to appear less intimidating. 'I'd suggest you lodge a formal complaint against the two who attacked you, but given they both claimed to have fallen down some stairs, and then one of them died shortly afterwards, that might be a bit counterproductive. If you can give us something better to link Fielding with the kind of crimes you've mentioned, then at least I can pass that information on to the NCA.'

Izzy was still defensive, but she seemed to consider his words.

'I don't have anything, but you could talk to Mirriam. She'll know more. That's why the Burntwoods crowd were protesting Fielding's conference, after all.'

An eerie silence fell on the room. Harrison's head snapped up at Izzy's last words and she stared at McLean for confirmation of what they had both heard.

'Did you say Burntwoods?' he asked.

'Yeah, Mirriam Downham and her merry band of witches. You know them?'

'I know them,' Madame Rose said. 'But I doubt many others do. The Downham Trust, of course. Their refuges are all over the place. And such an indictment of society that they are needed so much. But Burntwoods? I don't think there's many know it now.'

'Actually, it's come up in one of our recent investigations. So anything you can tell me about the place would be very helpful indeed. I was hoping maybe to pay it a visit soon.'

'Good luck with that. You'd never even find the front gates.' Izzy smirked as she spoke, making the words sound overly sarcastic. She tipped her head at Harrison. 'She might, though. And they'll probably let me back in if I ask nicely.'

McLean looked at Madame Rose for an explanation, aware that he wasn't going to get any sense out of Izzy. The medium shrugged. 'I'm afraid Lady Isobel is quite correct. No man can enter the grounds of Burntwoods House uninvited.'

It sounded like the mystic mumbo jumbo McLean had become used to from Rose, and he knew better than to press the point. 'I would like to speak to this Mirriam Downham if I can.'

'Of course. I will reach out to her.' Madame Rose made it sound like some arcane ritual. 'And if she's in Edinburgh anyway, then I'm sure she will come to you.'

41

'Not sleeping again, Tony?'

McLean looked up from his desk to see Detective Superintendent McIntyre standing in the open doorway. A couple of days on from his meeting with Izzy DeVilliers and he was still waiting for an update. He'd come in early, dawn still little but a threat, in order to get some quiet time to plough through the ever-growing paperwork and let his thoughts come together. So far he'd succeeded at the first, but the second eluded him. Too many different cases all banging up against one another, and still a frustrating lack of progress in tracking down the killers of Cecily Slater.

'There's a post-mortem I need to attend later this morning to keep our illustrious leader happy. Thought I'd get ahead with the paperwork before heading down to the mortuary.'

McIntyre cocked her head to one side. 'What have you done to upset Gail? More to the point, what's she done to upset you? "Illustrious leader" indeed.'

'I'm maybe being a bit unfair. Guess I don't much like being the centre of attention.' McLean pointed to the small conference table and the coffee maker in the corner. 'You want a coffee?'

'Aye. Thanks.' McIntyre followed him across the room,

pulled out a chair and sat down. McLean set a mug in front of her and took a seat himself.

'Sorry. Someone ate all the biscuits.'

'Someone?' McIntyre raised an eyebrow. She was going quite grey now, McLean couldn't help but notice. Not trying to hide her age.

'OK. There never were any biscuits. I take it this isn't a social call, or you'd have brought some with you.'

'No, it's not, sadly. There's never time for simply chatting, catching up on what everyone's doing, bringing insights to other people's cases. We're all too busy running just to stand still these days.'

'I like to tell myself it was always like this, but we only remember the few times it wasn't.' McLean paused to take a sip from his mug. This early in the day the coffee was fresh, although still not as good as the stuff Grumpy Bob brewed down in the basement. 'When do they want the investigation wrapped up by?'

'Am I that transparent?' McIntyre gave him a half-smile, too weary for a whole one. 'End of the week. If there's nothing new by then, it gets written up and sent for review. We need to reallocate staff, especially all these fresh-faced new DCs. They need to get a bit more experience in the field. Don't want them disillusioned before they've even started.'

'True enough. I'm just glad to see some new faces at all. Think they'll work out OK. Even if the ratio's getting a bit skewed now.'

'Ratio . . . ?' McIntyre frowned for a moment, then understood. 'Ah, yes. Is it a problem?'

'Why would it be? Male or female makes no difference to me. It's how they do the job that matters. Just need to keep an eye on things. Be aware of the potential, as it were.'

'Indeed.' McIntyre savoured her coffee for a moment, clearly steeling herself to some unpleasant task. Given she'd already delivered the news about the murder investigation being put on ice, McLean had a suspicion he knew what it would be.

'They're going to give the vacant DCI post to Kirsty,' she said eventually.

'Congratulations to her. She deserves it. Does she want this office, too? It's way too big for me.' And horribly close to the chief superintendent down the corridor.

'You're not angry about it, then?'

McLean looked at the detective superintendent in genuine bafflement. 'Why would I be? You know I never wanted to be DCI, Jayne. I was bumped into it when we had that nonsense with Forrester and his son. Detective Inspector is fine for me. It's not like I need the pay rise.'

That got a wry smile from McIntyre, albeit short-lived. 'That's good, because none of us are getting one. Kirsty's promotion hasn't been announced yet, so keep it to yourself for now. Gail's having a reception at her house in Stockbridge. She'll tell everyone there. All the senior officers are . . . I was going to say invited, but that's not going to work with you, is it?'

McLean shrugged, but said nothing.

'Call it a three-line whip, then. Everyone ranked Inspector or above will be there, plain clothes and uniform. I know it's a bit unorthodox, but apparently it's how she used to do things in the Met. Helen will send you the details, but I need you to promise me you'll be there. Can you manage that?'

At least he wouldn't be left alone with the woman. 'I suppose so, if it's to support Kirsty.'

'Try not to look so miserable about it, eh?'

McLean pasted a fake smile on to his face. 'Yes, ma'am,' he said.

'You do keep sending us the most interesting specimens, Tony. Please keep up the good work.'

McLean stood in his usual position in the mortuary examination theatre. Close enough to see the body and hear what the pathologist had to say, but not so close he could see the details when the scalpel came out. Today it was Tom MacPhail in charge, but Angus Cadwallader had come along to see him work. Brian Galloway's pale, naked body lay on the table in front of them.

'What's so interesting about this one?' McLean asked.

'Well, there's the fact that he drowned for starters.' MacPhail bent close to the dead man's head, pushed open his jaws and peered into his mouth.

'Drowned? He was in his living room.'

'Yes, but his lungs were full of fluid, poor chap. That's what did for him.'

McLean searched his memory for anything medical that might account for this, but had to admit his knowledge fell short. 'Is that . . . How can that happen?'

'Surprisingly easily, actually,' Cadwallader said. 'It's how a lot of people die of the flu. Their lungs inflame with the virus, secrete mucus that fills up all the little branches where the oxygen in your breath can cross into the blood, and the carbon dioxide go the other way.'

'But he didn't have the flu, did he? Isn't it a bit early for it yet?'

'Ah, Tony. Influenza can strike any time of the year. But you're right. He didn't have the flu. Something else triggered a massive and rapid inflammation in his lungs. It would have been extremely distressing, and reflex would have closed off his throat to stop him breathing in more liquid. Except that he hadn't breathed it in, and now he couldn't get it out. Dry drowning, they call it. More common in children, but it can happen in adults.'

'Any idea what caused it?'

'That's the million-dollar question.' MacPhail looked up from

288

his work, his white latex gloves smeared with blood and ichor, scalpel held aloft. 'He shouldn't have reacted badly to those painkillers you found, even if he'd mixed them with alcohol. Of course, he might have taken something else we don't know about, but the tests we've done so far haven't come up with anything suspicious. I've asked for the painkillers to be analysed just to be sure they're what's written on the label.'

'You think they might not be what they say they are?'

MacPhail lifted both hands in a shrug, narrowly missing Cadwallader with the scalpel. 'I'm no detective, but that'd be one way to kill someone and hide the evidence, wouldn't it? Swap his pills? But given they're in blister packs, it's unlikely. That's a lot of trouble to go to.'

'Anything's possible, I suppose. Who'd want to kill him though?'

'Well, anyone who likes decent music for a start.' MacPhail went back to the cadaver, still talking while he guddled around inside. 'Seriously though, it's a strange way for an adult to die, even one who's probably abused his body more than most.'

'But not something you've never seen before?' McLean asked.

MacPhail frowned in concentration, as if dredging the very depths of his memory. 'Once or twice, maybe. More often in kids, like I said. The thing is, that usually goes along with heavy inflammation in the lungs. This chap . . .' He waved his hand at the body, and for a horrible moment McLean thought he was going to dig the organs out and start showing him. 'There's a little inflammation, but he looks more like I'd expect if he'd fallen in his swimming pool while stoned, if you know what I mean. Except without the puckered skin and general dampness.'

McLean had left the mortuary fully intending to take the results of Galloway's post-mortem straight to the chief superintendent and let her decide whether or not to pursue the matter any further. The short walk back to the station had given him time to think it through a little more, so he diverted to Detective Superintendent McIntyre's office instead. In a reversal of their morning meeting, he was now the one knocking on the door frame.

'You got a minute, Jayne?'

McIntyre sat at her desk, half-moon spectacles perched on the end of her nose, squinting at a report. Judging by the two piles – one small, one large – she'd been working through a lot of them.

'A minute, an hour. Anything to get away from these damned things.' She closed the folder, but not before slipping a piece of paper in to mark where she'd got to. McLean noticed that she returned it to the larger of the two piles. More left to do than done. He knew the feeling all too well.

'I've just got back from the mortuary, checking in on Brian Galloway's post-mortem.'

'Galloway?' McIntyre looked momentarily confused. 'He's the one Gail wanted you looking into? How on earth would she even know him?'

'I tried asking her, believe me. She's quite good at not answering questions, so I thought I'd let you know first that the verdict is he drowned.'

That got him a raised eyebrow. 'Drowned?'

'Well, his lungs were full of fluid. Possibly a bad reaction to his painkillers. You know he'd apparently fallen down the steps of Fleshmarket Close a while back? Broke his nose and three fingers.'

'I don't like the way you say "apparently", Tony. What are you not telling me?'

'He was with a mate, who also took a tumble. Blew out his knee and ruptured a testicle. They were both treated at the Royal Infirmary. The thing is, there's no report of any incident like that in the Old Town that night.'

'So they weren't hurt enough to need an ambulance. Too embarrassed to call one even if they were.'

'There was, however, an attack on a young woman who made more than a good accounting for herself. Trained in self-defence, and perhaps a little bit more. She was jumped by two middle-aged men, dragged into a close off the Royal Mile. Same date, same time.'

McIntyre pulled off her spectacles and placed them on the desk, paying him more attention now. 'Have you interviewed this young woman? Is she a suspect in Galloway's death?'

'Yes, and no. She never reported the incident officially, claims she wouldn't be able to identify the men if she saw them again anyway. All she knows is what she did to them, which was pretty specific.'

'And pretty brutal, by the sound of things. You don't think she went back to finish off the job, then?'

'No. She didn't know the identities of the men, and she's got a cast-iron alibi for the night Galloway died. And before you ask, Galloway didn't succumb to his injuries. Tom was fairly sure about that.'

'Hmm.' McIntyre leaned back in her seat and folded her arms. 'So why are you bringing this sorry tale to me then?'

'Galloway's is the third unusual death since I came back to work. Not including Cecily Slater, which we know was murder.' McLean counted them off on his fingers. 'We had Steve Whitaker spontaneously combusting down in Meadowbank. Then there was Don Purefoy who somehow managed to get himself crushed under a rockfall that didn't mangle his body so much as squeeze the life out of him. And now Brian Galloway drowns in his living room.'

'People die every day, Tony. You and I know that better than most folk.'

'Aye, true. But they're not all past clients of Tommy Fielding though, are they?'

At the mention of the name, McIntyre reached forward and picked up her spectacles. She didn't put them on, but fidgeted with them for a while before speaking.

'What are you implying?' she asked.

'I'm not implying anything, Jayne. He's represented enough people over the years, it might just be a coincidence. But you know how I feel about coincidences. I've also heard a few rumours about Fielding recently that go way beyond the stuff he gets up to with his fathers' rights advocacy.'

'And you know how I feel about rumours, Tony.' McIntyre seemed to notice that she was playing with her spectacles, studying them for a few seconds before putting them down again. 'Fielding is also . . . tricky. You know what he's like. We all do. Poking around in his business without a very good, justifiable reason could blow up in our faces.'

'I'm working on it.' McLean saw the look of horror that swept over the detective superintendent's face, and quickly added 'carefully'.

'Just be sure that you are. And keep any suspicions well away from Fielding himself.' McIntyre shook her head as if not quite able to believe she was agreeing with him. 'You know he has the chief constable on speed dial, right? Plays golf with half of the Police Authority? What's your plan of action?'

'The young woman who was attacked? I'm trying to keep her name out of things for as long as possible. But she was one of the group protesting outside Fielding's conference. She's going to introduce me to her friends, give me the intelligence they've dug up on him. It might be tin-foil hat stuff, so I'll treat it with due suspicion. They claim he has links to some banned organisations. White Supremacist and domestic terrorism stuff, so I'll be sure to take it all with a good bagful of salt.'

McIntyre had her spectacles in her hands again, passing them back and forth, twisting the frame in a manner that was likely to lead to her needing a new pair soon. 'You know, it wouldn't surprise mc if she's right, this new friend of yours. Doesn't change the fact Fielding can and will make life miserable for anyone who annoys him.'

'I'll be sure to remember that when I speak to him, then.'

The snap was audible across the desk, and when McIntyre put her spectacles back down, one of the arms poked out at entirely the wrong angle. 'Is that wise?' she said through clenched teeth.

'Someone needs to explain to him why the protesters were released without charge. Thought he'd probably take it better from a senior officer than some young detective sergeant not long in the rank. He'll probably react better to a man, too, if any of what I've heard about him is true.'

'And you just happen to want to talk to him about three un-explained deaths.' McIntyre shook her head slowly. 'Be careful, Tony. You think a few months of suspension is bad? Well Fielding is worse. Much worse. If you piss him off, it won't just be you with a bit more time to spend in the garden. He'll take the whole of Edinburgh CID apart. Don't give him any reason to make our lives more difficult than they already are, OK?'

42

McLean had assumed he would find Tommy Fielding at the offices of his law firm, but a quick phone call redirected him to the nearby Scotston Hotel and conference centre.

'Mr Fielding runs regular advocacy seminars out of the hotel, Inspector,' the polite receptionist had told him. 'There's another one this weekend, and he likes to do his prep work over there. To be honest, I think he prefers it to the office.'

McLean remembered the Scotston, perhaps not particularly fondly, from his student days. It had been not much more than a step up from a doss house and knocking shop, renting rooms by the hour. Not that he'd ever been interested in rooms. It was the ratty Walter Scott bar that had drawn the more desperate students in search of a drink in the very small hours. As he stepped out of the squad car that had given him a lift across town, he was transported back all those too many years. An image of Phil Jenkins bent double, ridding himself of half a dozen pints of Guinness and an ill-advised kebab. McLean himself resting his hand on his flatmate's shoulder as much for his own physical support as Phil's moral. Happy times; he'd have to give Phil and Rae a call, since Emma wasn't around to do it for him. It had been too long.

Much had changed in those intervening years. This part of

town was no longer the haunt of prostitutes, at least not the sort who hung around on street corners and knew which hotels wouldn't ask questions as long as the money was right. The old railway marshalling yards and the McEwan's distillery were gone, modern office and apartment buildings rising in their place. He wasn't far from the tiny terrace house where Brian Galloway had breathed his last, nor the slick modern apartment block where the young lad who'd stolen his car had lived. Everything focusing down on Fountainbridge as if the dark secrets bulldozed and buried since the turn of the century were oozing back up into the light.

The hotel had changed, of course. A shiny polished brass plaque at the door identified it as part of a boutique chain now. The same chain, McLean noted, that ran Bairnfather Hall and was in turn owned by the Bairnfather Trust. There was another man he would have to visit and placate. Cecily Slater's murder investigation would never be closed; unsolved murders always remained open. But it would be, in the term so beloved of management, deprioritised. Perhaps in a decade or so he would revisit it in his retirement, having moved like Duguid and Grumpy Bob down into the basement. A prelude to the grave.

A smart-uniformed doorman opened the door for him, tapping the brim of his slightly absurd hat by way of greeting. McLean nodded his thanks and strode across the lobby to the reception desk. Echoes of his past kept coming to him, although the ancient and faded decor he remembered had been renovated and polished until it gleamed.

'Detective Inspector McLean. I'm here to see Mr Fielding?' He showed his warrant card to a young female receptionist, noting the slight tick that marred her face at the mention of the name. She got it under control with admirable speed.

'He's in the Walter Scott bar, sir. Over there.' She indicated the way, even though McLean knew exactly where it was and that Fielding would be waiting for him inside.

'My colleague Detective Sergeant Harrison might have been in touch. She was hoping to get a hold of some of the security camera footage after those protesters broke in and disrupted the conference.' He put as much emphasis as he could on the 'after'.

'I'm not sure, sir. That would have gone to security. I can check, but as we said to the other detective, we have no idea how those people got in.'

'I know. That's not what I was looking for.' He scanned the reception area, spotting a couple of cameras that covered both the entrance to the hotel and the door through to the bar. 'I was more interested in who was here with Mr Fielding. We know who the protesters were, after all.' He paused a moment before adding, 'I don't suppose you have a register of conference attendees, do you?'

The receptionist frowned ever so slightly. 'I don't think I could—'

'It's not a problem. I completely understand. You have to protect the anonymity of your guests, after all. Even those simply attending Mr Fielding's seminars. The last thing any of those men would want is the police asking uncomfortable questions. Forget I asked.' He gave the receptionist his best innocent smile, then turned and walked away towards the Walter Scott bar.

Much like the rest of the hotel, the Walter Scott bar was at once hauntingly familiar and yet utterly different. It didn't smell of weed, spilled beer and cigarette smoke for one thing, and the bottles behind the marble-topped bar held considerably more expensive spirits than he remembered. There was still a Guinness tap, Phil would be pleased to see, probably. The other few beer taps were of the chilled-to-tasteless, carbonated fizz variety that so many bars sold these days. Well, he wasn't here to drink.

Neither was anyone else, if the emptiness of the bar was anything to go by. Another difference from McLean's student days. Judging by the decor, the smart uniforms of the reception staff and the boutique nature of the place, it was too expensive for students and in the wrong part of town for the more affluent tourists. He looked around the empty tables and comfortable alcoves before finally spotting the man he had come to see.

Tommy Fielding sat on his own, slim laptop computer on the table in front of him, an empty coffee cup beside it. He had his phone clamped to one ear, gesticulating with his free arm even though the person he was talking to couldn't possibly see him. McLean wasn't there to eavesdrop, but the lawyer was speaking so loudly it was hard not to.

'. . . don't give a flying fuck what you think. You wanted the job done differently you should have said so.'

McLean turned away, caught the eye of the barman and ordered a coffee he didn't really want. On the other hand, he remembered that he had to go to the chief superintendent's reception that evening, so maybe the caffeine boost wasn't such a bad idea.

'Jesus fucking Christ, Reggie. It's like listening to a fucking broken record. No, it's not a problem. I'm dealing with it. Have I ever let you down before?'

The barman raised an eyebrow, his glance flicking towards Fielding, up to the ceiling and then back to McLean as he placed the coffee down on the bar. McLean raised one himself when he was told how much the coffee cost, but paid without further complaint.

'Look, I know that woman's sniffing around the company, but she can only buy a minority share. You still control the board so the most she can do is be annoying.'

McLean sipped his coffee and waited for the call to be over. The cup was empty and he was contemplating a refill, despite the cost, before Fielding finally managed to persuade whoever Reggie was that it was all OK and nobody was going to take his company from him, especially not some upstart woman who was probably a lesbian anyway. There had been some other comments that wouldn't have seemed out of place in a small-town rugby club locker room after a home defeat, peppered with enough foul language to make even Jo Dalgliesh blush. It was hard to imagine the man standing up in court and impressing both judge and jury, but then the best briefs were consummate actors after all.

'Mr Fielding?' McLean approached before the lawyer could begin another call. Fielding looked up, a frown of irritation disappearing swiftly from his face.

'Ah, Detective Chief Inspector McLean.' He stood up, presenting a hand to be shaken. Fielding's grip was firm but damp, and he wore an expensive suit that he somehow managed to make look cheap.

'It's just Detective Inspector now, remember?' He resisted the urge to wipe his hand on his trousers. 'You got the message I was coming, then.'

'An explanation as to why no charges are being pressed against the harridans who broke into my seminar and threatened my guests? I am eager to hear it, Detective Inspector.'

Fielding had made no indication that they should sit, and McLean was quite content to remain standing. If nothing else it should make the meeting short. 'You know how it is, Mr Fielding. Everywhere there's cutbacks. Too many demands on too few resources.'

'Are you suggesting these women get away with it simply because you can't be bothered sorting out your budgets?' Fielding put heavy emphasis on the word 'women', managing somehow to convey that he had utter disdain for them. But then McLean already knew that.

'Far from it. We take our duty towards protecting the people very seriously indeed. However, our investigations have discovered that the hotel entrance through which the women . . .' and here McLean put his own, subtly different emphasis '. . . came was not locked, and indeed was a public entrance to the building, albeit from the rear.'

Fielding's frown returned. 'They burst into my meeting room, screaming obscenities and threatening us.'

'So I'm told. However, I wasn't there to witness it, and apart from yourself nobody else has agreed to come forward and corroborate your story. My team had some difficulty in tracking down a list of the . . . what was it you called them? Oh yes, the guests. And those they did manage to speak to gave rather conflicting accounts of the events. The women themselves of course deny doing anything worse than stumbling into the wrong room when they were looking for the bar.'

Tiny beads of sweat had begun to form on Fielding's forehead now, and his skin had taken on that hue more normally associated with Glasgow lads after the first sunny day of spring. When he spoke, McLean was glad of the space between them as flecks of spittle almost covered the distance before falling to the floor like slimy rain. 'This is preposterous. You can't be suggesting I made the whole thing up? These women have been camped outside this hotel for weeks, screaming at anyone who comes inside, waving around banners with claims on them that are defamatory at best.'

McLean let the slightest hint of a smile show. 'It's not that I don't believe you, Mr Fielding. Quite the opposite. But you're a man of the law. You understand how these things work. We could press charges, send these women to the Sheriff Court, but you and I both know what the outcome of that would be.'

'So you just, what? Let them go?' This time one fleck reached

McLean's lapel, but he ignored it. The suit was due a clean anyway.

'Not at all, Mr Fielding. As you've no doubt noticed, the demonstrations have stopped. All the women involved have been officially cautioned. We have their details on file should they breach the peace again. If we had sufficient evidence, you can rest assured that we would have pressed charges. We can't have women bursting into private meetings and trying to disrupt them, can we?'

Fielding's eyes narrowed in suspicion. McLean was trying hard not to wind the lawyer up, given the warning he'd received from McIntyre. It wasn't easy though. There was something about the man, his haughty, puffed-up nature, that begged to be poked. Harrison certainly had the measure of him.

'Indeed not, Detective Inspector. They should know their place. And you can rest assured, I'm not happy with the situation even if I do understand your reasoning. I will be mentioning it to the chief constable the next time I see him.'

On the golf course at the weekend, no doubt. McLean inclined his head slightly to indicate he thought this reasonable. 'I'll let the new chief superintendent know too. I believe you know her? Gail Elmwood?'

Had he not been trained in interviewing suspects, with more than two decades of experience behind that training, McLean might have missed the almost imperceptible flicker that crossed Fielding's eyes at the name, the tiniest moment of utter stillness as the thoughts tumbled through his sharp, lawyer's brain. It was there though, plain as day if you knew what to look for. And if you'd set up the trigger on purpose.

'Well, I'll not waste any more of your precious time, Mr Fielding,' he said, before the lawyer could respond. 'Pleasure to meet you again.'

★ ★ ★

'Detective Inspector McLean, sir?'

McLean stopped mid-stride as he was heading for the door, turned to see the receptionist he'd spoken to earlier. She had one hand raised to catch his attention, in case her shout had been insufficient. He changed course and went to see what she wanted.

'Sorry to shout like that, sir. I wasn't sure when you would be finished with Mr Fielding, and I didn't want to miss you.'

'No problem, Ms . . .' He squinted to see the name on the badge pinned to her chest. 'Elaine?'

'You were asking about the CCTV footage from the lobby here. I spoke to Colin in security and he pulled it all on to a memory stick. It's all digital these days, amazing what they can do.' She held out her hand, and McLean saw both a tiny, company-branded USB memory stick and a neatly folded sheet of A4 paper. He glanced at the door to the Walter Scott bar before taking both and slipping them unobtrusively into his jacket pocket.

'A guest list, I take it?' he asked quietly.

'You didn't get it from me, sir.' Elaine straightened her uniform as if she'd just emerged from the stationery cupboard moments after her boss. 'Some of us were a bit uncomfortable with the conference, the sort of things that were being said and the way the guests treated us. Those ladies outside were much more polite, if you get my meaning.'

'I do. Thank you.' McLean tapped his pocket. 'And don't worry about this. No one will know where it came from, but it may prove very useful.'

43

The major incident room was in a certain amount of turmoil as the last few actions of the Cecily Slater investigation were tidied away. Someone had already taken down the photographs of the dead woman and the burned-out gamekeeper's cottage, which meant both that nobody had to see them any more and that they were no longer a constant reminder of the horrific crime they were supposed to be investigating. Somewhere out there the men, and McLean was as certain as he could be that they were men in the plural, who had done this terrible thing to a helpless ninety-year-old woman, were still walking free. Might even continue to walk free until they died. It wasn't the first time he'd had to wind up an investigation without any result, and every time the injustice left a bitter taste in his mouth.

'How did you get on with Fielding?'

Lost in thought, McLean hadn't noticed Detective Superintendent McIntyre follow him into the room.

'As well as could be expected. He wasn't happy, but he conceded the lack of evidence was a problem. That's got to hurt, really. He could have given us any number of witnesses, but he doesn't want to upset his base. Last thing any of them want is to be on our radar.'

'Well, at least I won't get an irate call from the chief constable.'

'Oh, don't count on it. I imagine he'll be in touch after this weekend's golf round. Unless something more urgent comes up.'

McIntyre arched a thin eyebrow. 'Oh aye? Something I should know?'

'Probably best if you don't, Jayne. Plausible deniability and all that.' McLean looked around, remembering why he'd come in here in the first place. 'You haven't seen DS Harrison, have you?'

'Janie's away with Kirsty on another case. Any reason why you needed her?'

McLean stuck his hand in his pocket and pulled out the memory stick. 'She was after some CCTV footage and I managed to sweet-talk it out of security. I was hoping she'd be able to have a quick look over it, but I guess there's no reason I can't do it myself.'

'Can't you get a constable to do it, Tony? That's what they're for, you know.'

'I could, but by the time I'd found them and explained what they're meant to be looking for, it'd be as quick doing it myself.'

'Oh aye? And what are you looking for?'

'A specific person in a small group of people at a specific time. Don Purefoy, to be precise.'

'Pure . . . ? Oh, right. The estate agent. Where was he seen?' McIntyre nodded at McLean's hand, still clutching the memory stick.

'Probably—'

'Best I don't know, aye. I get it. Plausible deniability.' The detective superintendent shook her head. 'I don't know why I bother, Tony.'

'Call it following up on a hunch. If it doesn't play out, then best nobody knows.'

'To save you from the embarrassment of being wrong? That's not usually bothered you before.'

'Not me, Jayne. You know I don't give a damn what other people think about me.' McLean waved a hand at the collected team of detectives, uniformed officers and support staff quietly dismantling the apparatus of investigation around him. 'It's this lot I'm concerned for. The fewer people know about this, the less chance of it getting back to the wrong person.'

McIntyre wasn't stupid. You didn't get to her level in an organisation like Police Scotland without being clever, although the time she'd broken a reporter's nose had been a lapse. Not that anyone who'd ever worked with her didn't think the reporter deserved it. Now McLean could see the wheels turning in her mind as she put together the various pieces of information and came to a perfectly valid conclusion.

'I wasn't joking when I told you to be very careful, Tony. This is not something you want to be wrong about. Hell, it's probably not something you want to be right about either. But I know better than to tell you to stop.'

McLean tilted his head in understanding, pocketing the memory stick as he turned to leave. 'I will be the soul of discretion, have no fear.'

'It's too late for that, Tony. Several years too late.'

McLean had almost reached the door before McIntyre spoke again, loud enough for everyone else to hear. 'And don't forget this evening. Seven o'clock.'

McLean stopped by the canteen on his way back to his office, aware that if he was going to spend the last hours of the afternoon staring at grainy CCTV footage on a tiny laptop screen he would need tea and at least a half-packet of biscuits. Somehow the day was mostly done, and he'd completely failed to eat any lunch. Emma would tut at him when he got home and immediately raided the fridge for a sandwich. Except that Emma was half a world away in the sub-Saharan sun, and he wouldn't be heading home until he'd suffered the torture that the chief super-intendent's reception was likely to be.

Mindful of McIntyre's warning, he closed his office door before slotting the memory stick into the laptop he'd borrowed from Mike Simpson in the IT department. He didn't expect the stick to be riddled with viruses, but you could never be too careful. And this machine had no connection to the building's network, so if something went wrong it could easily be contained. It took a moment to work out the unfamiliar program, and at first he was confused by the four different video files. Then it dawned on him that they must be for different cameras covering the same time, and soon enough the video footage expanded to fill the screen.

He recognised the view in the first file. The camera was mounted in the ceiling above the reception desk, pointing at the front door. People came and went, although there were surprisingly long stretches of nothing much happening at all. A timestamp ticked over in the bottom left corner of the screen, minutes flicking past like seconds as he viewed it on fast forward.

Nothing much happened until about half past five, when a commotion of people appeared from off-camera. Some made their way across the reception hall in the direction of the bar, but most simply left the building as quickly as they could. Members of staff bustled backwards and forwards, clearly dealing with the incursion into the conference room by Izzy DeVilliers and her friends. After perhaps twenty minutes a couple of uniformed officers entered, but mostly hung around the lobby doing nothing. And then, at about a quarter to seven, the front door opened and DS Harrison stepped in, dwarfed by the looming figure of Lofty Blane behind her.

McLean closed the file and opened another one. It showed a corridor, which if ancient memory served was the route from the Walter Scott bar to the toilets. It also led to the kitchens and other service rooms, judging by the occasional appearance of hotel staff about their business. McLean fast-forwarded the image to around the same time the mass crowd had erupted from the conference hall, and was rewarded by the view of Tommy Fielding and a group of five other men as they walked towards the bar. The angle of the camera wasn't good for identification, but he made a note of the file name and timestamp for future reference.

The third file was a camera mounted behind the bar in the Walter Scott, its fish-eye lens taking in almost the entire room but distorting the image at the same time. There was no sound on any of the files, so when McLean found the footage of Harrison and Blane as they spoke to Fielding and his friends, he couldn't hear what they were saying. It wasn't necessary to hear anything to understand the tone of it though. Fielding's face was a picture of barely constrained rage, his anger at having his precious little men's rights meeting disrupted by a bunch of uppity women compounded by the appearance of DS Harrison to deal with his complaint. The other men at the table were mostly obscured, except for a young lad nursing a pint of what looked like fizzy lager. Then, after a silent rant from Fielding which had Harrison almost rocking back on her heels, all of the men got up and left. And as they filed out past Lofty Blane, each one looked at the taciturn giant, their faces perfectly lined up with the camera as if they'd been posing for a mugshot.

'You beauty,' McLean muttered under his breath as he paused and screen-grabbed each face in turn. Then he switched on his own computer and brought up the file on Don Purefoy. It might have been strange that the man's body hadn't been completely mangled in the rock fall, but the fact that Purefoy's head had been left unscathed meant his face was easy enough to recognise, even if it was pasty white with death in the mortuary photo.

And there, on the CCTV footage, just as Harrison had thought, was the man alive. McLean increased the magnification, checking between the two screens just to be sure, but there was no mistaking it. Don Purefoy had not only been at the men's rights seminar, he was pally with the big man himself.

McLean remembered the sheet of paper the kindly receptionist, Elaine, had given him. He pulled it out, unfolded it and stared at the list, noting as he did so that the title at the top of the page said invited guests, not attendees. No way of knowing if they'd all been there, but the names were in alphabetical order, which made finding Purefoy easy. As he scanned the rest of them, Christopher Allan sprang out, mostly because he was right up there at the top. McLean didn't know what the man looked like, but Harrison would. Near the bottom of the list, between Charles Weston and Samuel Yates, was another name McLean knew, Steven Whitaker. Was this the same night he had gone home and somehow managed to set himself on fire? He'd have to check the dates.

His phone buzzed before he could do anything about that, and McLean picked it up, seeing the text from McIntyre reminding him of his appointment with doom. A glance at the digits in the top corner of the screen told him it was time to go if he didn't want to risk the wrath of the chief superintendent. He slipped the phone into his pocket, then picked up the guest list, intending to fold it up and put it somewhere safe. The last thing he wanted was to be asked how he had acquired it. As he went to fold it, another name caught his eye, nestled in among the Gs. Brian Galloway had been at the seminar too, which raised some uncomfortable questions. But it was the final name that had him staring in disbelief, even as his phone pinged another text. McLean remembered the phone call Fielding had been on when he'd first entered the Walter Scott bar, Fielding's assurances to someone he called Reggie. Well, there was a

Reginald on the guest list who might very well have been the same man.

Reginald Slater.

Lord Bairnfather.

44

McLean had to check the address he'd been given for the reception twice. He knew that it was being held at the deputy chief constable's home, which in itself had surprised him, but when he saw the house it piqued his curiosity even more. Elmwood was single, he knew. She'd not long moved up from London, so surely had to be renting. A chief superintendent's salary was on the generous side, and there would have been relocation expenses to tap into as well. Even so, the vast terrace house in Stockbridge must have been eating into her wages.

There was also the rather unsettling fact that he had been to this very house before, and not all that long ago. It had belonged to Alan Lewis, a hedge fund manager with a side interest in money laundering on a massive scale. Unless you counted hedge funds as money laundering anyway, in which case it wasn't a side interest at all. Gazing up at the facade of the building, McLean could pick out the windows that looked out from what had been Lewis's bedroom, and the en suite bathroom in whose bath the financier had died. Possibly from a heart attack, possibly from the curse of a vengeful ghost. Neither cause appeared on the death certificate though. As far as the world was concerned, Alan Lewis had committed suicide by electrocuting himself, rather than face the consequences as his dark dealings were brought to light.

The fact he had died in that bath might, of course, have made the house difficult to sell and cheap to rent, so maybe that was why the chief superintendent was here. It was disquieting nonetheless.

Two uniformed constables were on duty at the front door, looking bored and a bit grumpy. McLean could understand. Walking the beat would be far preferable to guarding your boss while she hosted a party. They both came to a sort of attention as he approached, but he waved for them to relax.

'Evening, sir,' one of them said as the other opened the door for him.

'You two do something to piss off your sergeant?' he asked, which at least got him half a smile from one of them.

'Something like that.'

'In which case, shouldn't you be asking me for ID before letting me in?'

The constable holding the door shrugged. 'We know who you are, Detective Inspector, sir. And that was a bloody nonsense, knocking you back after you shut down that gang out Penicuik way. Should've been a promotion, not suspended for months.'

McLean shrugged awkwardly. 'I didn't follow procedure. Can't haul my constables over the coals for cutting corners if I do it myself now, can I?'

'My point exactly, sir.' The second constable saluted, then motioned for McLean to go in.

It had been an odd exchange, a clever joke too, but as he stepped over the threshold, he was grateful for the small show of support. McLean stood for a moment in the relative safety of the inner porch. Beyond it, the large hall buzzed with conversation. Some people revelled in this kind of thing, but he would far rather be at home, in his favourite armchair with a dram of whisky and a good book. Although given the way his stomach was rumbling, some food might have been a good idea first.

Shadows danced across the wall as someone came across the hall towards the door. He couldn't stay in the porch for ever. Taking a deep breath, he set off into the fray.

'Tony, you're here. I was beginning to worry you might not show.'

Any lingering thoughts he might have had that this was a formal police reception to celebrate DI Ritchie's promotion evaporated as McLean saw the deputy chief constable striding towards him. She had discarded her uniform in favour of a figure-hugging black cocktail dress, and held a champagne flute loosely in one hand. In his work suit, and smelling like he'd been wearing it since five that morning, he felt immediately on edge. He had to remind himself that this was not a party, and he wasn't the socially awkward teenager who didn't think he knew anyone and certainly didn't know what to say to any of them even if he did. He wasn't here to socialise, whatever Gail Elmwood might think.

'I was told seven.' He looked at his watch without really seeing the time, shrugged. 'Might have got a bit carried away reviewing some evidence.'

'Well, never mind. You're here now. Come join everyone in the front room.' Elmwood slipped her free arm into the crook of his elbow before McLean could react. His instinct was to pull away, but he was also aware that this was her house and he was a guest, however reluctant he might be in that role, so he allowed himself to be steered across the hall and in through an impressively large doorway.

The room beyond was busier than he'd expected, at least two dozen, maybe thirty guests and an army of liveried waiting staff wandering around with trays of drinks. McLean scanned faces, looking for familiar ones. He recognised the chief constable, although they had only met once before. A few other senior officers would probably be more readily identlfiable if he hadn't been so adept at avoiding the regular strategy meetings his previous rank of detective chief inspector required him to attend. Over in the far corner, DI Ritchie and Detective Superintendent McIntyre were chatting away like two people who hope if they appear absorbed in their conversation they won't be interrupted by anyone else.

More surprising was the number of civilians present. Again, McLean was struck by the idea that this was more of an old-fashioned drinks party than an official Police Scotland reception. Before he could mention it, the chief superintendent had grabbed a glass of champagne from one of the waitresses and shoved it into his hand with such force a little liquid sloshed over the rim.

'Have a drink. Loosen up a little. We're here to celebrate Kirsty's promotion.'

McLean carefully extricated his arm from Elmwood's, transferred the glass to his now free hand, then wiped the other one on his jacket. He looked around for the waitress to ask for something soft, since he'd driven over, but she had disappeared.

'Ladies, gentlemen.' The chief superintendent tapped a fingernail against her own glass to bring the hubbub of conversation to a close. All eyes turned to her, and as they did so McLean could see the faces of the rest of her invited guests. There were a couple he remembered from the Safe Streets reception, and through a gap in the crowd he briefly spied Mrs Saifre at the back of the room. It made a certain sense that she would be here; Elmwood was exactly the type of person Jane Louise Dee would try to sink her corrupting hooks into. More surprising, though, was the man McLean saw standing beside her. What on earth was Lord Bairnfather doing here?

'Thank you all for coming along this evening,' Elmwood continued. She stood beside McLean, almost uncomfortably close still. So much so that he could feel the heat coming off her, smell the champagne on her breath as she spoke.

'It's been almost two months now since I arrived in this city. A stranger, unknown and unknowing. Each and every one of you here has helped me in one way or another. By welcoming me warmly,' and here the chief superintendent waved her glass in the direction of the chief constable. 'By managing the transfer from my predecessor,' she swung the glass around like a search-light until it pointed at McIntyre. 'By introducing me to this wonderful city. And this wonderful house.' The glass swung back until it wavered in the direction of Lord Bairnfather, which at least explained why he was there. 'And by keeping me on my toes, eh, Tony?'

McLean froze as Elmwood reached around his shoulders and pulled him to her, which had the unfortunate effect of upsetting her balance so that she ended up leaning heavily into him, almost falling over. Never particularly happy in the limelight, even so he had no choice but to either catch her and help her steady herself, or let her tumble to the floor in an undignified mess. The latter was sorely tempting.

'Oops. Silly me,' Elmwood said once she had extricated herself. 'I always forget how to wear heels after a week in sensible shoes.'

As she said those last two words, she darted a look across the room towards where Detective Superintendent McIntyre stood. McLean was sure he couldn't have been the only one who understood the veiled insult.

'Anyway. Where was I?' Elmwood stood up straight again, her attitude professional, not a hint of what he had assumed was a touch too much to drink about her any more. 'What we're really here for is to celebrate another milestone in the career of one of

Scotland's foremost female officers. Kirsty? Are you there? Or should I say Detective Chief Inspector Ritchie?'

The room spluttered into a round of applause that sounded more embarrassed than heartfelt. Was this something they did regularly in the Met? McLean couldn't be sure, but he doubted it. The contrast with his own promotion couldn't have been more marked. That had been born out of desperation after the then head of their branch of Specialist Crime Division had gone off the rails and almost beaten a man to death in the cells. There'd been no party, no presentation, and he'd been absolutely fine with that.

Newly anointed DCI Ritchie came forward as the chief superintendent beckoned her. She raised the ghost of an eyebrow at McLean as she passed him, and he took the opportunity of her being the focus of attention to slip away. He made it to where McIntyre stood before Ritchie began to give a carefully rehearsed impromptu speech.

'We should all be down the pub with the rest of the team,' he muttered.

'There'll be time enough for that, Tony. You can buy everyone a drink when the Cecily Slater case is wound down.'

'About that. How did we not know that Elmwood and Lord Bairnfather were connected? He's Slater's nephew. What if he decides to kick up a fuss?'

'Then I'm sure your new best friend will smooth things over. Really, Tony, you want to watch yourself with that one.'

'I seem to remember it was you insisted I come to this . . . thing.' McLean shrugged at the room. 'I can think of much better ways to be spending my evening, and I'm sure you and Susan can too.'

McIntyre grimaced at the mention of her wife. 'Sensible shoes, my arse.' She threw back the last of her champagne and looked around for another.

'Here.' McLean handed her his own, untouched drink. 'Never did much like the stuff anyway. Something to eat wouldn't go amiss though.'

Another round of applause dragged their attention back to Ritchie, who was being congratulated by the chief constable. As if by magic, the waiting staff who had been plying everyone with drinks now reappeared with trays of canapés. He grabbed what he could, but drew the line at filling his pockets when McIntyre suggested it.

'I'll pick up a kebab on the way home. Not hanging around here any longer than I actually need to.'

'Make an effort, Tony. It's only one evening, and it's not as if Emma's waiting at home for you.' McIntyre went to look at her watch, then realised doing so would tip her champagne on the floor. 'You heard from her much? She getting on OK?'

'Yes, she called yesterday. Sounds like she's having a whale of a time. Can't say that digging through trenches of decaying bodies is my idea of fun, but I think she was feeling a bit stifled here in Edinburgh. Change of scene's doing her a world of good.'

'You should go join her.' McIntyre must have seen the look of horror on McLean's face, as she quickly added, 'Once she's finished at the dig. Take a couple of weeks' holiday. Maybe a month. Go on safari or something.'

McLean opened his mouth to object, then closed it again. It wasn't all that mad an idea when he thought about it. Except that he'd just spent the best part of three months on suspension. Taking leave so soon after that wouldn't go down well with those overworked sergeants and constables who still gave him filthy looks when he passed them in the station corridors.

'I'll think about it. If I ever escape from this place alive.'

McIntyre rolled her eyes like the hammiest of actors. 'If you're that bored, just go. I'll tell Gail you were called away on urgent business. See, she's busy talking to that dreadful MSP right now. What's his name? Sits on the Justice Committee. She'll be distracted for ages.'

McLean was sorely tempted. He'd still have to run the gamut of the room to get from where he was to the door and back out into the hall. Perhaps if he made a show of talking to one or two people on the way it would look like he was mingling, or at least trying to. He looked around, searching for a suitable target, and spotted just the man.

'Thanks, Jayne. I owe you. I just need to have a quick word with someone first.'

'Surprised to see you here, sir.'

McLean pitched his voice loud enough to carry through the hubbub. Lord Bairnfather turned to see who had spoken, his mouth full of half-chewed vol-au-vent. The old man munched upon it industriously for a few moments before swallowing heavily, eyes narrowed as he stared at McLean all the while.

'Mac – something. Detective chappie. You're the one looking into Sissy's death, aren't you?'

'Detective Inspector McLean, sir. Yes. I'm SIO on that investigation.'

Bairnfather made an odd growling gurgle that might have been disapproval but might equally have been indigestion. 'And how is it coming along?' he asked, once the noise had subsided.

'If I'm being honest, sir. It's not. We have no leads, no clear idea as to why anybody would want to do such a senseless thing. If your aunt had any enemies, we've not been able to find them. And the fire left nothing useful for the forensics team to work with.'

That strange noise again, and this time McLean realised it was Bairnfather clearing his throat. 'You're closing the case, then?' His words dripped with disapproval, verging almost on contempt, but there was none of the anger McLean might have expected.

'Far from it, sir. Murder cases are never closed. We're review-ing what we have at the moment, and I've still got officers working on Lady Cecily's recent history. I just wanted to be candid. Unless something new comes to light soon, it may be a while before her killer is brought to justice.'

Bairnfather harumphed, but made no other complaint. McLean tried to read the man. It wasn't easy to see beyond the ruddy complexion and wobbling jowls, the standard features of a country laird. He was even wearing a tweed three-piece suit. Stick him on a grouse moor on the Glorious Twelfth and he'd fit right in.

'I couldn't help noticing that Gail – the chief superintendent – thanked you for this house. I wasn't aware you owned it.'

'I don't,' Bairnfather grunted. 'Well, not exactly. It's one of the company assets.'

'It used to belong to a fellow called Alan Lewis. Did you know him?'

'Know him? Of course I bloody knew him, McLean.' Some-thing about speaking the name brought Bairnfather up short. 'McLean. Of course. You were the one who found him, weren't you? Uncovered that money laundering racket he had going. I owe you a debt of gratitude then.'

'Oh? How so?'

'Lewis's company dissolved after he topped himself. Coward's way out, if you ask me. Picked up quite a few choice assets in the fire sale, mind you. This house was one of them. Probably paid only half what it was worth on the open market.'

'Does she know?' McLean indicated the deputy chief con-stable, deep in conversation with someone McLean had a suspicion might have been in a cave in the Moorfoot Hills back in the summer.

'Know what?'

'That Alan Lewis died in her bath?'

Bairnfather stared at him for a few seconds, his face a picture of puzzlement. Then he let out a great bark of a laugh that momentarily silenced the room. 'Good God, no. Why would I tell anyone that? Hard enough renting out a place this size as it is.'

'You could always sell it. Realise that hundred percent profit.'

Bairnfather shook his head slowly. 'That's not how my family does things, McLean. We're in it for the long run, not fly-by-night merchants like Lewis.'

'And the hotel business is very different from hedge fund management, I'd imagine.' McLean watched a frown of confusion work its way across Bairnfather's florid features. 'That is your main business, is it not? Hotels?'

'One of 'em, I suppose.'

'Only, I was in the Scotston earlier today. I remember it being a terrible place back in the nineties. You've done great things with it. Not surprised Tommy Fielding likes it so much. It's a great conference venue now.'

The frown changed from puzzled to wary. 'What are you up to, McLean? How do you know Fielding?'

'Know him?' McLean feigned innocence. 'I don't know him, sir. Had to go and see him about a small matter. The disruption to his most recent symposium. You must have seen the protests outside.'

Something like fear widened the old man's eyes for a moment. Then he seemed to collect himself. 'Heard something about it. You moved them on, I take it?'

'Eventually, yes. Sorry we couldn't do more sooner, but we have to work within the law.'

'Of course.' Lord Bairnfather shook his head ever so slightly, as if he disagreed. Then he looked past McLean to the far side of the room. 'If you'll excuse me, McLean. There's someone I'd like to speak to.'

318

McLean stood aside to let him pass, said nothing as Bairnfather elbowed his way in the direction of the chief constable. Well, it was bound to happen sooner or later. He glanced around the room, seeing the chief superintendent deep in conversation with Mrs Saifre. Heads close together, their body language was unambiguously conspiratorial. Another complication he could have done without. Not pausing to say goodbye, he slipped out of the room and made good his escape.

45

McLean was almost home, the hot chilli sauce and garlic aroma of the kebab he had picked up en route chasing away the last of the new car smell of the little Renault, when his phone ring tone boomed out through the speakers. A glance at the screen in the dashboard showed a name he would once have happily ignored, but now found himself surprisingly glad to be hearing from. He reached out and tapped the accept call button.

'It's a bit late for you, isn't it, Dalgliesh? I'd have thought you'd be tucked up in your bed by now.'

'Ha bloody ha, Tony. An' who's to say I'm no'? I could be snuggling up wi' some wee toy boy jus' the now while you're home all on your own.'

McLean didn't like the mental image that conjured. 'I'm in the car, actually. Won't be home for ten minutes yet. You just calling to brag about your sexual exploits, or was there a reason for this?'

A moment's silence, which was probably the reporter taking a drag on her foul-smelling e-cigarette. 'Aye, look at the two of us, sad old lonely buggers that we are. Working late into the night 'cause we've nothin' better to do.'

'I'm on my way home from a party, actually. Think I'd rather have been at work.'

'A party? Who am I speaking to and what have you done wi' Tony McLean?' Another short pause, another drag.

'Kirsty Ritchie got promoted to DCI. About time too, if you ask me. The chief superintendent threw a little reception for her. I think Kirsty would've been happier down the pub buying a round for the team. I'd have preferred that myself, but Elmwood's the boss. We have to do what she says.'

'Aye, well. It was her I was calling about. See when you mentioned her name and Tommy Fielding's to me. That was just desperation, wasn't it?'

'Am I that easy to read, Jo?' McLean glanced at the Sat-Nav. He didn't need it to find his way home, but it was useful for estimating how long it would take to get there, and how much charge the car would have when he arrived.

'Aye, you are. But you've got this annoying way of seeing things other folk can't, too. Took me a while to join up the dots, but there's a link true enough.'

'A link between the chief superintendent and Tommy Fielding?' McLean indicated without looking in his mirror, slowed and pulled in to the kerb. A car behind him he'd not noticed before revved its engine and blared its horn as it overtook. Through its back window, silhouetted by the lights beyond, he made out a raised middle finger as the driver sped away.

'Aye, and it's a good one too,' Dalgliesh said, blissfully unaware of the drama at the other end of the line. 'There's a juicy story in it, I reckon.'

'And are you going to tell me? Or was this call just so you could wind me up?'

'Fair enough.' Another pause, longer this time, and McLean could almost smell the sickly scented vapour. 'See your new boss was in the Met most of her career, aye?'

'Yes.' He looked down at the plastic bag holding his kebab. It was tempting to open it up and start eating, since Dalgliesh was clearly going to take her time telling him what she had found out. On the other hand, there was little chance of him not getting chilli and garlic sauces on the upholstery, and this wasn't his car.

'Well, she wasn't always a high-flier. Started off quite unremarkable, really. Made it to sergeant quickly enough, then seemed to stall. Now, your man Fielding, he was working in London around that time. Getting himself something of a reputation for defending men accused of battering their wives, marital rape, that sort of thing. He was winning a lot of cases, too. Word was he was dodgy as hell, used all manner of underhand tricks to win. Seems some tigers never change their spots, right enough.'

'Leopards,' McLean corrected.

'What?'

'Leopards never change their spots. Tigers are striped. Thought an educated woman like you would've known that.'

'Ha bloody ha. You know what I mean.'

'Sorry. How does this all tie in to Elmwood then?'

'I was getting to that before you went and interrupted me with your fancy zoological accuracies and stuff. See, there was this big case she was involved in. Prosecuting some fancy rich aristo who'd killed his wife. Bloke swore it was an accident, sex games gone wrong, whatever shit he could come up with. He had money, so he called in the best lawyer, which was your man Fielding. He not only got the man off, he ripped the Met prosecution team a new one. Fair enough, they'd bent a few rules getting their evidence, but the only way he could have known that was if he'd either been given or had stolen inside information.'

'The man who got off? What was his name?'

Dalgliesh didn't answer immediately, and McLean imagined he could hear her flicking through the pages of her notebook. More likely she was having a drink. He needed one himself, if only because it was never wise to eat a kebab sober.

'Here it is, aye. Chappy called Angus Trensham. Fourth Baronet Wisby or something. It's no' important. He died in a car crash a month or so after the trial collapsed. The thing is, there was an inquiry into why it all went wrong. The DCI and DI on the case both fell on their swords, a couple of senior uniforms too. Well, took early retirement, but it's the same thing. Only person who came away smelling of roses was young Sergeant Gail Elmwood. She was inspector within a month, superintendent a couple years later. Been on the up ever since.'

'And she owes that to Fielding, is that what you're telling me?' McLean tried not to let his disappointment show. It wasn't a clear link between the two of them, even if Elmwood had known of the lawyer for many years.

'Ach, you know me, Tony. I don't like to leave a story alone until I've shaken all the dirt out of it. I had a word wi' some of my old London contacts. No' that there's many still alive, mind. Kind of journalism they do's hard work on the liver an' makes enemies of powerful people.'

'But you found something.'

'Aye. Struck gold, you might say. He's no' much to look at now, but your Tommy Fielding was quite the charmer in his London days. Had a reputation for loving and leaving, as it were. Usually once he'd got what he was looking for. Maybe a quick shag, or maybe internal police investigation documents pertinent to a prosecution he was defending. Left on an unsecured laptop in a young sergeant's flat by the DCI she had been shagging in the hope of a promotion.'

It was McLean's turn to pause before replying, the implications taking time to trickle down through his brain.

'You're saying our chief superintendent had an affair with Tommy Fielding in London? At the same time she was sleeping with her boss?'

'Top marks to the detective chief inspector.' Dalgliesh

coughed, and McLean heard the distinct sound of her thumping her chest to clear it. 'Ah, no. It's just detective inspector now, isn't it? Sorry. Going the opposite way to Ms Elmwood, I'd say.'

'Do you think she knew? That he'd stolen information from her laptop?'

'Can't see how she couldn't know, but she kept it quiet. An' she was far enough down the pecking order that the shit didn't reach her. I'm guessing the DCI wanted it kept hush-hush too, given how his wife was expecting their second kid at the time.'

It took McLean a while to digest all the information Dalgliesh was giving him. He did his best to keep a lid on his growing excitement. If ever there was a way to persuade Elmwood to leave him be, this was it. Except that he knew he would have to tread very carefully around the subject. She was chief superintendent, after all, and in a position to make his life very difficult should she choose.

'You going to press with this story any time soon?' he asked after a few more silent moments.

'No' just yet. Don't think anyone else even has a sniff of it, and I'm waiting on a few more bits and pieces to come through. Wouldn't mind a chat wi' the cheatin' DCI, but it's unlikely he'd talk to an old hack like me.'

McLean knew a plant when he saw one. This time he was happy enough to grasp it. 'You know who he is, though.'

'Aye. And where. It's no' all that far from here, as it happens.'

'What if I was to give him a call? Maybe let you know what he had to say afterwards.'

'Aww. You'd do that for me?' Dalgliesh faked soppy gratitude. 'You've changed, Tony. An' no' for the worse.'

'Well it's just possible I might owe you this time, so if I can help your story without breaking any rules I will.'

'I'll ping you the details in a text. Gotta go now. That's my toy boy back from the lavvy.' And without another word the line went dead.

McLean hoped that Dalgliesh had been lying about the toy boy, and the fact that the text with contact details for ex-Detective Chief Inspector Simon Martin arrived before he had even parked and plugged the Renault in to charge suggested she was pulling his leg. Then again, Dalgliesh was a law unto herself, and he really didn't want to know anything about her private life. Ever.

Mrs McCutcheon's cat was lying in the middle of the kitchen table as he entered the room. She eyed him with a 'what time of night do you call this to be coming home?' look on her face, which he ignored. Cecily Slater's cat, if that was who the creature had truly belonged to, lay beside the Aga, purring contentedly to itself. Herself, McLean remembered. The vet had given her the once-over, declared her in need of worming and microchipping but otherwise fit and healthy. Probably between five and ten years old, but with no indication of ever having had kittens, so also probably spayed when very young. Looking at her, he had the distinct impression he had somehow acquired a second cat when he'd never even intended having the first one. Well, it wasn't as if they ate a lot, and there was plenty of room for everyone.

He had reheated his kebab in the microwave and poured himself a pint of beer, poised ready to eat even though he knew it was late and would lead to indigestion and a sleepless night, when his phone rang. Glancing at the screen, McLean didn't recognise the number. It was an international call, and he was about to cancel it on the grounds that whilst his car had recently been in an accident, he himself had not, when it struck him that it might be Emma using someone else's phone. He thumbed the screen to accept the call, lifting the handset to his ear.

'Hello?'

'Hi, Tony. Hope I'm not calling too late. I always get the maths wrong in my head when I try to work out time differences.'

Not Emma, but Hattie. Professor Turner. For a moment, McLean's blood turned to ice. What possible reason could she have for calling that wasn't bad news?

'It's no bother, Hattie. I was just about to eat, but that can wait. Something up? Is Em OK?'

'Oh God. I'm so sorry, Tony. What must you think? Emma's fine. Don't worry. No. I was just calling to say we're going to be home rather earlier than anticipated.'

'Something come up?'

'Doesn't it always? Emma's trying to sort it, but I think she's fighting a losing battle. It's the paperwork. Always is. They swear blind everything's fine and you'll be whisked from airport to dig site without even seeing any over-zealous officials, but every single time I come to Africa it's the same. You have to have all your paperwork done, sure. But you also have to pay every single pen-pushing, rubber-stamping bureaucrat who puts himself in your path. And it's always him, never her. God save me from this . . .' Turner trailed off just as McLean had assumed she was getting into full flow and taken a drink from his glass of beer. He swallowed it down too quickly and almost choked.

'So the whole thing's fallen through because you didn't bribe the right people?' he asked after a moment's silent wheezing.

'Don't use the B word, Tony. Not on an open line.' Professor Turner sighed. 'And anyway, this time I don't think any amount of money would have saved the day.'

'What's gone wrong?' McLean counted the days, and the few phone calls from Emma, in his head. As far as he was aware they'd arrived at the dig site and started working weeks ago.

'We had a visit from one of the local politicians. Well, I say politician, but mob boss might be a better description. Maybe tribal chief. He didn't have a problem with the dig and the results we've had so far, but he couldn't get his head around the fact that I was in charge and more than half my crew are women. Kept asking to speak to the boss man. Emphasis on the man bit.'

McLean remembered his conversation earlier in the day with Detective Superintendent McIntyre; her suggestion he take some leave and go out to join Emma after her work was finished. He'd dismissed the idea pretty much out of hand, but then why not?

'I could always come out and pretend,' he said.

Hattie laughed. 'That's a kind offer, Tony, but it's a bit too late for that. Our invitation has been withdrawn, apparently. Emma will give you a call once she's got the flights sorted out. She has the patience of a saint, that one. But then she's put up with you all these years so that's hardly surprising. Helps that she's travelled through these parts before, too. She's busy calling in a few old favours, which is why I got lumped with phoning everyone to let them know. Meg's next on the list, so I'd better call her before she gets started on the booze. We'll see you in a week or so.'

McLean thanked her for calling him, wished her well and then hung up. He looked at the congealed mess of spiced lamb, salad and sauces, glistening in its pitta bread and still contained by the environmentally disastrous expanded polystyrene box. It had seemed a good idea at the time, but now he felt too weary for food. He'd managed to grab a few canapés at the chief superintendent's house, so it wasn't as if he'd not eaten anything since breakfast. The beer on an almost empty stomach had given him a fuzzy edge that should at least mean getting to sleep would be easy, although the quality of that sleep might be up for debate. Draining the last of the pint, he closed the lid on the takeaway, then glanced over to where the two cats were staring at him like they'd never been fed in their entire lives.

'You can have it for breakfast. And out in the utility room. It's bad enough when you leave mouse entrails all over the kitchen floor. I don't want to come down to kebab everywhere.'

McLean shoved the container back in the single use plastic bag, wrapped it tight and shoved it in the fridge. He rinsed out his glass and set it on the rack to dry, then took up his phone from the table and headed off for bed. As he walked up the stairs, he thought about Hattie's call, the news Emma would be home soon. Much sooner than expected. Their relationship had been through a rough patch recently, starting with her miscarriage if not probably before. For a while now it had felt a bit like they were two people orbiting each other distantly, living in the same house but otherwise barely communicating at all. And yet, as he pushed open the bedroom door and switched on the light, he found himself sad to see the wide bed empty, and very glad indeed that it wouldn't be so for much longer.

46

'**I**'m very disappointed in you, Tony.'

Yet another early morning. McLean had hoped to be in his office and hard at work before the chief superintendent had even left her home. Given the state of the reception when he'd slipped out the night before, it had seemed a fair assumption she wouldn't be in first thing. As it was, he'd managed an hour before the summons to her office, every one of the dozen or so steps along the corridor feeling like the walk of shame he remembered from his hated boarding school. Called up in front of the headmaster for some imagined misdemeanour.

'Is there a problem?' he asked, once it became clear Elmwood wasn't going to tell him what had disappointed her. He knew, of course. Or at least he could narrow it down to two or three things, possibly a combination of all of them.

'You sloped off without saying goodbye last night.'

'An important phone call.' The excuse was out before he'd fully considered the ramifications, but fortunately the chief superintendent wasn't interested in details. At least not right away. She'd been sitting behind her desk, but now she stood, smoothed down her uniform, and gestured for him to join her in the casual corner.

'You also upset poor old Reggie Bairnfather. Making unfounded allegations.' As she spoke, Elmwood set about pouring coffee for two, which suggested this dressing-down wasn't going to be too harsh.

'I was just a little surprised to find out where you were living, ma— Gail. I . . . knew the previous owner, Alan Lewis.'

'I know. Jane Louise told me all about it. Apparently he killed himself in his bath. My bath. Can you imagine that?'

McLean almost didn't catch the quick mention of Mrs Saifre by her first names. He was surprised by the excitement in Elmwood's voice, the mischievous glint in her eye, the apparent delight rather than horror at the discovery.

'I don't really need to imagine it. I saw it.' He didn't add, 'I set it up so it looked like suicide because nobody would believe a vengeful ghost had scared him to death and almost did the same for poor Janie Harrison.'

'Gosh. I suppose that means you've been in my bedroom.'

McLean chose to ignore the slightly lewd suggestion, waiting for the chief superintendent to sit down before doing so himself.

'That's not why I'm disappointed though, Tony,' Elmwood said, as she arranged herself on the sofa like a young lady fresh out of finishing school. 'I'm very disappointed that there has been no progress on the Cecily Slater murder. We've spent a great deal of money so far for very little return.'

McLean had been savouring his coffee, but the chief superintendent's words gave him pause. Not that her concern about the lack of progress was a surprise, far from it. Jayne McIntyre had warned him the investigation was going to be mothballed by the end of the week. It was the mention of budgets that jarred. In all his dealings with Elmwood so far, money had never come up. She had found the budget for half a dozen new detective constables and was pushing for more funding to come east. It rang false that she would want to wind down the Slater investigation because it was expensive. And that made him wonder what the real reason was.

'It's not been an easy case,' he said. 'Bad enough her body wasn't found for a week and the weather destroyed most of the forensic evidence. She was a recluse, had been for years. It's almost impossible to find anyone who's been in contact with her recently, let alone anyone who might have harboured such a powerful grudge.'

The chief superintendent nodded, her face serious for a moment. 'I understand. Some cases are like that. And it's not as if it's actually closed. I want you to pull everything together and we'll get an outside team to review it. You'll need to reassign the team to other duties.'

McLean took a sip of coffee to stop his reflex instinct to complain. This wasn't a battle he could win, he knew that. It hurt all the same. Cecily Slater's death had been fuelled by a hate that wouldn't simply go away. If they didn't find the people responsible, someone else would suffer the same fate soon enough.

'You got my report on Brian Galloway?' he asked, by way of pushing the conversation along.

'Yes. Thank you, Tony. I'm very grateful to you for doing that. His death could have been quite . . .' She searched the air for the right word. 'Sensational? Everyone knows Mad Bastard, but only a few people knew Brian Galloway. I heard the press were sniffing around, going to make something lurid out of it all. Thought it best to get ahead of them.'

On the surface, Elmwood's words sounded reasonable, plausible even, but McLean could see the lie easily enough. Nothing to be gained from exposing it though. Not now, at least.

'The pathology isn't conclusive, but they reckon he had a bad reaction to a mixture of prescription painkillers and something else he'd taken to help himself sleep. It's tragic, but I hear the band's last album is back in the charts.'

The chief superintendent narrowed her gaze for a moment, as if trying to work out whether or not he was taking the piss. McLean kept his best poker face on, and she finally relented.

'Well, this has been fun, hasn't it?' She put her barely touched mug of coffee down and stood up in one fluid motion, bending perhaps a little closer to McLean than would be considered polite at his end of town. One hand briefly flirted with touching his knee, but then she pulled away, giving him space to stand as well.

'I'll get the Slater investigation into shape by the end of the day,' he said, receiving a brief nod before Elmwood retreated to her desk. McLean let himself out, the tension falling from his shoulders as he walked the short route back to his own office. He wasn't so foolish as to believe he was off the hook though; the leopard didn't change its spots that easily, and neither did the tiger. Should he have confronted her about Fielding there and then? No, it was too soon. There was too much of their past history he hadn't uncovered yet, most of all the reason the chief superintendent seemed keen to keep it a secret.

He paused at his door, pulled his phone out and navigated through the screens until he found the text from Dalgliesh. A name, a number, answers. But he couldn't make that call here, in the building and not more than a dozen swift strides from the woman he wanted to talk about. Shoving the phone away again, he set off, unsure exactly how much distance would ever be safe.

In the end, the station car park had to suffice. McLean sat in Emma's little Renault ZOE, stared sightlessly out of the windscreen, the chief superintendent's words going round and round in his mind. He could understand them shutting down the Cecily Slater case; it was going nowhere after all, and showed little sign of any sudden breakthrough. No, it was the excuse of budgetary reasons that still rang false with him. It was stupid, really. If Elmwood had simply said close it down, he'd have reluctantly complied. But she had to go and over-explain it, that was how he knew it was a lie, and he couldn't help but see the invisible hand behind the order. He'd spooked Lord Bairnfather at the reception and annoyed Tommy Fielding earlier that same day, then added to his tally by upsetting Elmwood as well. Hardly surprising he was being punished. A black mark against his record of successful investigations, and a ninety-year-old woman whose killers would walk free.

Or was there something more sinister at play? A thread that turned a series of unlikely coincidences into something more deliberate?

He retrieved his phone from his pocket and flicked through the screens until he found what he was looking for. He'd been expecting to have to copy the number over, perhaps even writing it down on a scrap of paper first, but the phone seemed to know what it was doing better than he did, highlighting the line in the text from Jo Dalgliesh. Clever little thing. He tapped it, and the ring tone echoed through the empty car even as he held the handset up to his ear.

'Martin residence, who's speaking?' A woman's voice, sounding a little tired if he was any judge. Although that might have been the echo effect of the hands-free system.

'Oh, hello. This is Detective Inspector Tony McLean, from Edinburgh CID. I was wondering if I might speak to Mr Simon Martin?'

A moment's silence, followed by the scratchy crumpling noise of a handset being pressed against material to mute what was being said. Presumably a woolly jumper, since it wasn't part-icularly effective. McLean could distinctly hear the woman's voice shout 'Simon? It's the police. Some detective from local CID? I don't know, do I?' The scratchy noise ceased, and the woman's voice came back clear again. 'He's on his way.' Then silence.

McLean stared out the windscreen at the empty car park. He should probably switch off hands free just in case. He'd barely tapped the screen before a voice sounded, only in the handset this time.

'Hello?'

'Mr Martin? I'm sorry to bother you. It's Detective Inspector McLean here. From Edinburgh CID. Well, Specialist Crime, but that's just another name for the same thing.'

'Hah. It's nice to hear some things never change. They do love messing around the department names, don't they? Was there something you wanted, Detective Inspector? Only I don't know if you realised, but I left the force a couple of decades ago. Retired completely last year.'

'I do know that, sir. And I'm sorry to disturb you. I was just wondering if I might be able to ask you a few questions about Gail Elmwood.'

If it hadn't been for the icon on the dashboard screen indicating that a call was still in progress, McLean might have assumed Martin had hung up, such was the silence that followed. He waited it out, knowing that the longer the man stayed on the line, the greater the chance of his agreeing to talk.

'That's a name I've not heard in a while,' Martin said finally. 'A name I'd hoped never to hear again, if I'm being honest.'

'I take it you're not aware that she's currently serving as chief superintendent based in Edinburgh, then.'

Another silence, but shorter this time. 'And let me guess, she's making trouble? You a drinking man, McLean?'

'I'm a detective inspector with twenty-five years' experience, sir. What do you think?'

Something like a chuckle echoed down the line at that, which was an improvement on the silence. 'I like to go to my local of

334

an evening. Gets me out of the house, gives Jean a bit of free time now she can't send me off to work every day. Can't manage it tonight, but this is your number, right? I'll drop you a text in the next day or so. Buy me a drink, and you can explain to me why a time-served detective inspector wants to know about his boss's past, and if you're really lucky I might tell you what I know about her.'

47

Low grey clouds threatened rain and the wind whipped at the tops of the narrow conifer trees as McLean drove Emma's little electric Renault through the gates of Mortonhall Crematorium. Beside him in the passenger seat, DS Harrison had spent the short journey from the police station furiously sending and receiving texts, presumably in an attempt to explain to DCI Ritchie why she wasn't available for the next couple of hours. Kirsty would accept it, of course. Harrison had been the first plain clothes officer on the scene, and had led the early stages of the investigation. If anyone should be there to pay her last respects and apologies to the dead woman for their failure to bring her killers to justice, it was her.

It had surprised him to learn that Cecily Slater was to be cremated; McLean had assumed there would be a large Bairnfather family crypt somewhere for her to be laid to rest alongside her illustrious ancestors, and a long drawn out funeral service in St Giles's Cathedral. But then he remembered how she had lived her life, and the most likely reason she had fled Bairnfather Hall in the first place, as a seven-year-old girl. Perhaps ashes scattered somewhere peaceful would be preferable to an eternity in the company of her abusive father.

Not many people had turned out to see the old lady off. Lord

Bairnfather was there, of course, avoiding McLean's eye. His estate manager, Charlie McPherson, had accompanied him, along with Tam Uist and his wife. A few other people waited in the cold car park for the previous funeral to finish, the large figure of Madame Rose among them.

'Good morning, Tony. Janie,' she said as she approached the car. 'Thought you two might be here for this.'

'I was senior investigating officer. Still am, technically, since the case hasn't been closed. We try to show face at these things when it seems like the right thing to do. I have to admit I'm surprised to see you here. Did you know Cecily Slater well?'

Rose shook her head. 'Not well, no. She shunned society, didn't much care for people really. I think the last time I spoke to her at any great length must have been in the sixties.'

'But you've come to her funeral?'

'Some ceremonies must be borne witness to. This is one. Will you accompany me inside?' Madame Rose gestured towards the building, its doors now being opened for the mourners who had begun filing in like well-trained ants. On the other side, a different group would be making their way out, their short time slot over. Such was the business of death.

Inside the crematorium was much as McLean remembered it from his last visit. How many years was it now since he'd said a final goodbye to his grandmother? The room was far too large for the congregation, which at least meant he could avoid Lord Bairnfather. There had been an ominous silence from that quarter since their brief conversation at the chief superintendent's house, but McLean knew a reckoning was on the cards sooner or later.

'I don't think the Cecily Slater I knew would have liked such an ostentatious coffin,' Madame Rose said, as they sat near the back and waited for the ceremony to start. 'She was never one to make a fuss. That's what made her so powerful.'

It was an odd thing to say, even for Madame Rose. McLean

hadn't thought much about the coffin, sitting at the front of the chapel waiting for them. Sometimes coffins were brought in after everyone else, sometimes they were already there, and one looked pretty much the same as another, didn't it? There was no time to ask what the medium had meant by her words, though. As the community celebrant stepped up to the lectern to speak, a last group of people hurried in and squeezed into the row beside them both.

'Oh good. You made it,' Rose whispered, and when McLean looked around to see who her friends were, the nearest one waved. Izzy DeVilliers had tidied herself up considerably since they'd spoken a few days earlier. Her hair was still a short-cropped, spiky red mess, but she wore a loose-fitting black cotton jacket over a simple, dark, ankle-length dress and plain white blouse. The transformation from the surly teenager was quite impressive.

'Hi, Tony. Hey, Janie.' She even smiled as if she were pleased to see him, although that might have been meant for Harrison. Then she was shushed by the person sitting beyond her. McLean nodded a quiet greeting and turned to face the front again, but not before seeing a tall, thin woman with straight grey hair that fell well past her shoulders. If he hadn't seen her in photographs already, he would have known Mirriam Downham at once. The only thing that troubled him was that those photographs had been taken more than half a century earlier and she looked exactly the same.

The service was mercifully short, overseen as it was by a community celebrant who had clearly only heard the name Cecily Slater a day or two before. McLean felt that familiar mix of horror and dread as the curtains drew together to hide the coffin on its way to the furnace. Was it really fifty years now since he'd watched his parents go that same way? Near enough as didn't matter.

Outside, the promised rain had arrived, albeit half-heartedly. Few people hung around to chat, heading straight to cars as swiftly as they could. Tam Uist came up and told them there was to be a wake at Bairnfather Hall.

'His Lordship said to tell you. All who knew his late aunt are welcome,' the farmer said, eyeing Madame Rose, Izzy DeVilliers and Mirriam Downham with a certain trepidation. To DS Harrison he gave a warm smile of recognition before trotting back to his lord and master.

'I wouldn't set foot in that house in a hundred years,' Mirriam Downham said, the first words McLean had heard her speak. Quite unusually, Madame Rose had not yet introduced her.

'Ms Downham, I presume?' McLean said.

'Doctor Downham, but it will do. And you are Anthony McLean, if I am not much mistaken. You have your grand-mother's eyes.'

'I . . .' There wasn't much he could say to that. As far as he was aware, nobody had ever made the comparison before. 'You knew her?'

'Not well. We corresponded from time to time. And she supported the trust, for which I remain grateful. I understand you wanted to talk to me?'

'I did, yes. About Cecily Slater, in fact.' McLean held out his hands to catch the rain, growing ever more persistent. Behind them, the crematorium was already filling up for the next service. 'This isn't maybe the best place.'

'Agreed. I need to arrange to collect Sissy's ashes, first. They are to be scattered at Burntwoods, not placed in the Bairnfather mausoleum. She made that abundantly clear.'

'Perhaps we could meet back at my place,' Madame Rose suggested. 'I'm sure you all have much to talk about.'

Downham turned to look at the medium, her face utterly unreadable. The rain had damped her hair, making it hang even straighter, but she seemed quite unperturbed at getting wet.

'That's very kind of you, Rose. Perhaps you could take young Isobel with you and I'll meet you all there.'

Tea at Madame Rose's house was never much of a chore, especially if you didn't mind being stared at by cats and surrounded by esoteric clutter. McLean couldn't help thinking it was infinitely preferable to expensive canapés and booze at Bairnfather Hall. The medium had produced an enormous cake, and enough tea to drown in. After a damp drive across town, being in the warm and dry was a welcome change, too.

They were all in the living room where McLean had first met Izzy DeVilliers. The young woman sat on the sofa next to Harrison as if they were old friends, and she seemed like a completely different person. It wasn't just the funeral clothes, but her entire deportment, and it wasn't hard to see the reason why she was behaving herself.

Mirriam Downham sat close to the fire, as if she needed its elemental heat to survive. She held her cup and saucer in long-fingered hands, balanced elegantly in her lap, but had politely declined Madame Rose's offer of cake. Beside her, on a low table, a small cardboard box contained the ashes of Cecily Slater. McLean had the impression that she wouldn't let them out of her sight until they had been scattered in the grounds of Burntwoods. Possibly not even then.

'I'm surprised that Lord Bairnfather didn't object.' He indicated the ashes with a slight nod of his head.

Downham stared at him for a moment down her long, straight nose. It was like being back at his hated boarding school and facing up to Matron.

'What he doesn't know can't hurt him,' she said, then took a sip of her tea that was clearly intended to signal the end of that subject. McLean let it slide; there were more important questions to answer.

'You said that Ms Slater made it clear she didn't want to be buried in the family mausoleum. Might I ask when she told you this?'

'I've known Sissy Slater almost all of her life. From the very first, she always said she wanted to be brought back to Burntwoods when she died. I suspect however that you mean to ask when last we spoke of such things.' Downham made it sound like a foreign concept, as if she were more used to communicating through telepathy, or the reading of cards. 'She called me about six months ago, I'd say. We didn't speak often, but Sissy knew she didn't have long left. She was anxious to put her affairs in order before the end. All of her affairs.'

'There was no mention of it in her will.' McLean tried to recall the salient details, buried deep in the case notes somewhere. There hadn't been any instructions for dealing with her mortal remains, but then often those sorts of things weren't covered.

'You've seen it then, I take it?' Downham's face, not exactly filled with good cheer to begin with, took on a sour look.

'It was reviewed as part of the investigation into her death. If anything had seemed amiss it would have been followed up, I'm sure.' McLean made a mental note to dig out the relevant notes and go over them himself, and damn the chief superintendent's order that the investigation be mothballed. 'Is there something about the will that we might have overlooked, Dr Downham?'

'I cannot say. I was never party to it. I only know Sissy meant to put things in order. Whether she managed or not, I have no idea, although the fact I had to personally intervene to obtain these . . .' Downham gently patted the box of ashes '. . . might suggest that she was thwarted.'

'A shame then that her end came sooner than expected, and in such a horrible fashion,' Madame Rose said.

Downham turned her imperious stare on the medium. 'Not at all, Rose. Sissy knew exactly when, where and how she would die. That was always part of her covenant. I would have thought you of all people would know that.'

Madame Rose looked suitably chastised, something McLean wasn't sure he'd ever seen before. From his brief encounter, he had already come to the conclusion that Mirriam Downham was not someone given to idle talk. She thought about what she was saying and who might hear before speaking her mind.

'Her . . . covenant?' he asked, ready to be told to mind his own business. Instead, Downham leaned forward in her seat and fixed him with a stare it would be difficult to break.

'What do you know of the persecution of witches, Detective Inspector?'

It was McLean's turn to pause before answering.

'I have to confess perhaps not as much as I should do. King James the Sixth and First had a bit of a thing for witchcraft when he came to power at the end of the sixteenth century, didn't he? Witches coming from Denmark in sieves, stuff like that? We . . . by which I mean men and the establishment . . . spent the next hundred years or so persecuting perfectly innocent women, torturing confessions out of them and burning a fair few at the stake. Think I read somewhere that in Scotland we tended to strangle the witches first before burning them, unlike down south where they like to burn them alive. Could be wrong there, though.'

Downham stared at him for a moment with those piercing black eyes that drilled right into his thoughts, her face blank until the faintest whisper of a smile ghosted across it.

'A little cold and heartless, but actually that's pretty much the gist of it. Always a power play, always the men keeping those uppity women in their place.' She paused, placed her cup and saucer on the table beside Cecily Slater's ashes. 'Those uncounted poor innocents. Tortured, murdered, butchered, and all because they had the temerity to stand up to men. To be different.'

'Is that all it takes, then? To be a witch?' It was Harrison who asked the question, although McLean had thought it. The detective sergeant was focusing on Downham with an intensity he'd not often seen in her. Something about the old lady fascinated her.

Downham's smile was like a knife slash in a bloodless face. 'Need it be more? Any woman can be a witch. Young Isobel here is well on her way. As are you, Janie Harrison.'

'I . . .'

'You serve your community selflessly, you are motivated by justice for everyone, not simply your paymasters. You have a good soul and it shines brightly. So yes, I'd say you are a witch. You could be much more, if you want to be.'

'I thought there was a wee bit more to it than that,' McLean said.

Downham laughed, an oddly bird-like trilling sound. 'Yes, of course there is. And that is the covenant Sissy entered into. The power that she contained is free now. You have seen it, even if your male eyes cannot really understand what they have seen. Soon, though, it will need someone new to sustain it. And whoever it chooses, she will become a true witch.'

A silence fell upon the room then. McLean's grandmother might have said an angel was passing overhead, even though she had no time for religion. Harrison fiddled with her phone, trying to ignore the texts that kept flashing up on the screen.

McLean considered his empty teacup, the plate from which he had eaten his delicious slice of cake. Well, two slices of cake if he was being honest. 'Is that why they killed her, then? Because she was a witch?' he asked.

'And now you begin to understand something of our eternal struggle.' Mirriam Downham gave a single, slow nod in his direction by way of acknowledgement.

'Do you know who they are? The men who killed her?'

This time the old lady shook her head once. 'If I did, I would have told the police, although there are few of your kind who would listen. Like much of Sissy's life, her death is a darkness to me, and believe me when I tell you I have tried to see.'

McLean found that he did believe her, at least that she'd tried. The rest of the talk of witches and darkness was apt for Madame Rose's parlour but not particularly helpful for his own line of work. There was one other thing he needed to ask.

'How about Tommy Fielding? You've been camped outside his conference for weeks, and Izzy here has made some fairly serious allegations about him.'

'Do I think he killed Sissy?' Downham's posture was always upright and correct, but she seemed to straighten even further as she considered the question. Even though that wasn't what McLean had meant.

'I wouldn't put it past him,' she said. 'If he knew what she truly was. I don't think there's any way you would be able to prove it, though. If I cannot see what happened, then your science and your forensics won't help you.'

McLean wanted to say that such pronouncements weren't exactly helpful, but in truth he hadn't expected much more. 'Well, for what it's worth, my science and my forensics are going to keep trying anyway. We might not find who murdered Cecily Slater, but we'll be taking a closer look at Fielding now. You have my word on that.'

Mirriam Downham stared at him for a while, her eyes dark, face unreadable. Finally she smiled, truly friendly for the first time since McLean had met her.

'I do believe you will, Detective Inspector. I do believe you will.'

48

The major incident room was empty when McLean let himself in later. Going to Cecily Slater's funeral had been important, if only to meet with the enigmatic Mirriam Downham. But it had wasted most of the day, and now an evening of paperwork beckoned. At least Em wouldn't complain about him coming home late.

A buzz in his pocket signalled the arrival of a text, and he was reminded of DS Harrison's frantic scrolling through messages as they drove from Rose's house to the police station. She'd have to get herself better sorted if she wasn't going to burn out trying to do everything for everyone. A couple more detective sergeants on the team wouldn't hurt either.

Fishing out his phone, he peered at the screen, struggling to make out the tiny letters, and to work out who it was from. The name was there, Simon Martin, but it took a while to remember who he was. The invitation to meet for a drink later was welcome, nevertheless. Even if it meant McLean would have to get stuck in to all the work he'd not done while drinking Madame Rose's tea.

One thing had come out of that conversation he could follow up straight away. It bothered McLean that he couldn't remember the name of Slater's solicitors. It would have been one of the first actions of the murder investigation to identify them and view any will the old lady might have made. If nothing of interest had turned up, that would probably explain why he'd missed it when reviewing the case.

He could have gone back to his office, but that ran the risk of bumping into the chief superintendent. Instead, Mclean settled himself down in front of one of the workstations, logged in and began searching through the system for the relevant details. It didn't take long to find, although he was disappointed to see that only a detective constable had been sent to speak to the lawyers. The name of the firm didn't ring any bells either. DCF Law weren't one of the city's old and established firms, which was a bit of a surprise given the Bairnfather connection. Bringing up another window on the workstation, he tapped the name into a browser and followed the links to the corporate website.

DCF Law worked out of a modern office block in Fountain-bridge. They seemed to specialise in corporate and family law, as far as his tired eyes could scan from the screen. He really needed to get them tested. Searching the annoying drop-down menu cunningly hidden within the company logo, he finally found what he was looking for, brought up the list of partners. And there it was.

John Donaldson, Andrew Cartwright, Thomas Fielding.

McLean clicked back to the report. DC Stringer had spoken to an associate partner by the name of Penelope Threadworth. She'd given him a copy of Cecily Slater's will, which left the entirety of her estate to her nephew. It had been drawn up in the mid eighties by Carstairs Weddell, the same firm of solicitors McLean himself used, and not updated since. There was a breakdown of Slater's assets which amounted to very little. The cottage belonged to the Bairnfather Trust, and it seemed all her bills were looked after by it too. A codicil to the will mentioned one other fact about the trust of which McLean had not been aware. Cecily had been both a trustee and a beneficiary. Her nephew, Reginald Corslaine Slater, now Lord Bairnfather, was listed as the other trustee, and presumably also beneficiary.

McLean recalled the telephone conversation he'd overheard. Tommy Fielding speaking to his friend Reggie. He knew better than to jump to conclusions; it was perfectly possible Fielding knew two Reginalds, and did work for both of them. It was a coincidence though, and McLean didn't like coincidences.

He speed-read the report of Stringer's interview with the solicitor. She seemed to have been helpful, had provided everything the detective constable had asked for, but there were tantalising gaps in the information. He needed to know more about the Bairnfather Trust for one thing. Were there any other trustees? And who would be appointed to take Slater's place? How much money was at stake here? Downham had suggested Cecily Slater was keen to put her affairs in order. And yet her will remained unchanged in over thirty years.

'Oh, Tony. It's you. Thought I saw a light on.'

Startled, McLean looked up from his workstation to see the chief superintendent standing in the doorway. So much for hiding from her. She stepped inside, letting the door swing shut as she walked towards him, an unnecessary sway to her hips. Not quite sure why, he closed down the browser window with Fielding's name on it before she could see the screen.

'I was just checking something,' he said, as if the explanation were necessary. Elmwood put a hand on his chair, fingers lightly brushing the fabric of his jacket as she leaned in close to have a look.

'I thought all the case notes had been filed for review.'

'They have. Just wanted to settle my mind on something that came up in a conversation. I went to the funeral this afternoon, got chatting. You know how it is.'

'Is that why you weren't in your office all day?' The chief

superintendent stood up, turned and perched herself on the edge of the desk, one leg raised so that her uniform skirt rode up her thigh. It was such an artless movement, McLean almost laughed. A woman half her age might have been able to pull it off, maybe.

'Yes.'

'And it wasn't something a sergeant or a constable could do? Only, I notice DS Harrison was missing all afternoon too.'

McLean looked up at the chief superintendent's face, not even trying to avoid her gaze. 'I've no idea what DS Harrison's been up to today. I thought she was working with Kirsty on something. It's not like I own her or anything.'

Elmwood raised a perfectly trimmed eyebrow. 'You know there's station gossip? About you and the young DS?'

'It's been brought to my attention. As have all manner of rumours, malicious and otherwise. I try to rise above it all.'

'And yet you persist in working closely with her.'

'I'll work with any detective worth their salt. Harrison's one of the best to come up through the ranks in a while. It'd be stupid not to use her just because of station gossip, and anyway, if I stopped now they'd all just say we'd fallen out or something. Besides, I worked with Grumpy Bob for years and nobody ever suggested we were a couple.'

Elmwood laughed so hard she slipped off the desk and had to put a hand out to steady herself. It rested on McLean's shoulder for too long before she finally took it away.

'I'm glad I didn't let them sack you, Tony. You're by far the most interesting thing in this dreadful place.' She shrugged, straightened her skirt. 'Anyway, I'm off home. Unless you fancy a drink?'

Drink. The question reminded McLean of the text from Simon Martin. 'Sorry. I almost forgot. Prior engagement. If I don't hurry I'll be late.'

★ ★ ★

McLean had almost choked when Simon Martin, ex-Metropolitan Police Detective Chief Inspector, had told him the name of his 'local'. Martin had retired to Edinburgh because his wife's family had come from the city and she had inherited a sizeable house in Newington. Martin had always been a keen golfer, so the chance of living within walking distance of a half-decent course had been more than enough reason for him to accept her suggestion they leave England and return to her home city. All this and more McLean learned in the first half-hour of their meeting at the club house of Prestonfield golf course, which also happened to be the favourite watering hole of ex-Detective Superintendent Charles Duguid.

'Not sure I've ever met him,' Martin said when McLean brought up the subject. 'Does he play here regularly?'

'Play? Not so much. I think he's more of a social member.' Although McLean couldn't think of many people less social than Duguid. Fortunately the man himself was not in the members' bar that evening. At least not yet. He couldn't help glancing up at the entrance every time the door swung open.

'I'll have to try and make his acquaintance.' Martin leaned back in his chair, pint of beer in one hand. He was a short fellow, but wiry. Like a featherweight boxer, or a junkie, McLean couldn't make up his mind which. He seemed affable enough, but they hadn't quite managed to home in on the reason for the meeting yet, and that might prove more tricky.

'So Gail made it all the way to chief super, eh?' Martin broke first. 'I guess it was always on the cards. If she didn't get herself either fired or killed, she was always going to climb to the top.'

'You don't mind talking about her?' McLean sipped from an extraordinarily expensive glass of fizzy water.

'It's been, what? Twenty years since I last spoke to her? More, I think.' Martin shook his head. 'It was a mistake, difficult time in my marriage and she exploited that. Luckily my wife is very understanding. And I got out of the job, too, which pleased her no end.'

'So the rumours about an affair were true, then?'

'Ah, you're good, McLean. I'd forgotten what it was like to be interviewed by a well-trained detective. Getting old and slow.' Martin took a long draw from his pint, wiped foam from his lips with the back of his hand. 'Yes, we had an affair. Well, more of a fling, who am I kidding? She was twenty-five and I was the wrong side of forty. What red-blooded man wouldn't, if he was offered?'

'But you think she was only interested in you as a means to furthering her own career.'

'I didn't at the time, of course. Well, maybe a bit. She's – was – very easy to be around. Good company, you know? Always knows the right thing to say. Christ, you should see her work a room full of politicians.'

'I have,' McLean said, recalling the Safe Streets Campaign. 'And I've seen her switch on the charm, too. It's like being caught in a spotlight. Disconcerting.'

'You married, McLean?' Martin leaned forward, his gaze flicking down to McLean's hand and its lack of rings.

'I was engaged once. A long time ago. She . . . died.'

'I'm sorry.'

'Don't be. Like I said, it was a long time ago. I have a partner. We've had our ups and downs, but we're working things out.'

'She know about Gail?' Martin asked.

'As in her existence, yes. There's nothing else to know, really.'

Martin took another drink, but McLean could see the old man's eyes on him the whole time. 'She must be losing her touch, then,' he said, as he placed the glass back down on the table.

'She's chief superintendent in charge of all policing in Edinburgh and the Lothians, and I'm a DI, recently knocked back from DCI for failing to follow procedure and pissing off too many politicians. There's no good reason why she should be interested in me. I can't do anything for her.'

'I don't know. Maybe she's changed. Maybe she's looking for someone to settle down and grow old with.'

'Why not Tommy Fielding, then? He's living in Edinburgh now.'

McLean had thought the name might spark a reaction, and he was right. He was wrong about the nature of that reaction, though. Far from anger, hearing the lawyer's name brought first a smile and then a burst of laughter so loud it disturbed the other drinkers and earned them both a withering glare from the barman.

'Fielding? And Gail? After what he did to her?' Martin shook his head so vigorously McLean thought his spectacles might have flown off. 'No, no, no. You've got that relationship all wrong. She despises him even more than I do, which is saying something.'

'But she—'

'Fell for exactly the same game she was playing on me. Fielding's just like her. He uses people and then throws them away when he no longer has need of them. He worked his charm on her and for once she fell for it. Maybe she thought she was playing him, but we all know that's not how it ended up, eh?'

'The laptop.'

Martin's eyes narrowed. 'You're remarkably well informed, McLean. Who've you been talking to?' He didn't wait for an answer. 'Yes, the laptop. Thing is, I didn't leave it at her place. She borrowed it, along with my password and security tag. That was a lapse on my part and I got hung out to dry for it. But if she hadn't taken it in the first place, then Fielding wouldn't have seen what was on it. He'd probably still be a failed divorce lawyer taking out his misogyny on cheated wives. And I'd have retired on a Detective Chief Super's pension and a broken marriage.'

'That case made Fielding's career? I thought he was already going places.'

'Yeah, probably. Guys like him always seem to prosper, don't they? And he was a nasty piece of work. Didn't really know what men's rights activists were back then, but that was what he was doing. Whipping up hatred for feminists, putting women "in their place".' Martin used both hands to emphasise the phrase, but didn't quite go the whole rabbit ears. 'He was clever about it. Never too brazen, and certainly not in court. But see him with a client during an interview? Christ, it made me feel dirty just being in the same room.'

'So there's no way he'd have got back in touch with Elmwood, then. For old times' sake?'

The laughter was quieter this time, but no less hollow for that. 'Neither of them would piss on the other if they were on fire. Way I heard it – and you'll understand I was out of the Met by then, working in IT in Cambridge until I retired up here – way I heard it, soon as she could, she started making life difficult for him. Payback, I guess. And the higher she climbed, the more influence she could bring. That's probably why he came back up to Scotland.'

'He must be overjoyed to hear she's our new chief super-intendent, then.'

Martin picked up his glass, drained what was left in it, then thumped a light belch out of his chest. 'I imagine he's furious. If I were her, I'd be watching my back.'

49

Janie Harrison hung her coat on the hook in the hall and bent down to unlace her boots. Kicking them off at the end of the day was one of life's little pleasures. It had been a long day too, an odd one. She still wasn't sure what had prompted her to join the boss at the old woman's funeral. A sense of duty, perhaps? A wish to apologise for their failure to catch those responsible for her death, certainly. It had been worth it in the end, though. Seeing Izzy dressed up like a proper lady was a laugh, but meeting Mirriam Downham had been something else entirely.

There was something about the woman, an inner strength maybe, that was utterly fascinating. Janie had tried to stop herself from staring, knowing it was both rude and unprofessional. But she hadn't been able to, and had hung on every word the woman had said. Even the nonsense about witches. Better not tell Manda about that, or she'd come home one day to find her flatmate had bought them both pointy hats and decorated the place with pumpkins.

A light knock at the door stopped her before she reached the kitchen. Janie peered through the peephole to see who it was, then quickly opened the door.

'Hey, Izzy. Thought you'd gone back to stay with Madame Rose.'

Izzy still wore her funereal clothes, although she'd pulled on a coat that was so large it must have belonged to the medium.

'I have. Just popped round to pick up some things. And to give you this.' She held up a bag with the logo of a very expensive local delicatessen on it. 'And this, if you can manage it.'

Izzy stepped aside to reveal a case of wine on the landing behind her. And not a cheap cardboard box either. This was one of those wooden ones with French writing stencilled on the side.

'Wow. Thank you. Thought you didn't have any money?' Janie ushered the young woman into the hall, then fetched in the case. It was reassuringly heavy and the words 'Château Pétrus' sparked a memory.

'Stuck it all on Charlotte's credit card,' Izzy said, with all the innocence of a teenager. 'Sure she won't mind. Probably won't even notice.'

Janie laughed as she grabbed the kettle. If Manda had been home already she might have been tempted by wine – although probably not the bottles Izzy had just brought – but she was parched and tea would slake her thirst without getting her drunk.

'I take it Doctor Downham's gone back to Burntwoods now,' she said, as Izzy opened up the bag and started putting things from it into the fridge.

'Yes. She and Rose don't exactly get on. I mean, they're not enemies or anything. They're civil. But you can tell neither of them particularly want to be in the same place. Like they're the wrong side of a pair of magnets, if you see what I mean.'

Janie stopped in the act of filling the kettle. 'Actually, yes. I do. That's a very good way of putting it. They both seem to have a lot of time for the boss, though.'

'He's weird, and they both love weird. Like, I never expected him to be driving around in a piddly little electric car, but he does. It's like he doesn't care what anyone thinks about him.'

'Well, you're right about the not caring bit, but not the car.

His got nicked a week or so back. That's his other half's he's just borrowed.'

'So what's he drive then? BMW, I bet.' Izzy went through the cupboards, fetching out pot, teabags, mugs, as if she had lived here all her life.

'Alfa Romeo Giulia Quadrifoglio.' Janie watched Izzy's face for any reaction. It was highly unlikely a nineteen-year-old woman would have any great interest in or knowledge of cars, but she had asked.

'Sounds a bit weird and posh. Much like your boss, I guess.'

'Well if you think that's weird, he used to drive around in a fifty-year-old classic until it got smashed up a couple of years ago.'

'Really? Like that bloke on the telly?'

'Well, it was another Alfa, not a Jag, but aye, I guess so.' Janie poured tea into two mugs, handed one over.

'Mirriam liked him, anyway. And she doesn't have much time for men.'

'You surprise me. Is she really a witch? Like, black cat as a best friend, riding around on a broomstick, pointy hat?'

Izzy giggled like a little girl. 'She looks a bit like that, but I don't think I've ever seen her with a cat, and certainly not a broomstick. That's not what witches are about, Janie. We're about balancing forces, life energy, keeping tabs on the spirits that most people don't believe in any more.'

'We?' Janie blew on her tea, took an unladylike slurp.

'Figure of speech. I stayed there a while. Burntwoods, that is. Learned a lot of stuff. Probably should have stuck at it. Would have saved my half-sister a world of trouble if I had.'

Harrison knew the story. No need to ask. She sipped her tea again, enjoying the chance to relax. Enjoying Izzy's company too. She'd miss her, even if the flat wasn't really big enough for the three of them.

The moment was spoiled as her phone buzzed in her pocket: a text. Probably Manda asking if they wanted anything picked up for supper. Janie pulled it out, thinking pizza might be good, then frowned when she saw who it was actually from. What it said.

'Something up?' Izzy asked.

'The boss. He does this. Quite often.' She tapped the screen to show the full message, read it a couple of times, then clicked the phone off and put it away again.

'Looks like something important,' Izzy said.

'Possibly. Could probably wait until morning, but I think I might go and have a quick drink. There's a bar not too far from here might be worth my while visiting.'

'Drink? But you've just made tea.' Izzy lifted her mug to prove the point.

'Aye, but it's a bit late for tea, really.' Janie went out to the hall and started pulling her boots back on. Izzy followed, fetching both their coats from the hooks.

'I should do this on my own. It's sort of police business.'

Izzy was about to say something, but the noise of a key in the lock distracted them both. The door swung open to reveal Manda Parsons fumbling with her bag. She looked at them both for a second. 'Just in or going out?'

'Janie's off to the pub,' Izzy said, and a broad smile spread across Manda's face.

'Pub? Excellent idea.'

It was just as well there was an entrance to the Walter Scott bar direct from the street. As Janie led Izzy and Manda inside, it occurred to her that Izzy's last visit had involved being taken away by uniformed police officers, so coming in through the foyer and past reception might not have been the smartest move. Even with a hat pulled down over her scrappy red hair, she was quite striking to look at and easily recognised, although the funeral clothes might throw people. Janie scanned the room quickly, spotting an empty alcove to which she shooed them both as swiftly as she could.

'Christ, I've not been in here in an age. It's fair changed a bit.' Manda paused halfway there, gawking at the decor like a tourist in the Sistine Chapel.

'Come and sit down.' Janie grabbed at her forearm and got her hand, then pulled her to her seat. 'OK. What's everyone drinking?'

Orders taken, she went to the bar, looking around to see if Tommy Fielding was about. It was a long shot, but she knew he lived across the road in one of the anonymous modern apartment blocks that had sprung up around Fountainbridge, and she knew from her conversations with some of the guests at his fathers' rights seminar that he held regular meetings here at the Scotston with smaller groups. If they were meeting tonight, then there was a chance she might see him. And then what? Ask him about Cecily Slater's will? Coming to the hotel had seemed a good idea half an hour earlier, but Janie was beginning to wonder what had come over her.

'What can I get you, love?'

The arrival of a smartly dressed bartender interrupted her thoughts. Janie reeled off the order. Pint of Stella for Manda, red wine for her and Izzy. They should all probably get something to eat too, but when the drinks arrived and she learned how much they were costing, she hastily revised her plans to ask for a bar menu.

'Make them last, OK? Need a second mortgage to drink in this place.' She put her spoils down on the table, complete with a couple of bags of crisps that should have been family sized packets given their price.

'Why'd you drag us all the way here then? There's plenty

better pubs on the way.' Manda expertly prised open the first crisp packet and folded it out so they could share.

'Wanted to see if someone was here,' Janie said, then turned her head swiftly away as Tommy Fielding came in through the door from reception. 'And it seems like he is.'

Manda stared shamelessly. 'Reckon he's a bit old for you, Janie. Dresses well, mind.'

Janie risked a look, and saw Fielding talking to the barman who had served her, ordering a round for the three men with him. She recognised one of them from the last time she'd been here. The young lad with a thing for seventies horror movies. The other two had their backs to her, but she could tell they were older and richer. More like Fielding himself.

They took their drinks to a table on the far side of the bar. Fielding sat with his back to Janie, the young lad next to him and the other two men facing her. She didn't recognise either of them, but her attention was mostly taken up by the young man anyway. His body language was fascinating. He held himself awkwardly, clearly uncomfortable in the company, but also desperate to be there. He almost clung to Fielding, hanging on the older man's every word. Standing, the young man was the taller of the two, but seated he bent his back, almost crouching down so that he could look up at the lawyer. A strange dynamic indeed.

'So what's the story with them?' Manda asked.

'The one with his back to us is Tommy Fielding,' Izzy answered before Janie could say anything. 'I think the two older guys are Anthony Swale and Jeremy Scobie. They're both lawyers and scumbags like Fielding. The young lad? No idea.'

'How on earth . . . ?'

'Know your enemy is the first rule of war, isn't it? We weren't just standing outside shouting slogans and waving signs, you know. If you'd asked, we could have given you intel on these MRA idiots that'd keep you busy for months.'

'Might just take you up on that.' Janie sipped at her wine, trying to keep herself inconspicuous while watching Fielding and his little group of sycophants.

'My round,' Manda said, her beer finished long before either Janie or Izzy had got far with their wine. She forced Janie to swap seats and headed to the bar. While she was gone, Janie watched as Fielding pulled out his phone and stared at the screen. He seemed to stiffen, then relax, before putting the phone away and saying something to his friends. They swiftly downed their drinks, got up and left, the young man hanging back until Fielding dismissed him with a wave. Then the lawyer pulled out his phone again, tapped away at the screen to send a message, and put the handset down on the table in front of him.

'Jesus wept. How can anyone afford to drink in this place? I could've got myself drunk for a week on the price of that one beer. Daylight fucking robbery.'

'It's night-time, Manda,' Izzy said.

'That just makes it worse.'

'Well, cheers anyway.' Izzy raised her glass and clinked it against Manda's. Janie barely noticed, her attention focused on Fielding. He was drumming his fingers on the table as if waiting for someone. Then he stopped, looked up at the door through to reception. A figure had just entered, and of all the people it might have been coming to meet the lawyer for an evening drink, this was the last one Janie would have guessed.

'Isn't that—?' Manda started to say, her hand beginning to point. Janie grabbed her and pulled her close in a pretend lovers' clinch, desperate that neither of them be seen as the chief superintendent walked up to a now-standing Tommy Fielding and embraced him like an old friend.

50

G ary can't understand what's going on.

He'd been to one of Fielding's meetings, same as he's done every week since he first met the lawyer. This time it had been a smaller group, but it changed week on week, he was finding that. The two other men there looked like they'd known Fielding a long time, old friends. Both of them were lawyers and both were older than him but they'd not talked down to him. Far from it. They'd shared their experiences at the hands of the biased courts and the even more biased media, and with each new revelation Gary's anger had burned brighter. When it had come to his turn, he worried that his own story of betrayal might seem pathetic, but they'd all been outraged on his behalf. One of the men, Anthony he thought his name was, had even promised to look into the lawyer who'd tricked Gary into signing that fateful document. The one that lost him his house, his child, his job and God knew what else besides.

And then everything had changed.

Some of them had gone for a drink after the meeting. More stories from the courts and the endless list of injustices done to men who were only trying to provide for their families. Gary was glad nobody asked him to buy a round. His money's almost run out and he's behind on the rent already. They were winding up anyway, but then Fielding gets a text that obviously means something. Gary can't see what it says or who it's from. Fielding tells them he needs to cut things short, and it's only when the other two get up to leave Gary realises it means he has to go too.

That's when he sees the redhead. The bitch from the protests. Sure, she's dressed herself up a bit smarter, and she's got a hat on to hide her hair, but he'd recognise her any day. She shouted in his face, accused him of being in league with paedos. That's not something you forget in a hurry. Last he heard she'd been arrested and thrown in a cell. So why's she sitting in a little alcove off the main bar along with a couple of young women who must be lezzies given how close they're sitting together? He turns back to tell Fielding, but the lawyer's on his phone and the other men have gone. It'll have to wait until tomorrow.

But it bothers him, all the same. One of the lezzies looks familiar too, though he really can't place her. Still, he knows that there's something going on, so instead of heading back to his grotty little bedsit in Gorgie and the constant whining of the landlady, he finds a corner of reception to sit and watch.

It doesn't take long for something to happen, but it's not what he was expecting. Not at all. The flunky in the ridiculous uniform hurries to the front door, pulls it open just in time for someone to come in. Instinctively, Gary tries to hide, make himself invisible, even though the woman who has just entered has never seen him before. He's seen her, though. On the news, in the papers, and in photographs Fielding's shared with him and the others. This is the queen bitch, the one who runs the cops in Edinburgh. The cops who arrested him for assault when all he'd done was give Bella the slap she deserved for nagging him to go change Wee Mary. Fielding's told him all about her, the things she did to him in London, the way she screwed her way to the top of the police and the men she shat on, careers she destroyed, on her way up. He hates everything about her.

So why is she coming to see him? Why here? Why now?

From where he sits, Gary has a good view through the open door to the bar and Fielding's table. He can even see the little alcove across the room where that redhead bitch is chatting with her lezzie friends. That's when it hits him where he's seen the other one before. Here. In this bar. With that giant bastard who was so tall he had to stoop through the doorway. She's a cop, for fuck's sake. Not locking the bitch up in a cell but taking her out for a drink.

Gary's anger is burning bright now. He's on his feet, striding across the reception area towards the bar, ready to defend Fielding when the police corner him or try to arrest him. But they don't do that.

The one on the far side of the bar looks like she's snogging her girlfriend, but Gary's not so easily fooled. She's hiding from her boss, using the clinch to stop herself from being recognised like Captain America and Scarlett Johansson in that movie. It stops him in his tracks, and just in time too. The senior cop, the top bitch, sees Fielding at the same time as the lawyer spots her standing just inside the bar. Gary's expecting angry faces, arguments. What he gets is Fielding standing up swiftly and embracing the woman like an old friend.

Like a lover.

They chat briefly, and then Fielding's grabbing his coat from the back of the seat. Gary's almost caught out, but he ducks down the little corridor that leads to the gents as the two of them walk out arm in arm. They're so engrossed in each other, they barely notice the doorman opening the door and wishing them a good evening. And they certainly don't see Gary as he darts out behind them to follow.

They don't go far, just a couple of hundred metres down the road to where one of the new glass-walled apartment blocks glows in the night. Fielding taps at the keypad beside the door, the lock buzzes, and the two of them go inside. Only one reason Gary can think of for them to do that, and it makes no sense.

He hears footsteps on the pavement and shrinks into the shadows, unnoticed as the three women walk swiftly by, chattering away. They carry on down the road until the next set of traffic lights, cross, and make their way back along the other side. When they reach the apartment block, the one who's a cop pulls out her phone and plays with it for a while. They're arguing, but from where he is, Gary can't hear what they're saying. Then they set off again, back towards the Lothian Road.

He watches them go, then stares up at the building. It's impossible to see into any of the apartments from where he stands, and he's no idea which one is Fielding's anyway. They've always met at the hotel.

It's cold out, a fine drizzle working its way through his coat and deep into his bones, and yet he can't stop staring up at the apartments. Out here is slightly less miserable than going home. Fucking damp little shithole's not his home anyway. His home was taken from him and these fuckers pretended to care.

How long he seethes, Gary doesn't know. The anger keeps him warm even as the smir slicks his hair to his head and drips begin to fall from the tip of his nose. And then the front door clicks open. She steps out, the woman, the copper, the witch. She looks one way, then the other, as if expecting someone to come and pick her up. Then with a little shrug, she heads in the same direction the three other women went.

In his mind, Gary rushes across the road and confronts her. Or he makes it to the door before it has swung shut, gets his foot in it at the last moment, goes up to Fielding's apartment and has it out with him. Only he doesn't know which one is Fielding's apartment, and the door has already closed. The woman's too far away to catch up with too.

Miserable, angry, not even enough spare change to catch a bus, Gary hunches his shoulders against the rain and slouches off towards Gorgie.

51

Early morning, and McLean was surprised to see the major incident room fairly bustling with activity. For a moment he thought that maybe some well-hidden clue had been unearthed and the investigation into Cecily Slater's murder had gained new impetus. Then he noticed that a couple of IT technicians were unplugging computers and rolling up lengths of cable. An admin support officer was carefully wiping names and other unwanted comments off the whiteboards. Files were being packaged into boxes, ready to be shipped down to the basement and Grumpy Bob's tender mercies. Everything was winding down.

'Have you seen DS Harrison?' he asked the first uniformed constable to come within range. He knew the detective sergeant's shift had already begun, but she hadn't been in the CID room either.

'Think she went out with the new DCI, sir. Not sure where.'

McLean thanked the constable, cursing inwardly. He'd texted Harrison the night before to tell her about the connection between Fielding and Slater, or at least Fielding's law firm and Slater. He'd hoped to have her set up a meeting with the other partners, but he couldn't really complain if Kirsty had nabbed her before he got in. He remembered when Ritchie had first turned up in Edinburgh, a fresh-faced young detective sergeant looking to break out of the goldfish bowl of Aberdeen. He'd been her superior then, and now she was the one giving orders. Other officers might feel aggrieved at that, but somehow he found he didn't really care.

The door clicked open and a tired-looking DC Stringer shuffled in, scratching a thoughtless armpit. He looked like he'd overslept and not taken the proper time or care to dress himself before rushing to work. It didn't matter for what McLean wanted done.

'Morning, Constable,' he said, getting the startled reaction he'd hoped for.

'Oh. Morning, sir. Late one last night and I slept right through the alarm.'

'Boozing with your mates, was it?'

Stringer gave him a slightly shocked, slightly astonished look. 'Don't drink, sir. But I was with my mates, right enough. We were playing *D&D* and lost track of time. I'll make it up at shift end.'

'Don't worry. I wouldn't want to come between a Paladin and his campaign. You can make it up by sorting us a pool car. I need to head out to Bairnfather Hall Hotel and have a word with His Lordship.'

Stringer stared a little longer than was perhaps necessary, eyes a little wide before he pulled himself together. 'On it, sir. You want me to give you a call when it's ready?'

McLean checked his watch, wondering how many other senior officers were in already. 'Give me half an hour. I'll meet you in the CID room.'

'His Lordship is not receiving any visitors at the moment. Did you make an appointment?'

Apart from a little more discussion of Dungeons and Dragons than he'd perhaps wanted, the journey out to Bairnfather Hall had been uneventful and swift. A pity the same could not be said for their reception, once McLean had presented himself to the day manager and then passed on to Lord Bairnfather's personal assistant.

'Perhaps you could tell him that it concerns the murder of his aunt, Lady Cecily. I have new information about the case that he might want to hear.'

McLean hadn't met the personal assistant before. This new barrier between him and what he wanted was a young woman in an unflattering business suit who had yet to give him her name. She wore her hair tied up in an intricate knot high on the back of her head, and stared at the world through a pair of rimless spectacles, all the while maintaining a look on her face of horrified disgust at what she was seeing.

'His Lordship does not like to be disturbed whilst taking his breakfast,' she said. 'Perhaps if you could come back later?'

McLean took a deep breath, held it a moment, then let it out again slowly. 'Or I could ask him to accompany me to the station for a more formal interview.'

The personal assistant held his gaze for just long enough to let him know that she wasn't intimidated by him. Then she nodded minimally.

'Come. I will inform him you are here.' She turned away and strode off towards a door marked 'Private: Staff Only'. McLean raised his eyebrows at DC Stringer, then the two of them followed.

Through the door was every bit as opulent as the part of the hotel frequented by paying guests, which made McLean think this was the Bairnfather family's private suites rather than the route to the kitchens and staff quarters. The personal assistant walked with the same brusque efficiency she showed in all her movements, and by the time they had caught up with her, she was knocking at an unmarked door. If a command to enter came,

McLean didn't hear it, but the woman pushed on through all the same, ushering them into a large room dominated by a vast dining table. Silver domes covered plates of food, enough to feed a small army if they weren't merely for decoration.

'What is it, Ashley? Can't you see I'm eating?'

The voice came from the far end of the table, but the view of Lord Bairnfather was obscured by an arrangement of quite spectacularly vulgar flowers and several enormous silver candlesticks. As he followed the personal assistant down one side of the table, McLean finally saw the man himself, sitting in a large chair at the end. He had a napkin tucked into his collar, the starched white cotton already pocked with stains from his breakfast.

'I'm sorry to disturb you, Your Lordship. It's the police. About Lady Cecily.'

Bairnfather scowled at the woman, but his face darkening when he saw McLean. He dabbed at his lips with the napkin and then beckoned him forward.

'Detective Inspector. What an unexpected surprise.' He stared past McLean at DC Stringer. 'Not got the tall chappie with you today?'

'Detective Constable Blane is taking some time off for paternity leave, Your Lordship. This is his colleague, DC Stringer. I'm sorry to disturb your breakfast. Most important meal of the day, I know. But some things have come to light that need swift attention, and I thought it best to come straight over rather than waste time going through channels.'

Bairnfather grunted something unintelligible through a mouthful of food, then spoke before he had swallowed. 'Heard that about you, McLean. Gail said you could be a bit terrier-like when you smell a rat. Have a seat. I'm sure Ashley will get you a coffee. Then you can ask me whatever it is you need to know.'

'Actually, this won't take a moment. It concerns the

Bairnfather Trust. I understand you and your aunt were both trustees and beneficiaries.'

Bairnfather had lifted a fork of what looked like very fine kedgeree to his mouth, ready to eat, but he placed it back down on the plate carefully, then dabbed at his lips with his soiled napkin again. All the while he fixed McLean with a far more calculating look than before.

'What's this about, McLean?'

'Just clearing a few things up, that's all. I was wondering who would succeed your aunt as trustee now. Tommy Fielding perhaps?'

Bairnfather's face went as white as the non-stained parts of his napkin. 'I really don't know what you mean, Detective Inspector.'

'You do know Tommy Fielding, though. Has an annoying habit of calling you Reggie on the phone? Senior partner at DCF Law? They looked after your aunt's legal affairs, didn't they? Do you know when she switched from using Carstairs Weddell? Old established law firm like that must have been sad to see a client like her go.'

The colour seeped back into Bairnfather's cheeks in odd splotches. He ripped his napkin away and flung it on the table like a petulant child. 'I'm not sure I like your tone, Inspector. Coming into my house and throwing accusations around like that.'

'I'm sorry. I wasn't aware that I'd made any accusations.' McLean turned to DC Stringer, standing at the far end of the table. 'Did I make any accusations, Constable?'

It was unfair, dragging the young lad in like that. He was clearly uncomfortable in this setting.

'Get out, McLean. I've had quite enough of your baseless insinuation. Bad enough that Sissy's dead and you've utterly failed to find out who's responsible.' Bairnfather's petulant child imitation had taken on a desperate edge now. He struggled to push the heavy wooden chair back, and when he stood with his hands pressed knuckle down to the wooden tabletop he wasn't a great deal taller than when he'd been seated. McLean knew he wasn't going to get anything more from him, though. It didn't matter; what he had learned was more than enough.

'We'll not waste any more of your time, Lord Bairnfather. Thank you for your help.' He turned to where the nervous personal assistant, Ashley, stood stock-still but for her fidgeting hands. 'We'll see ourselves out.'

'Be sure that you do,' Bairnfather yelled. 'And you can be sure I'll be speaking to the chief constable about this. I'll have your job, you know.'

McLean paused at the door, but only for a moment. And when he muttered, 'You're welcome to it', it was quiet enough that only he could hear.

The drive back to the station took a little longer than getting out had done, mostly because they hadn't spent long enough at Bairnfather Hall Hotel for the rush hour traffic to subside. There were routes into the city where it never really did any more. McLean tried to call DS Harrison while DC Stringer drove, but her phone went straight to voicemail. He pinged her a text instead, then settled back in his seat as they inched slowly along the Gorgie Road.

'What was that all about, sir?' DC Stringer asked after they'd been silent in the car for a good twenty minutes.

'Lord Bairnfather?' McLean realised that it was the first time the detective constable had met the aristocrat, and given Stringer's background it had probably seemed rather strange. 'First time I spoke to him, he came across rather differently. He's extremely rich, very well connected, and he gave the impression he was distraught at his aunt's death. Nothing we turned up in the initial investigation suggested he was in any way involved. He had very little to gain and a lot to lose from her murder. Least, that's what we thought. Turns out it's not quite as straightforward as that.'

'How so?' Stringer asked, then swore as a car swung out of a turning into the flow of traffic in front of him without warning. McLean braced himself against the dashboard with one hand.

'For starters, he's using Tommy Fielding as his personal and business lawyer. Nothing wrong with that on the face of it, but it's a coincidence and I'm not overly keen on those. There's also the Bairnfather Trust itself. I don't know the full details, really need Lofty to look into that, but it was set up originally to avoid death duties on that massive pile of a house and the estates surrounding it. Lots of old families have done the same down the years, I'm not going to argue the morality of it. All I know is that the trust is extremely wealthy. It owns the hall, not Lord Bairnfather. It also owns the Scotston Hotel in Fountainbridge, and I dare say a great deal else as well. Two people controlled how that money was invested, Cecily Slater and Lord Reggie there. As long as they both agreed, then everything's fine. But if old Cecily decided she didn't like the way things were going? I'd say that was starting to look like motive.'

'You think he'd kill his own aunt?' Stringer asked.

'Not with his own hands, no. And not without cast-iron deniability either. Men like him don't make that kind of mistake. And think about the murder. Cecily Slater was beaten almost unconscious before having petrol poured on her and being set alight. That's rage at work, not some hired hit man.'

'Which goes against what you're saying then, doesn't it?' Stringer said, then added 'Sir,' for good measure in case he'd overstepped his authority.

'On the face of it, yes. Slater's murder being so brutal makes it seem unplanned. Spur of the moment. Except that she was an old lady who lived on her own in a cottage in the middle of the woods. She barely interacted with anyone, so it's hardly likely she'd have pissed someone off enough for them to track her down, beat her up and burn her to death. There had to be a reason she was chosen, same as there had to be a reason for the violence used against her.'

Stringer shook his head slightly. 'I don't understand where you're going, sir.'

'OK. Bear with me here. This is wild speculation based on a few things I've heard recently. Someone's been stirring up men's rights activists. Radicalising them, forming them into a loose army of angry men all nursing a grudge against women. You know what an incel is, right?'

Stringer nodded slowly. 'Aye. Involuntary Celibate. What we used to call Billy No-Mates. Like those nutters in the States who go and shoot up nightclubs and schools and stuff.'

'The same. I reckon it was a bunch of them who killed Cecily Slater. It would have been the final part of their indoctrination. A rite of passage if you like. Once your anger's been stoked that high, once you're that committed, there's no turning back. You'll do anything for your cause.'

'Makes a sick kind of sense, I guess.' Stringer sounded like he was having a hard time getting his head around the idea, which McLean took as a positive sign.

'The thing is, though, why her? And why now? You might argue that she was an easy target, but she was also unknown to almost everyone. Look how hard we've tried to build a background on her. Weeks of work and we've virtually nothing. So how did our incels know about her?'

'And you think it's to do with Lord Muck there? His trust fund?'

McLean shrugged as Stringer eased the pool car into the station car park and alongside Emma's little Renault ZOE, still sipping electricity from its charging point. 'It's all very circumstantial and tenuous right now, but it's the best we've got.'

'Isn't the whole case meant to be going to review and then to the archives anyway?'

'Aye, it is. And I'm not happy about that. Seems hasty. Pressure from high up to sweep everything under the carpet. And you'd think Lord Bairnfather might be upset that we've not found his dear aunt's killers, but I get the impression he'd be happier if the whole thing went away too.'

McLean climbed out of the car, shivering at the change from the warm interior to the bitter chill wind that whistled around the high walls of the building. He had almost reached the back door, hurrying to get out of the cold, when his phone started buzzing away in his pocket. He pulled it out, saw Harrison's name. Juggling with screen and security keypad, he almost dropped the phone on to the concrete steps, but managed to catch it and slap it to his ear as he pulled open the door.

'McLean,' he said, somewhat unnecessarily.

'Sir. Harrison here. Are you anywhere near the station?'

'Just heading up the stairs to my office now. Did you get my message about setting up a meeting with Fielding's law firm?'

'Aye, sir. About that. You might want to hold off on it for a wee while.'

McLean looked behind him to see DC Stringer push through the door. He was staring at the screen of his own phone, frowning. 'Why? What's happened?'

'It's Fielding, sir. He's dead.'

52

McLean had Stringer drive him back across town to Fielding's address, which was just as well since there was nowhere to park anywhere nearby. A forensics van, a couple of squad cars and Angus Cadwallader's British Racing Green Jaguar were parked on a double yellow line outside the soulless modern glass-walled apartment block, and a pair of uniformed constables were busy diverting pedestrians from the front door.

'Morning, sir. It's the third floor you'll be wanting,' one of the constables said to him before he could even present his warrant card. He struggled to remember her name, even though he knew she was friends with Harrison. Settled for a nod of the head and 'thanks', before going inside.

The ground floor of the building was given over to high-end retail space, on one side an expensive office furniture showroom, on the other what McLean would have called a barber's shop, except that it seemed far too clinical and modern for that. Both had their own entrances, leaving a wide foyer for the residents to access their apartments on the upper floors. At the far end, windows looked out on to a small plaza hemmed in by more tall glass buildings. A door with a security keypad beside it opened on to stairs, and opposite that another door was marked 'Security'. McLean tried the handle, but it was locked. He thumbed the button to call down the lift, but before it arrived, the door to the stairwell clicked open and DS Harrison appeared.

'Jay told me he'd dropped you off, sir.' She held the door open for him. 'We're keeping the place locked down for the moment. At least until the pathologist's had a chance to see whether it's suspicious or not.'

'How is it not suspicious?' McLean asked. 'He's dead, didn't you say?'

Harrison half shrugged, half shook her head. 'It's . . . weird, sir. And there's more. She . . .' She stopped talking as a paramedic came down the stairs towards them. 'Best if I tell you after you've seen.'

'How was he found? I didn't think there was a Mrs Fielding.'

'There's no',' Harrison said. 'But he has a cleaner come in every morning after he's gone to work. She'd already done most of the flat before she found him in the bedroom.'

'That's going to please forensics if it comes to it. Nothing like a nice, freshly cleaned crime scene to work with. The cleaner still here?'

Harrison shook her head. 'She took a bit of a turn. Kirsty— DCI Ritchie said to send her home with a constable after I'd spoken to her. We'll follow it up once the doctor's given her the OK.'

'Is Ritchie in charge then?'

'Aye, sir. She's upstairs wi' the pathologist. Think they're waiting for you to show up, actually.'

Intrigued, McLean followed the detective sergeant up the next two flights of stairs and out on to a wide hallway. There were only two apartments on this level, Fielding's being the one with its door wide and a couple of uniformed officers standing outside. One of them held a clipboard, and the other handed him some paper overshoes and a pair of latex gloves 'just to be on the safe side'.

'I'll wait out here, sir,' Harrison said as McLean signed himself in. He pulled on the overshoes and snapped on the gloves, glad not to have to go for the full paper overalls, hood and mask. Then with a last glance over the hallway, he stepped inside.

From his encounters with the lawyer before, McLean had come away with the impression of a man who spent money to show that he had it, rather than from any innate sense of taste. The apartment only served to reinforce that appraisal. It was expensive, largely open-plan and filled with sleek, modernist furnishings that were a vulgar expression of wealth over comfort. The wall opposite the entrance was glass from floor to ceiling, looking out on to the street through vertical blinds. Across the road, an old church stood empty, its windows boarded up, its walls scrawled with graffiti. From this height, he could see down into the remains of a graveyard, which perhaps wasn't the nicest of views, but at least meant the neighbours were quiet.

Noises from an open door reminded him of why he was here. McLean turned slowly, taking in the room, looking for anything that might have been out of place. Then he remembered that the cleaner had already been through this main space, so it was unlikely there would be any clues to be found. It certainly looked like a room that nobody really lived in.

The bedroom would have been large by modern city apartment standards, but with several people in it including the deceased, it felt small. Sharing the same glass wall as the main room, the blinds on this side of the divider had been closed, leaving only the light from an overhead fitting and a couple of bedside lamps. All attention was on the king size bed and the figure lying sprawled on it. As McLean took in the scene, it wasn't hard to understand why.

Tommy Fielding lay naked on top of his sheets, one hand spread limply over his crotch, as if covering his modesty even in death. The other hand reached up behind his head, where a silk tie had been fastened round his neck, then looped over the bed frame, the free end draped over his half-curled fingers. His dead eyes stared at the ceiling.

'Well that's not exactly how I imagined starting my day,' McLean said. All eyes turned towards him, except for the pathologist, who was bending over the body, peering at Fielding's head.

'You got the message then, Tony.' DCI Ritchie stood on the other side of the bed, arms folded, face sombre.

'Aye, I was out talking to this one's boss.' He nodded at the body. 'Was going to be speaking with him next, but I guess that's not happening now. What's the story? He do this to himself?'

Cadwallader stood upright with a great deal of groaning, then turned slowly to face McLean. 'Hard to say without having a more detailed look at him in the mortuary. Certainly looks like a bit of auto-erotic asphyxiation gone wrong. I think Kirsty has other ideas, though.'

McLean looked to the DCI for clarification. 'How so?'

'There's just a couple of problems. Here.' Ritchie led him to a half-open door, beyond which was an en-suite bathroom. The large mirror above the basin was clear until she reached a latex-gloved hand for the tap and turned it on. Steam billowed up from the scalding hot water, misting the glass and revealing letters, words.

'. . . ying breath I cur . . .' McLean turned his head to one side as if that would make more of the message readable.

'With my dying breath I curse thee.' Ritchie switched off the tap. 'Don't want to upset the forensic techs any more than necessary. We'll get them to analyse that. Maybe pull some prints from the glass.'

'You said a couple of problems. I take it that's only one of them, then.'

'Aye, and not the worst.' Ritchie gave a nod of her head to indicate they leave the room. 'Come on. I'll fill you in.'

McLean followed Ritchie out through the bedroom, casting one last glance at Fielding as he went. The words on the mirror could have been a sick joke for all he knew, more than likely a misdirection. But something about them struck a chord, as did the fact that Fielding, like his three associates Whitaker, Purefoy and Galloway, had died in what appeared to be an unlikely and unfortunate accident. He didn't like coincidences at the best of times, but four deaths went far beyond that.

He wanted to ask who had found the message and how, but Ritchie led him to the far end of the apartment's main open-plan living space before he could speak. Fielding's work area was sparsely furnished around a modern steel and glass desk and a chair that looked like it couldn't possibly be comfortable to sit in. A slim laptop computer lay open on the desk, a few reports and printouts beside it. Fielding's briefcase sat on the floor, open, and McLean could well imagine this was an area the cleaner might have been told to leave alone. Either that, or the lawyer would normally have packed all this stuff away and taken it with him to work. If he'd not been dead, and all.

'What's going on here, Kirsty? Why's nobody want to talk in front of civilians?' McLean tapped a latex-gloved finger on the desk, partly distracted by the names printed on the report folders.

'Fielding did have a visitor last night. But it's complicated.'

'Complicated how? Why haven't they been brought in for questioning already?'

Ritchie gave him a look far more old-fashioned than her years. 'Because his visitor was Gail, Tony.'

'Gail? Wait. Gail Elmwood?' McLean asked the question even though he knew it was stupid.

'I know. It's mad, right? But they were seen. The two of them came back here last night. Together.'

'But she hates him.'

That got him a raised eyebrow, or what passed for an eyebrow on Ritchie's face. She'd lost both of them rescuing him from a fire several years ago and they'd never really grown back afterwards.

'Hates him? Who have you been talking to?'

McLean gave her the briefest of rundowns on what he'd found out, first from Dalgliesh and then from Simon Martin. 'Of course, it might all be bollocks, and I can't believe she'd have got the job in the first place if she was as corrupt as some folk think. Martin's got an axe to grind, even if he says it's all water under the bridge. It's fair to say she's known Tommy Fielding a long time, though. Now you're telling me they met last night and that's him dead. Does she know?'

'That's the million-dollar question now, isn't it, Tony?' Ritchie ran a weary hand over her short-cropped hair, let out a sigh. 'I'll have to speak to her. Or maybe ask Jayne to.'

McLean nodded his understanding. As long as it wasn't him breaking the news. He glanced down at the reports on the desk.

'I'll speak to his colleagues, will I?' He remembered to phrase it as a question to his DCI, reaching out and picking up the top folder as he spoke. Someone was going to have to take on Fielding's caseload anyway.

'Aye, might as well. Let's get an idea of what he was doing in the past forty-eight hours.' Ritchie smacked herself on the forehead with the heel of one hand. 'Fuck, he's mates with the chief constable, isn't he? We're going to have to make sure this is done absolutely perfectly.'

McLean only half noticed. The writing on the front of the second folder had been obscured until he'd picked up the first, but now he could read it quite plainly. A name that was almost too convenient to have been left here by accident.

Cecily Slater.

By the time he made it back down to the ground floor of the building, the door to the security room was slightly ajar and light shone from within. McLean tapped on the wood, before sticking his head through the gap to find DS Harrison and an elderly gentleman in the ill-fitting uniform of a private security firm. The detective sergeant stood while the man was seated, both looking at a couple of flat-screen monitors showing security camera footage.

'Anything interesting?' he asked as Harrison looked around to see him.

'Aye, sir. Harry here was just making a copy for us.'

The elderly security guard twisted in his seat, greeted McLean with a smile and a nod, then went back to what he'd been doing.

'It helped that your lovely colleague here knew what time Mr Fielding and his friend left the Scotston Hotel.' The guard tapped a couple of buttons and the right-hand screen flickered to reveal an image of the lobby, a timestamp in the corner ticking up from half past nine the night before. It didn't take long before the image showed the front door swing open and two people walk in. If he hadn't been able to see their faces, McLean might not have believed that it was the same Tommy Fielding and Gail Elmwood he had heard such lurid tales about. They clung to each other like teenage lovers, almost stumbling to the lift and chatting animatedly as they waited for it to arrive.

'Nothing much happens for about an hour.' Harry the guard tapped the keys again, the only thing on the screen that changed being the timestamp. After a moment, the lift door opened and Elmwood stepped out alone. She paused for long enough to straighten her jacket and roll her shoulders, then walked to the door and out of the building.

'Is that the only camera? There's nothing on the landing upstairs?' McLean asked.

'Oh, aye. I'll put that up next, but it's much the same thing.' Harry the guard tapped his keyboard with two crooked arthritic fingers. The screen jumped, this time showing the wide corridor that served the two flats on the third floor. McLean watched as the couple went to Fielding's front door, and then inside.

'Again, there's nothing happens until about an hour later.' Harry tapped and the screen jumped once more. A couple of seconds, and Fielding's door opened. Elmwood stepped out, pulled the door closed behind her without looking back, and headed for the lift. It must have still been sitting at the third floor as she barely had to wait at all before it opened and she stepped inside.

'Well, at least we know what time she left. And he didn't wave her off or anything.' McLean stared at the screen, the scene unchanging save for the slow ticking timestamp in the corner. 'What about the other flat on that floor? Nobody come and go last night? Have we spoken to them?'

Harry tapped his keyboard a final time, reached forward and plucked a memory stick from the slim box underneath the screens. As he handed it over, McLean noticed it bore the same logo as the one on his uniform.

'Nobody there just now, sir. Terrible story, it was. Young lad, nice chap but more money than sense. Seems he lost control of his car up the road there.' Harry the guard nodded his head in the vague direction of the Lothian Road and Tollcross. 'Such a terrible waste.'

53

'News coming in of the death of leading lawyer and men's rights activist Tommy Fielding . . .'

Gary stares at the screen, mouth open in disbelief. It's got so bad now he hardly gets up before ten in the morning, slouches about in his boxers and a hoodie against the cold. Can't afford much heating, can't afford anything better to watch than the crappy little screen on his knackered old laptop. At least the neighbour's too stupid to put a password on their Wi-Fi, otherwise he'd not even have that. Clicked on the news and this was the first thing he saw.

'. . . Senior partner of DCF Law, Fielding was apparently found dead in his Fountainbridge apartment by a cleaning lady early this morning. Police have yet to issue a statement other than to confirm the death and that they are looking into it . . .'

Fuck. He was there. Just last night. He sat with Fielding and his two lawyer mates in the bar. Drank with them. And then that bitch came along and ruined it all. No. Not just her. There were others. All those polis bitches spying on him, spying on Fielding. Waiting 'til he was alone and they could fuck him over. Just like Bella fucked him over. Like all those women thinking they were better than him, better than all of them.

'. . . Colourful and controversial career, first in London, where he came to prominence following . . .'

Gary shuts off the noise by closing the laptop lid. He doesn't want to know. Doesn't need to know anything about Fielding's past. The lawyer was there when it mattered. He was helping. Going to get Gary back with his wee girl. Get him his job back too. Now that's all gone to fuck and they did it. Those witches killed Gary's hope. Killed him. She killed him.

'So what are you going to do about it?'

Gary should be surprised. He's alone in this pokey wee one-room flat. Hasn't had any visitors since Bazza helped him move in. Only the wart-faced old witch of a landlady constantly pestering him for rent. Well fuck her. Only, not fuck fuck her. That'd be gross. She's like, eighty or something. And hideous.

Gary shakes away the thought, looks around. There's nobody here, and not exactly anywhere they could hide anyways. He can even see into the wee shower cubicle toilet space that's probably not health and safety compliant. He's left the door open because otherwise the smell gets so bad you can hardly breathe in there. Better to let it out, isn't that what Bazza always used to say?

'You just going to sit here moping, Gary?'

The voice is in his head, but it sounds like Tommy Fielding. Well, not exactly like Tommy Fielding. It's like the way the lawyer used to speak to him, only with a different accent.

'Tommy's no use to me any more, Gary. He let them in and they destroyed him.'

'Let them in? Who's them?' Gary speaks the words out loud, even though there's nobody to hear him.

'The witches, Gary. The evil hags who sold their souls to the devil. Fornicated with him in exchange for ungodly power over men. You know who I am talking about.'

And Gary does. The young redhead screaming at him, calling

him disgusting names. The queer pair in the pub, one a cop, the other who the fuck knows? And the queen bitch, head of the polis.

'Yes. Her. She's the one you need to focus on, Gary. The one you need to destroy.'

'I . . . Destroy?'

'Would you let her get away with it? With everything she has done? Her and all the others?'

With the words come images, feelings, sensations. Gary sees Bella holding a wailing Mary, body turned away from him as if he's some kind of monster. Bella's poisonous lies already infecting Mary's innocent soul. He sees a woman he's never met before but instinctively knows is Jim's wife, the woman who took his twin daughters from him and persuaded the judge their father was a child molester. He sees other women and knows who they are, what they have done, the scheming, the lies and injustice. They stand in rows, their numbers swelling, all scream-ing at him like the protesters at the meeting. All baying for his blood. And in that moment he knows that they are a cancer growing in the heart of good society. They are not women, but witches. An evil abomination that must be swept from the face of the earth lest good men like him drown in their terrible filth.

There is no rumble of thunder. No drum roll or magic explo-sion. There is only Gary, but changed. Something has opened his eyes to how things really are. Without another thought, he stands, turns and walks out of the shithole that is all the witches have left him. He knows what needs to be done.

54

'How is it we didn't know that the young loon who stole my car lived in the same apartment block as Tommy Fielding? The same bloody floor.'

McLean stood in Detective Superintendent McIntyre's office, back to the window wall and the grey winter skies outside. For once the office door was closed, the only officers present him, McIntyre, DCI Ritchie and DS Harrison. They'd seen Fielding's body off to the mortuary an hour earlier, Cadwallader promising he'd get to it as soon as was practicable and let them know the outcome. His initial estimate of time of death, given as grudgingly as ever, had been sometime around midnight, which took a bit of the heat off Elmwood, but not all of it.

'We haven't been watching Tommy Fielding, Tony. He's not been part of any investigation until you suddenly started taking an interest.' McIntyre sat at her desk, leaning back until her head almost touched the wall. 'I'm still not entirely sure why you did that anyway.'

McLean looked to Harrison for back-up, then realised that was unfair. 'We should have been watching him, though. We should have interviewed him and the other partners in his law firm the moment we knew they were handling Cecily Slater's affairs. He had her file in his apartment.'

'Which you'll get to look at in due course, Tony.' McIntyre was annoyingly calm where McLean felt agitated. Something was about to break, he could feel it. Even if he couldn't say what, or how he knew.

'The more important question right now is what we're going to do about the chief superintendent.' Ritchie sat at the conference table, Harrison next to her. McLean knew he should take a seat too, try to calm down and look at the situation rationally. For some reason he was finding that hard to do right now.

'Where is she now?' he asked.

'Gartcosh, sweet-talking our friends in the NCA. She's not due back until late afternoon, so we've a bit of time to work out our strategy.' McIntyre stood up, crossed the room to the conference table and pulled out a chair. 'Sit down, Tony. You're looming. If you start pacing, I'll start calling you Dagwood.'

McLean smiled, even though the jibe stung, and did as he was told. Only once the four of them were seated did the detective superintendent speak again.

'The way I see it, we've a suspicious death on our hands, and the last person to see the deceased alive was our own station chief. Is that right?'

'Fielding's death might not be suspicious,' Ritchie said. 'And I'm sure Gail's got a perfectly good explanation for her visit last night. She was only there for an hour.'

McLean held his tongue. He knew that Elmwood had treated Kirsty well. Apart from her strange obsession with him, the chief superintendent had treated pretty much everyone in the station well. Now wasn't the time to wade in with accusations.

'There's still the matter of his connection to Cecily Slater.' Harrison filled the silence that had followed Ritchie's input, and McLean was pleased to see that the detective sergeant felt confident enough to do so. He'd not have had the nerve when he was her age. But back then chances were none of the officers in this room would have been women, and the air would likely have been filled with cigarette smoke too. Small changes, but none of them for the worse.

'What are you smiling about, Tony?' McIntyre's voice cut through his wandering thoughts.

'Sorry, Jayne. Just thought of something from way back. Not relevant.'

'Well concentrate on the matter in hand. You can start by explaining to me exactly what the connection is between your dead woman in the gamekeeper's cottage and Tommy Fielding.'

Where to start? 'We know his law firm were dealing with all her legal matters,' he said. 'They held her will. Unchanged, apparently, since it was drawn up by Carstairs Weddell in 1984, after her brother died. Given that Carstairs Weddell are still one of the top law firms in the city, especially when it comes to dealing with families like the Bairnfathers, it strikes me as a bit strange Cecily Slater would have taken her business away from them.'

'Who were the beneficiaries of the will?' McIntyre asked.

'Just her nephew. Lord Reginald. And since she never nominated a successor, he gets to decide who's appointed to her post on the board of the Bairnfather Trust, too. My guess is he was going to get Fielding to do it.' McLean clasped his hands together, wished he had more information and less speculation. 'I think this all comes down to money. It usually does.'

McIntyre raised an eyebrow at that, but nobody said anything so McLean carried on.

'I don't begin to understand how these things work – I'd need Lofty to look into that and I'm not about to bother him just now. But the fact is that Lord Bairnfather stands to take control of the trust that manages the family estate. I don't think he particularly needs the money, but his aunt's veto on what the trust could and couldn't do? What if she were about to pass that on to someone else? Someone her nephew couldn't control?'

'Mirriam Downham.' Harrison made it a statement, not a question, but then she looked straight at McLean with an expression that confirmed his suspicion she'd make a good detective chief superintendent one day. 'Is that not quite a leap?' She paused and then added: 'Sir?'

McLean almost laughed. 'Complete speculation, but we've got nothing else to explain why she was killed. We know she had told Downham she was going to put her affairs in order. And yet the will provided to us by DCF Law is more than thirty years old.'

'So, what?' McIntyre asked. 'You think Fielding saw what she was doing and told Lord Bairnfather? Destroyed her latest will, knowing that his firm had the earlier one still on file? Set a bunch of violent thugs on her before she could do anything about it?'

'Well, that was what I was going to ask him. In a roundabout way. Not going to be able to do that now, but I'd still like to talk to the other partners in his law firm, and I need to see those folders he had on his desk.'

McIntyre rubbed the weariness from her eyes, then looked around the group, taking her time to come to a decision. 'OK, Tony. You go speak to the lawyers. Janie, I'd like you to go to Fielding's apartment and fetch back anything you think might be relevant. Folders, computer if he had one. On the face of it, we're looking for any reason that might explain his death, but if there's information about Cecily Slater in there, highlight it.'

McLean was already on his feet, and Harrison stood up to follow him. 'And what about Elmwood?' he asked.

McIntyre let out a heavy sigh and rubbed her eyes again. 'Leave her to me.'

DCF Law occupied a floor of the office block directly across the plaza from where Tommy Fielding had died, which must have made commuting to work a breeze. McLean had barely shown his warrant card to the efficient receptionist before he was being whisked through to a conference room where two men were deep in conversation. They stopped as soon as they saw him.

'Detective Inspector. It's been a while.' The nearest of the two men stood up, crossed the room, offered a hand to be shaken. McLean thought it possible he might have met him before, but he couldn't recall where or when. He had to be either Donaldson or Cartwright.

'Has it?' he asked, hedging his bets.

'Andrew Cartwright,' the man said. 'I used to work with Jonas Carstairs. Terrible what happened to him.'

A brief flash of recalled image, from a lifetime ago. An elderly man, friend of McLean's grandmother, his throat cut and a piece of his own liver shoved in his mouth. McLean shuddered at the memory, surprised at how clear it was. How visceral. For a moment he could still smell the hot iron tang of the blood, hear the lazy buzz of the flies as they feasted.

'Terrible indeed, Mr Cartwright. And now we have another unexpected death to deal with. Your partner, Mr Fielding.'

'It's come as something of a shock.' The other man, presumably John Donaldson, stood up and came around the table to greet McLean. 'They told us he died at home, but nobody's said how it happened. Was it suspicious?'

'I can't really confirm anything at the moment,' McLean said. 'We're gathering information right now. As you say, Mr Fielding's death was unexpected, so we have to look into it.'

'Well, if there's anything we can do to help?' The man who was probably Donaldson indicated a chair at the conference table. 'Why don't you have a seat and Dot can bring us some coffee.'

'I shouldn't be long. Just a couple of questions for now. It might come to nothing if the post-mortem tells us he had an undiagnosed heart problem or something.' McLean sat down, waited for the two partners to do the same. 'When was the last time you saw Mr Fielding?'

'Yesterday afternoon. We had a partners' meeting here. Finished about half three, I think. He seemed fine then. His usual belligerent self.'

'Belligerent?'

'Did you ever meet him, Inspector?' Cartwright asked. 'Tommy was a first-class defence lawyer. Exactly the kind of man you wanted fighting your corner when the odds were stacked against you. But . . . how can I say this without sounding harsh about a dead man? He was very combative at times. Didn't suffer fools much. We've lost a few promising junior lawyers to his temper before.'

'I've met him a few times before. He cross-examined me in court a while back, and I bumped into him at a function at the North British. Most recently, I spoke to him a few days ago. At the Scotston Hotel.'

'Ah yes. Tommy's second office. I sometimes wonder why we bother paying the rent on this place. He's more often there these days.' Probably Donaldson waved a hand in the general direction of the hotel. 'At least it's not far, if we need to send one of the interns to fetch him.'

'Do you know why he favoured the hotel so much?' McLean asked.

'Well, it's handy for his seminars and conferences, for one thing. And it belongs to the Bairnfathers. Tommy's been working very closely with them for years now.' Cartwright frowned as he spoke. 'I suppose someone will have to inform Lord Reginald. Don't imagine he'll be too pleased.'

'I thought you said Fielding was a defence lawyer,' McLean said.

'Oh, he is. Was.' Cartwright shook his head once as if still not quite accepting the fact. 'But he met Lord Reginald at one of his fathers' rights things. I think that's what he said. They seemed to get on, and the next thing we've got all of the Bairnfather Estate's legal business. Not going to look that gift horse in the mouth, am I?'

'And that would be why you were acting for Lady Cecily Slater's estate following her death, I take it.'

Probably Donaldson stiffened. 'Is that relevant?'

'I don't know. But Fielding had her file on his desk at home. You know she was murdered? And the investigation into that is still ongoing?'

'You don't think Tommy had anything to do with that, surely?' Cartwright asked.

'Was he . . . ? Do you suspect foul play, Inspector?' Probably Donaldson added. 'Those women protesting outside the hotel seemed very hostile.'

'I don't suspect foul play, no. And certainly not some kind of angry mob baying for blood. It's not like that at all. I'm simply trying to put together as much information as I can about what Mr Fielding was doing in the time leading up to his death. It'll go into a report for the Procurator Fiscal, along with the results of the post-mortem, and that will be the end of it, I expect.'

Cartwright appeared to relax a little, taking McLean's words on trust. Probably Donaldson was more wary though, still sitting forward, his posture tense.

'Was Fielding the only one working for the Bairnfather Estate?' McLean asked. 'I mean, is there someone who can easily pick up where he left off? Run with it? I know Lord Bairnfather's not an easy man to keep happy.'

Probably Donaldson's shoulders slumped at the question, his defensiveness melting away. 'There's a couple of secretaries will be able to help, but Tommy kept on top of all that stuff himself. It's going to be a nightmare picking through all the pieces. It's something we touched on yesterday at our meeting, actually.

Same as we did at every meeting, to be honest. He was very defensive when it came to his clients. Detrimentally so, as we both told him time and time again.' He shook his head slowly, 'And now it's come to bite us on the arse. Just like I told him it would.'

McLean considered the pair of them. They might have been lying to try and protect the reputation of their firm, but it seemed unlikely. Fielding had struck him as the kind of man who kept secrets, even from his business partners. Maybe especially from his business partners.

'Well, that's probably enough to be going on with. Thank you for your time, gentlemen.' McLean stood up, took a business card from his pocket and slid it on to the conference table. 'If you do think of anything else that might be relevant, or come across something when you're reviewing Mr Fielding's business, do let us know. Soon as we have cause of death confirmed, I'll pass that on, and you will of course be kept informed of any other developments too.'

'One thing before you go, Inspector.' Probably Donaldson pushed back his chair and rose to intercept McLean before he could leave. 'You said Tommy had some work at home? Might we have those folders back soon? And his laptop?'

McLean smiled his best shark tooth smile. 'As soon as possible,' he said, reappraising just how much Probably Donaldson really knew of Tommy Fielding's activities. The lawyer was almost certainly right. This was going to bite DCF Law on the arse, and hard.

55

The major incident room had about it the air of somebody's house halfway through moving home. Fielding's death had brought a halt to the process of winding down the Cecily Slater investigation, but there wasn't much evidence of it going into reverse. At least not yet. If it turned out the lawyer had accidentally choked himself, and the only link with the dead woman was his being her solicitor, then the room would be mothballed until the next serious crime. McLean didn't imagine that would be long in coming.

He found DS Harrison and DC Stringer huddled around one of the few workstations that hadn't been unplugged and wheeled away by the IT technicians. Spread out on the table beside them, the folders that had been sitting on Fielding's desk were now marked with little yellow Post-its, which meant that somebody had read through them.

'Find anything interesting?' McLean asked, which made Stringer jump. Harrison's nerves were much stronger. Or she was simply used to being crept up on.

'Sir. You're back then. Go OK with the lawyers?'

'As well as can be expected. I think they knew Fielding was pursuing his own agenda, but were happy to turn a blind eye as long as the money kept coming in.'

'Lawyers, eh?' Harrison rolled her eyes, then turned back to the folders. 'I've had a quick scan through these. Really wish Lofty was here, mind. He's got an eye for the detail'

'And?'

'Slater's file is just stuff to do with her will. Powers of attorney, that kind of thing. I did notice something, though.' Harrison picked up the file and flicked it open to the first marked page. 'There's a copy of a letter here. Routine stuff. But it refers to the will being redrafted.'

McLean peered at the typed page, but he'd never been all that good at legalese, and his eyes were tired. 'When was this?'

'Letter's dated six months ago, which would put it around about the same time Slater got in touch with Mirriam Downham about setting her affairs in order.'

Hardly a smoking gun, but it was something. 'Anything else?'

'There's some correspondence about the Bairnfather Trust that's probably worth following up.' Harrison flicked through to another page. 'Again it's an oblique reference, but reading between the lines I get the feeling Slater had put her foot down about something and Fielding was trying to persuade her to change her mind. That one's from a couple of months earlier.'

'So potentially we could have Fielding asking Slater to approve something to do with the trust that she doesn't want to. Slater making moves to protect herself. Possibly even reassigning her power of attorney to someone else. And Fielding suppresses all that. Keeps the paper trail to a minimum, and kills the old girl before she can kick up a fuss?'

Harrison shrugged. 'It's pretty much what you suggested, sir. Pieces seem to fit, but there's nothing conclusive. Just speculation.'

'What about the laptop?' McLean scanned the table but couldn't see it.

'Serious security on it. Which you'd expect from a lawyer's computer. Same with his phone. I've sent both of them down to Mike in IT forensics, but we're treading on thin ice, sir. Unless Fielding's death turns out to be suspicious, we probably shouldn't be poking around in his personal stuff.'

McLean had to admit that Harrison was right. Even if everything was deeply suspicious as far as he could tell. He checked his watch. 'Angus should be starting the PM in an hour or so. I'll head down to the mortuary and see what he can come up with for us.'

'You want us to carry on going through this?' Harrison waved the folder about.

'No. Leave it for now.' McLean focused on the spotlessly clean whiteboard for a moment, then remembered the thing he'd been going to ask. 'The other people who were drinking with Fielding last night. Anyone spoken to them yet?'

'No, sir. We thought going through this was more important. They'd all left before . . .' Harrison looked around the room to see who else was in there, then decided not to finish the sentence anyway.

'But you know who they are, right?'

'Aye. Well, two of them. Izzy recognised them. She's got contact details and everything.'

McLean shook his head. 'I don't want to know. Just speak to them and find out what they were doing there, where they went afterwards. The usual stuff.' He turned to leave, but was pulled up short by DS Gregg, who was standing directly behind him and had the look of someone who's been waiting for the right moment to interrupt.

'Before you do that sir, the cleaner's in interview room one. Melanie Naismith. You said you wanted to speak to her soon as she arrived?'

'The cleaner?' For a moment he couldn't think what the

detective sergeant was talking about. 'Oh, right. Yes. The cleaner. I'd better go and talk to her then.'

When McLean entered the interview room, Melanie Naismith was sitting in her chair, eyeing up the walls and sparse furnishings as if they could do with a good dusting. She was probably right, although he had no idea how often, if ever, the interview rooms were cleaned. This was at least one of the nicer ones, with a window that had a view and a radiator that more or less worked.

'Thank you for coming in, Ms Naismith. I imagine this must be very difficult for you.'

'Worked in a care home gone fifteen years. Ain't the first dead body I've seen. I was mostly shocked 'cause I thought I'd walked in on him having a wank.'

McLean suppressed the smirk that wanted to spread itself across his face. 'Had you worked for Mr Fielding long?'

'I didn't work for him. I cleaned his flat. Same as I clean a lot of folk's flats. Some big houses too. But if you mean how long had I been cleaning his flat for, about two years, maybe a bit more?'

'How often do you clean it?'

'Every day during the week. Mr Fielding likes it all neat and tidy when he comes home. Liked, I should say.'

'And you had a key to gain access when he wasn't in.'

'Key for his door. Code for the front so I didn't have to bother Harry every time I wanted to get into the building.'

'You cleaned other flats in the block, then?'

'A few.'

'Is it usual for your clients to give you access like that?'

Naismith shrugged. 'Some do. Others watch you all the time, like they think you're going to try and steal things. I've had folk leave money in plain sight, jewellery sometimes. Just to see if I'm tempted. I don't normally work for them long, though. Spent enough of my time wiping assholes. I don't much care to clean for them too.'

McLean found himself warming to the cleaner. It could have been an act, but her no-nonsense attitude felt sincere. 'Could you go over this morning's routine for me, please? What time did you start?'

'I was in the building at six. The Simpsons live on the top floor and I had to do them first. Dolly's off sick. She's one of the other cleaners, Dolores O'Brien, if you can believe that. So I was covering for her too. Mr Fielding's gone to his work by half eight. Well, normally he would be. So I was probably in there around then.'

'And you didn't notice anything unusual?'

'Aye, well. He's normally quite tidy. Puts stuff away and loads the dishwasher. He must've had a visitor round 'cause there was two wine glasses on the coffee table, and the bottle was lying on the floor empty. The sofa cushions was all over the place, too. If you asked me I'd've said he'd had a woman up there. Only if that was the case, why would he . . .' Naismith trailed off, her imagination finally catching up with her.

'But you tidied up anyway,' McLean said.

'Aye, that's my job. I usually start in the kitchen and work my way round the living space. Y'know how it's all open plan 'cept the bedroom.'

McLean nodded that he did, even though it hadn't really been a question.

'Well, that's what I did. Left the stuff on his desk 'cause that's no business o' mine. Straightened up the living room, put the cushions back, loaded the dishwasher and put it on. That's when I went into the bedroom, and, well, you know what happened next.'

'Did you notice anything unusual in the room?' McLean

asked. 'Aside from the obvious, that is.'

'Don't ask much, do you, Inspector? A grown man, naked as the day and lying dead on his bed with a tie around his neck? I really don't think I saw anything else at all. Could have been a brass band playing in the corner and I'd probably have missed it.'

McLean had to concede that. She was a cleaner, and even if she'd seen and dealt with dead bodies before, it would still have been a shock. 'So what did you do next? I mean, did you call 999 straight away? Did you use your own phone or the house phone?'

Naismith narrowed her eyes in thought for a moment. 'I used my own phone. Called 999 like you say. Then I went to the kitchen and poured myself a glass of water. My heart was going a hundred mile an hour.'

'And you waited there, in the kitchen, until the first police officer arrived? You didn't go back for another look?'

This time Naismith's face took on a pained expression for a moment, as if some momentous internal struggle were ongoing. McLean left her the time she needed.

'Aye, well. You know how it is. I'd seen him, like I said. Knew he was dead. But what if he wasn't, aye? What if he was just un-conscious? Maybe I could help him. I mean, I was a care nurse, I know what to do, right? So, aye. I went back in. But soon as I saw him there, I knew. Like, I'd known before but your mind kind of goes blank and then your brain starts filling in the pieces. And you wonder, did I really see that? And what if this? Aye?'

'It's quite all right, Ms Naismith. You haven't done anything wrong. All I'm trying to do is put the pieces together and work out what happened to Mr Fielding.'

'Well if you ask me he tried to wank while choking himself and it all went wrong. Stupid sod. That's two flats in that building I'll no' be cleaning again.'

'Two? You cleaned the flat across the hall?'

'Aye. No' as often as Mr Fielding's place, but he'd ask me to do it every once in a while. When he had new tenants in.'

McLean considered the information and whether he should pass it on to the NCA. Chances were they already knew, and hadn't thought to tell him. So much for all this liaison work Elmwood was supposedly doing.

'Shame really,' Ms Naismith continued, talking to herself as much as McLean. 'Neither of them were all that much work, and the pay was good.'

'Not much work?'

'Aye, the rented flat was empty most of the time, and Mr Fielding was very tidy himself.' The cleaner frowned, recalling something. 'There was that mess a few weeks back, though. Took some cleaning, I can tell you.'

'Really? What was that?'

'Well, Mr Fielding usually left all his clothes in the laundry basket to be washed. Only this one time he'd shoved everything in himself and overloaded the machine. Men, eh?' She flicked her head back in a 'what can you do?' gesture. 'Took me ages to sort it all out, and some of the clothes were fair ruined. No idea what he'd been doing, but they reeked of smoke and stuff. Must've been at some bonfire or something, only it smelled horrible, y'ken? Like when someone sets fire to a carpet.'

McLean hardly dared breathe, let alone ask the next question. 'You wouldn't know exactly when this was, would you?'

Naismith scrunched her forehead into a frown, trying to think. 'It was a while back. Before the bad weather set in, but I couldn't say for sure.'

'And the clothes?'

'Och, they were ruined. I put them in a bin liner and chucked them out.'

56

Sitting in a cramped meeting room at the offices of MacFarlane and Dodds, Solicitors and Notaries Public, Harrison was beginning to wish she'd sent DC Stringer on his own to interview Anthony Swale and Jeremy Scobie. Admittedly her attitude to them was biased by their association with the men's rights movement their dead friend ran, but their attitude towards her was condescending, verging on outright rude.

'I'm not entirely sure how you came by the information, Detective Sergeant, but it's hardly a crime to have a drink with someone in a bar, you know?' Swale peered down his nose at her, head raised slightly as if being in the same room as a woman caused him physical pain.

'Frankly I'm appalled that you would have someone of the standing of Tommy Fielding under surveillance at all. When did we become a police state?' Scobie's mock-affronted tone put Janie's teeth on edge, but she swallowed her annoyance and plastered a fake smile on her face.

'Do you deny being in the Walter Scott bar at the Scotston Hotel last night, Mr Swale?' Janie didn't let the man answer before turning her attention on his colleague. 'And Mr Scobie, I can assure you Mr Fielding was not "under surveillance" as you put it. He is dead, though, and we need to trace his last movements.'

Both men startled at her words, which suggested to her the news hadn't reached them yet. Well, she didn't feel sorry for breaking it to them this way. If they'd offered coffee she might have been in a better mood. Biscuits would have helped, too.

'Dead?' Scobie regained his composure quickest. 'When?'

'How?' Swale asked.

'He was found dead in his bed by the cleaner this morning. It appears not to be suspicious, but we'll know for sure once the post-mortem has been done.'

'How did he die?' Swale asked again.

Harrison put on her sweetest smile but didn't answer. 'So, gentlemen. We know that you both attended one of Mr Fielding's little get-togethers at the Scotston yesterday evening. We know you both joined him for a drink in the bar afterwards. What time did you leave?'

Scobie looked at Swale, something like worry passing between the two of them. 'You know he had a lot of enemies?' Swale said. 'Those women who protested outside the hotel, for one thing. Heard you let them go after a bunch of them broke in and disturbed the peace. What if it was one of them did him in, eh? How will that look?'

'Mr Swale, I can assure you that none of the women in question were anywhere near Mr Fielding at the time of his death. We don't even think it was suspicious, but as you so rightly point out, he was a man who courted controversy and had, as you say, a lot of enemies. We would be remiss in our duties if we didn't investigate, even if it turns out to have been nothing but natural causes. So again, please. What time did you leave him?' Janie wasn't quite sure why she asked the question, given that she already knew the answer. Perhaps because it was making them uncomfortable.

'I guess it must have been the back of nine? Quarter past

401

maybe?' Swale finally relented. He had begun playing with his fingers like a smoker in need of his fix, although Janie got no scent of either tobacco or vape off him.

'Aye, Tommy got a text from someone. Said it was important and he needed to cut the evening short. Otherwise we'd have been there another hour, maybe.' Scobie drummed his fingers on the table. 'There's a point. Who was he meeting? Have you spoken to them yet?'

'Was it just the two of you in the bar, then?' Janie asked, again ignoring the question put to her.

'No, there was that young lad Tommy'd taken a shine to,' Swale said. 'Got kicked out by his girlfriend on some made-up assault charge. What's his name again? Harry, Barry. No, Gary, that's it.'

Janie raised an eyebrow. 'Gary who?'

Scobie pulled out his phone and swiped the screen awake. Tapped at it a moment, then turned it so Janie could see. 'Gary Tomlinson. Aye, he's a good lad gone through a rough few weeks. Tommy was going to see about getting him visiting rights for his wee girl.'

Swale looked sideways at his colleague as if surprised that he knew so much about the man. Janie took down Tomlinson's number, frustrated that there was no address to go with it.

'Thank you.' She smiled again, but only because she knew it unsettled the two men. 'Now, have you any idea who it was Mr Fielding was meeting?'

Swale shrugged. 'He only said it was an old London contact recently moved up to Edinburgh. It was obviously very short notice, but important. And he didn't want us there. We both walked up to the Lothian Road. I got a taxi home. Jeremy was going to do the same.'

Janie nodded, as if this information was important and useful even though she'd only really wanted to speak to these two to find out the identity of the third man. She pushed her seat back and stood up.

'Well, thank you, gentlemen. You've been very helpful. And I'm sorry to be the one to break the news about your friend. As I said before, we don't think his death is suspicious, but we need to trace his movements and speak to anyone who saw him yesterday. I'll make sure you get an update as soon as we can confirm cause of death. And if you think of anything that might be helpful, please do let me or my colleague know.'

DC Stringer understood the prompt, pulling a business card out of his jacket pocket and sliding it across the table. These two were far more likely to call a male officer than a female one. Not that Janie would have put much money on them calling anyone other than the most senior member of the Police Authority that they played golf with. Or possibly a friendly MSP. Well, she'd deal with the fallout from that when it happened. For now, she'd got what she wanted.

'We need an address for this Gary Tomlinson,' Janie said as they left the offices of MacFarlane and Dodds. Outside, the light was fading fast, even though it was barely mid-afternoon. Edinburgh was a lovely city in the summer, with its seemingly endless soft evening light and crisp, bright early mornings, but you paid for that in the winter when sometimes the sun hardly seemed to bother rising at all.

'On it, boss,' Stringer said, without a trace of irony. He had his phone out and was already tapping at the screen as they walked to the pool car.

'Knock it off, Jay.' Janie stopped mid-stride, forcing the detective constable to turn and face her.

'What?' he asked.

'Enough of the "on it boss" nonsense. Just because I got promoted. I'm a DS, not your boss.'

Stringer paused a moment. 'OK, Sarge.' He couldn't quite keep the grin off his face this time.

'I give up.' Janie unlocked the car and climbed into the driver's seat. 'You got anything yet?'

'Control centre are running the name. Not too common so we should hopefully get lucky.' As he pulled his seat belt on, Stringer's phone buzzed and he peered at the screen. 'Here we go. Gareth Tomlinson. Twenty-six years old. Arrested for domestic violence three months ago, but the charges were later dropped. Sounds like our man. Address listed in West Pilton.'

'Stick it in the Sat-Nav then. We'll go see if he's home yet.' Janie started the car, shoved it in gear and pulled out of the parking space.

'Shouldn't we call him first? See if he's home right now?'

'And spoil the surprise?' Janie shook her head. 'Don't think so.'

The drive from the lawyers' West End offices didn't take long, and would have been even quicker had they not been diverted around roadworks at the Western General Hospital. Soon enough, Janie was cruising slowly along a potholed road, lined on both sides with council housing blocks, searching for the right number. Slightly better than Muirhouse to the north west, this part of the city was still not somewhere you would want to leave your car parked for long if you liked its wheels attached.

'There we go. Number fifteen.' Stringer pointed, and Janie pulled to the kerb.

'We'll not be long,' she said as they both climbed out, looking around for signs of life. The street lights had come on, and a gentle wetness hung in the air that might have been rain or might have been haar drifting in off the Forth. Most of the windows glowed with light too, so there was a good chance somebody would be at home even if Gary Tomlinson wasn't. She locked the car, hoping it would still be there when they got back, and then the two of them ventured up the short path to the building.

Janie remembered growing up in a council block not dissimilar to this one. An open corridor ran from the front of the building through to a patch of drying green at the back, two flats leading off it on the ground floor and a stone staircase climbing to another pair upstairs. It was always a bit of a lottery as to which flat was the one you were looking for, although these ones seemed to have passed out of council ownership some time ago. There were no signs to indicate who lived on the ground floor, but upstairs one door had a buzzer beside it with a name scrawled underneath. Peering closely, Janie saw that Tomlinson had been scrawled out, and MacDonald written underneath in black biro.

'We know what Tomlinson's bidey-in's called?' she asked, as she pressed the bell and heard a loud 'ding-dong' from inside.

Stringer shook his head, and before Janie could say anything else, the door popped open a fraction, held in place by a stout chain.

'Whut youse want?' A young woman peered through the gap at them, her brow furrowed in suspicion. Janie pulled out her warrant card and held it up.

'DS Harrison. This is my colleague, DC Stringer. We're looking for Gareth Tomlinson?'

The name turned the suspicious frown into a furious one. 'He's no' here, is he. Fucker should be in jail for what he did to me, only that weasel lawyer said it'd be better if I just told him to go an' never come back. Near enough broke my jaw, the bastard.' She lifted a hand to the side of her face as if even though there was no obvious bruising any more the injury still pained her. Three months on, there was every possibility it still did, and the mental scars would take even longer to heal.

'I'm sorry. We have his address still registered here.'

'Aye, useless fucker can't even get that sorted. What youse want him for? Gonnae lock him up this time?'

Janie shrugged. 'Maybe. Depends what he got up to last night. You wouldn't happen to know where he's living now, would you?'

'What am I? His fucking secretary?' The young woman closed the door, and for a moment Janie thought she'd blown it. Then she heard the sound of the chain being unlatched, and the door opened wider.

'Here.' The young woman had fetched a pad from a table just inside the door and was scribbling something down on it. She tore the top page off and handed it to Janie. An address in Gorgie, and the same mobile number that she'd got from the lawyer, Scobie.

'Thanks. And I'm sorry we disturbed you, Miss . . . MacDonald?'

The young woman's gaze flicked in the direction of the doorbell, then back up to Janie. 'Aye,' she said, and then a small child's wail began to echo through the flat. 'Gotta go. That's my Wee Mary wanting her feed.'

She made to close the door, then stopped at the last moment, bent down and picked something up off the floor. When she stood up again, she was clutching a small pile of letters, which she shoved in Janie's direction. 'Gi' him those when you see him, aye? And tell him the next lot's getting burned.'

57

'Subject is male, Caucasian, fifty-four years old. One hundred and seventy-eight centimetres tall, eighty-three and a half kilograms in weight. Initial examination shows the body to be in reasonably healthy condition. Subject's neck shows bruising and abrasion consistent with the silk necktie found tied around it at the scene of death. Petechial haemorrhages in both eyes are another indicator of asphyxiation by strangulation.'

McLean barely listened as his old friend worked diligently around Tommy Fielding's body. Laid out on the cold examination table he didn't look all that different to how they had found him in his bedroom, except that the tie had been carefully removed and taken away for analysis. What they might be able to determine from it was anyone's guess, but his gut feeling was it would be inconclusive.

He kept on coming back to Melanie Naismith's words. A team was even now raking through the store at the back of Tommy Fielding's apartment block, in the vain hope the bags that the cleaner had dumped in the maintenance area had not made it as far as the industrial wheelie bins for collection. Or that nobody had emptied the bins in the past couple of months. Given the amount of rubbish piled up, it was just possible they might find the smoke-damaged clothes, even if McLean would have to buy Manda Parsons a case of whisky to make up for her having to rake through all that foetid waste. But even if they did find something, then what? He had a hypothesis, but it was far-fetched even by his normal standards.

'Are you paying attention, Tony, or just standing in the mortuary because you like it here?'

McLean focused, aware that he'd allowed his mind to wander too far. Cadwallader had bent over the body, gloved fingers gently manipulating Fielding's neck.

'Sorry, Angus. A lot on my mind.'

'Clearly.' The pathologist straightened, grimacing as something in his back gave a click audible even over the hiss of the air conditioning. 'As I was saying, the abrasions on the neck are consistent with the silk tie. There are however other marks, very slight bruising that suggests he may have been throttled first. Could have been rough sex play, but equally could have rendered him unconscious, then the tie was used to finish him off.'

'Do you have an accurate time of death?'

Cadwallader sighed, perhaps a little over-theatrically. 'I can give you a range, but nothing more accurate than within a couple of hours. Given the state we found him in, and the cause of death, I'd say somewhere between ten p.m. and midnight. Certainly no later than one in the morning.'

McLean opened his mouth to ask if Cadwallader was sure, then closed it again before he insulted his old friend.

'Is that a problem?' the pathologist asked.

'We know he was alive at half-nine. Janie Harrison saw him leave the bar in the Scotston Hotel, and we've CCTV of him arriving at his apartment block not long after. The problem is he wasn't alone.'

'That would explain the fact he appears to have had sex before he died, which makes the onanism a little unusual.' Cadwallader waved a hand at the dead man's shrivelled genitalia. 'We'll swab for DNA, but if you already know who it was, then maybe it's not necessary.'

McLean shook his head, wondering when life had become so complicated. 'Oh, it's necessary, Angus. Very much so. The person he was with? Who left alone an hour after the two of them entered the building, so very much within the murder window? Our very own chief superintendent.'

Cadwallader looked at McLean, then at the body, then back at McLean again. 'I see. Well. I'd better get those swabs tested on the hurry-up then.'

It took far longer to drive back from West Pilton to Gorgie than going the other way. Janie stared at the unmoving traffic on Queensferry Road and wondered whether she would have been better off heading out to the bypass and back in again. Or maybe walking.

'Isn't evening rush hour traffic meant to be away from the city?' she asked, as they finally managed to negotiate the round-about on to Belford Road, only to be faced with yet more angry red brake lights.

'Probably the trams,' Stringer said, helpfully. He had his phone out and was pecking away at the screen with one finger. Finding out something useful, Janie hoped, although more likely playing some game.

'Seems Mr Tomlinson has something of a reputation,' he said after a moment and another hundred metres.

'Oh yes?'

'Nothing official. Putting his girlfriend in A and E's the closest he's ever come to a criminal charge. But he's had a few warnings down the years. Aggressive behaviour, drunk and disorderly at the footie, that sort of thing.'

'How did he get away with it this time, then?'

Stringer peered at his screen again. 'Miss MacDonald's lawyer persuaded him to sign over the flat to her, and agree not to seek visitation rights for his daughter. Still has to pay maintenance, though. Jesus. I almost feel sorry for the bloke. He got shafted without any lube, for sure.'

Janie looked across at the detective constable, but he was so fixated on the tiny letters on his phone screen that he missed her scowl.

'Sorry for him? He's a violent thug who broke her jaw.'

'Almost broke her jaw, but aye. He's a piece of shit. And I only said I almost felt sorry for him. He really got screwed over by her lawyer.'

'Who was it? Her lawyer, that is.' Janie eased through a gap in the traffic and cut across the road to a side street that might be a quicker route, but then again might not.

'Hang on. I need to scroll down a bit.' There was a short pause while Stringer tried to find the information. 'Oh. That can't be right, can it?'

'What can't be right?'

'Says here that she was represented by DCF Law. Isn't that Fielding's firm?'

'Aye, it is. But Tomlinson was with Fielding last night. No way they'd be having a drink together if Fielding didn't want him there. And why would Fielding's firm represent the girlfriend? He's usually fighting the father's side, isn't he?'

'Search me.' Stringer swiped at the screen, then clicked off his phone and put it away. 'Guess we can ask him when we get there.'

'You think someone told him?' Janie zipped through a set of traffic lights as it changed to yellow, hoping she wouldn't have to explain herself to Traffic.

'Who, Fielding?'

'No, Tomlinson. I mean, yes, both of them. But if Tomlinson found out it was Fielding who got him kicked out of his nice wee flat in West Pilton, lost him access to his daughter. Well, he'd be pissed off, wouldn't he?'

'Enough to follow him back to his place, wait for Elmwood to leave, then what? He's not on the CCTV footage. No way he went into Fielding's flat and throttled him, then set it up to look like a sex game gone wrong. He's a building site labourer. Left school at sixteen. Handy with his fists, brain not so much. He's hardly likely to come up with a scenario like that.'

Janie had to admit that Stringer was right. They didn't even know if Fielding had been murdered or simply strangled himself while trying to rub one out after a visit from his ex. She indicated, pulled sharply across the road again, this time earning herself a middle finger and blast of horn from a driver coming the other way, and pulled into the street where Tomlinson lived. The only place to park was a double yellow line, so she would probably have to explain herself to Traffic anyway.

'OK. Let's see if second time's a charm.'

The front door to the tenement was locked, an elderly intercom system showing a series of names, none of which were Tomlinson. Janie picked one at random, pressed and waited. There was nothing to indicate that the system worked, no light, no audible buzz and certainly no answer. She moved on to the next button, then a third. As she was about to press the fourth, the door clicked and then swung open to reveal a fearsome-looking elderly woman, waving a bamboo walking stick like a weapon.

'Bloody kids. Get— oh.' She put the stick down, leaning on it with one arthritic hand.

'Good evening, ma'am.' Harrison gave the woman what she hoped was a friendly smile as she presented her warrant card. 'Detective Sergeant Harrison. I was looking for Mr Gareth Tomlinson?'

The woman sniffed so noisily Harrison feared she might

hawk and spit next, but instead she swallowed heavily before answering.

'Top floor left.' She stood to one side to let them in. 'He's no' there, mind.'

'He's not?' Janie asked.

'No. Went oot a while back. No idea where. Left his door open, though, if you want a look.'

Janie turned to look at Stringer, who shrugged.

'Should probably ask if you've got a warrant, like. But he's two weeks behind on his rent, so help yourself.' And with that, the woman walked away, disappearing back into her ground-floor flat.

'Charming,' Stringer said as the two of them climbed the stairs.

'But helpful. Sort of.' Janie had the small collection of envelopes in her hand, just in case, but when they reached the top landing, it was clear the landlady had been telling the truth. One of the two doors stood slightly ajar, the lights still on inside.

'Mr Tomlinson?' She knocked on the door anyway, then pushed it all the way. It opened on to a single room bedsit, or what the estate agents would call a Studio Flat. It smelled of stale body odour and takeaway food, something more pungently rotten underneath like the bass note to a concerto of stench. An unmade single bed shoved in one corner, small single armchair and low table opposite the narrow dormer window that gave a stunning view of the taller tenement on the other side of the street. Behind the door, someone had artfully inserted the most basic of cooking facilities, and in the last corner, a small built-out cupboard housed a shower, sink and toilet.

'Compact and bijou,' Stringer said.

'Nowhere to hide, at least. And the landlady said he'd been gone a while so it's unlikely he's popped out to grab his evening meal.' Janie poked at an empty pizza box lying on the table beside an elderly laptop. Its screen was blank, but when she jabbed a button it lit up. A website showing a paused video news clip that seemed incongruous until she saw the sidebar of shame filled with images of scantily clad female celebrities.

'What's he been watching? Porn?' Stringer crossed the room in two short strides, leaning down to get a better look at the screen. Janie found the cursor, clicked play.

'Tommy Fielding, leading men's rights activist and lawyer, was found dead in his Fountainbridge apartment by his cleaner early this morning . . .'

Janie tapped the trackpad and the video paused. 'Well I guess he's heard the news.'

'Heard it and headed straight out. In such a hurry he didn't even remember to lock the front door?'

58

'This just come in from forensics, sir. I know Kirsty's in charge, but I thought you'd want to see it.'

McLean had barely stepped into the major incident room, fresh from his walk back from the mortuary, when DS Gregg came bustling up with a sheet of paper. The rest of the room lacked the same sense of urgency, but then they had been packing up the Cecily Slater case for a couple of days now, so that was hardly surprising.

'What is it?' he asked, at the same time as he took the page and scanned it.

'Fingerprint analysis of the mirror in Fielding's bathroom. You know, the ghostly message?' Gregg waved her hands around in a very loose approximation of something spooky, but McLean barely noticed. Top marks to the forensics team for turning it around so quickly. No doubt someone had made it clear that the chief constable himself was likely to be taking an interest in the case. It was just a shame that the results weren't particularly helpful.

According to the report, the team had found remarkably few fingerprints around the bathroom, all of which seemed to belong to Fielding himself. The writing on the mirror appeared to have been done with one index finger, an almost perfect print picked out at the end of each letter where that finger had been lifted to move to the next one. The only problem was that the print was also Tommy Fielding's.

'He wrote it himself?' McLean asked, even though he could see well enough.

'Apparently.' Gregg shrugged. 'Is it important?'

McLean scanned the report again, searching for any mention of when the writing might have been done. The only indication of timescale was a small note at the bottom confirming that the cleaner had wiped down all the surfaces in the bathroom the morning before Fielding's death. He remembered her telling him she cleaned every day, so she was obviously diligent about her work.

'It's odd. Not sure what to make of it, to be honest.' He looked past Gregg, across the room, not seeing the faces he hoped to see. 'Harrison and Stringer still out chasing up the men from the pub?'

'Far as I know. The chief super's back, though. Went straight up to her office. No' sure if anyone's spoken to her yet about . . . well.'

'Have you seen Kirsty about?' McLean asked. It was easier than approaching Ritchie's office and risking an unprepared meeting with Elmwood. But that was just being stupid. McLean knew he had to grasp this nettle or risk getting stung. 'Forget it, Sandy. I'll go find her.' He waved a hand at the incident room and the officers slowly packing things away. 'Tell this lot they can knock off early. We'll know better what's going on by tomorrow. Wouldn't want to have to put it all back together again.'

'Aye, sir.' Gregg accepted her new orders without question, bustling off to carry them out. McLean glanced around in case either Harrison or Stringer had magically appeared, but they were all still absent. He pulled out his phone and rattled off a quick text to Harrison as he left the major incident room and went in search of his new DCI.

He'd only made it halfway to her office when the shouting started.

'I've never heard so much fucking rubbish in my life.'

McLean didn't really want to go into Detective Superintendent McIntyre's office, even though the door was open. A little further up the corridor, the chief superintendent's secretary, Helen, was sitting at her desk, transfixed. McLean caught her attention, hooked a thumb at the door, and then raised both hands in a gesture he intended to mean 'should I go in?' but which could have meant anything. Or simply made him look like an idiot. Helen merely shrugged, then shook her head and held both hands up to indicate she wanted nothing to do with it. Fair enough, this was way above her pay grade.

'You can't possibly think I'd have anything to do with—'

McLean chose that moment to reach out and knock at the open door, much more loudly than he would do normally. The effect was instant, and more or less as he had hoped. The chief superintendent stopped shouting, but the expression on her face as she rounded on him was one of such fury he feared he might blister under its heat.

'You're behind this, aren't you, McLean? What is the meaning of this outrageous—'

'Jayne, ma'am.' He stepped into the room and then very deliberately closed the door behind him. Elmwood stood in the middle of the room, shaking in her rage. McIntyre was leaning against her desk as if prepared to scuttle behind it for safety should the need arise.

'I've just been at the mortuary, getting the details on Mr Fielding's cause of death.'

In the silence that followed he could hear the tick of the clock on the wall.

'He was strangled. Possibly by the tie, by his own hand as it were. But there were other marks on his neck. Angus thinks someone could have choked him with their bare hands until he fell unconscious, then did the thing with the necktie to make it look like an accident. Auto-erotic asphyxiation gone wrong. Those are his preliminary findings. We'll know more once all the tests are in. But I've known Angus a long time, and he's usually right first time.'

'I still don't know—'

McLean held up his hand to stop the chief superintendent from speaking. 'Before you say anything else, we know you were there. We know you met him in the Walter Scott bar around half nine, walked back to his apartment and stayed there until about half past ten. You were seen by multiple, reliable witnesses, and we have security camera footage from the apartment block lobby. Denying it isn't going to help.'

'I didn't kill him. He was fine when I left. The bastard.'

'That's useful information,' McLean said. 'But until we can prove it, you are at the very least a person of interest.'

'This is ridiculous.' Elmwood looked from McIntyre to McLean, then back again. She held out her arms, wrists pressed together. 'What are you going to do? Cuff me and throw me in a cell?'

'I really don't think that's necessary, Gail. But you understand as well as I do that you can't be anywhere near this investigation. Not until we know exactly what happened to Mr Fielding.' McIntyre crossed the room, taking the chief superintendent's hand. 'We have to be seen to be doing everything right here.'

Elmwood almost flinched at the detective superintendent's touch. She turned away and focused on McLean, the earlier anger gone now, replaced by earnest supplication. 'Tony, surely you must believe I'm innocent?'

'Fielding used you, back when you were a sergeant. You never forgave him for that.' He couldn't help himself, even though he knew it was mean to kick someone when they were down. 'And yet you met up with him last night. Went back to his flat and had sex with him.'

'Used me?' Elmwood narrowed her eyes, staring at McLean as if she might be able to see his thoughts. 'Is that the best gossip you could come up with?'

'Well, maybe it went both ways. Mutual support with a bit of mutual loathing thrown in. Let's just say the two of you have had a long and complicated relationship, shall we? Culminating in a . . . liaison last night.' McLean enjoyed the flinch his choice of word brought. 'Tell me, ma'am, do the words "with my dying breath I curse thee" mean anything to you?'

If he'd been hoping for a reaction, he was disappointed by the one he got. Elmwood's face went from angry to confused far too quickly for it to have been an act. She knew nothing about the message on the bathroom mirror, so maybe she was innocent after all. At least of Fielding's murder.

'What on earth are you talking about?' she said eventually.

McLean told her about the writing, failing to mention the forensic conclusion that it was Fielding himself who had done it. 'We've no evidence of anyone else entering the flat until the cleaner arrived the next morning. Fielding's death is suspicious. We have to investigate, and you can't be involved in any aspect of it. By all rights we should be calling in a team from another region to do this.'

'So, what? I just go home and lick my wounds?' Elmwood dropped herself into one of the chairs that had been pulled out from the conference table.

'Actually, that would probably be the best idea,' McIntyre

said. 'Go home, Gail. You can have a couple of days off while we run everything down and prepare a report for the PF. I doubt anyone will even notice you're gone.'

McLean grimaced, not wanting to be the one to break bad news. 'Actually, that might not be true.'

'Oh?' Elmwood tilted her head in an accusatory manner, which given what McLean was about to say was probably fair.

'The press already know Fielding's dead. And they also know about your history with him.' He held up a hand to stop the chief superintendent before she could complain. 'Not about last night, but about your history. London, all that stuff.'

Elmwood narrowed her eyes at him. 'How is it you know this?'

'Because one of Edinburgh's finest muckrakers told me. The press have been digging into your past ever since you arrived. It's what they do.'

'Dalgliesh?' McIntyre asked.

'The same.'

'And you're one of this hack's sources, are you?' The ice in Elmwood's voice would have chilled a perfect Martini.

'We have history, but I don't talk to the press without official sanction. I've not told Dalgliesh anything about you.' McLean heard the defensiveness in his voice and hoped neither Elmwood nor McIntyre noticed it.

'Go home, Gail. Let us do our job, aye?' McIntyre said, and finally the chief superintendent relented.

'Fine. But I want to be kept up to speed on developments, OK?' She turned on McLean. 'And if this Dalgliesh fellow so much as breathes any rumour, you can tell him I'm not afraid of suing, right?'

McLean nodded, feeling it unnecessary to point out that Dalgliesh was a woman. 'We'll need to post an officer outside your door.'

Now the heat came back into the chief superintendent's face. 'What? You think I'm a flight risk? Where the fuck would I go?'

'I don't think that's necessary, Tony.' McIntyre stepped in to calm things down. 'I'm sure Gail will be happy to call in regularly. Won't you, Gail?'

Elmwood glared at both of them, but McLean could see her considering the options. She was trapped and she knew it, but she also knew he and McIntyre were her best hope. Standing tall, she adjusted her uniform jacket, squared her shoulders, then without a further word, she strode to the door and left.

McLean was still waiting for the call from Elmwood's driver to say that she had been delivered safely home when he heard a knock at his open office door. Glancing up, he saw DS Harrison standing half in, half out of the room.

'I heard about the chief super, sir,' she said. 'Did you really threaten to throw her in a cell?'

'One of these days I'll find out who's behind all the station gossip and kick them so hard they'll not be able to sit down for a month.' McLean shook his head. 'And no, I did no such thing. We all agreed it was best if she went home, took a bit of leave while we sort things out.'

'House arrest then,' Harrison said. McLean was going to object, but then he remembered that after Elmwood had left McIntyre's office he'd persuaded the detective superintendent to assign a uniformed officer to guard duty outside the Stockbridge house anyway.

He shrugged. 'If that's what we have to say to keep the papers happy, I'll go with it.'

'Just as well there's someone on the door, anyway. I think we might have a problem.'

'Oh?' McLean sat up a little straighter.

'Fellow by the name of Gary Tomlinson. He was in the bar

with Fielding last night, and the day Izzy and her mates broke into the seminar. I spoke to his ex, and it seems Gary's a bit free with his fists around women. Which is why she's his ex and he doesn't get to see their wee girl any more.'

McLean felt a tingle of something unpleasant on the back of his neck. 'Go on.'

'According to the other two who were in the pub, Fielding had got right pally with Gary these past couple of months. Spending a lot of time with him, promising to help him get access to his kid.'

'Isn't that what Fielding does? It's kind of his thing. Was his thing, I should say.'

'Aye, right enough. But this is where it gets weird. Apparently Gary got stiffed by the lawyer his ex used. Threatened he'd go to jail, then got him to sign away everything to have the charges dropped. But here's the thing. There weren't any charges. It never got that far. And the ex's lawyer? He works for DCF Law.'

'That doesn't make sense. Why would Fielding's firm screw this bloke over, then Fielding . . .' McLean stopped talking as the pieces began to fall into place.

'Aye. What better way to radicalise someone? Just like Izzy said.'

'Did you speak to him? This Gary . . . ?'

'Tomlinson, sir. And no. We went to his place. His new place. But he wasn't there. According to the landlady he just upped and walked out. Left his front door open, lights on, laptop on the table showing a news bulletin about Fielding's death.'

'So he knows. I guess he'll be upset. Maybe gone out to get pissed?'

'And leave his flat unlocked? Door open? He was in the pub with Fielding last night, sir. Him and two lawyers Izzy identified for us. They all left before Gai— the chief superintendent arrived, but what if he'd not gone home? What if he was hanging around and saw her with him? With Fielding?'

McLean frowned, trying to squeeze all the different snippets of information into something resembling a sensible whole. 'How would he know who she was, though? I mean, she's not exactly high profile. You and I know her, but the average man on the street?'

Except that she was high profile. The English copper come to Edinburgh. Elmwood might not have known who Jo Dalgliesh was, but Dalgliesh sure as hell knew the chief superintendent. He picked up his phone, meaning to call her, then instead stood up and slipped it in his pocket.

'Come on then. Let's go pay our boss a visit.'

59

It's almost as if he's a different person.

Gary hadn't understood before quite how much he had been suppressing his rage. Controlling it. Keeping it inside. All to stop the poor feartie women from feeling threatened. Well he's done with that shite now. No more laughing at his weakness. They've pushed him too far, and now they're going to pay.

She's going to pay.

There's a freeness in him as he walks the city streets, heedless of the damp haar that fills the air, the drops of water that glisten on every surface, reflecting the street lights and the glow spilling out of shop windows. He feels more alive than he has in days, months, years even. Without knowing why, he bursts out laughing, and the sound only spurs him on.

It is dark when he reaches her lair, although he has no memory of the journey. He doesn't think about how he knew where she would be hiding; those kinds of questions are un-important now. The street is quiet, as these rich streets always are. A few of the other houses have lights on, barely showing behind thick curtains or closed shutters, but hers is dark. She is in there, though. The uniformed police officer standing at the front door confirms it.

'Wait,' the voice in his head whispers. So he moves back into the shadows beneath the dripping branches of the trees, shoves his hands deep into his pockets, and waits.

It doesn't take long. Or maybe it's hours. Gary neither knows nor cares. The voice has given him purpose, and now he understands what it was that drove Fielding. These witches have become too powerful, infiltrated right to the heart of things. Like a cancer spreading through a body, unseen and deadly. And like a cancer it needs to be cut out before it spreads even further.

Burned out.

The barest sound reaches him in the shadows, a chirp as the police officer receives some message. Gary watches the man bend his head to his shoulder, speaking into a handset. Moments later, the officer glances once at the door he has been guarding, then hurries down the steps and along the street.

Gary waits until the officer has disappeared before emerging from the shadows. He skirts around the parked cars, across the road and then down the narrow mews entrance that will take him around the back of the terrace. There are gardens here, more trees for cover, high stone walls keeping neighbours apart. He counts back until he identifies her building. An old coach house takes up most of the space, with a wooden access gate set into the wall beside it. There is no reason it should be unlocked, and yet when he turns the handle it clicks smoothly, opens to reveal a neat path up to the back door, lit only by the glow of the city refracted through the thickening haar.

Closing the gate behind him, Gary walks up the path as if this is his own home. And why shouldn't it be? Why should this woman, this murderous harlot, this witch, have such a place when he's forced to live in a pigsty bedsit? He has as much right to be here as any man. More right than her.

It doesn't strike him as odd that the back door opens to his touch. Gary is beyond noticing these things. He steps into a utility room that is small by the standards of these terrace houses, but still twice the size of his single room across town. Beyond it, the kitchen is bigger still, kitted out with sleek stainless-steel fittings, granite worktops, no expense spared. He eyes the block of knives on the counter, but he has no need of such weapons. Moves on further into the house.

The silence is so total he wonders if she has left through the front door while he's been coming in the back. He stands in the middle of the vast central hall and listens. Even the city cannot make it inside, its never-ending murmur held back by thick stone walls and secondary glazing, muted by the mature trees that grow all around this exclusive enclave.

'Who the fuck are you?'

The voice doesn't startle him. Nothing can startle him any more. Gary turns slowly and sees her on the stairs, halfway down from the landing above. He moves swiftly, but not at a run. She can't escape him and they both know it.

'Get out.' The words are a command, but her voice betrays her. Her gaze darts to the hall below, and he knows she has left her phone there. He smiles, says nothing as he climbs the stairs.

'What do you want?' And there's the pleading, the attempt to bargain as if he couldn't take whatever he wanted anyway. She backs away, heels uncertain against the stairs. He keeps coming, never taking his eyes off her, never giving her a moment. Flustered, she trips and falls heavily, a cry of pain as she turns an ankle. Gary can smell the fear on her now and it is wonderful.

'You won't get away with this.' She lashes out at him, but he catches her by the wrist, jerks her upright so that they are close.

'Tommy says hello,' he says. Then punches her hard in the face.

60

'Isn't there supposed to be a constable on the door?'

McLean stared up at the dark facade of the terraced house, searching for any sign of life. It was late enough that most people would be home by now, but not so late they'd be in their beds. On the other hand, a lot of these big houses were empty, bought as investments or tax boltholes by wealthy bankers and foreign plutocrats. Even so, the street felt unnaturally quiet as he parked the car and climbed out, not helped by the thick haar that drifted eerily past the street lights.

'Should be, sir. You want me to get on to Control about it?' Harrison asked.

McLean nodded, leaving the detective sergeant to make the call as he crossed the road and approached the front door. He could see only the reflected street lamps in the glass of the windows, no lights on inside. Only the incongruously modern doorbell and intercom at the front door was illuminated. He climbed the short flight of stone steps, peering down into the light well of the basement level. Nothing obvious in the shadows below, so he pushed the button.

No answer, and no sound from within. Given the thickness of the door, and the fact there was an inner porch to further insulate any sound, it wasn't surprising he could hear nothing, but McLean pressed the button again, straining his ears for any sound just in case.

'Apparently there's been a bit of a barney at one of the pubs on Brunton Street, sir. Constable Peters was on duty here, got called off to help out. Somebody must have OK'd that, I guess. Apparently patrols have been coming down here regularly just to keep an eye on things.'

That would explain it, although McLean wasn't happy about the situation. He pressed the button again, and still there was no response.

'Heavy sleeper?' Harrison suggested. McLean doubted it. He pulled out his phone, found the number and dialled. A moment's pause, and then he heard the tone through his handset.

'Is that ringing inside?' Harrison leaned forward, pressing her ear to the door. 'I think I can hear a mobile ringing in the hall.'

McLean thumbed the screen to end the call.

'Stopped now,' Harrison confirmed. 'That's not good, is it?'

'Not really, no.' McLean tried the door, but it was locked. 'Get on to Control again, can you? This is a rented property, so the agency should have a spare key. If they can't get it here in fifteen minutes, we'll use one of our own big red ones.'

'It's a bit late, isn't it?' Harrison said, but made the call anyway.

McLean pressed the doorbell again, then called Elmwood's phone. Now that Harrison had pointed it out, he too could hear it ringing, the tinny noise echoing in the large hall. He let it carry on until it kicked into voicemail, then hung up. A few metres along the pavement, a gate in the iron railings opened on to steps leading down to the basement. It reminded him curiously of the tiny flat where Steve Whitaker had met his grisly end, only the light well here was considerably larger. There was no entrance to the house, only three windows all with shutters closed. Dead leaves littered the flagstones as he walked from one end to the other, and as he trod through them the rustling noise brought to mind winters past, heavy coats, woolly hats and bonfires.

Bonfires. McLean sniffed the air, catching the faintest whiff of smoke. Or was he imagining it? He kicked up a few of the leaves, in case it was their decay that he could smell. But that was a different scent. He walked to the nearest window, felt the glass for warmth. An old wooden sash, it wobbled slightly as he pressed against it, but it was firmly locked against intruders. As he turned away, he thought he heard a noise, faint as a whisper, like the cracking of dry branches underfoot. He stopped, straining to hear anything over the omnipresent dull roar of the city. Even muffled by the haar, it still made focusing on any particular sound all but impossible. Had he imagined it? The night was certainly one for playing on his fears.

'Twenty minutes is the best they can do,' Harrison said as McLean emerged from the steps back out on to pavement level. 'Lucky one of the secretaries was working late.'

'Call in a squad car with a big red key anyway.' McLean climbed the steps to the front door again, bent to the letter box and pushed it open. Beyond, he could see only the dark shapes in the unlit front porch. The inner door was closed, only blackness beyond. Once more he thought he heard something, turned his head to listen through the opening. His fingers slipped and with a clatter, the flap sprung shut. The noise rang loud, blotting out anything else.

'Can you hear movement inside?'

Harrison pressed her head to the door, paused for a few seconds as McLean's hearing slowly came back. When she stood up again, she shook her head.

'Quiet as the grave. But this place gives me the creeps anyway. Of all the houses in the city she could have chosen to live in, why pick this one?'

McLean knew what the detective sergeant meant. Harrison

had almost died in this house, touched by something neither of them were quite prepared to accept could exist. What other trouble awaited them within its forbidding stone walls?

'Here.' He pulled out his car keys and handed them over. 'You go wait for back-up or this late working secretary to turn up.'

Harrison looked at him suspiciously, but took the keys anyway. 'What are you going to do, sir?'

'There's a mews entrance up the way.' McLean pointed to a gap in the terrace further along the street. 'I'm going to have a quick look around the back.'

'Shouldn't we both wait?' Harrison's tone wasn't exactly hectoring, but for some reason it put McLean in mind of his grandmother when she'd been less than impressed with something he'd done. He knew he should heed her advice.

'Just going to have a quick look,' he said. 'I'll be back in a minute.'

The haar that had drifted in off the Firth of Forth thickened as McLean made his way along the street and down the narrow entrance to the mews. There were no street lamps here, and the few lit windows at the backs of the houses added an ethereal glow that only served to deepen the shadows. The air hung heavy with the scent of damp stone, oily cobbles and leaf mould, and somewhere on the edge of it all, he caught the smell of wood smoke. Most likely someone nearby had a wood burning stove in their house. This part of the city was meant to be a smoke free zone, but that didn't necessarily mean the local residents all followed the rules. These were wealthy people, and experience had taught him they were the ones most likely to ignore petty things like not burning logs brought down from their second home in the countryside. Unless it was someone else doing it, in which case they would complain loudly to the authorities.

It was hard to tell from the back lane which of the houses was which. The upper storeys were lost in the swirling fog, and the squat coach houses of the mews further obscured the view. McLean counted garage doors until he thought he had the right one for the chief superintendent's address. Alongside the incongruously modern garage door, a wooden door was set into the garden wall. It should have been locked, and yet when he tried the handle, it clicked and the door swung open. Mist billowed through the opening like smoke, and brought with it that tantalising scent again.

He pulled out his phone, brought up Harrison's number, and dialled as he walked through the back garden towards the house itself. The call went straight to voicemail, which probably meant the detective sergeant was talking to someone else. It should have logged his attempt, possibly even notified her he had called, so he rang off and put his phone away. She'd ring him back as soon as she was done.

Unlike the front door, the back door opened at ground level to a paved area. In the pitch black McLean stumbled on an uneven flagstone, almost falling arse over tit. He reached out to steady himself on the frame, and felt the door itself give slightly. Not just open, but ajar. Had the chief superintendent fled? Left even her phone behind so that she couldn't be traced? Gone in such a hurry she'd not even remembered to close the back door?

Taking his phone out again, McLean tried Harrison's number. Once more, straight to voicemail. Inside, he tried the light switch, but nothing happened. Not good. He knew he should go back, wait for the squad car that was surely on its way by now, but there was that faintest scent of smoke, and could he hear something? He trained the soft LED glow of his phone's torch ahead of him so that he could step inside without fear of tripping over again.

The laundry room felt cold, the fog from outside having

seeped in through the slightly open door. As he moved further into the house, so the temperature rose and the air began to feel dry. McLean stepped into the kitchen and played the torch around, revealing a large room with modern fittings that somehow looked bare. He almost dismissed it as being the minimalist work of some grossly overpaid interior designer, and then he noticed that there were no chairs around the table.

A noise from the doorway distracted him, something creaking in the narrow passage that led from the kitchen to the hall. McLean pointed the torch that way, but its beam cast too little light to see much. He crossed the room on light feet, tense as he listened for any more sounds, but there seemed to be only the general creaking expected of an old building.

The light switch by the door didn't work, and now he thought about it, McLean couldn't hear any telltale hum from the large American-style fridge across the room. Someone had cut the power. Was it Elmwood herself? Had she done a runner? But why leave the back door unlocked, then? Why switch off the power?

McLean shook the thoughts away. There was nothing to be gained from playing the hero; the events of the summer and all the idiotic blame-spreading fallout from them had taught him that. He tapped off the torch light, slid his phone in his pocket and started to retrace his steps.

A low moan echoed in through the other door. The one that led to the front hall. McLean froze, tensed, straining his ears to hear. The noise came again, human, suffering. What the hell was going on?

Moving slowly, fingers brushing the wall to help him navigate the almost total darkness, he stepped silently out of the kitchen and along the corridor. There should have been a couple of antique side tables, memory told him, but his hand passed through empty space. There should have been old paintings hanging on the walls, but they were not there. Someone had cleared everything out of the corridor, along with the chairs from the kitchen.

Another door stood ajar, blackness beyond it almost complete. McLean knew it led to the basement, but in the darkness he could sense nothing. Then that low moan came again, wounded and woozy. He edged past the open door, carried on until the corridor opened out into the hall. There was a little more light in here, the reflected glow of the city coming in through the glass cupola three stories up. Even so, the scene made no sense.

Furniture had been dragged from every room, pictures ripped from the walls, chairs heaped one atop another in a huge pile that reached almost to the edges of the hall. Even if it hadn't been fast approaching Guy Fawkes night, McLean would have recognised the stack for the pyre that it was. And there, at the top of it, in the place of the infamous would-be regicide, gagged and bound to a sturdy bed frame, was the chief superintendent.

'The actual fuck?'

McLean mouthed the curse, even as he was moving towards the stack, searching for a way to get to the chief superintendent and cut her down. She still wore her work clothes, but her face was a mess, black around her nose that was almost certainly blood, and dark bruising under her eyes. Judging by the size of the pyre, she must have been out cold for hours, but now she was slowly coming around.

Another low moan forced its way past the gag in her mouth. Her head swayed as she tried to take the weight of it, and as she raised her chin, McLean saw a thin strip of something tight around her neck. A recent conversation came back to him then, taking tea with Madame Rose and Mirriam Downham. The tradition in Scotland to throttle the accused so that they were unconscious before burning them to death for the crime of witchcraft. Whoever had seen to Elmwood was not practised in the art, then.

Skirting around the edges of the pyre, he pulled out his phone and hit the screen to call Harrison again. It went straight to voicemail. What the hell was she playing at? McLean killed the call and turned towards the front door. He could unlock it, let her in along with the back-up that must surely be here by now.

A man stood directly behind him, face sheened with sweat, hair matted with it. His wide eyes were mad and bloodshot, and he carried a bottle of what looked like white spirit in one hand. McLean barely had time to react before the punch came out of nowhere, a jab to the face boxer-style. It caught him on the turn, snapping his head back and spinning him around to sprawl on the ground among the broken picture frames and smashed chairs. His phone slipped out of his grasp, skittering away into the darkness. Before he could even begin to rise, before he could even shout for help, the air whooshed out of him as the man kicked him hard in the stomach. McLean rolled away as best he could, trying not to vomit as he gasped for air. He needed to shout, alert Harrison to what was happening, but it was all he could do to even breathe.

He sensed the next kick more than saw it, twisting away so that it grazed his shoulder. Had he been less dazed, he might have grabbed the foot in passing and sent the man tumbling. Instead, he pushed himself away, weak legs refusing to let him stand. The man was a shadow, almost invisible in the gloom, but instead of coming in for a killing blow he seemed to recede. There was a scraping noise that penetrated even the ringing in McLean's punch-drunk ears, and then a powerful reek of paint thinners filled the air.

'No.' McLean pushed himself to his feet, fighting the urge to throw up, and the dizzying whirl that threatened to have him tumbling to the floor again. He could barely see anything over the spinning stars in his eyes, and the reek of white spirit only made things worse. He was still gasping for air, still not able to muster much more than a hoarse whisper.

Another noise, and with it a bright flare of light that wasn't anything to do with the blow he'd taken to the head. McLean squinted against the glare as it illuminated the man's face. He stood close to the pyre, almost in it, and stared up at the lolling form of the chief superintendent.

'All the witches must burn.' His voice wavered as the match in his fingers flickered in anticipation of greater things. McLean was already moving, the last of his strength carrying him across the hall in what he hoped was a straight line. Even though his lungs felt empty, he forced out an angry roar, reaching for the hand that held the match as he smashed into the man. But his fingers closed on empty space. The two of them fell together, rolling away from the pyre in a tangle of limbs as the room lit up bright with fire.

'No!' McLean lashed out with a weak fist, catching the man in the side of the head. Almost casually, his attacker swatted him away, pushing himself to his feet with an ease McLean envied. Gary Tomlinson. It had to be him. McLean was all too aware that his attacker was half his age, strong from a decade of working on building sites, stronger still from whatever mad rage was coursing through him. There was no way to win this fight fairly. Where the hell was Harrison and that back-up?

Pivoting on his elbow, McLean lashed out with a foot. His hip screamed in pain, but somehow he managed to connect with Gary's leg as he brought it in for another heavy kick. The man fell backwards with an angry yell, but the move brought McLean's head round to the fire that was greedily climbing up the pyre towards the chief superintendent. He heard the crackle of his own hair catching, and instinct pulled him back. He brushed away the flames with one hand as the other one found the floor, levered himself into a crouch just in time to see Gary coming for him again. He launched himself upwards with all his remaining strength, catching his attacker in the midriff. The two of them fell to the floor once more, tangled together, and McLean used his momentum to smack his forehead into Tomlinson's face. He felt the crunch of nose breaking, and then his attacker fell still.

No time to rest, the air was choking bad, the flames leaping eagerly at the dry wood. McLean thought his ears were ringing with the blows he had taken in his brief fight, but as he focused he realised it was screaming. He scrambled to his feet, swaying from the exertion. Stumbling to the nearest window, he grabbed a long, heavy curtain and heaved. For an agonising few moments nothing happened, then the whole curtain rail pulled away from the wall and he fell backwards, momentarily smothered by the heavy velvet.

It took too long to fight his way out of the fabric's embrace, his strength almost gone. The room was unpleasantly hot now, and somewhere over the roar of flames McLean could hear a rhythmic pulsing sound. Unimportant, he could deal with that later. He gathered up the curtain and flung it over the pyre. Flames licked at the edges, finding something new to feast upon. There was no time to spare.

Taking his life in his hands, he stepped on to the curtain, finding a balance in amongst the burning stack. The chief superintendent had fallen silent now, head bowed, hair almost all gone. Was she still alive? McLean put his arms around her and heaved. He'd expected resistance from the ropes that tied her to the bedpost, but the flames had already weakened them. She fell against him and, unbalanced, he tumbled backwards. He landed on his back, the fall and the weight of the chief superintendent both driving the air from his lungs. The back of his head clattered against tile and the flames seemed to dim around him. Elmwood's face rested on his shoulder, her skin blackened and blistering. What a stupid way to go, burned to death in the embrace of a woman he wanted nothing to do with.

And then the weight lifted off him as someone carried the chief superintendent away. Another face loomed over his, upside down, as other figures swarmed in his peripheral vision. DS Harrison looked both worried and livid.

'Thought you said you weren't going in on your own, sir.'

61

Fire engines blocked the no-longer quiet street, the crews going about their skilled work as they attempted to contain the blaze. Watching from the back of an ambulance, McLean wondered whether Lord Bairnfather was adequately insured, and if the owners of the properties either side would sue.

'Apart from the hair, I reckon you're fine.' The paramedic who had been checking him over stepped back and pulled off his blue plastic gloves. 'Probably going to be coughing for a day or two, but I don't think you got too much smoke. Might have been a better idea if you'd not gone into a burning building in the first place.'

McLean took his admonishment, aware that it was justified. 'Not the first time I've been told that, though in my defence this time it wasn't on fire when I went inside.'

He stood up carefully, aware of the many bruises that were going to make life fun for the next few days. At least he'd have a next few days to moan about them in, so that was something. The chief superintendent had been whisked away to hospital, and all anyone would tell him was that her burns were horrific.

'You OK, sir?' DS Harrison stood up straight as McLean

approached Emma's little Renault ZOE. It was boxed in by two fire engines, so there wasn't much chance of them going anywhere in it any time soon.

'Should see the other guy,' he answered.

'I did. From the look of him you had a few anger issues.'

'They got him out OK, then?'

'Aye, we dragged him out soon as we knew we couldn't control the fire. These old places don't half go up quickly.' Harrison glanced at the building, then back at McLean.

'It was Tomlinson, right?' he asked.

'Looked like him, from what I could see. Finding out about Fielding's death must have tipped him over the edge. No idea how he knew where the chief super lived, mind.'

'Nor why he fixated on her. You know he was trying to burn her as a witch, right?'

'Just like poor Cecily Slater.' Harrison stood up straight. 'Here, you don't think he . . . ?'

'I don't know what to think any more, Janie. I just want to go home.' McLean looked down at the car, then up at the nearest fire engine. 'Looks like I might have to find a taxi to take me, though.'

In the end, Harrison managed to persuade a squad car to give McLean a lift home, while she stayed at the scene. But as the car headed uphill towards Queen Street, he changed his mind and pointed the driver in a different direction. Traffic was mercifully light, and the thick haar made it feel like they were moving through orange glowing clouds, which only added to the sense that he had temporarily stepped out of reality and into some other realm. In short order the car pulled up outside a large house in Leith, but as he walked the short distance from the lane to the front door, the feeling only intensified.

'Tony, come in, come in.' Madame Rose greeted him at

the door as if she'd been expecting him for hours. Stepping over the threshold was like waking up. The dull throb of his burned face, the ache of his bruises and the hundred other little pinpricks of pain reminded him that he had been in a fight for his life, in a burning building.

'Here.' Rose took his arm just in time to prevent him collapsing to the floor. Delayed shock, a part of his brain told him, even though it felt unlike any shock he'd experienced before. McLean was grateful for the support, and let himself be led through to the ground-floor kitchen. Izzy DeVilliers was in there, doing the washing-up, a sight so incongruous McLean almost collapsed again. She took one look at him and grabbed a dishcloth to dry her hands.

'I'll put the kettle on, shall I?'

'Thank you, Isobel dear.' Rose pulled out a chair and only let go of McLean's arm once he was safely seated. He didn't feel quite as bad as she was treating him, but it was nice to be pampered for a change.

'I'll be fine,' he said eventually. His voice suggested the opposite, but it was only dehydration. Nothing a hot, sweet drink couldn't fix.

'Aye, I reckon you will.' Rose sat down on the opposite side of the big table that dominated the centre of the room, while Izzy busied herself making a pot of tea. 'You want to tell me what happened?'

McLean managed a smile. 'And here's me going to ask the same question.' He paused a moment, gathering his thoughts as best he could. It was a bit like herding cats.

'Tommy Fielding died last night, not long after he left the hotel where young Isobel here saw him, with our own chief superintendent hanging on his arm like a lover.'

Izzy brought the pot to the table and set it down. 'Did he suffer? He deserved it, the scumbag.'

'Isobel.' Madame Rose used her scolding voice, but it washed off the young woman like rain.

'He was strangled, best we can tell. Possibly by the chief superintendent, although that's a puzzle I've still to work out. I imagine the end was quite frightening for him. Not as frightening as it was for poor Cecily Slater, though. Certainly not as painful.'

McLean held Rose's gaze as she carefully poured three mugs of tea. He'd already seen from her expression that nothing he'd said was surprising to her.

'I don't know this man, Fielding, but I know his type. He claims – claimed – to be a Witchfinder, which makes me think there was maybe more to him than you understand, Tony. Or should I say, more to him than you're likely to accept?'

McLean knew what was coming next, knew he'd rationalise it by the morning. For now he was content to drink tea and relax in this warm kitchen.

'Cecily Slater was a witch. A very powerful one. You know this. Mirriam told you as much.' Madame Rose leaned forward, arms on the table, massive hands cradling her mug. 'When such as her die violently, things rarely go well for those who have done the foul deed. A witch's dying curse cannot be stopped. At least, not until its work is done.'

Brian Galloway, Don Purefoy, Steve Whitaker. Another name appended itself to the list almost as if someone else was thinking McLean's thoughts for him. James McAllister. All of them disciples of Tommy Fielding. All of them so warped by his words, his twisted logic, their own hate and anger, that they would help him murder a defenceless ninety-year-old woman. All of them dead, their ends baffling. Weird. And then the words on the mirror, written by Fielding's own hand.

'With my dying breath I curse thee.'

Madame Rose dipped her head slightly in acknowledgement. 'Something like that, yes.'

'But why go after the chief superintendent?' McLean asked. 'Why try to burn her as a witch?'

'That was not Cecily.' Rose paused a moment, taking a drink of tea. McLean found himself mimicking her action, and the warm, milky liquid soothed both his throat and his mind.

'Then who?' he asked, before the unwanted implications began to fall into place. 'Oh.'

'Told you he was a bastard, didn't I?' Izzy said.

'Isobel dear. What have I told you about bad language?' Madame Rose tutted her displeasure, then turned her attention back to McLean. 'But she isn't wrong. Men such as him gather around them the power to control and influence the weak-minded. That power does not die with them, no more than Cecily's died with her.'

'So you're saying Gary Tomlinson was possessed?' Well, it made as much sense as anything, although McLean doubted it would stand up in court.

'If you must use such a crude term.' Rose smiled, lifted her mug again but didn't drink this time. 'I'd say more that he gave himself totally to the hatred, and now it has consumed him.'

'So what about Cecily?' McLean asked. 'You know I'm sceptical about all of this, Rose, but if she, her spirit, whatever, killed all those men, where is it now? Has she gone? Has it gone?'

The old medium didn't answer straight away. Her gaze had been on him throughout their strange conversation, but now McLean saw her focus fade for a while, as if she was searching for something deep in her memory. Or listening for something beyond the range of normal hearing.

'Cecily is at peace now,' she said finally, her eyes flicking momentarily in Izzy's direction before coming back to him. 'And now the spirit seeks a new vessel.'

McLean took another drink, surprised to find that his mug

was nearly empty. The tea had been exactly what he needed, but he wasn't sure he could remember the last time he had felt so tired. He had come here because he knew that being alone with his thoughts was not a good idea immediately after the events at the chief superintendent's house. He'd also hoped for a few answers, even while knowing they'd be neither straightforward nor satisfactory. On that score at least he hadn't been disappointed, but now it was time to return to something resembling reality.

'I'll call you a taxi,' Madame Rose said, as if she could read his thoughts. Perhaps she could.

62

'You look like shit, Tony. You know that?'

McLean turned away from the one-way mirror separating the observation booth from interview room two. Detective Superintendent McIntyre stood in the doorway, shoulders slumped, looking every bit as tired as he felt.

'It's only a bit of singeing. The hair will grow back.' He lifted a hand and lightly brushed the frizzy patch on the back of his head where he had come too close to the flames. Given the circumstances, it was a miracle that was all that had burned. Well, that and yet another suit fit only for the bin.

'He saying anything?' McIntyre gestured towards the glass. Beyond it, Detective Sergeant Harrison and Detective Chief Inspector Ritchie were attempting to interview Gary Tomlinson. If McLean and McIntyre were frazzled, then the young man looked even worse. His face glowed red where the heat of the flames had burned his skin, and dark black bruises circled his bloodshot eyes, the result of McLean's own Glasgow Kiss.

'Not a squeak, but then I don't think he will.' McLean gently touched his forehead, feeling the slight bump that was all the bruising he'd earned for his troubles. His cheeks were ruddy from the heat, too, but he couldn't see them.

'What was he doing there?' McIntyre asked.

'Aside from the obvious? Who knows?'

'I heard Fielding had taken him under his wing, so I guess he figured he owed him payback.'

'There's more to it than that, though. Fielding was radicalising him. Same as he did for the goons who helped him kill Cecily Slater. Steve Whitaker, Don Purefoy, Brian Galloway. Probably Jimmy McAllister too. They all fell under his spell, and he twisted them until they'd do anything he asked them to. Our Gary in there was just the latest in a long line.'

'That's . . .' McIntyre paused for a moment as if searching for the right words. 'That's quite an allegation, Tony. Do you have any proof?'

'About them killing Slater? No. Not that could be used in a court of law, at least. And it hardly matters either, since they're all dead. That poor bastard though?' He nodded at the figure staring sightlessly at the wall. 'I wouldn't be surprised if he ends up in a secure psych unit for the rest of his life. He's been twisted so thoroughly he probably thinks he was doing God's righteous work.'

McIntyre stared for a while, so close to the glass that her breath misted its surface gently as she breathed. 'You sound like Rose,' she said eventually.

'Well you're the one introduced me to her, remember?'

'Touché.' McIntyre conceded the point with a smile.

'The other point, though, about Fielding radicalising men for his fight against the rising tides of feminism? We've got him fair and square there. Not that it matters, since he's dead.'

McIntyre turned to face him, her back to the glass as she raised a questioning eyebrow. 'Oh yes?'

'Mike Simpson down in IT cracked the security on his laptop, and there's all sorts of interesting stuff on it. Seems he really was a leading light in the more militant wing of the men's rights movement. Our friends at the NCA are just itching to get stuck in to it all.'

'Why is it you don't sound as happy about that as you should, Tony? You're not a closet misogynist, are you?'

McLean smiled at the joke, even though the movement made the skin on his face ache. 'You know me, Jayne. Hate women in powerful positions. Can't stand working with them at all.' He shook his head. 'No, it's the other stuff we found on his laptop that's going to cause a few sleepless nights. There's a lot of email correspondence with Lord Bairnfather about Cecily Slater's will. At the very least they conspired to suppress her most recent changes, particularly her nomination of a successor to her role as trustee of the Bairnfather Trust. The name Mirriam Downham comes up quite a few times. Can't imagine that being terribly popular with a man like Lord Reggie. He might even have been complicit in his aunt's murder, though I doubt we'd ever make that stick.'

It didn't take McIntyre long to see the problem. 'And he's filthy rich, with a lot of powerful and influential friends. You do know how to pick them, don't you?'

'Almost makes me wish the chief superintendent were still here,' McLean said. 'She was always good at navigating those choppy waters. And soothing ruffled feathers.'

'Any news on her condition?' McIntyre asked.

'She'll live, I'm told. Burns take a long time to heal, though, and they leave nasty scars. Her clothes protected her in the main, but her hands and face are badly damaged. Mentally, who knows how she'll cope? And there's the small matter of her and Tommy Fielding still to address.'

'You still think she killed him?'

'I think she had motive and opportunity. But that's not enough to prove it.'

'I don't get it, though.' McIntyre shook her head slowly. 'I

445

mean, I understand they had history, but from what everyone says they both loathed each other. Why would she . . . ? She seems so . . . ?'

'It's about power, Jayne. I'd have thought you'd understand that. Elmwood – Gail – can be charming. God knows she turned it on me from the first we met. But it was always about power. And manipulation. Fielding's just the same. Using that horrible charisma of his to mould like-minded people to his will. Preying on their insecurities and stoking their hate. The two of them were almost perfectly suited. Sure, they hated each other, but hate can be just as intoxicating as love. Why else do exes so often end up screwing each other's brains out then regretting it the morning after?'

'I always forget you have a degree in psychology, Tony.' McIntyre glanced away from him as she spoke, her attention drawn by the nothing that was unfolding in the interview room. 'So you think Gail and Fielding were just having a hate fuck, nothing else?'

'No, it's more than that. They were using each other, must have been for years. He contacted her about Galloway, for starters. There's no other explanation for how she could have known. What are the chances it was Fielding having a word in the chief constable's ear that got her the job up here in the first place? Problem is, she stood to lose more than him if it ever became public knowledge.'

'Sounds like a motive to me. Something like that wouldn't just destroy her career; it could land her in jail.'

It was McLean's turn to shake his head. He considered the writing on Fielding's bathroom mirror, and the things Madame Rose had told him while he was still in shock the night before. 'Motive doesn't equal guilt, and forensics leave us with reasonable doubt. I can't see it going to prosecution. No, as far as the world's concerned, Tommy Fielding's death was misadventure. A wanker to the end.'

McIntyre laughed out loud, then covered her mouth lest the sound travel through to the interview room beyond. If it had done, Gary Tomlinson gave no indication he had heard.

Neither of his two rescued cats were in the kitchen when McLean let himself in and dumped his briefcase on the table. He didn't recall having left the light on either, but it had been a very long day, beginning with aches and pains well before dawn, so there was every possibility he'd forgotten. He filled the kettle and hefted it on to the hotplate, then set about fetching teapot and tea for a much needed cuppa. Beer and something from the takeaway could come later.

It was about the same time he realised the teapot was missing that he heard the voices filtering through the closed kitchen door from the hall beyond. Something about the sound, the cadence of the words he couldn't make out, relaxed him at the same time as it lifted his weary heart. He hurried through to the library, certain of what he would find there and not disappointed.

'Surprise!' Emma leapt out of her chair to greet him as he entered the room. He barely had time to make out that there were other people present before she had wrapped him in a tight hug. McLean held on as if his life depended on it, both to Emma and the moment. He didn't want to let her go, lest all the horror of the past few weeks come crashing back. And was that a dampness he could feel pricking the corners of his eyes, a lump threatening to form in his throat? Christ, but he'd missed her.

'Well look at you,' he said, once the embrace had finally been broken. Africa seemed to have suited Emma. Her face was tanned, a smear of freckles cresting the top of her cheeks. She'd cut her hair even shorter than he remembered, the spikiness of it making him think she'd maybe done it herself, with blunt scissors. Despite the heat coming from the lit fire, she wore several layers of shapeless clothes as if she was freezing. But she glowed with an excitement he'd not seen in her for a long time.

'I don't know, Tony. I leave you alone for what? Two months? And look at you.' A frown creased her forehead and she took a slower step towards him, one hand reaching out to gently touch his face. He'd not really noticed how taut and burned his skin was, but her fingers brought little pulses of pain he did his best to hide.

'It's nothing. Just got a bit too close to the fire.' He took Emma's hands in his, as much to stop her fussing over him as anything, then turned to greet the rest of the group. Madame Rose and Izzy sat side by side on the sofa, and McLean was surprised to see Mirriam Downham in his favourite armchair. Huddled a little too close to each other on the smaller sofa sat Manda Parsons and a rather embarrassed-looking Detective Sergeant Harrison.

'Anything left in that pot?' he asked. 'Or should I be looking for something stronger?'

'Here, let me. You sit down.' Emma directed him to the only empty armchair, then set to fetching him a mug of tea. McLean did as he was told, glad to get the weight off his feet, although when he had his mug and noticed Emma had nowhere to sit, he almost got up again. She squeezed in beside Madame Rose and Izzy before he could muster the energy to move.

'Well I can't say this isn't pleasant,' he said, once he'd had a slurp of tepid, tannic tea. 'But I'm a detective, and there are far too many clues here for me to think this is purely a social visit.'

'You can blame me for bringing Rose and Isobel.' Mirriam Downham leaned forward in her seat, the better to be seen. 'I'm sorry we interrupted your reunion. We won't stay long.'

'Has anyone spoken to you about Cecily Slater's will?' McLean asked.

'Indeed they have. I had a call from a rather nervous lawyer early this morning, and another from young Janie here this afternoon. I thought it only polite to come and thank you in person.'

McLean wanted to say he'd just been doing his job, but he stopped himself at the last moment. He could hear his grandmother chiding him from beyond the grave. Accept the compliment; don't downplay it.

'I suspect there'll be a fair few more lawyers in the coming months,' he said.

'Of course. There always are. I don't imagine young Reginald will give up without a fight, but I've been besting the Bairnfather lords for many years now.'

'I'm sorry we can't pin her murder on him too. It might have been Fielding and his band of zealots who did the deed, but he's every bit as guilty.'

Doctor Downham tilted her head in partial agreement. 'Sissy had her justice, in the end. I think we both know that.'

McLean opened his mouth to respond, but was interrupted as the two cats sauntered into the room. Mrs McCutcheon's cat sniffed at the tray with the tea things on it, ever hopeful there might have been tuna sandwiches to steal, then stalked off and curled herself down in front of the fire. The other cat, most probably Cecily Slater's, but also possibly some random stray that knew a good thing when it saw one, stood in the space between the sofas and armchairs, the tip of her tail twitching at full mast. She raised her head, turning it slowly this way and that as if sniffing the air, searching for something. Then she leaped gracefully into DS Harrison's lap, purring a deep, low rumble and butting her head against the detective sergeant's startled hand.

'I . . . ah . . . I'm a wee bit allergic to cats?' she said, her voice rising at the end of the sentence as if even she weren't entirely sure. She picked up the animal gingerly, her lack of experience as obvious as her fear of getting scratched, and placed it back on the floor. It cocked a quizzical head at her, then sauntered off to join Mrs McCutcheon's cat on the rug in front of the fire.

'Interesting,' Downham said, in a manner that reminded McLean of one of his old psychology professors. Then she slapped her long, thin hands down on the arms of the chair and levered herself upright. 'But we've taken enough of your time here, Detective Inspector. My thanks again. Should you ever need it, you will find a welcome at Burntwoods. Now we must leave. Come, Rose, Isobel.'

'We should probably be going too. Let you and Em catch up, aye?' Harrison stood up swiftly, Manda Parsons taking a little more time. McLean hadn't even finished his tea, but given how it tasted that wasn't necessarily a bad thing.

'You want me to call a taxi?' he asked, but no sooner were the words out than he heard the crunch of car tyres on gravel outside.

Madame Rose gave him a conspiratorial wink and patted him on the arm. 'We'll be fine, Tony. Just leave you two to get reacquainted.'

In moments they were gone; three in a taxi heading for Leith, two on foot walking towards Bruntsfield. McLean closed the door and let out a long breath he hadn't realised he'd been holding. He crossed the hall and went back into the library, where Emma had curled herself up on the sofa at the end closest to the fire. Cecily Slater's cat lay in her lap, purring contentedly as she stroked its head.

'Found a new friend, I see,' he said, as he went to the hidden cupboard and helped himself to a stiff dram. Anything to take away the taste of tannin. He held up the bottle for Emma to see. 'Want one yourself?'

She shook her head, patted the cushion beside her. 'Sit down, Tony. Before you fall down.'

He did as he was told, not realising quite how worn out he was until he was finally able to relax. Emma leaned in and they sat there together for a while, silent save for the sound of gentle purring. McLean felt like he could have sat there for hours, enjoying that one small moment of peace. But nothing lasts for ever, and too soon Emma sat up a little straighter, pulled away far enough that she could face him.

'Right then, Anthony McLean. Are you going to tell me just what you've been doing with my car?'

63

The darkness is soothing, warm like the womb. She floats in it carelessly, watching and waiting, listening to the quiet noises of the house as it breathes. It is good to be free of the pain, the weariness of long years and a body grown tired and old. She was done with being Cecily, more than ready to move on.

But not straight away, perhaps.

She has earned some respite, she thinks. A chance to rest and recover, now that her vengeance is complete. True, her nemesis died at another's hand, but such is life, and death. His end was sweet joy to witness all the same, and it has brought with it an unexpected bonus. Blindsided, he acted foolishly, too swift in seeking his retribution. And now he is trapped. The mind he possessed was not ready, not strong enough to contain him. How long will that body survive? How long will modern medicine keep it alive? Will he live ninety years like Cecily? If so, then she is in no rush. She has time to choose, time to make plans and change the world.

Beside her the other spirit stirs, turns, settles and falls back into slumber. This is a safe place, a secure and most welcome refuge. They have both of them done well to find it. Although it is perhaps not surprising given the family that has lived here, that lives here still.

She sniffs the air, tastes the scent of those who have passed through here so recently. Some already have the knowledge, the wisdom of ages passed down from soul to soul. They see her for what she truly is, but keep that secret to themselves. Of the others, almost any would make a fine union. All but the master of the house. He is an ally, that rare thing in this world, a genuinely good man, but he is no vessel.

But the others? Which one would agree to take on her mantle? Which one would assume that great power, and with it that great responsibility? So many to choose from, and all so strong.

She is in no rush. For once, she is safe. And her old foe is weakened, trapped. She can afford to take her time.

She will wait, for now, to be reborn.

Acknowledgements

This book is very much a product of lockdown, even though the actual restrictions had very little impact on my rural and isolated life. You can't write contemporary fiction in a bubble though, and the constantly changing and ever-worsening news made it hard at times to concentrate on the work. I don't think I would have managed it without the regular emails from readers who had enjoyed Tony McLean's previous adventures and took the time to let me know. There's nothing quite perks a writer up like being told their words have been appreciated. So thank you, all the readers out there. You make what we do worthwhile.

Rural and isolated my lifestyle might be, but a small army of other people have helped in the making of this book. I am as ever totally indebted to my amazing agent, Juliet Mushens, and her tireless assistant Liza DeBlock. Thank you both. I'm so glad it's all about ME now!

The team at Wildfire have done great service over the past year too. Thank you Alex, Ella, Jo and Serena. Your enthusiasm keeps me going. A big thank you to Sarah Bance, whose swift and detailed copy editing weeded out my worst errors. And a thank you and farewell to Jennifer Leech, whose heroic publicity efforts included bribing booksellers with chocolate and me with gin. Works every time.

A big thank you to Ian Hanmore, too, for his audio narration over the course of the series. More than anyone else, he is the voice of Tony. And Madame Rose and Kirsty Ritchie and Janie Harrison and, and . . .

And last, but never least, a huge thanks to Barbara, whose surname I stole for my detective all those many years ago.

Biography

James Oswald is the author of the *Sunday Times* bestselling Inspector McLean series of detective mysteries, as well as the new DC Constance Fairchild series. James's first two books, NATURAL CAUSES and THE BOOK OF SOULS were both short-listed for the prestigious CWA Debut Dagger Award. WHAT WILL BURN is the eleventh book in the Inspector McLean series.

James farms Highland cows by day, writes disturbing fiction by night.